RIGHT OF PASSAGE

To my mother and father
who loved each other
and fought against the forces,
internal and without,
that worked to separate them.

RIGHT OF PASSAGE

Lee Jenkins

This is a work of fiction. Reference made to the lives of actual people, and to events, has been imagined.

First published in 2018 by Sphinx, an imprint of
Aeon Books Ltd
12 New College Parade
Finchley Road
London NW3 5EP

A portion of this novel appeared in a different form in *The Village Voice*. Grateful acknowledgment is made to the editors of *The Village Voice* for permission to reprint this material.

"The Road Not Taken" by Robert Frost from the book *The Poetry of Robert Frost* edited by Edward Connery Lathem. Copyright © 1916, 1969 by Henry Holt and Company. Copyright 1944 Robert Frost. Reprinted by permission of Henry Holt and Company. All rights reserved.

British Library Cataloguing in Publication Data

A C.I.P. for this book is available from the British Library

ISBN-13: 978-1-91257-302-8

Typeset by Medlar Publishing Solutions Pvt Ltd, India

Printed and bound in Great Britain by TJ International Ltd. Padstow

www.aeonbooks.co.uk

www.sphinxbooks.co.uk

ONE

When I was a child I helped my mother in the garden behind our house. We would get down on our hands and knees and scour the ground for weeds, or anyway I would try to do this, crawling along in a race to see who could spot the most and not trample on the collards. I had on my overalls with the two straps going over my shoulders and no shirt, and she had on what looked like an apron for a top and shorts, which bared her legs, allowing her knees to make imprints in the soil. She liked to dig her toes into the soil and squish it between her toes and invite me to do the same. She liked to sit against a large oak and split one of our own watermelons with a large butcher knife she had bought for that purpose, and we would eat it and spit out the seeds.

She sometimes spoke to the tree as if it were a person, or even something more powerful, requesting that it please not mind our sitting against it enjoying its shade, and it seemed to me the tree sometimes spoke back to her, so respectful she was of its presence. It is probably from this that I came to conceive of the idea that objects in nature were not just alive or dead, as in whether the fruit tree was alive or dead and would or would not bear fruit any longer, but that it was a living being, and was involved in its own decision to bear fruit. Later on, in her mental illness, she spoke in earnest to trees and to invisible presences, powerful unseen forces. She liked to let me rest my head against her thigh after we had eaten, and we would look skyward as she sometimes stroked my head and I looked at her extended leg with toes rutting the soil. Her toes looked like little wee-wees, what she called mine, and what I thought my father had, only bigger and longer. She and my father would stand me at night before the toilet, while I was mostly asleep, and sort of tickle me, "Go wee-wee," they said. Then they would flush the toilet. "Did he go?" he or she said afterwards, as I would be put back into bed.

Sometimes she and I saw scampering chipmunks, whom she addressed, "Well, Sir, look at you, Sir!" They looked like little hyped-up chieftains, with pasted-on stripes down their backs, scurrying in and out of the portals to their underground kingdoms. She never wanted to hurt them, even though they ate our goods. She only wanted to talk to them, which she always did with a kind of ironic pleasure, the same way she sometimes talked to me. We pulled some of the carrots we had grown, some with twin roots, and nothing was sweeter, and she would sometimes take me up and hold me against her breast, the way it used to be when I was still nursing; and if I had wanted to, I could have put my mouth on one of those brown globes again. But it was already enough just to be held like this and feel such warmth and intimacy. I know now she was a country girl who enjoyed the physical delights of nature and may have been somewhat ashamed of her earthiness when my father married her, brought her into town, and placed her in what passed as the heroic, tortured self-sufficiency of a middle-class Negro neighborhood in 1935. I'm talking about schoolteachers, small businessmen, insurance agents, craftsmen, *educators*—at the Negro university nearby, with their master's degrees and doctorates from Oberlin, Fisk, and Columbia—along with the inevitable supporting cast of domestics and laborers, and the lawyers, doctors, dentists, shopkeepers, and undertakers who served them. It was the county seat and the capital of the state, and race relations rose to the level of benign and unthreatening tolerance touted by the progressive voices of the community. It didn't hurt also that a black university and white one existed at opposite ends of the town. I never knew the degree of menace from which I had been protected until the civil rights movement dramatized it or the newspapers drove the reality of it home, such as with the Emmet Till murder of 1955, upping the ante on the routine limitations and humiliations of Jim Crow segregation. I hadn't appreciated the place of impoverishment that had been reserved for us that was experienced by so many of my black countrymen, such that being black had become synonymous, in the minds of both blacks and whites, with being poor and deprived.

My mother and her twin were the youngest of eight siblings reared in a frame house on 100 acres who had used a hand pump to wash themselves. And at that time no electrical lines had yet been strung that far off the main road back up in there to the little settlement of two or three black-owned farmsteads. Yet she was enrolled in the university when my father met her, ending up teaching grade school for many years in the county. It was she who subscribed to *Life, Look, The Saturday Evening Post* and *National Geographic*, which I spent many Saturday afternoons sitting in the swing on the front porch reading (looking a lot at pictures of half-clothed natives in Africa). *Ebony* and *Jet* or *Negro Digest* were also there, but she thought that reading *Life* or *The Post* made us members of the mainstream. Others in the community were more radical. When I grew older I realized that a certain Mr. and Mrs. Thorpe, who were socially prominent in our community, had been people of this type. They had statistics on all the atrocities, the numbers of lynchings that still occurred, intimidation and brutality on the part of hate groups and of the regular (white) citizenry and the authorities. The Thorpes were members of an organization called the Community Improvement Association (the CIA); and it was improvement not just of our Negro community but

3

the larger civic community (as in Dr. King's Beloved Community). Meetings were held to which do-gooder whites could be seen crossing their lawn to attend, ministers and civic leaders. Their big dog, a German shepherd named Storm, who lived in their house and not in a dog house like most of the dogs of our neighbors, would greet them as they came.

My father was an engaging man constantly in contact with people, a resourceful man, also, highly emotional, excitable to the point of instability, probably what we'd call now a male hysteric. He was a contractor who loved building houses and, after he developed respiratory problems, an insurance man who loved selling policies, speedily moving up to district manager, and who also loved a drink. His death was a blow which I could not assess. Something had been taken out of me—and, like the impact, the picture, of the grotesque, crumpled heap of metal in which he died, the thing itself was still unassimilable. I'd heard my mother say, speaking years later to my father's sister, "The boy like to have gone out of his mind." I hadn't thought *that* at the time, merely having been numbed, emptied, silenced.

* * *

"The thing arrives tomorrow," grandfather said, with blunt precision. The family to the boxed gift planned a visit. I am lying in bed with him, my father's father, in my bedroom, my limbs separated from his by the sheet between us, an acute impossible body. He had been referring to the coffin containing his son's body. The adults went to see it, but I stayed home. I never saw it, as cosmetic work had had to be done on it as a result of the head-on crash at ninety miles an hour. The next day they brought in certain articles, laid them on my table, a watch, a satchel emptied of its paper. They were now my possessions. Grandfather watched my eyes fill. I felt the manner of being held by a stiffening old man. I shuddered, yielding to the force in him. He wished nothing more than the holding. In myself I aspired to a worthiness, something strong in me that would survive him, and the unforgettable imprint of his limbs. That he had been a high school principal, and then a professor—in his retirement years a street and a high school had been named after him, in his little Florida town—a black man who had accomplished something in life—meant everything to me. Considering this, it was not the first time I had thought, how could the grandfathers—who had been direct descendants of the slaves, if not slaves themselves—have been more powerful than the fathers?

But my father too had been an example of something empowering, of determination and possibility, just as other black men in our neighborhood had been. After he died, on my way home from high school, walking through the university campus, I found myself entering the chemistry building and walking down the halls as if I were a college student who belonged there. I was also involved in the Sputnik-fueled amateur rocket building craze at the time and had seen a model of my own blast off. How did I get the fuel, the sulfur, charcoal, zinc dust, potassium compounds, nitrates, and oxidizers needed to fly it? When I walked past the chairman's office door one day the door was open and he looked out and saw me.

"Chris Hinson," he called out. I came back and looked in. "I knew your Dad. I hear you're flying rockets." He knew me as he probably knew all of the children in the neighborhood.

"Yes, sir. I flew one last week." I saw it again in my mind's eye, three feet long, one and a half inches in diameter, resting skyward-pointing on its launching pad as we watched from maybe thirty yards away. (*Popular Mechanics* had published various how-to-build designs for the amateur rocket enthusiasts.) We had painted it green with red bands. Inserted in its tail were matches with a coil of wire wrapped around them and a line leading back to the dry cell battery. I then connected it. When ignited the solid fuel would be consumed in

5

so many fractions of a second and we would hear the swoosh-ing blastoff (or explosion!), but we knew to already be looking skyward where it would already be, if it hadn't blown up, a speck in blue, plumes of smoke in its wake. A parachute with a spring mechanism was supposed to deploy at the apogee of its ascent. It didn't; and instead of the lovely floating descent we expected, it plummeted, as the other had done, back to earth, 200 yards away in the field out behind my house. But we had pierced the sky again and sent our hearts aloft. Nothing like the Atlas, though, that grey-coated concentration of energy like a clothed thunderbolt, the vehicle poised to toss aloft our country's hopes after the comeuppance of the beeping Sputnik that could actually be seen when it made its passage overhead. But the mighty Atlas would do it! Poised, as it began its ascent on those dual blasts of fire, the clamps holding it in position would snap away—the voice of mission control crying Lift Off! We have Lift Off!—and it would make its stately ascent, sort of momentarily pausing, it almost seemed, as if to say good-bye, the most complex and powerful manmade thing we had yet witnessed, the humming of its myriad components, the engineers said, like the respiration of a living thing. Something of this grandeur was in our minds when we looked at our own little rocket.

"Tell me about it," Dr. Ellis, the chemistry department chairman, said. So I came back and sat down, not knowing how much I had missed my Dad, though I see now that he knew. He found time to talk to me on other afternoons. He took me down the hall and introduced me to the chemical supply clerk, who dispensed chemicals through a widow to the students for the experiments they were doing, authorizing me to be a recipient of the bounty from those vast stores, supplementing what I got from the supply shelves of my high school.

* * *

Behind our house, next to the garden, was my father's workshop, full of machines that cut lumber with stacks of lumber on rafters overhead. He took me back out there sometimes on weekends. I loved the profusion of tools with cabinets full of nails, screws, and wondrous implements. The sawdust on the floor gave off the sweetest smell, like the smell of comfort, if good feeling could have a smell.

"Stand back," he said, "over there." I stood ten feet away behind him while he fed a plank into a machine that shaved it smooth by slicing away curling ribbons of wood. The machine had revved up to an intense preening and had slowly subsided, when he cut the switch, into a contented whir of an engine satisfied with its performance. It was like the sound of the world beginning. "This is going to be a cabinet for Mrs. Thorpe," he said, the lady I knew of who had a big lawn and a big dog that guarded it, who had interracial meetings at her house. When he mentioned her cabinet I thought of the sign at the top of our driveway up on a post that had our name on it in large letters, J.E. HINSON, GENERAL CONTRACTING AND FINE CABINETRY. It wasn't from looking at that that I first knew I could read, but from the ice truck. The ice man would come down our street on certain days, selling blocks of ice for the ice boxes people had, at a time, 1945, when home refrigerators were not yet in common use; and written on his truck was COLD ALONE IS NOT ENOUGH, ICE DOES IT BEST. I knew cold and I knew ice and I knew best, but I couldn't figure it out, pondering, until I asked my father.

"That means cold weather isn't enough," he said.

"Enough what?"

"Cold. Not cold enough. So we buy ice."

It came to me then, that idea, and I knew that I could read, and it was also at that time when I looked up again and knew that HINSON was also my name. He said to my mother afterwards, "The boy can read."

7

"Sure he can," she said. "Probably got it from looking at the funny papers, and he just turned four." Now maybe I *had* gotten some of it from looking at the comics! Yet she used to read to me every night, just as she had done with my older sister, and we looked at the books together, and we would also make up and tell each other stories, about the day's events or imaginings— just as we did when we had lain under the tree in the garden. She had often told me a series of stories about a certain Little Bear, and his exploits, a stand-in for me. It was wonderful to reenact the things that I, Little Bear, had done that day. She had seemingly not even thought to credit this as a factor involved in my progress, so self-effacing she was, except in her dealings with her netherworld. I suppose she thought that what we had been doing had been done not just because you were supposed to do it, but because it had been fun to do it. Yet she was proud. She picked me up and showed me the newspaper.

"What is that word?" she asked.

"Tallahassee," I said, pronouncing it exactly. It was where we lived. I'd heard it many times. I loved the way the letters were like the sounds they made. They grinned at each other.

"What does it mean?" he then asked.

"Where we live," I said.

"What *is* it?" he continued.

"I don't know. What? The name?"

"Name of our town, yes."

"Oh, I knew that."

"What is the other word," she asked. She showed me, but I could not pronounce it.

"DEM-o-crat," she said. "*Tallahassee Democrat*, the name of the paper." Then she kissed me on the mouth, her eyes glowing, I imagined, as if she thought I was something delicious to eat, and I also didn't mind being as tasty a morsel as she wanted me to be. Then he started talking to her about something:

"Where in hell *are* the *Dem-o-crats*? After all that trouble, they endorsed that cracker again …" I knew it was about politics

8

but didn't know about what. But I learned later that my Dad himself knew how to be politic in his dealing with people.

I was on a Greyhound bus once, traveling for the first time to Atlanta to visit my sister, about sixteen years old in 1958. My father met the driver and placed me in his care, a man to man affair (trumping the racial affair?), with his hand on my shoulder. I saw the hair-trigger grin of the driver's compliance, his blue eyes like they were encased in ice though he was smiling handily in agreement.

"This is my boy. Going to Atlanta by himself. Look out for him if you can."

"Sure thing, I'll do that." The white man looked at the black man like two southerners who completely knew the rules and understood each other, as they might approach the Coke machine at the convenience store, the white man first, the black man after, the black man, if need be, slowing up to ensure that the white man does arrive first. And the white man could take as long as he liked—he was *supposed* to spend some self-indulgent time doing it—before he relinquished access to the machine to the colored one. Now my father *knew* this, of course, but it didn't mean the rules of etiquette were violated by his asking. On the contrary, appealing to the white man's generosity could secure his protection of me, and he would feel the claims of his idea of noblesse oblige, and we would feel appreciative and in his debt. Even more radically, we might even like each other somewhere for daring to try to establish human bonds!

However, the recent passage of the new Federal Interstate Passenger Law invalidated the segregation statutes for interstate travelers, allowing me to sit wherever I wished, since I was traveling from Florida to Georgia. Somewhere in me was the desire to test the law, though I'm sure my father hadn't suspected this. I looked at the windowpane and saw briefly there the image of a dark-skinned prince, and then I looked through the window and saw my father walking away, without having

9

bestowed the parting wave or glance I had expected. The morning sun sketched a fading hairline, a forehead, and un-hurtful eyes, like mine. It was like one of those scenes of an epiphany, in which I saw him in clarity. It is the image I take away of him, since that moment, seen in retrospect, was the last time I really saw him (no matter how many times we looked at each other afterwards), that year being the year of his death.

The bus quickly filled on our journey through Florida. The whites continued moving on backwards, and the blacks got up and swelled from the rear, assessed my lonely island, its atmosphere, as a blond man deposited his gear—his smile egalitarian in idea. As we became interracial seatmates, in a kind of howl the driver appeared, pounding his fist into his palm.

"Get on back, boy, I mean to look after you like your daddy said." When I continued to stare at him—I'm sure I was quite frightened and couldn't have moved in any case—he reached right across my seatmate and grabbed the shoulder of my coat and pulled me into the aisle.

"It's OK! It's OK!" said my seatmate, tossing his blond hair back into place as he was ignored by the driver. The driver directed me toward a seat in the rear, in the black space, next to a black woman who couldn't look in my direction.

"There, now, that's a good seat, ain't it?" His grin returned, like something he had read about in a manual. I sat on with upraised head, thinking of what manly but un-heroic, life-preserving thing I could have said.

"You all right?" the woman next to me asked. I nodded my head, as all right as I was going to be. She spoke with a mixture of sympathy, outrage, fearful submission but moral superiority that was familiar to me. "Luckily he didn't do no worse," she sighed. I would not have told my father about what happened on the Greyhound bus, though as soon as I got my bags and saw my sister and her husband, Mordecai, who had been a civil rights activist, I told them. He went right back to find the driver to tell him that what he'd done had been illegal. Already he was making a scene. He was angry, his eyes flashing. I thought how good it was too that he was big, black, and powerful looking, the very epitome of the threatening Negro, come at last to unleash his vengeance; and I think that the driver was afraid of him, though he said that he didn't care about what Mordecai said. Then he said that he hadn't done anything. Hearing this I could see the woman who'd sat next to me pipe up with, "Yes you did! And you know what you did." Then my former blond seatmate affirmed that accusation with, "That's right!" and an emphatic toss of his hair back into place. Mordecai seemed to be blocking the driver's egress, so the driver backed up and took another route, his own gear in hand, and disappeared into the station.

What would my father have done? He would have been angry but would have been thinking about how the driver had violated his word and their agreement, and I'm sure the driver would have said exactly that he had kept his word by making an effort to properly look after me. Then my Dad would probably have wanted to pursue the process of securing legal redress. He might or might not have gotten in the driver's face like Mordecai did.

In my twenties I learned that my father's mother had died of tuberculosis before he was a year old. What must it have been like to have the most vital needed thing here one minute and gone the next without even having the language to say what was missed. What would I have been like if my mother had died when I was one? He approached everyone with the expectation of being loved. He seemed sometimes immature to me. But he was hard working and self-sacrificing. He had probably been infected with TB from infancy and it had remained dormant all his adult life until doing the work in his shop activated it. He appeared one day with a mask on, accompanied by county health officials, and then he went to the sanitarium for three years. When he came out he went into the insurance business. I watched my mother negotiate with the white men who came to purchase the machinery in his shop. How could I have known what was the matter with me? Seeing my father led away wearing a mask, my mother's calmly hysterical watching eyes, my younger sister and I being given free lunches at school under the benign generosity of the principal, seeing in the eyes of my friends some sort of look signifying "TB," my sitting under the watchful eye of my fourth grade teacher, after school, making up some math problems that she just couldn't understand why I could no longer do, tears slowly dripping down on the ruled paper.

* * *

At fourteen I acquired my restricted driver's license and started acting as a kind of chauffeur for my father. I think he liked to have me with him, just as he liked to have me mind the office when he and the secretary were out. He took me himself to take the road test, the anxiety we shared about what I might encounter muted. In his pride I don't think he wanted to acknowledge the ways in which the labyrinthine operation of racist designs could impede my progress or dim my hopes. There were plenty of people waiting when we arrived, black and white. While waiting some of us examined one of the new police cruisers parked nearby, with its hood up, said to sport a modified version of a Ford Thunderbird engine, formidable-looking components (a 350+ horsepower high performance V8, four-barrel carburetor, 10:1 compression ratio). By now, with the people assembled around it, the whole thing had become an impromptu demonstration, and a trooper got into the cruiser and started up the engine, gunning it discreetly, but sufficiently to produce that full-throated, propulsive roar that defined the authority of the internal combustion engine, scattering debris in every direction where the dual exhaust pipes curved downward toward the ground. I supposed it got ten miles per gallon (gas was 28 cents a gallon), but what malefactor could outrun it?

When my time came my name was called and I was beckoned by a trooper to follow him. It seemed that actual state troopers conducted the road tests. He was a sandy-haired young man with the florid complexion of an orange, of middle height, with a compact build. He wasn't wearing a gun or other equipment, but his shirt and trousers were official-looking, with a stripe running down the side of the leg, and his wide belt fit snugly around his waist.

We drove and went through some maneuvers. I think I did them well enough. I used hand signals to indicate turns, and when I had to back up, I was able to do so in a reasonably straight line. All the while he wrote up my performance on a clipboard. I, however, felt confident, and immediately I thought that such an attitude was precisely what I should not show to him. When we pulled up to the point from which we'd departed, he told me to stop. He said that I had failed and that I would have to come back. The way he'd said it, as if he had no obligation to explain himself, hurt me into utterance.

"What did I do wrong?" I asked. It wasn't a defiant statement, so much as it was a genuine inquiry. He turned and rested his grey eyes on me, flecked with changing color the way some of the marbles were that I used to play with. He then listed some things which we both knew were spurious. We simply continued to stare at each other. I think it might even have lasted a full minute. We both knew that something of some moment was transpiring, and it was up to him to say what it was. His stare wasn't cold. It was more one of surprise, and then one of examination, of himself, maybe, and of me, and my stare was one of respectful waiting for my right to a reply. He then said, and I knew he was going to say it:

"Come on in and get your license." He didn't say it with apology; it was just a statement he wanted to make. So I went in, got my license, and didn't have to take the parking test, and I when I got back I didn't know what I was going to tell my father. My father could see, just as others watching could, that I hadn't taken the parking test, but when I got into the car, showing him the papers, he just beamed at me and said nothing further. Then, about ten minutes down the road, he said:

"I see you didn't take the parking test."

"Yeah."

"Must have really liked your driving."

"He told me I had failed—and then changed his mind."

"He's that nasty son-of-a-bitch, messes with everybody, the white people too. My heart sank when I saw you had him." There was silence.

"I just stared at him."

"Son-of-a-bitch changed his mind?"

"Yeah."

"Now *that* is something!" He laughed, and then, for the first time that day, I did too.

I thought of a day when a classmate had accosted me with, "You better tell your dad to stop drinking. He was high as a kite yesterday and took a nap in our living room when he came in to use the phone! His car was in a ditch."

Another time he was high, sitting in the dining room with Uncle Louis after a night of drinking, maybe two in the morning. Somehow I had been awakened and had come downstairs—maybe they had called me. He was reeling and sitting at the same time, full of bathos, anguished that his children didn't love him any longer, he said, because I wouldn't come over, when he invited me, to hug him. I think this scene had been instigated by Uncle Louis, an unrepentant drunk, who seemed to get a smug, perverse pleasure out of sharing his affliction—and addiction—with another, seeking as well to promote it in the other, at the same time that he viewed the character weaknesses that emerged in the other with a clinical and amused detachment. My father wanted me to come to him, but I remained rooted to the spot where I stood.

"How you gon' ignore yo' father like that?" Uncle Louis asked, reeling. But he had a mischievous, if not vicious, glint in his eye. I continued to stare off to the side, as if I were studying with some acute scrutiny the intricate lace-work of the table cloth where it hung off the side. My father stared at the floor, perhaps at the patterns in the rug, as if we were mates with different ways of looking at the ironic horrors of the universe. And then my mother came out of the kitchen. She herself had a drink in her hand, and inside had probably been mixing theirs.

"Chris," she said, "go to bed. Go on!" I went back upstairs, but not before I saw her turn on Uncle Louis, her eyes like flares. "YOU, shut your damn mouth." And then, to my father, "and you! ..." But she couldn't continue.

"Hey! Ease up," Uncle Louis said to her.

"Leave 'er alone, Lou," said my father. "The whole thing sucks."

I went back upstairs and lay on my bed. My sisters were awake in their room because I could see the light go off under their door. They (or in any case my older sister) had probably pretended not to have been awake when my father had called me downstairs. I couldn't sleep, of course. After Uncle Louis left, the two of them came up to my room, and stood in the doorway, at which point I too pretended to be asleep. Later, when I got older, and couldn't sleep for a multitude of other reasons, I would play music, an abiding source of solace for me, keyboard music by Bach, perhaps, in which a pianist probed the depths of all sorrow and hope, or introspective longing; or something delicate and soothing, say, by Fauré, as I am one of those people who loves that kind of music.

* * *

"He like that kinda music."

"Dies Irae and shit." They laughed.

"No, man, BhaaAhk—like you going to cough up some crap—and Cho-Pan, some kind of jackleg comedian, in spats," said another. They laughed. This was after choir practice in high school after we'd been rehearsing a short choral piece by that same Bach, the pronunciation of whose name they had just been ridiculing. They were jocular, in a good mood, and still slightly embarrassed at having heard what their sweet tenor voices could do when pushed by our no-nonsense choir director. She made them sing their lines individually, like soloists, and we all knew our comparative vocal strengths and weaknesses. Then we all became aware of what the power was of an ensemble when we put together the individual parts into a thrilling whole. She made them do rousing AHhhhhmens instead of ARrrrmens, sounding, she said, like rabbits. Moreover, some of them took piano lessons, as I did, and played instruments in the high school band.

"Say it again, Chris." This one, Mike, and I both played coronet in the band. When my father, after having spoken to the band director, had actually brought my new instrument down to the school, and all of us admired it, the next week Mike's father had bought him one, too, in place of one of the well-used ones provided by the school.

"The Cincinnati Symphony is playing Brahms's E Minor Symphony up on the campus this Friday, Max Rudolf conducting." I had earlier said this to the choir director. I may have done it just to hear the sound of my voice saying it and their reaction, knowing that the director would approve. They laughed and I laughed with them.

"Damn that shit is boring!" said one, to back-slapping approval.

"And the next thing you know, you be ridin' around with Miss Billie," said another.

"'Those *buns*!, honey,'" two said in unison, with laughter, slapping each other's palms, referring to a well-known, flamboyant, homosexual student, an esthete.

"Listen to you dumb bunnies!" said our director-teacher, suddenly, who had been listening to us. "I think I'm going to

16

have to get some tickets for the choir and take attendance on Friday." They howled in protest. For me it had begun with Bizet's L'Arlesienne Suites which my mother had purchased after clipping a coupon in *Life* magazine touting the virtues of such music and remonstrating how a cultured home should not be without it. She was the perfect customer for whom such advertisements were intended, not being able to make very discerning judgment about such music herself but believing that her possession of it indicated that she was able to do so, and that one should aspire to be able to do so. I had loved it, playing long-playing records on our new console.

"It won't make you any smarter," said Mike, maybe taking up my gambit.

"Chris is already smart. Maybe that's how he got that way," said the teacher. "How's your piano practice coming, Mike? Think you could learn something from listening to some great musicians?"

"I listen to Louis Armstrong and Miles Davis," said Mike.

"You SHOULD listen to Louis Armstrong and Miles Davis, and other musicians as well," said the teacher.

"He never listened to no Louis Armstrong and Miles," said another, having a long-standing beef with Mike's smart-alecky aptness.

"I bet Chris hasn't ever listened to any E Minor Symphony either," said Mike. He had the same timbre to his voice that he had had when he told me about my dad's napping in his living room.

"Well, I'm going to," I said.

"They ain't never liked each other," said another. "Both like the same girl, and both got a crazy brother and sister." It was true that we had a mutual interest in the girl—(she and I used to speak with our eyes in fourth grade crafts hour when we sat and looked across the table at each other as we molded figures in clay)—though her interest in us was decidedly one-sided, to his disadvantage; and the family tragedy we shared meant the recognition of an unwanted and shared familial pain as the basis of a mutual and humiliating identity. Mike's older brother as a child had caused the rotting timbers of an abandoned chicken coop to fall on his head, rendering him mentally impaired and eccentric in behavior, while I didn't even know the cause of my younger sister's infirmity, only that at age three she had sustained some kind of brain injury. It was curious how this was a situation I had had to accept while at the same time never really giving it the kind of thought that the pain of it required. It was as if Mike and I couldn't forgive each other for being the twin reminders of an affliction for which there was no solace or remedy. I don't think I taunted him, but he did taunt me. As a last straw, he once made fun of my movements when the bandmaster had us practicing the steps of our routine on the field. Before I knew what had happened, my hand had shot out and struck him at the collarbone. Actually, I had, uncharacteristically, *decided* to do so, and with that decision came a movement of my hand almost of its own accord. I dared him to tussle and he backed away. Some of the usual crew were watching, wondering what had gotten into me, trying to egg him and me on. They were delighted to see a brawl, where they least expected it, but the two of us just walked away by mutual consent, with no real taste for blood. Yet for a moment I had been intrigued by the idea of—and was poised to bring it about—being the recipient and deliverer of blows, to the head, eye sockets, nose, and mouth, with bloodied faces and knuckles, maybe some broken teeth spat out in bloody, frothy discharges, and so on.

However, an unspoken factor in the dispute with Mike—this just occurred to me—was something as seemingly irrelevant as it was omnipresent, the many-layered issue of skin color and caste identity. The immediate presence of white ancestry expressed itself in his fair skin, hair texture, and eye color, which in turn usually conferred—and in my world was indicative of—privilege and advantage, in opposition to the brown-skinned, curlier haired, and more ambiguous expression of the white ancestry that could be seen in almost all my classmates and in, I once read, all African Americans, 15–20 percent of whose blood was white. We were African Americans in culture as well as appearance and did not look like Africans anymore than we could go back to an African homeland and fit in there. Mike should have therefore had the girl—she was brown-skinned and pretty, who spoke with her eyes, like someone else I knew with whom I used to lie under a tree!—and he was supposed to have had all the good looks and all the smarts as well. But this was not the case, in his ongoing contest with me, and therefore a source of continuing irritation and antagonism.

* * *

The remaining years in high school seemed an agitated blur. I took to senior prom the same girl who spoke with her eyes but also now had a lovely musical voice. It was her voice that had the power of insinuation now, not so much her eyes, which were used now to accent what she said. I was the senior class president, a somewhat shy one, and the salutatorian at our graduation exercises. Having made the highest score on our twelfth grade achievement examinations, I was granted a full scholarship to the local Negro university, FAMU. My mother certainly wanted me to go there, so that I would still be in town near her, not to mention that she would not be called upon to make a financial outlay. I did not want to go there, however. I wanted to go away, not to Columbia or Yale—or even the *white* school in town, Florida State, with my state-granted scholarship—but to Fisk University, in Nashville, Tennessee, a highly rated historically black university—as they called them. To go there seemed to me a matter of pride as well as practicality. Fisk turned out more Negro students who went on to achieve PhD or medical degrees than *any* other institution. It was the first Negro institution to be granted a *Phi Beta Kappa* chapter. It had the famous Fisk Jubilee Singers who had sung before Queen Victoria as ambassadors promoting the cause of Negro higher education. It drew a cadre of proud, strongly aspiring, and capable Negro men and women, from all over the country, urban centers of successful middle class accomplishment as well as ghetto impoverishment, students from small cities and rural farm life. Where else could such a group of Negroes be assembled with so much energy and hope? I wanted to be a part of it.

* * *

I want to speak about two important relationships I had during my college years which were both friendships and love affairs, one with a guy (not what you're thinking) and one with a girl (probably exactly what you're thinking). It is fall 1960 and I am sitting in my dorm room, waiting for my friend Ed to arrive. When he does and I open the door, I see a solidly built, not too tall, somewhat disheveled looking, somewhat sallow-complexioned young man who looks like a hockey player (or a football player, which was one among the many other things he was). Everything about his appearance or inner self seems contradictory. He is the smartest, the most sensitive and gentlest person I have yet met. He would risk his life to save a stray cat darting in front of traffic. He is tormented, and he doesn't just drink beer but frequent hard liquor. He has a strong brow, and bright, soft-brown, watchful eyes that shifted back and forth as he looked at you, the way I imagined a child's might as he attended to what the teacher had just written on the blackboard and the version of it he had scribbled in his notebook. This was not disconcerting. Rather, it made you feel that this was his way of paying attention to you. I felt that he was the first really "gifted" person I had ever known, and it was a privilege to associate with him. He had learned French (because he felt he ought to) and Russian (because he wanted to) at the selective, progressive high school he had attended in Philadelphia, and was said to be perfectly fluent in both. He was supposed to have a photographic memory. He knows as much about jazz, about Miles Davis and John Coltrane, and Ella Fitzgerald, as he does about Mozart and Tchaikovsky, Leontyne Price, and Mirella Freni. He stays up all night reading, and he does differential equations on a pad he always carries in the breast pocket of his shirt, not only just for fun, but also as an unremarked means of keeping his mind engaged. And it didn't seem strange, and was completely wonderful, that he was a black guy like me who possessed these qualities. He joined SNCC and was a Freedom Rider while he was in high school, and though he is not a music major, he exercises a forceful baritone in one of the school's choirs and on occasion is a soloist. Whatever he does he cannot help himself being completely engaged in it. Here we are on one of our weekend excursions:

"I think we gave him a shock," Ed said, as we made our way into our favorite night spot, The New Dawn, at the outskirts of the campus bordering a little business district that soon gave way to a residential area. We saw that our favorite table was available and sat down, this time only the two of us where normally, on a Friday evening, we might be a group of three or four, though the others still might come. Ed had been referring to a mathematics professor we'd just encountered in the liquor store, where we'd gone to purchase, not Smirnoff, Ed's habitual choice, but a bottle of grain alcohol, ethyl absolute, 180 proof.

"Dr. Courtney," Ed had said, with mischief, "a surprise seeing you here."

"Yes," said Dr. Courtney, "the same could be said of *you*, Mr. Kavanaugh." He seemed amused. "I'm getting some scotch, and what are you here for? Is that Mr. Hinson with you?" I smiled sheepishly. The clerk, a bearded man wearing a dashiki, smiled also; he was familiar with us and no doubt with the professor.

"A pint of grain," Ed said.

"Absolutely," replied the professor. "Powerful stuff, rocket fuel, isn't that right?"

"Sir, a pleasure on a whole higher order."

"No doubt, Mr. Kavanaugh. See you in class on Monday morning." He took his purchase and left, placing his brown-paper-bagged bottle into his briefcase, while Ed took his, a pint, and put it into his trouser pocket.

"Of course he knows we drink," I said, as we sat at our table.

"Yeah, but seeing him there is like seeing your mother, getting her bottle of chardonnay." He laughed. He extracted a Camel and I a Marlboro. He lit both with a lighter and we inhaled deeply, blowing smoke into the already smoky room. Where he held the unfiltered Camel I could see the yellowed, discoloring stains on his fingers, like a callous. On the jukebox was a familiar voice singing, *"Don't be cruel,"* penetrating the noise made by the patrons, and when the waitress arrived we ordered hamburgers, fries, Pepsi Colas and ginger ale, for the alcohol, the bottle of which Ed kept out of sight.

"He thinks I won't ace that exam on Monday," Ed said.

"We shouldn't stay here all night then." If the others came we might not leave until 2 a.m., and probably quite drunk, imperiling the whole weekend for studying.

He looked at me. "How're we doing, Chris. How's the state of the world. Are you happy?"

"What? With the universe?" He was being amusing, ironic, but he wasn't teasing.

"With your life." Saying nothing, I thought about this. I'd had the advantage of a supportive environment and the privilege of realizing myself, going to college, and beyond, in spite of having had personal misfortune in my family, a crazy mother, an invalid sister, an alcoholic father, a fear of asser- tion, a character disorder, the always barely suppressed fear of being looked down on as a Negro and treated as less than an equal. I imagined he was going to go in that direction.

"Are you?" I replied.

"You think there'll ever be parity? Not just racially. Economically? Socially? You see the state of the world. Most people don't have a damn thing, and it's hard to know if they even know it. Haiti, India, China, and a million pitiful African villages, not to mention Montgomery, Alabama, if and when their overlords let up on them."

"You try to live a good life yourself," I said. "Things change slowly. You wouldn't have wanted to be in Mississippi in 1840, would you? Even the white boys wouldn't have wanted that."

"*Some* damn well would!" We laughed. Then we were silent. "You think we'll ever really have anything … the Negro race respected like other people. Are the African countries gonna make it? And the Jews and the Arabs? And the Christians and everybody else—who're all gonna go to hell anyway—and all the Hispanics and other mixed-blood people who hate the blacks and hate each other in their desperate attempt to be white, when, as George Wallace used to say, there's not a dime's worth of difference between them."

I looked at him. "And you?"

"I'm trying. We could use some black Einsteins." He looked at me, then he looked away in his habitual way, and then back again, and grinned.

"That's not what I meant."

"But isn't that what we mean? Being the Man at last."

"You had a hard day?" He wasn't speaking out of sadness or bitterness. He spoke as if these were concerns he thought about when he went to bed at night, like a math problem he might be considering with the hope of an answer in the morning.

Our food came and we began to eat. On the jukebox was a well-known ensemble of five family members, singers and instrumentalists, the youngest of whom, the lead singer, was singing in a high falsetto voice—or maybe it was still his actual voice—"*You'll be all alone*," if you continue to reject true love that's being offered.

"You think they're doing a good job by us at school? Would you have rather applied to Brown or Columbia?"

"And been the usual one or two of us there?"

"Yeah."

"I think they're doing all right by us."

"What's your estimate of the degree of incompetence in the ranks? 20 percent?"

"That's too high. Probably about what it is elsewhere."

"What's that? That could vary radically."

"I don't know ... three out of twenty-five?"

"12 percent."

"We've got good, hard-working people," I said. "Look at Dr. Courtney."

"Spends, maybe, some time at the liquor store, 'cause he ain't at MIT, or some such place, Vanderbilt."

"Maybe."

"And I'm sure he still might have some trouble in downtown Nashville trying to buy a decent pair of shoes at an upscale joint, the kind he might want to patronize. What's he gonna say: 'But I have a doctorate in mathematics; I'm one of a select few,' and then pull a blackened diploma out of his pocket." Ed laughed, like he might if he were watching some very funny white people doing vaudeville in blackface—footage of which I had once seen—with thick red lips and widening whites of the eyes, boisterous exuberance, utterances such as *I is* ... and *No you ain't!*

"But he *is* one of a kind," I said. "How many math PhDs of color you think get turned out each year? A hundred? Twenty? Ten? None?"

"Which kind of color?"

"The African variety," I said.

"Doesn't that include everybody, regardless of their *color?*" He had looked away and returned with a sly grin.

"Most recently—*our* kind of color," I replied, returning his grin.

We poured ourselves a drink, a capful or two of grain in about eight ounces of ginger ale. On the jukebox was a triumphant, familiar female voice declaring, in a most sincere and poignant way, "*I say a little prayer for you!*"

"It's a hard thing, man," Ed continued, "just going about your business. I was walking down the street, behind this girl—I hadn't even noticed her—and she looked back and saw me—"

"Sober?"

"Sober—and picked up speed. I kept my pace, and the next thing you know she took off and disappeared around the corner. Went into a store."

"In the day, with people around?"

"Evening."

"Mistook you for her boyfriend, trying to get back together with her."

"It was a white girl."

"Same difference."

Ed took a drink, squinting from the strong vapors that made his eyes water. He said: "Humans are beautiful, men and women, and especially women, who will always be objects of esthetic wonder. Men didn't create that; nature did. The girls wear hot pants and halter tops and expect you to look the other way, when I'm walking down the street minding my own business, and they're coming toward me. Can I help it if they're worth looking at? They ought to be pleased, not angry. All they think is some guy wants to shove his prick into them." We drank and thought about this.

"But isn't that true," I said. We thought some more about it.

"And even if you did, it's not what they think—I'm not talking about the psychos. What can you do with the fact that women are so wonderfully made, so 'express,' as Hamlet said. He was talking about the perfection of the human form, men and women both, so beautiful that it almost makes you want to cry, and they're just being themselves, like peonies in a field."

"Aren't there women who understand that?"

"Really? I think it's virtually impossible to understand, to be completely understood, by anybody. I think we're not capable of understanding each other, really. We just agree, to stave off further trouble."

"No shit? Do *I* understand *you*?"

"There's an ache in my heart and a hard-on too, not for her, but the idea of perfection she represents. You understand that? Would she understand that? How would I convey it? Like wanting to kiss your sister because she's your sister. You see in her the thing you share that both of you are trying to perfect."

"What's that?"

"The agony of being alive and the little things that offset it—a pretty face, or the look in your eye right now, that makes me feel good, and want to bless you."

"Go ahead. You look like my mother does when she wants to kiss me."

"Can I?"

"I don't know. Can you?" I saw that for him not to do so would be to say no to possibility, so he go up and sort of leaned over to say something in my ear and kissed me on the cheek. He sat down again and took a long drink. On the jukebox was a wondrous voice addressing his *"Cherie,"* saying *"I … I, I … I, I love you!"* In that moment it penetrated our consciousness.

"You ever put any money into that thing?" he asked. "Is there a song on it for me?" He started to croon in a melodious baritone, some lyrics and a melody he felt coming to him at that moment. He did not pause as he thought it up, as it seemed simply to come whole:

> *I saw her at the table*
> *Her eyes were quick and low*
> *But she held our hidden glances*
> *And our hearts began to glow.*

Then, he said, the chorus kicks in with, "*No, No, No!*"

We laughed. He was looking at a table where a woman was looking back at us. We had seen her before. She was sitting with her girlfriend. "We ought to invite them over," said Ed.

"Go for it," I said. He got up as casually as if he were going to the john, just as he had done when it seemed he was coming to whisper something in my ear, and went over and brought the two back with him. They sat down and we introduced ourselves. They were Joan and Janice, clearly older than we were, at least in their thirties.

"We've seen you before," I said.

"This used to be our neighborhood place," said Joan, "but the students have taken it over."

"That's us," said Ed. "Can we get you anything?"

"How about a Heineken," said Joan, speaking to Janice.

"Sure," said Janice. "Were you singing a song."

"Wanna hear it?" asked Ed. "We just came up with it, looking at you."

"Something original?" asked Janice.

"Probably," said Ed. He looked at me and then began, changing the singular to plural, and I followed. We held the words at the ends of each line, for maximum effect. We swelled in volume as we continued, achieving some harmony, and people turned in their seats to watch us and listen. When we finished there were whistles and applause:

> *We saw them at the table*
> *Their eyes were quick and low*
> *But they held our hidden glances*
> *And our hearts began to glow.*

"Oh, that's great!" said Joan. "You made that up? You talking about us?"

"But you haven't heard the chorus yet," said Ed, "which goes, *No. No. No!*" They laughed heartily. Joan was plump, brown-skinned, with a low-cut black dress with plunging neckline, while Janice was slender and fair-skinned, in a red pants suit. Both wore wedding rings.

"Did you really make that up?" asked Janice.

"On the spot," said Ed.

"That's interesting," said Joan, "unlike some men we know." They looked at each other and laughed. Joan was pretty, with sensuality in her plumpness, and her smile was sweet and innocent. She had been the one who had looked back over her shoulder at Ed.

"What're you majoring in?" asked Janice.

"I'm in physics; he's in psychology," said Ed.

"You don't look it," said Janice.

"How're we supposed to look?" I asked.

"Uptight," said Janice.

"We are," said Ed.

"In that case we won't hold it against you," said Joan. "We had some crazy teachers once. They were the most fun."

"Though I don't know if they kissed each other," said Janice. The two of them laughed.

"But you never know," said Joan.

"What if we did?" asked Ed.

"You did—we saw you, but no problem with us," said Janice.

"But it ought not to be a problem in any case," said Ed.

"I know. People are narrow-minded," said Janice.

"But I think you guys were just playing around, right?" said Joan.

"Oh, we were dead serious," said Ed.

"You mean, you're gay?" said Joan.

"Do you think so?" I asked.

"No," said Joan.

"Why?" I asked.

"Jesus, you guys are really—strange," said Janice, laughing.

Ed said: "Not so strange we couldn't make love to you, though, I bet."

"Oh, I believe you could!" Janice declared.

"But could you *love* us," asked Joan.

"The men you know can't?" asked Ed.

"We're talking about you," said Janice.

"What's your impression?" I asked.

"I don't trust impressions," said Janice. "But I will say you sing nicely."

"You inspired us," said Ed.

"That says something good," said Joan, "that maybe women matter to you."

"They do," I said.

"The way you matter to yourself," said Janice.

"I might not matter to myself," said Ed.

"Well, you're the professors; it's on you to figure that out," said Janice. "That's what you're going to be, right, teachers—professors?" A certain tension had been removed.

"Is that a good thing to be?" asked Ed.

"Well, yes," said Joan. "You can be smart, get your PhD, like Dr. King, and still be real, and deep, too, like Malcolm X, all at the same time."

"And still know how to party," said Janice.

"We're trying," said Ed. "So what do you two do?"

"I'm a legal assistant, in a law office," said Janice.

"She works downtown, the only colored one in there," said Joan. "You should hear some of her stories."

"And you?" I asked.

"I work in day care, with little kids," said Joan.

"We've seen the two of you in here," said Ed.

"Likewise," said Janice. "You guys hang out with your other friends."

"We grew up around here," said Joan.

"Then you got married?—we couldn't help noticing your wedding rings."

"Oh, that's just for show," laughed Janice.

"You're not married?" I asked.

"Yeah, we're married," said Joan.

"Still for show," said Janice. "I mean, it only represents what it does."

"What's that?" asked Ed.

"Hope," said Janice. "You're looking for one thing and you get something else. Still you hope."

"And if one of them came in here now and saw us talking to you …" Joan's voice trailed off into silence.

"You could say we went to high school together," said Ed.

"*They're* the ones we went to high school with," said Janice.

"But you stay married," I said.

"You stay married to hope," said Janice, "unless, you know, he hurts you."

"Maybe you'll find out differently when your time comes," said Joan. Into this moment intruded a mellow voice on the jukebox, crooning, *"Your precious love …"* "If only they mean it when they say it," said Joan.

"Just lies," said Janice.

"Maybe it's his version of hope," I said.

"What's he doing to sustain it? I still got my ring on," said Janice. It didn't sound like bitterness, so much as simply a matter of fact statement.

"Any children?" I asked.

"None," said Janice.

"I want some," said Joan, "but they don't come."

We spent another twenty minutes or so talking like this with them before they had to get up and go home. They thanked us and told us to keep on singing. We could be the singing professors, they said. We left after they did, our mood somewhat subdued. As a tonic we had another drink. Outside we walked down the street and became enlivened again, in the state of being pleasantly high. We passed by a respectable-looking edifice, the marquee next to it announcing evening vespers and worship. I think it was African Methodist Episcopal.

"Let's go to church," Ed said, extraordinarily amused by the idea. "I could use some spiritual uplift, and maybe it's time to cleanse the Temple again."

"Probably it's too late," I said, having an inkling of what might be in the making in Ed's mind. Nevertheless, we continued, mounting the steps. When we arrived at the first landing, and stopped, slightly swaying from the cessation of our motion, we could see a figure—probably female—huddled under a blanket sitting with her back against the stone wall at the side of the stairs. When we drew abreast of the figure a narrow palm, seeming to address us, extended itself from under the blanket. It hovered there, as if weighing its portion of the displaced air.

"Son-of-a-bitch!" I heard Ed mutter under his breath. He reached into his hip pocket, got out his wallet, and extracted a bill. In reaching to put it in her palm, he almost tipped over the neat-looking little shopping cart, parked next to her, tightly packed with her belongings.

"Lady,"—he said it with the greatest delicacy—"please take this." He placed a $20 bill in her hand, and the hand closed around it and withdrew back under the blanket. We paused a moment longer then resumed our ascent, at which point we heard a light, thin female voice say, "Thank you, Sir." Then we marched on up the stairs, jerked open the doors and stood swaying before the congregation. We were not the repentant inebriated sinners, pitiful and pitiable, come to plead salvation for our souls that some worshippers had imagined to their disgust. On the contrary, Ed began a loud, sustained assault, shocking and outrageous. At once he jeered at the vanity and self-importance of the officiating minister, whose upturned face had a questioning look of shock and disbelief. Ed challenged him to say at once if he thought he was worthy of any

31

divinity's grace. He called upon him to cease his inept ministra-
tions, to come down from the pulpit, take off his stupid robes
that made him look like death itself, so suitable for his dead
doctrines. Let him strip himself naked, let him come down
from there and walk the streets of the real world, defiled, full
of human wreckage and misery. Let him do so in rags, with all
the humility he could muster, like the example of his master
the Christ, he said, then raising his hand, pointing his finger,
who, if you met him, *you* wouldn't recognize him, since he'd
be consorting with derelicts and junkies! And by the way, he
concluded, there's a starving lady outside this edifice sitting
on the steps. Maybe one of you good people could go out and
help her. Then, as if for the first time addressing the minister
directly, he said: "Do you really think God is on your side?
Jesus *really would* be out putting his hands on all the people
you despise, doing so with soulful, piercing eyes, in the halls
of power and community centers, where people don't believe
they're one human family; in the GHETTO, people using
and abusing, where children ain't got no daddy, or mommy
either—'Suffer Little Children to Come Unto Me.' That's where
He'd be. Consorting with ladies of the night—or other *jobless*
people—admonishing them, sure, but suffering along with
them. Just about the last thing *you* would be doing."

This and more resounded in my ears, which were burning.
So was my face. I could not retreat, shrink away into my body,
so I found myself instead detached from it, hovering above.
Every perception was coolly distinct and precise. I heard
Ed's sharp staccato breathing and his rapid-fire disgorging of
words, insanely reminding me of an ax-wielding woodsman in
a forest, sweat-beaded and sublime. I was not surprised by his
inspired elocution. He had made himself perfectly understood,
and I could only admire him for that. But the enormity of our
act began to press in upon me. I imagined that we would be
struck by lightning, I imagined that we would be beaten sense-
less, I imagined that we must have looked like the very devil

to the array of outraged faces which confronted us, now being roused as if from a numbed stupor.

It wasn't long before church attendants moved against us as one man, literally lifting us off our feet, propelling us back out through the massive wooden doors and flinging us down the steps where we lay, bruised and bleeding. Ed had not resisted this, in a way that I knew he certainly could have. We were tolerably sobered for the moment. I saw that we should leave, and I made efforts to lead him away. It was clear that the men were ready to give us a beating. The look in their eyes was indescribable. They seemed as much outraged as wounded, glaring still in disbelief. They did not appear to have words equal to their feelings. Even profane ejaculations would not have sufficed (to utter them would seem to put them on the same level as the brutes they were dealing with), though I thought that the tension in their bodies hungered for physical discharge—some of the blows and kicks we had already received. It was at this point that we heard a sweet, thin voice, but with surprising carrying power, declare, "Oh, don't hurt them!" We looked up, momentarily taken aback, and saw her, an obviously grand-motherly face, uncovered now, though not creased, that went exactly with her youthful sounding voice and long, gray-streaked braids. It did not seem possible that this was the same head that we had earlier seen cowering under the blanket. But our attention was quickly withdrawn from her back to the situation at hand, the churchmen seemingly dismissing her as some kind of aberration. Ed and I roused ourselves and went up the street and, to my relief, noted that we were not being pursued. "Tomorrow you'll see that bastard riding in his Cadillac—just like my father!—as if nothing had happened," said Ed, "the damned hypocrites."

We seemed completely sober now, as we approached a small park of three or four benches adjacent to a bus stop, in which sat a couple past middle age. We sat down. Ed produced a pack of cigarettes, took one for himself, offered me one, and lit both with the flip of his thumb on the mechanism of his little silver lighter. We sat and smoked silently, staring into space, in the vicinity of the couple, who returned our gaze uneasily, scrutinizing us from head to toe with quick flitting glances. Ed produced a handkerchief and gingerly dabbed, with nicotine-stained fingers, at the back of his head and the bridge of his nose. The handkerchief came away faintly stained with blood. Ed stared at it but said nothing, as if he were looking down the bottom of an empty glass. Seemingly uninjured, I found only that I needed to brush myself off and tie my shoelaces. I felt guilty as I watched Ed put his handkerchief away. Ed said, in a neutral tone, "I think one of those bastards must have hit me." I didn't know, though I remember the strong grasping fingers that locked onto me like talons and lifted me bodily away. A furtive glance told me that Ed was staring intently ahead, in the direction of the couple. He appeared to be in a trance. I also looked at the couple and saw that they had become afraid. I thought how they were what our own parents would have looked like. The couple presently got up and moved toward us in the direction of the exit, shrinking away from us as far as possible, as if walking on a tight rope, bracing themselves against a strong wind. Ed, seeing this, suddenly roused himself. He rose from his seat and approached them in a shambling urgency. "Don't go," he said. "You don't have to be afraid of us." Saying nothing, they hastened their departure, the woman instinctively placing her hand across her bosom in a protective gesture. Ed, almost imploring, continued: "We wouldn't hurt you! That's the last thing in the world we would do." But they were rapidly moving toward the bus stop, looking over their shoulders back at the two of us, and I could see that the bus was coming. It stopped, they got into it and rode away. "Probably going to church," said Ed dully, "or coming home from it." He flung away his cigarette in disgust and began walking down the street. I had to stride quickly to keep up with him.

I was unpleasantly aware of feelings of pain and shame about what we had done. The night was calm and peaceful. The street lamps, like giant bowling pins in top hats, cast an ineffectual, hazy glow along the shrubbery-bordered sidewalk. Ed said: "The only divine thing, the only thing capable of being honored, is the human spirit, in you and me, forever and ever. There isn't anything else. The guy on the cross is a powerful image, a powerful image of suffering. Isn't that what the world is, has been, and always will be doing? But love isn't triumphing in this world, hate is, and self-interest, and stupid religious intolerance, not to mention hypocrisy." This he delivered in both a solemn and fervent manner, as if he had been praying; and as we walked along, I could see tears flowing down his cheeks. "You think they would have let us in there—in their filthy 'holy' sanctuary, if we hadn't been 'respectable' looking—even though we also looked like poor suffering bastards reeking of drink seeking repentance—'CUSE ME, I mean *salvation*." He laughed. "Shopping bag ladies? Those other ragged, pitiful, crazy bastards with their hands out, begging. Homeless families? They don't even let 'em into the place. They sleep outside on the steps, when they don't just shoo 'em away like human garbage. Ain't that a bitch! If there were a God, He would have died of horror and shame by now, at all the crap done in his name. Jesus! Can't they see themselves? Look at those creatures who actually burn Christ's cross, that Lamb of God, in the name of their lunatic hatreds. Sons-of-bitches! Divine wrath should have incinerated them on the spot! And the sad, sad thing about it is they die just like you and me. There's no reckoning in the end. Hell is a natural human idea. A very attractive idea. Some justice ought to be coming down in the end. But it's a lost cause, hell is. Think what it would be like if they really knew, if they really knew, that in the end what they did to others would be done to them. Simple, pure, precise. I could love the world then, and honor it, and take my chances like the next guy, because there would be real accountability. What you did would be done through choice, and would *count*. The world would have order and justice in it. No more fictions and lies! We would have to trust ourselves, stand up and be real men in this universe. And we would get what we deserve, a fulfilling of our glorious humanity, instead of pitiful quacks and their spiritual apparatus."

I saw how the profane in him was as extreme as the spiritual. As we turned a corner, we could see the array of lighted windows in the dormitory. I didn't know what to make of this night, but I certainly would never forget it. And it had begun to be clear to me the severe nature of Ed's disturbance, the ease with which I'd allowed myself to be sucked into it. Ease? I had willingly embraced him almost as a lost soul mate, suddenly found, a beloved brother I had never had. But I had to quit this kind of behavior. Moreover—it seemed somewhat a crass thought, alongside the concerns with which Ed was grappling—my grades were beginning to suffer, in this, still, our freshman year. Yet I understood Ed's disturbance.

One Sunday morning weeks later, I emerged from the dorm with a group on the run trying to make breakfast before the doors closed. It was a bright sunshiny morning, cold, before the Christmas holidays, and we burst out the doors and down the sidewalk, on the run, where, at the curb in the gutter, a body lay, arresting our motion. "Good Lord, it's Ed," someone said, as I turned to him, somehow suspecting as much. Ed, soiled, but otherwise unhurt, lay in an alcoholic slumber. We took him back in and put him to bed, fearing pneumonia. I sat by his bedside and waited for his roommate to return. When the roommate returned, without Ed's awakening, I went out for breakfast.

Later that afternoon Ed appeared, embarrassed, with bloodshot eyes and trembling hands. He had always had a tremor, but this was the worst I'd seen. "How do you feel?" I asked. "Shitty," he replied, "and I can't sleep. I haven't been able to sleep in days. I keep having this dream, and I wake up in a sweat.

There's this giant red blob—imagine that, a red blob, like in horror movies—there's this red blob creeping up on me, absorbing everything in its path, eating things up, disintegrating things, everything in its path. A giant protoplasm, hungry, and it's headed for me. I can't sleep … Jesus, I'm tired, Chris. You think I could sleep in here? Your roommate's away, isn't he? Let me sleep in here. I need somebody with me." I agreed to this, hoping Ed wouldn't soil my bed, which is where I put him, not in my roommate's, who in any case wouldn't have minded, who was a civil rights activist at this moment probably engaged in the planning of some life-threatening action. I myself had work to do, as a matter of fact, a mathematics assignment. Perceiving this, Ed wanted to help. "You aren't in any shape. Just lie down," I said. Ed protested, "No, man, I can always do that. That's my meat." I declined Ed's offer, though we all knew of his exceptional performance on the college boards. Mathematics was his god, and he served with the most unpretentious, yet exacting, devotion. It was not about *this* that he was arrogant, since he never called any attention to it.

Not more than thirty minutes had passed when he awoke with a shriek, trembling, as he shrank away on the bed into a corner, as if he were looking at something, a coiled rattler on the floor. He came to himself and said out of tormented eyes, "The thing's going to get me." He was as helpless as a child. I knew that what Ed wanted was for me to hold him. I climbed into the bed, my back against the wall, and did so. It was frightfully uncomfortable, but it quieted him. After minor adjustments, he began to sink down into sleep again. Here we are, I thought, and what a sight this would be. What Ed needed was psychiatric help. What *I* needed was psychiatric help—didn't everybody? But a man who's been drinking since fourteen is already far gone. What had happened in his family? He only spoke of this obliquely, as about his mother's chardonnay and his father's hypocrisy, a man who had achieved prominence in the black Church, one of the main routes of black male achievement. And here Ed was, just as he was, utterly and completely and self-destructively wrought.

After a while Ed began to snore, in deep guttural exhalations, but I was afraid to move, lest he awaken. Yet I was stiffened; both my legs were asleep. I gingerly disengaged myself and got out of the bed. I stood before the recumbent form, sorrow and pity clutching me. I had held him in my arms, soothed him into quietness. He had clung to me. It brought tears to my eyes, but I was as helpless as he was. I went back to work, as best I could, after a brown paper bag dinner, through the afternoon and into the night, while Ed continued to sleep, rising once to go to the bathroom. Thus it remained when I turned out the light and went to bed. Ed was chastened and grateful when he woke up the next morning. He thanked me for simply being a friend. There was also something else he seemed to want to communicate to me. He said, "Last night I remembered a time when I was happy, when I was a kid at a place my parents had outside Philadelphia. A kind of farm up on a hill, with a barn. We went there on weekends and in the summer. They thought I hated leaving town to go there, but I loved it. I'd look out of my window and see the sun rising. An apple tree was out there, that flowered in the spring and gave applies in the fall, Macintosh, I think. The streaks of red would start showing through the clouds, and the sun would push up past the horizon. That's when the birds would start singing. In the beginning, you might say, God had intended something beautiful, and it just all went downhill from there … I was thinking of the place, or I dreamed it, last night."

For the rest of the school year, I saw less and less of Ed. School officials had intervened, contacting his parents, giving him a therapist, with the consequence that his allowance had been drastically cut, though he still managed to find money for drink, at which time I would lock my door and pretend I wasn't in, when Ed knocked on it. One time I found myself paying Ed a visit, having previously observed him walk soberly up the hall to his room. He had a half-full bottle of something that had started out as water. This he passed successively through other empty bottles, giving each a vigorous shake. Ed began to drink, satisfied with his efforts. "Did you save all these bottles for this?" I asked. "What do you think?" was the reply, "and maybe I'll give my shrink a taste too." I smoked a cigarette and left. Ed seemed in the process of descending to some level of hard, bare imperviousness where he could not be reached. I noticed, though, that in front of him was a little pad with mathematical equations on it. In downing his drink, he had looked at me in that quizzical way, then looked away, then back at me, and had said, "Everything sucks." In it I heard the echo of my father's statement, *The whole thing sucks*, what *he* had meant, the particular part of his human inheritance as a disappointed and humiliated black, joined with the general, maybe, what everybody grapples with, *who is there to love me*? to which Ed would have added, as I would, *Who is there to understand me in this loneliness*? I saw then how it was that the familiar lure of drink had been a compelling force, like something hereditary, something I could succumb to in relating to Ed, even though I had never been a drinker.

It developed that I slowly acquired a new set of friends and had little contact with Ed, though we still lived a few doors away from each other. I had begun to write articles for the campus newspaper and to associate with a literary crowd, people regarding whom it was ironic that Ed probably had more literary ability than they, and he would look at me with the understanding that we shared this knowledge. He accused me of being a false friend, though always without heat, as if by not doing so in anger he never acknowledged the actual break in our friendship, while at the same time he kept open to me the option of changing my mind. Or at least I think that's the way it was.

* * *

The second relationship I had was with Della, the girl who should have been my wife, who was my first real girlfriend, the girl with whom you discover for the first time what your mettle is or whether you're a worthy person in your own eyes. I am sitting in my dorm room thinking about whether I should get up right now, take a bus to her house (she lived in town) and undo everything that has just transpired regarding our decision not to try to maintain our relationship after graduation that spring, since I would be in graduate school in Iowa and she would be working as a chemist with Bristol Myers in Illinois. It had been decided, I had decided, like slipping a $100 bill into a slit in your strongbox, where it can no longer be retrieved, yet you wanted it back as soon as it left your hand. It is 10 p.m. and I can hear bells announcing this from some tower on the campus, perhaps Jubilee Hall. Instead of getting up and going, I find myself putting a record on the record player.

I am listening to Gabriel Fauré's Opus 50 "Pavane," and then his *Requiem*, beautiful ethereal music, giving voice to poignancy and regret. With the "Pavane," it always seemed to me that some great gracious thing was being recalled, something deeper than nostalgia, because the thing that was trying to be recalled would forever remain unknown. I thought that it was a remembrance of an original state of perfection, where what *was* was inseparable from what was *good*—the floating protoplasmic potential in the womb, for instance. I thought of the innocence and wonder of a child, lying in the crib, looking up and out at the attending face in all its mysterious solicitude. It held me in such a way that if I were to cry out, I wouldn't know, beforehand, whether the sound I'd make would be of pain or joy.

Della was smart, willful, pretty, a feminist in the way that many black women have always had to be, claiming their right to self-assertion, if they wanted to survive, not simply as women or black women but as human beings. The writer Alice Walker had seemed to affirm this idea when she didn't want to call it being a feminist so much as she wanted to call it being a womanist.

40

We arranged a foursome one night. It was a residential area some distance from the Fisk campus. Both Della and Mary lived off campus, had been born and raised in the city. Nevertheless, securing the apartment had been a coup of some kind, and they were proud of having brought it off. We would go to it, set soft lights and music, drink, dance, talk and sleep briefly together, the long awaited and expected raison d'etre of our coming together in the first place.

Kevin and Mary sat amused in the front seat of the car while Della and I satirized the anticipatory motions of lovemaking in the back. I groaned and panted, tried to put my hand down her blouse, as she brushed it away. The two in the front had the settled appearance of a married couple, already sure of each other. Now I know that Della had planned, that night, to yield up her virginity, bind me to her, secure from me a pledge that mated me to her, and to her family—whom I'd already met, frequently had dinner with, and *liked*—and the life we would make together, the two children we would have, of course, the nice house, after we'd finished graduate school and gotten good jobs. I saw it already, laid out, and something in me rebelled.

There was an assortment of music on the stereo, rock, rhythm and blues, mood music, and we performed the gyrating, contorting rock steps, interspersing these with what we made to be the equivalents of waltzes and polkas, whenever the music allowed, all our movements governed by the ongoing, jerking influence of The Twist. As the motion continued, Kevin closed with Mary and propelled her into the bedroom and closed the door.

We lingered on the floor, kissing, until the music ceased, then went to the couch and sat down, continuing with a long impassioned kiss, as we stretched out on the couch, with the beginning now of a sense of the inevitable and a new and tender and slightly frightening quality. I felt how sumptuous she was, yet I felt within me the beginnings of a disquieting realization that the intercourse I must have with her was not wholly desired, I could not say why. But the momentum of our action had continued, and we lay now sufficiently unclothed, I on top of her, as I continued to experience the ever increasing inner shrinking and withdrawal of desire, until we lay prone, quietly unmoving.

"What's the matter?" she asked gently.

"I don't know," I said. "I can't," with a finality which surprised me. But it was also as if I'd said, "I won't," an implication not lost on her.

"Don't you want to?" she asked, in a kind of burning, pleading, intensity. "I do." I didn't know what to say; I didn't know what was happening.

"I'm sorry. Maybe I've had too much to drink." Was this true? I didn't think so. I tried to stroke her furrowed brow, which annoyed her, and she began to lean away from me, as we became aware of sounds and movement coming from the other room. I began to think of the extent of my innocence. I hadn't given any thought to contraception beforehand, and I imagined the thought she gave it was not to have any tonight. Yet I knew what I should have expected of this night—knew fully, yet had never once thought of it until now. But the matter of contraception wasn't the issue. It was something else—what?—to make love to her would be to take a wife? To accept something real and serious about the two of us? Well, I desired her, yet I couldn't make love to her.

Della, putting on her clothes, looked at me with sorrow, compassionately, but nevertheless with a detachment, as if some damage had been done me that needed repairing, and she was not sure what her role was in correcting it. "Maybe some other time," she said, "when we're alone. It might be better." I saw her luminous moist eyes. I saw how she had been hurt, and was struggling to dismiss whatever gnawing thought that led her to think that she had been the one at fault. I reached for her hand, she withdrew it; I reached for it again, holding it firmly in my grip this time. There was defiance, desire, and a

42

plea in her eyes. You could read each separate one. Her grip tightened in my hand, even as I felt the pull of an urge in her to draw it away. However, I now felt in place of the shrinking away in me something else, strong and pulsating, an urge to sink myself into her nevertheless, as if it were something I, still in my unclothed state, must offer her. I think it came about as a result of her resistance, her will to pull away, and we both seemed to be aware of this. She stared at me. At that moment we heard a certain recognizable sound of a squeaking, rhythmic give and take that the action of bodies might make on a couch pressed against a wall.

"Damn you," she said softly. There were tears in her eyes. She got up, went for the door, opened it, and left. I thought how I must quickly find my shoes, pants, and shirt, put them on and go after her. Outside was a residential area of houses bordered by sidewalks in front with periodic outcroppings in the walkway where the roots of the oaks had raised up the concrete. I went out after her looking I'm sure disheveled. I could see her walking slowly but steadily down the block as she approached a crossroad with a wooded lot at the left. Her pace was such that I had the impression she had been hoping I would follow her, but she did not stop when I called her name. When I reached her, I called her name a second time, put my hand on her shoulder and she stopped. Her head was bowed. I turned her around and kissed her, and she did not resist. She did not put her arms around me, but her mouth pressed back against mine. The urgency I had felt earlier returned, and I propelled her right through an opening in old, neglected privet hedges which formed a border around a lot at the corner. This done, however, she began to pull me down upon her, and we almost toppled down in a grassy twig-strewn area near the remains of a flowerbed. Next we were naked and lying on our clothes. It seemed like the farther I wanted to sink into her, the more I made up for our anguish and pain, as she took hold of it and guided it further within. We mounted and surged until the insurmountable building up and arrival of the sweetest discharge occurred, as her mouth fell away from mine and my fingers relaxed their grip on her buttocks. We had not consciously spoken, but as we lay, still holding each other, a middle-aged man and a woman thrust their heads right through the opening in the hedges, first he and then she. They looked expressionlessly and then withdrew, but as if they knew what they'd find, and then his head appeared again, "Maybe… you should finish that at home?" he said, and then they left. For the first time she smiled.

"We're finished," she said. She had grass and twigs in her hair, and her full-bodied form, still lying there, with her long, full, shapely legs, made her look like a woodland nymph.

We returned holding hands. Kevin and Mary had come out and were having tuna sandwiches and Pepsi. They looked at us and smiled. We joined them.

"I'm famished!" said Della. Her eyes were bright.

"Yes," said Mary.

"We took a walk," I said.

"I know what you mean," said Kevin.

* * *

The thing is, she was a completely desirable catch, in the way that a black woman could be sought after, possessing the qualities desirable to a black man. She had humor and she was a good sport. If I didn't support her she would support herself, and if I were successful she would be appreciative, always supportive and never give me flak, even if I had drawbacks or personal failures of character. I would really have to hurt her before she turned on me. She was good-looking, intelligent, congenial, and fair-skinned, of an old, established, black middle-class standing. She was a chemistry major and had already been recruited by a chemical firm responding to the burgeoning new cadre of black college graduates. The school

44

year was almost ending, and all we talked about was graduate school and the prospects of jobs beyond. She already had a job, and I was set to go to the University of Iowa to write plays in the creative arts division there.

"Are we going to get engaged?" she asked one afternoon late in the school year, as we sat on the porch of her house in one of those old black neighborhoods in Nashville. We sat in a swing and looked down a tree-lined street of elms. We were aware that Kevin and Mary had announced their wedding plans for June this time next year. Her mother appeared through the screen door, the spitting image of Della, a middle-aged, overly plump but well cared-for version of a good-looking black female, brown-skinned like me.

"Would you like more lemonade?" she asked, looking at me. She had a tray with glasses, cut lemons, a bottle of gin and a pitcher of real lemonade. She set the tray down and stood outside the door as if she were an expected participant in our conversation, to which undoubtedly she had been listening. "You can let yourself go now and have a drink now that school is over." She sat down in a wicker chair next to the door looking like she could be Della's elder sister. She looked at me and smiled, with playful, light-colored eyes, like my mother might when she was pleased with something I had done.

"I loved your play they did at Fisk," she said.

"Just a reading," I said.

"It was good, though, and you got a scholarship to go to graduate school." She got up, went to the tray, poured herself a glass of lemonade over ice. "Chris?" She motioned to me. I agreed to have a glass, so she poured me one, with a substantial amount of gin in it.

"I'll have one, Mama," said Della. What sounded like the residue of a child who had had to ask permission for many things was still resonate in her voice, not completely mitigated by the assurance of a confident young woman. "With rum," she said. The amount she got was half of what I got.

45

"You should come more often, Chris. You can always have dinner here. Della won't be here for long." She gave a sort of long, constrained sigh.

"Thank you," I said. In the last month I had visited three times, as many as in the past two years, since we had become interested in each other.

"Della is going to take that job with Bristol Myers."

"I know," I said. "A good salary."

"They were *very* interested in me in my interview" broke in Della.

"Of course they were, a smart black girl with a straight A average. In chemistry and biology no less," she added. "But!—is that real security?" She looked at me.

"You don't really know anything about it, Mama."

"You should get a PhD in biochemistry! You should have gone to medical school! The whole world has become possible to you! You should take advantage of it." She took a drink of lemonade. "You can't trust anything. You should fix it so you set yourself up in the best way."

"You never know how far she can go there," I said, not wanting to have her enlist me on her side against Della.

"I believe they're just going to use them, take advantage of them, and have window dressing to boot."

"Ma, you think you know everything. You never listen to anyone."

"Ask your father! They finally let him move up to the office at the factory after twenty years. The only one. Time for a black man."

"But he knows the business inside out," Della said.

"I got my MA, I got tenure, I have a union, I get regular salary increases."

"He makes more than you do, Ma."

"*Now*, he does." She looked at me. "Chris, I guess you're in the family now." She had that wry, playful look again.

46

"But you're going to be in Iowa and she's going to be in Evanston, Illinois?"

"Yes," I said.

"It's going to be long distance?"

"Ma, why don't you stop? You wouldn't expect him to give up his plans and come be with me. He doesn't expect me to give up my plans and come to Iowa."

"I don't expect any such thing," she said. "You know what I expect."

"Chris and I'll work this out."

"Of course," she said. "I'm out of order anyway." She got up and went inside. It was late evening as we sat in the swing, looking at shadowy figures approach and recede on the sidewalk. The street lights came on.

"Shouldn't we?" She placed her hand in mine.

"We could, but we shouldn't."

"You don't want to?"

"You know how hard it would be to keep it up."

"You don't want to try?"

"I don't want to start something that we can't keep." She studied this for a long time, then withdrew her hand.

"Then I don't either." She got up. "There's always something resistant in you. You should think about that."

"I think about it all the time."

"Then *do* something about it, because I'm tired of dealing with it!"

"Talking like that won't help me."

"You make people feel bad."

"You're making *me* feel bad!"

"You're giving up everything!" She had been standing, looking at me, as I looked back at her. Then she moved to go into the house. "I'm going in now, so bye, bye. You should be getting back to your dorm." She blew me a peck of a kiss. Her eyes were bright and glistening as she went in. I imagined mine were also, as much from regret as from an inability to understand my own fatal indecision or, better, inhibition.

* * *

There had been no woman since Della, not even through two years of graduate school, at the Midwestern university where I'd gone with the intention of becoming a playwright. I had, however, read a lot and met interesting people, one among whom was a great classics scholar with a joint appointment in the theatre arts and classics departments, the former department the one in which I was enrolled. In the theatre arts department the classics scholar tried out his translations of the Greek plays with the theatre group, and then published them in the lovely little blue-backed Crofts Classics series. He also taught courses in theatre history and dramatic literature. In one of these courses in which I was enrolled, I waited one day after class, as the papers were being given back from the first examination, and the drone-call of names was proceeding, for my name to finally be called.

I had come to understand how I could be viewed with sympathy and even unexpressed pity for being a struggling black student who had made it so far. Not that the white kids hadn't struggled either, many of them working class and/or just off the farm, *real* farms, but they seemed to think that their disadvantaged state was of a different order from what they imagined mine to be—a benighted or blighted status that defined a condition of being, whereas they were simply experiencing difficult circumstances from which they hoped to extricate themselves through the hard work and sacrifice that the boon of higher education presently required. As I waited for the return of the papers I was thinking—as I imagined everybody else was thinking, though there never seemed to be any basis to this idea—that the best papers were at the top and the worst at the bottom, especially as all the white faces came and went and the

48

solitary black one, mine, still remained standing—impassively, like a sheep with lowered eyes, waiting for the undoing. After what seemed an eternity—it was a lecture class that must have numbered thirty students, and the professor himself read the papers—there were only the three of us left, a blonde girl, the professor, and myself. The blond girl looked at me as she was handed her paper, and then the professor, his eyes flitting from the girl to me, turned to me and exclaimed incredulously, quite unconscious of his implication, "You!" But by this time, however, I knew I had triumphed.

"Was it that bad?" I asked innocently. I hoped it had been the best damned paper he'd ever read.

"On the contrary. Quite on the contrary." He had become aware of the effect of his surprise and had recovered with a resurgence of generous feeling. "I wanted to see whose it was. Yours was so interesting. It was one of the best. You seemed to say so much in so little space, where others write a lot and still don't get it right." He was English, actually I thought I had heard, Welsh, and he spoke with the appeal of an accent. I wondered if he could be responsive to me without the awkwardness of the racial history I shared with my countrymen. Regarding the length of the paper, I wanted to say that perhaps that was only an illusion, since my writing (I printed in very small, but quite legible, characters) was so small, and indeed took up less space, but might actually have contained more words, but I didn't say so. I remembered then that the professor's own handwriting was a flowing, cryptic calligraphy, bolder, not as agitated as mine, but just as tiny. But it almost seemed that the professor was now shy of me, though genuinely interested, and had turned upon me his pleasant but strikingly enigmatic smile, like that of the grinning Cheshire Cat in *Alice in Wonderland*. We left the classroom in conversation, and for the remainder of my stay there I would occasionally drop in to his office to chat. I did this probably out of loneliness, the need to be special and to be connected to someone powerful who had shown an interest in me. Here is an exchange we had once:

"I read your play."

I looked at him, surprised. Everybody must have known everybody there. I hadn't given it to him, and it was only now being gotten ready for a reading.

"Didn't believe a word of it. Want my advice? Stop that silly imitation and write about something you know, not sociology, but something in your imagination that's familiar and alive, compelling. Like what it means to be a black boy here not daring to write the truth. People you know. People who're proud, exempt from welfare, but perhaps find a hard time making it, who still go to college. The way they interact with the others. Am I right? Who come to see a professor like me daring to find some support and understanding. Don't you find that interesting? What's in a brown skin that's human like a white one?"

I was both shocked and delighted, and maybe a little angry. "'In a brown skin that's human like a white one?' Yours is orange," I heard myself saying. He looked right at me and nodded his head, not in the least disturbed, brushing away some fine particles that had fallen on the shoulders of his jacket. He had some sort of skin disorder. I knew what he was talking about. What I'd been writing about in college, that Della's mother had liked, I wasn't writing about any longer.

He laughed. "I'm a strange Welsh phenomenon."

But now I wanted to appease him, saying, "In your translations you capture the evocative everydayness of those monolithic Greek characters."

"I make 'em real, you mean?"

I had asked him once what the sound of classical Greek was like. No one knows any longer, he said, but this is what it could have sounded like, and he burst into extemporaneous song, beginning at a point in the text that pleased him, reciting Odysseus's arrival upon Phaiakian shores, having fought with the breakers and cast the magic sash of Ino back into the water.

50

The Greek sounded wonderful—it certainly was *Greek* to my ears—and yet it sounded like something I knew. The swimming Odysseus sees the outline of land at last, but it is unapproachable, since the swift flowing current of the river he's now in might still dash his body against the jagged rocks at the shoreline. *My Lord, I come to you as a suppliant*, says Odysseus to the river, *and the river heard him and stayed his course.* I had never read this passage without tears welling up in my eyes. I saw it as giving expression at the most fundamental level to the obligation we bear to be concerned about the well-being of others, with whom we are kindred. No wonder the professor had burst into song. The ever-struggling, ever-resourceful one had emerged from the center, the mysterious life-giving source, fought the waves in the journey through the birth-giving process, facilitated the working and the benevolence of the attending elemental processes or powers, and had *arrived*. He had been willing to do his part, but he had done all of his part that he could now do, and the rest was up to the attending fates to do theirs—as an example of the original, always present synergy or synchronicity? The fundamental pity felt by complementary parts of a whole? I thought it an expression of the attentive responsiveness that seems basic to human interaction—the mirroring, like what happens when, talking to someone, we mimic their actions—he raises his hand to his face, I raise mine, in a split-second faster than thought; he shifts in his chair and I shift in mine, almost as if we were doing it simultaneously. It seemed a universal phenomenon, built into the molecular structure of things, what Homer, in his simplicity, at the dawn of time took for granted when he had Odysseus pray to the river and indicated how the river had heard him. *He dropped to the ground and kissed the grain giving soil*, the only place fit for a man to play out his drama, not back there with Circe, but here in this place of struggle and accomplishment. It was just *such* a story, a story that I loved.

It came to me later how my father hadn't come back from *his* journey, to be the man he was supposed, and much needed, to be; and I imagined, in a different way, that this was also part of Ed's problem, though *his* father had at every moment been present in his life.

My second year I lived off campus in a house rented with two other students, one a graduate student in my department and the other an undergraduate, a disheveled student named Sheridan. It was a small, five room two-story house on one of the main streets of the campus, where Sheridan, Brock, and I lived cheaply, comfortably, and negligently. Sheridan had money; Brock and I had fellowships; I had a car and Brock a large motorcycle, a BMW. We ate lots of eggs and chicken and chops, oppressively broiled. Sheridan, tall, languid, and beautiful, took LSD, looked at you out of the haunted, deadened eyes of a shade. Brock was blond, short, wore glasses, but had a compact, kinetic build, and sitting astride his black BMW he seemed as if he were energizing it rather than the other way round, providing the propulsive charge.

Brock, a sensitive tough guy, never wore undershorts, or undershirts, eliminating half the need of going to the washhouse, as we used to call it at home, and it was the word he had used, though he was from Utah. He was very smart, a popular teaching assistant, in the habit of seducing the Midwestern girls he could entice into the house. They were all wholesome looking, blue-eyed, hair the color of corn, with high florid complexions, and he was pitiless. They were merely fair game, and really, as Sheridan had told him, beneath him. At this he laughed his constricted sardonic chuckle, or maybe it was a snarkle, a sound like what you'd imagine to be emitted by a good-natured hyena. He was a free man, he said, having already gone through his first divorce, from a woman who, also, it seemed, had been beneath him—that is, intellectually.

The second semester, Brock and I moved, this time farther out into a house in a quiet residential area. I had the downstairs and Brock the expansive upstairs attic, which was more private. That's when Barbara, Brock's new interest, came visiting. She was intrigued by Brock the way Daisy had been by Gatsby. Already interested in a man of the proper station, she continued to make her visits to Brock's attic. Later, after I'd left school, in an exchange of letters with him, I learned that Brock had loved her but she couldn't marry him. I thought about Barbara's rejection of Brock because I had known her and seen what she appeared to feel for him. I thought about the principle of social exclusivity and the weight it carried, as well as its self-regard and duplicity. She had told me, one time at a club when I had had more than a few, how much more charming I was then than when sober, how much more pizzazz I had. And in that moment I'd also had the distinct impression that she'd also been ready for me to approach her, that she would have offered me a night's remembrance in a kind of tribute to the romantic high charge of our momentary, fortuitous meeting of minds (or bodies). Not that I wasn't interested. But I was afraid, fearing to find that I had manufactured the whole thing out of my own alcoholically induced suppressed desires. I know that this is not the way most men would think of the situation, certainly not how they would have acted. I had looked at her, on one occasion when she and Brock descended from the attic, after I'd heard the muffled reverberating thumping of her slender bottom on the ceiling, and smiled in greeting as I would have at any other time, and she had returned it without the slightest implication or registering of a mood, idea, or feeling. Her face was as blank and pleasant as could be, no more than if I'd just seen her wash it. I thought it was because I did not count, that, as a black fellow, I didn't matter. Later I realized that, to her, it was the matter which didn't matter, whether I counted to her or not.

I saw her once as I was going into a coffee shop. We entered together and sat at a booth. She was both friendly and self-assured, able to put you at ease in an awkward situation not

53

just because she always seemed to know what to say but never seemed to be ill at ease herself. It was as if you could accept yourself and not have to pretend, tell the truth about anything and not be ashamed, or not feel morally judged. The next thing I knew we were talking about intimate things—why I had not been able to commit to Della, for instance, what it was like being a lonely black guy—at least *she* wondered whether I was lonely—at school. She acknowledged that she was thinking of getting married, but she wasn't married yet! Brock was a fine, intelligent man, and so much fun to be with. A good lover, I said mischievously. She looked at me with her clean, innocent smile. Not too noisy for you, was it, Chris? I'm cool, I said, but such blushing I could do I'm sure I was doing it. You're really a nice boy, she said. Now the fantasy I had was that because I was black she thought that my experience as such made me more sensitive to moral ambiguity and less ready to find fault with people, find fault with *her*, more accepting of the plain facts of a situation without too much elaboration. Was this an accurate perception?

After having chatted for more than an hour, we suddenly became aware that darkness had descended, as we looked out the window of the diner. She had to get going, and I accompanied her out and up the street. She had secured an apartment in town and, as she approached it, she invited me in. In the same way that it had been a pleasure talking to her, feeling at ease, so had it been walking with her. But even in this university town, as elsewhere—everywhere else in the world!—a black and white interracial couple—a black man with *any* white woman—still attracted attention, not withstanding the many deliberate pairings of this kind that were seen here. You could not help the following of your eyes in their direction. So as the two of us walked I had a sense of a shared need to cultivate an appearance of naturalness, normalcy, even nonchalance. And, to our delight, it *was* natural. We, the couple in question, were tall, slim, and attractive looking, in animated conversation, and the man sometimes supported the woman at the waist as they stepped off a curb, crossed a street, and stepped back up on the sidewalk. She sort of leaned against him as he did so, the two of them smiling as they proceeded.

When we stepped inside her apartment, we entered a space that was unpretentious, tasteful, restrained, and moneyed looking, the way you might feel looking at the exacting accuracy of a period setting in a fashion magazine, not an abstract idea but a warm and inviting living space. She made coffee and we sat down and talked some more.

"It's nice talking to you, and so different from what it's typically like here for me."

"I could say the same," I said.

"I don't think you know that I'm in the theatre arts department here too, acting, directing—"

"No!"

"Yes! I saw your play, but I'm not one of the ones involved in the reading of it."

"Yes. What'd you think?"

"It's interesting. The reading will help you see it, what's good, what isn't, what needs rewriting." I said nothing to this, though I wanted to say more.

"You've got talent, though. You'll be finding your way. I've got to do that too."

"What, exactly?"

"Find my way. I got away from the East Coast, coming here. I'm doing it all on my own."

"Career wise?"

"Chris? You know what an heiress is?" I just stared at her. "Of course you do. But what is it? Something wonderful? Something not real? A manufactured thing? That's what it is, what I am, to the tune of $20 million dollars."

"Wow!"

"Wow!"

I started laughing, and said, again, "Wow!"

"You laugh, I cry." Then she laughed.

"I'll take the $20 million," I said, in a take on the situation. I didn't know exactly what she was talking about but was beginning to get an idea.

"No, you probably wouldn't be helpless."

"You never look helpless to me!"

"I'm a good actress."

And *a beautiful one*, I thought, so I said so.

"But a useless person."

I began to understand her, a beautiful, useless thing, she said. *Like an orchid, maybe*, I thought, so I said it.

"You got it!" Now her eyes really were bright and moist. "Unless in a rainforest. Nobody expects anything, it's just there." But even in saying these things she never lost her composure. It was *almost* as if she *were* acting a part, but a part she couldn't say no to. "You understand, don't you … Chris. I wouldn't say Brock does. I have a sister who lives in Rome, married an Italian who runs a pharmaceutical company. They hire people like your girlfriend, Della, except that they aren't black. Yet." I could see that she really was disturbed about something. I had started to think: Was $20 million *that* much, though of course (I assumed) she had it in her hand. But *having* it wasn't the problem, it seemed. Having been bred to be its hapless beneficiary, that was the problem.

"Do they know who you are here?"

"Some know."

She slipped her feet out of her shoes, extended her legs under the coffee table in front of her and crossed her legs at the ankles. Then she took up a sheaf of papers from the table. "This is a script I've got to finish learning tonight." She smiled at me. "Chris, thank you for coming and our talking." She got up, accompanied me to the door, smiled her clean, pleasant smile, kissed me on the cheek, and said goodnight.

* * *

I want to speak about a situation that developed while Brock and I were still living with Sheridan. I had had to take over the care of a cat when Sheridan, to whom it had been given, found himself unequal to the task. The coed, Sheridan's friend, had brought and left the cat in Sheridan's absence, to be reluctantly relinquished to, and reluctantly received by, me. The coed was a pale, slender blonde, with the narrowest nose I had ever seen. She had moved and the new landlord allowed no animals, but that had not deterred her until the cat had been discovered. Now she had to quickly find another home for her cat.

Referring to her cat, Argos, she said, "He's very temperamental sometimes, and he likes to be close, like a dog, but he'll eat almost any kind of cat food. You *will* look after him until Sheridan comes, won't you?" she asked. "Of course," I replied. "I'll look after him when Sheridan is here, too, if you like. I'm used to cats, dogs too." Here I was lying, about the cats at any rate, but somehow I had to try to allay the girl's fears, ease her distress. "I'll take good care of him," I heard myself saying. "He won't go lacking for attention." "I'll have to go," she said. "Please tell him to call me when he gets home." I said that I would do so, and let her gingerly deposit Argos into my arms. I was pleased that Argos didn't resist, but nestled comfortably in my arms as if he belonged there. This seemed to surprise her, the one comforting sign perhaps she had been looking for which nevertheless was startling to her.

I'm sitting now in the kitchen in the house that Brock and I were able to rent, with Argos, alias Cat, in my arms. It was Sheridan who'd dubbed him Cat, and he had become mine.

He craved closeness as the girl had said and slept at the foot of the bed and, when judging me to be asleep, came up onto my pillow. He was content to stay inside and look out the window. Brock found this amusing, declaring that I was deliberately making the cat as frustrated as myself, suggesting that while I could make use of the Vaseline in the large jar on the dresser for a purpose he need not mention, the poor cat had no such recourse. I didn't comment. I *mainly* employed it as a deterrent to dry skin. Yet Brock had persisted.

"And I bet a lot gets built up too," he said.

"A lot?"

"Don't you guys manufacture a lot, considering the size?"

"About as much as you guys."

"Nothing extra?"

"Want to compare?" I didn't know what to expect, but I also didn't see why there should be any real difference either. I hadn't realized how irked I had been by his statements.

"You want to produce some?" he said, smirking.

"We can do that. You can use some of my Vaseline."

Ordinarily, it would have been nice to have owned up to the desire to have been well-endowed in the area Brock was referring to—all the boys I knew had wanted to, of course— but I imagined the implication Brock gave it (and he did not need to have been aware of this!) could only be that its possession was conceived of in terms of brute inheritance, not really a strength, like being admired for having the power and grace of a superb athlete without the appreciation of the intelligence, discipline, and self-sacrifice that went into the making of such an accomplishment. A body or a prick only, never a mind. You could, though, as a black, be a soul, as in soulful, but that had more to do with having mustered the fortitude necessary to endure deprivation and modulate the existential angst. This was something positive, perhaps vicariously to be identified with. It said something about the resilience and staying power of the wounded spirit, but the emphasis was still on the idea of the ones who carried the wound, the wounded unfortunates, who had nevertheless been able to make poetry out of their suffering, as in the Blues, as in what did I do, to be so black and blue?

Brock stepped forward: "Ready when you are." The amused look on his face was also mixed with one of a keenly focused interest. I extracted my penis and held it, as the bulk of it hung limply over my index finger. Brock did the same. He stepped forward and placed it next to mine. Both were flaccid and limp, like a chicken's neck revealed inside the freshly unwrapped package, and Brock's was of that color. I thought, this really is absurd, but I was not going to back down. Also, there was something rather exciting about it, to see what the outcome would be, something you would only think of in fantasy, or in the movies.

"Uncircumcised," said Brock, looking at the two juxtaposed objects.

"Yes," I said.

"Look how dark yours is," he said, "darker than your skin color."

"You too, darker, where the skin bunches up like that." As we held the flaccid objects in our hands, and somewhat massaged them, they grew thicker, to a size approaching tumescence that satisfied us. I looked Brock in the eye. "See any difference?" He didn't answer immediately.

"You must have known in advance." He was looking right at me, a serious statement.

"I'm surprised at you, having such stereotypes."

"You must be the exception."

"Maybe you're the exception."

"If so I take it as a compliment," he said. Later I thought: Suppose he and I *were* both larger than usual—he was happy to be so. I didn't have memories of the actual size of other men—you usually kept your eyes averted in public rest rooms, showers, or locker room activity. Brock was implying how this bore out the mythic equivalency of size with potency. *Did* women like it bigger, or did they also like affective resolve, and the way it was deployed? I remembered the joke about one guy, both big and long, who, when sitting on the toilet, had to keep it raised up lest it hang down in the water, and he was white.

I could see that Brock and I didn't want to go any further, as tumescence subsided, yet there was some sort of sense of shame involved that a manly urge sought to banish, so that neither one of us could let himself turn away.

"Get that sucker back up!" he said, apparently not referring to me so much as to both of us. I could no longer look at him, nor he at me, so we both turned away in order to be privately engaged. He seemed to be performing an action of single decisive strokes, making successive downward motions, similar to rapidly peeling back the sections of a banana, a real jerking off, while I engaged in quick back and forth motions, seeing how the euphemistically referred to action of beating your meat seemed entirely appropriate. We were exerting and stroking, a grunting physical expenditure of effort, at the same time conscious of a need not to make a sound. It seemed absurd, and began to be laughable. The levity rekindled a surge to completion.

"That sucker is coming!" he gasped, and discharged on the kitchen table. I saw how in the throes of that operation all other systems were shut down, you could hardly even talk—except for the vocalizing of various familiar, guttural sounds—though he had managed to make his statement and make it coherent. I followed him, in the grip of a similar surge, and deposited my puddle next to his. He was red-faced, heavily breathing, with an indescribable grin. There were two viscous, whitish accumulations, definitely resembling human discharge of some kind, thickish, off-white, glutinous substance in a watery solution reminding of a yoke (though not so intact and of that color) in egg white. I reached for the Kleenex box and handed it on to him.

"Same color," he said, seemingly astonished.

"Same amount," I said, relieved.

"You could knock up a few females with that," he said. "And they'd be getting the best from both ends, right?" I nodded. Then, through an unspoken mutual consent, and a kind of mutual tribute being paid, we put our spent penises back into our pants and walked away.

I wished Brock had been home the day the garbage man had come visiting right up on our back porch. The barrels of garbage were supposed to have been moved out to an assigned pick-up area. We took turns transporting them. Brock and I were normally very conscientious about this, wishing to keep up proper appearances. The garbage man had arrived morally indignant. Seeing me, his suspicions had been confirmed. He just launched right into it. "It's just like you people to keep the garbage on the porch, breeding vermin." I looked at him, stunned. Recovering my composure, I knew—and bitterly reflected on this without regret or surprise—that the conversation would quickly degenerate into the deepest antagonism. He was tall, well-built, ruddy-complexioned, Germanic, I thought, with thinning blond hair, and his garbage detail was composed of other fellows who looked the same, not a black or brown face among them. He looked scornfully at me, out of querulous, glittery-blue eyes, with an unsurprising heaviness and irritability. I felt immediately that I knew him, knew of him, knew what he was like, and if I should suddenly have called out his name—Herman or George, Bauer or Eberhart, in the correct combination—he wouldn't even have been surprised himself, just like I imagined he would have been thinking of a Leroy or Tyrone, Jones or Johnson, in reference to me, because we already had a long and intimate history together in which we knew our complementary roles (even if we had never personally enacted them together), and now I couldn't help but try to reverse them.

"You won't find any rats or roaches here," I said. "But you might find some out there where all this crap is spilled by you people before it gets tossed into the truck." He was taken aback by this, but recovered with a forceful rush of words.

"That's because we have to do five or six cans at once from one house, all slimy and filthy."

"That's because we eat well, and aren't concerned with what's left when we discard it, because people like you are supposed to be there to take it away. And besides," I was glad of the thought at the moment, "not all the cans out there you so carelessly mishandle are ours."

His eyes narrowed, as if squinting in bright light. "Why don't you people do right and stop tearing things down all the time? I came all the way from Alabama to get away from you people. This is a nice neighborhood, and we want to keep it that way."

"We? Who?" I said. He had made me angry, but in my pride I didn't want this revealed. Yet I really wanted to get to him. "*You* don't live here. Now if you want to know, it's my room-mate's turn to take out the garbage." I wasn't certain of this, but I wanted to say it, wanted it to be true. "He'll be home in a minute. You'll be glad to see he's a white boy, probably whiter than you." He stared at me a long time, and replied now, cool and malevolent.

"*You* won't ever be nothing but a nigger, black boy."

"I won't ever be black enough to do what you're doing. Think you're white enough to figure it out?" The garbage man cursed, wheeled, and turned away. "I didn't think so," I said after him. But he then turned back again and came toward me, flinging back the screen door. I stepped back as he raised his fist to my face. This is it, I thought. If he swings at me I will have to try to deflect or counter it, then give him all I had, coming back at his broad, flushed, open, unprotected face, with his chin thrust out in that ludicrous fashion—obviously he hadn't been fighting much either—an uppercut, or something between the eyes, like a knuckle thrust into pie dough. Instead, his fist still up, he offered a clinched-teeth, dismissive grimace:

"I ought to kill you," he said.

I just stared back at him, returning his grinning contempt. "Try it," I said. We locked eyes. They—at least mine did—grew parched in the unblinking staring. He cursed again, turned and left. Outside, he spoke again, through the screen door, with jabbing expostulations of two thick fingers that seemed ready to penetrate the screen, or even my chest. Looking at the two thrusting fingers, I thought of the comic strip *Dick Tracy*'s thick black .45, his weapon of choice.

"Somebody ought to report you fucking people. You're just like animals. You don't know how to live."

To his back, as he walked away, I replied, "Why don't you just hop back onto your stinking truck and let it take you out of here." I had not realized, then, that I was shaking. I saw that he had not really wanted to fight, and certainly I hadn't. He doubtless was stronger and more forceful than I (though not taller), but I'm sure I was quicker; and actually he might not have been stronger, but I think he took his strength for granted in reference to me; but there also seemed a guilty recognition of something, that indeed he was the garbage man, and I wasn't.

There was another encounter I had courtesy of the unmarried woman, or widow, who lived in the most imposing house at the corner, at the circle where the drive turned around through a dead end and went back down again. I would drive my car down the street, up around the circle and back again to be parked in front of the house, turned now in the direction I would be headed in when I next departed. But the car, as a result, was therefore parked, so to speak, on the wrong side of the road. The woman objected and called the police, who arrived early one morning, somewhat apologetically.

When I first saw them approach the house, one bright, sunny morning, through the glass screen front door, their authoritative posture, the glinting impenetrability of their sunglasses, the attending suggestion of irrevocable force, and, consequently, of menace momentarily conspired to produce a sinking in my stomach from a vision of the arrival of nightriders or the Gestapo come at last to claim me too. They were, however, as convivial as if they'd come to pick up a buddy for the after-hours baseball team or a workout at the gym. The complainant was a crank, they said, but nevertheless knew the law. I must cease parking my car in that fashion. She had made other complaints before, and they had to be called away from more important duties to take care of them. I said I understood. They winked at me and made their exit, their sea-green sunglasses glinting in the sunlight as they went toward their patrol car and got into it. I had seen the woman through my back window, working in her flower garden of an entire afternoon, wearing slacks and, sometimes, her own miniskirt, and when she leaned over she would not bend her knees.

It was my neighbors across the street whom I liked, because they liked me—a man, woman, and their twin, pixie-like daughters. When I drove up in the car, as was no less the case when Brock roared up on the BMW, they would all wave greetings. They worked in their yard just as the woman at the top of the hill did.

One morning the wife appeared at our door, equally as early as the policemen, with a large bowl of chocolate chip cookies she'd baked, because she knew that two young students, away from home, might have a craving for such. But especially glad did she seem in being able to deliver them into my hands. She spoke with infectious enthusiasm. Was I from the South? What a good thing it was I was able to attend as fine a university as theirs here in town, and what was I studying? Did I like it out here in the Midwest or would I go back home? And such a nice looking student I was, too! And what a winner we had in Dr. King, a great man. I felt her sincerity and enthusiasm, and I talked to her at length, thinking that since it was true that we lived on the same street, it might not really be true that we lived on different planets.

Having her at close inspection, I saw how able-bodied she was, like a pioneer woman, maybe. I graciously accepted the cookies as she insisted that I try one immediately. They were delicious. I thanked her; she promised that, at another time, she would bring over some more. About the lady up at the circle, she said, confidentially, that I should take no notice of her; she was an eccentric already known to have called the police about her own neighbors' dogs and cats who strayed across her lawn. I watched her stride back down the walk in her sandals.

* * *

After two years of graduate school without taking a degree, in 1966, at twenty-four years old, I didn't pursue my studies any further, took no job, entertained no prospects for the moment, and returned home—or rather to my sister's house in a suburb of Atlanta, where I expected to be taken in as I would be at home. I couldn't go home right now, in my present state of incompleteness. It would be an admission of defeat to my long-suffering mother and my invalid younger sister. You know what it's like to disappoint your mother. If you've had a good relationship with her you feel you've betrayed yourself and the good family name. If you've had a bad relationship with her, she makes you feel you've betrayed her out of your own neglectful self-regard.

As I think about this, I am in the upstairs bathroom in my sister's house. It's about two in the morning. The house is quiet in a late spring slumber. The others have been asleep some time: my sister, my brother-in-law (who was not working late that night), my two nephews. I drew a tubful of water—something I hadn't done since childhood—and stretched out in it, inflating my lungs to see if I would float. Nothing to do now but get into bed and wait for sleep, under the light covers, the soft and peaceful southern night like a benign presence outside my window. I looked out the window at the scene, a subdivision of neatly ordered one- and two-family homes designed for black people in the midst of the transition from working and lower middle class upward to whatever they did not know yet was the limit of their dreams. These were the ones who had escaped, through luck and hard work. They were the vanguard of the new professionals, beneficiaries of a will to succeed and the new affirmative action initiatives in hiring. I liked looking down on the manicured lawns and orderly rows of shrubbery, the late model cars and boats in the garages, peaceful, protected, and safe. Since I was looking, I cast one obligatory glance at the house where the interracial couple lived—or visited, rather, with what must have been the parents of the husband. I had seen the woman from my window, as she sometimes worked in her mother-in-law's yard, just as had the rest of the neighborhood—although my sister had refused to take any notice of her. She was a pretty blonde, a southern one, too, as I ascertained from her reply when I passed by once and spoke to her. I liked the way her husband looked, and I liked the way they looked together. I wanted it to be the case that their relationship looked good, whether it was, or wasn't, in fact.

I was under the cool sheets with the soft breeze lifting the curtains at the window. No sound in the house; no sound from the bedroom, across the hall, where my sister and her husband lay. Feeling hunger pangs, I eased down the carpeted stairs, past their always curiously opened bedroom door, down to the kitchen and refrigerator. Pots of cold vegetables and meat and casseroles—fare for two growing boys and a man, all of them big eaters. She, though, seemed to live off a pittance, and numerous cigarettes. She had had a family at twenty years old. Graduating from college, in her innocence, she had done the usual and acceptable thing. At twenty-four I had been to graduate school and back again, still didn't know what I wanted to do, was floundering in uncertainty, sustained only by my own self-regard. Neither she nor her husband questioned my intentions, whether I would look for a job or continue to read books and look out the window, since it was not to be expected that I would continue to do this indefinitely.

To warm up leftovers might interfere with the dining regimen, never haphazard, which had already been anticipated in some way. But there was a bowl of fried chicken. A breast, a piece of bread and a soda would satisfy me. I took my fare and sat down to eat at the table in the kitchen, alone, in illuminated silence, looking out of the kitchen window on a kind of embankment that had been shored up by a brick wall. The foundations for the houses here had been scooped out of a cliff, the area between the backs of the houses and the brick wall providing enough space, I imagined the developers had thought, for a reasonably sized barbecue party. Immediately, on the other side of the brick wall, the remains of the cliff rose upward into a wooded area where night creatures, rabbits and raccoons or opossums, still roamed within yards of the expressway leading into downtown Atlanta. I looked upon the cliff and my sister's ongoing efforts to plant ground cover and flowers to retard erosion and to lay esthetic camouflage upon an eyesore, and I was happy to see that the raw red Georgia clay had begun to grudgingly yield to her onslaught—because that is what it had been, the bringing forth of soil and shrubs and earth-shoring staves and boards to be fixed into the ground.

So I looked at the hill, splashed now in moonlight, with a kind of satisfaction, with a ridiculous kind of sweetness to my solitude, a kind of reprieve from psychic care, that made me love the hill and its challenge. It was like I wanted to have a vision. Well, I *had* had one once but didn't want another of that kind, the result of what happened when I first smoked pot. As a student gazing out the window, I saw the leafy green ivy on the building as a gray, swarming mass of protoplasm, sucking the life out of the brick. Then there was the idea of the cobblestones leaping out of the curb, like self-guided smart bombs, smashing into the heads of pedestrians as retaliation for eons of having been stepped on, trampling their glory, when they should only have been raising the spires of cathedrals. I saw a maelstrom of them, flying in every direction. What to make of this? Sometimes I was one of those people who, at a dinner party, or with the boys in the locker room, or in the presence of the authoritative figure, found my heart constricted and my words compromised in the moment of their issuing out of my mouth. Always, there were endless qualifications, and not those, maybe, of the coward, but of the man who wished to be *fair*, that is, civilized. I was beginning to see that the greatest fairness is the service rendered to myself, but in order to do that I had to know myself. I was afraid, of my anger, of my striking a pose, calling attention to myself, which meant that I was afraid of my life.

* * *

Sitting in the kitchen, I wondered at the mystery of looking out the door into the night. I opened the door and stood there. A slight breeze brushed my face. The night was there but nothing frightening. What I wanted to do, I thought, was dissolve into it, waft away—and disseminate a beneficence of spirit upon all the sleeping souls who lay now in the pride of their vulnerability, as I looked out at the houses in the neighborhood and the windows of some in which lights could still be seen.

Looking out, though, I *was* frightened for a moment before I realized what the two luminous iridescent discs were that were moving toward me with the deliberation of an animate creature. It was Cat, my cat, who continued his advance until he had emerged out of the darkness into the light and had placed two delicate paws against the screen door, meowing rather questioningly in greeting. He wanted to be let in. I opened the door and Cat advanced more boldly, in his striped pajamas, rubbing against my leg like a lover, and then against the kitchen table legs and over against the cabinets and back again. Mordecai, my sister's husband, didn't appreciate cats and desired that Cat, whom he called Tom, be banished from the house. Cat now had a whole neighborhood to explore, rather than the confines of the house back at school, a situation Brock would approve of. The beast was utterly given over to sensation, the way no human ever could be. How they would pity us if they knew our divided natures, maybe dominate us, too, if they knew the slender hold we had on our vaunted birthright, never wholly possessing it, never wholly living out of it, never ever whole, as an animal always is, wholly itself.

TWO

I woke up at about ten o'clock in the morning, lounged in the bed another hour, and got up at eleven. Julia, my sister, had long since left for work; the children, still in school, had also long since departed, and Mordecai, who operated a janitorial service, and worked at night and sometimes in the afternoon as well, had managed, apparently, to be off somewhere on an errand. Mordecai ought, as Julia would have said, to be home sleeping. Since Mordecai had been home early in bed the previous night, he might have said that he could allow himself this early morning excursion. She was afraid of his falling asleep, at six and seven in the morning, speeding down the expressway, on his way back home from a night's work. He would not admit that he was also afraid. And I, having already been pressed into service, accompanying him in those gray early morning hours, kept my heavy eyelids open. One advantage of graduate school was that you got used to staying up all night and all day too. But I found that the physical drudgery I'd now come to experience was more taxing by far than any amount of sustained mental exercise in a study. It made the body ache and disposed it to sleep in an exhaustion and fatigue that seemed life-threatening, whereas all-night study simply deadened the mind and cramped the muscles. Under these circumstances, sleep was refreshing and restorative, but not life-preserving, in the sense I'd now come to know it. I'd already found out what it was like to sweep hundreds of square feet of office floor, carry to and fro large trash bins, wax floors with powerful machines that had minds of their own and would not submit to operators weak in the arms and the shoulders; what it was like to clean plate glass windows and venetian blinds, dust furniture and clean out bathrooms, maneuver my broom in restaurants behind the counter in tight grimy spaces, fascinated by the vermin which inhabited some of the places.

I found myself surprisingly strong and hearty and even liked the work, liked that I worked just as fast as my brother-in-law, a big powerful man. What remained was to expand, to hire more men, and make more money. As it was, he was doing well. He was surprised by this and pleased with himself, almost not daring to think further, as it involved investment in more machinery and trucks, and the managing of men and schedules. His clientele was mostly black, his men were black and so was he, and he feared that business had a way of going up and down, in response to economic forces. He sought advice from me, imagining that my schooling gave me some mysterious wisdom and foresight. I could not help him, could only encourage him. This was at least Atlanta. A black man could with reason succeed in ways he could not elsewhere. All he had to do was have the nerve to seek out a larger loan and then see if he got it.

I dressed and prepared for breakfast. I could have cereal, fruit, eggs, and sausage; but whatever I had, I would have to prepare it. I resisted this notion in favor of going out to get it. I could get into my car, drive up the expressway, get off and descend along wide avenues into the heart of the black business district, to eat in a favorite little restaurant on Hunter Street. Afterwards, I could walk up and down the streets, browsing in shops, or I could spend some time visiting the cluster of black colleges in the area. Six or seven colleges, universities, up on a hill, well known, at least in my world, all of them for black people! One of my friends, with whom I'd gone to college, was now on the faculty at one of them. It was a beautiful sunny morning, not hot, and if I didn't find my friend, I could sit in one of the college squares, on a bench with pigeons flying by, and watch people. I had put on a sport coat and tie because, for no reason, I was feeling good that morning.

I arrived at the restaurant and found a parking space directly in front of it. It was a cozy place that featured "home cooking," just as did every other restaurant of its kind in the vicinity. I found a booth near a window and sat down, waiting on my favorite waitress, Gladys, to come serve me. I was pleased that she had taken a fancy to me.

"What you want this morning, college boy?" Gladys said, approaching me in her mock-tough manner. "You want some grits, you want some eggs—scrambled—you want some ham and home fries, right?" Though she gave an indication of having written this down on a pad, she also yelled the order back to the cook, without having consulted me, then looked at me, amused. "That's what you want, ain't it?"

"You forgot the coffee," I said, "and perhaps some toast—no jelly."

"Of course, I wasn't finished. You want it before, after, or in-between?"

"I want it whenever you want to give it to me." I too was in a good mood, and then, surprised, I heard myself saying, "I want whatever you got."

"*Do* you?" said Gladys, wickedly. "What you think I got you want?"

"Go out with me sometimes. I'll show you." Saying this was a continuation of the surprise, and I almost smirked. She scrutinized me for a second, then called to the other waitresses.

"You hear that. He wants me to go out with him tonight." They all turned and laughed, and the other customers grinned at me.

"I didn't say tonight."

73

"Then when?" she replied. "You think you can handle me? You think you old enough? How old you?"

"Old enough."

"How old you?" she repeated.

"Twenty-four. How old are you?"

"How old you think I am?" She was interested in hearing what I would say.

"Twenty-four," I said. I knew she wasn't any older, though she might have looked it.

"OK, I am. But I've lived longer." Groans of protest rose from the rear. "You sure have," the voices said. But I could see that she was pleased that I hadn't taken her to be older than she was.

"See, I knew 'college boy' had some sense." A certain tension had been removed and I saw that we felt at ease with each other again.

"How you know I'm a college boy?"

"Ain't you in school here in town?"

"No, I am not."

"Well, you ought to be. My oldest boy be in fifth grade this year. That's a *smart* boy. I intend for him to go to college, right here in town, to Morehouse, Dr. King's school."

"I hope he does." I imagined him, an exasperatingly energetic kid with a shiny black forehead and large bulbous eyes, like his mother's.

"You didn't go to college?" There was a hint of disappointment in her voice.

"Yes. I went to college. I went to Fisk."

"Oh, *Fisk*. That's a good school too."

"Yes."

"I wanted to go to college," she said. "Couldn't do it. Couldn't afford it anyway. I had to leave high school. But I went to night school. Got my diploma too."

She left and returned with my breakfast, and I began eating. It was hearty food and inexpensive, but my money would soon run out, and I accepted no salary from my brother-in-law. The heavy fare at first made me slightly nauseous, the workings of my wretched digestion, abetted by cigarette smoking. The wave of ill-feeling soon passed and I ate with relish from the heavily laden plate, gulping it down with hot draughts of coffee.

I finished eating and sat pensive for a while, smoking a cigarette and looking out the window at the car, the parking meter, to see if the time had run out. The meter had had time on it when I arrived—just enough, I thought, to allow me to eat breakfast. But unfortunately, my view was at such an angle that the red tag in the meter's window could not be seen—if there were one, and there should not be one yet. I thought of how—had I read this in the papers somewhere?—white radicals at eastern universities used to cut off meters in the middle of the night, load them into the trunks of cars, and drive off with their booty to be added to some revolutionary kitty, perhaps the metal to be melted down to make slugs, perhaps the metal casing, on the contrary, to be used as a bomb, packed with coins, to be blown back upon the world of their mothers and fathers in a spurious shower of contempt for their filthy lucre. I signaled for the check, and Gladys arrived with a flourish, the flesh of her backside swishing in her tight uniform like water in a plastic bag.

"You don't want no more coffee?" she asked.

"No, thank you."

"You ate that faster than you usually do. You in a hurry this morning? You come in later than you usually do."

"There're some places I want to go."

"What time you going to pick me up?"

"I thought you said I was too young for you."

"You are. But that's more your problem than mine. I'll have to think about this anyway. When you coming in again?"

"In a few days. Maybe tomorrow."

"I'll let you know then, college boy. What's your name anyway?"

"Chris …"

"What?"

"Chris—Christopher."

"Oh. That's a nice name. I'll tell my husband that."

"Of course," I said, game. It had never occurred to me that the one she'd *had*, or might still have, was still with her.

"What you think I am?" she said indignantly. "Of course I have a husband. Didn't you just hear me say I have kids? I have a husband. He in New York, however. He was suppose to send for me. I told him it was a mistake to go up there. You can't get no jobs. People starving to death on welfare. Live miserably. Down here we get along, and treat each other right. I don't mean whites and blacks—that's just the way things always are—I mean blacks and blacks. You understand me, right? They dying up there. I wouldn't go now even if he was to send for me. You ever been to New York?"

"Once."

"Horrible place, isn't it?"

"In some ways. Absolutely fantastic in others."

She narrowed her large eyes, staring levelly at me, as if she were scrutinizing a familiar object she had taken for granted, now wanting to examine it more closely. "Really? You sound just like the men do when they getting ready to up and quit things and go to New York, Chicago, or De-troit, some such place, looking for something they ain't gonna find."

"I'm not going anywhere, Gladys. You don't have to be critical of me."

"What you do for a living?"

"I thought you said I was a college boy?"

"You ain't got no job?"

"I'm independently wealthy."

"A real man still needs something to do."

"I'm a philosopher," I said, aware that I would persist in speaking in this way, no matter what I ended up saying. "I meditate on what was, is, and has to be."

"Sure you do. Like those boys—I won't call them men—on the benches outside, drinking out of brown paper bags."

"OK, Gladys."

"Goodbye, Christopher." She winked, all charm again.

I watched her return to her work, attending to her customers, a hostess, vivid, serviceable, appreciated in her domain, dispenser of good cheer and fare. What did I want and what did I have to offer? I saw myself in a ridiculous light as I weighed my conversation with her, my self-serving persistence in carrying forward my proposition to her. Could we amuse each other? We could go to a movie or club, see a show, have a few drinks and come home, where she probably lived with her mother—and I could see her children. I left the restaurant and got into the car, just as the red flag of the parking meter snapped into place, a mute accusing eye, as if I'd been winked at by a eunuch.

I drove up the street, turned onto one of the college lanes, and found, surprisingly, a parking space. It was a pleasant walk to the campus, past residences, until the beginnings of the encroachment of the campus—fraternity houses, white clapboard school buildings, institutional-looking brick structures, ideological and social organizations whose names began with the prefix, "Afro-." I was on a campus walk now, with students coming and going, carrying books, with expressions that seemed to mark their sense of themselves as a chosen group.

I passed into a building where I knew my friend's department was housed. When I approached the secretary and inquired, she announced that "Dr. Johnson's office is in Temporary Number 10, room 5. It's just outside to the side of this building. The row of silver trailers." I said that I didn't want his office; I wanted to know where his classroom was. "He's in class now, probably," she said, "if he's holding it—today's the last day of classes—and it'll be over in about"—she looked at her watch—"fifteen minutes or so."

"Good," I said. "Where's his classroom?"

"Go out in the hall, turn right. Number 3315," she said. I didn't want to be awkward as I continued looking at her, but she was absolutely intriguing. She was as black in complexion as tar, shiny, glisteningly black like a polished ebony carving, yet had, like an Indian's, a head of thick straight glossy black hair, with a strange, almost iridescent, sheen. She had gray-blue eyes (I thought they were real), and she lifted up her face to meet my gaze as I looked at her. She was beautiful, and on one of her fingers was a ring on which was imbedded the half-moon crescent insignia of the Nation of Islam. She was, I guess, a Black Muslim, though she wasn't wearing a headscarf. The name plate on her desk, incredibly, identified her as "Miss Georgia Peach. Secretary." As I stood staring, she said again, "Down the hall on the right. Room 3315."

"Thank you," I replied. I went down the hall, found the room, and looked in through the glass inset. I could see my friend, Derek, sitting on the edge of a table, before an overcrowded class, gesticulating as if in a mime. Next he rose up to pace, his back receding from my view as he approached the opposite side of the room, turned, and began approaching the other side again, closer, when, seeing me, he stopped, grinned, nodded his head toward the door, and said something I couldn't clearly hear, at which point the class laughed, as they looked to see the face in the glass rectangle.

The entire front row was occupied by trouser-less and mini-skirted women, who extended (or crossed) a variety of short, thick, and long legs, shapely and spindly, in a bewildering display of ankles and sandal-clad toes. I supposed that Derek could not have had on the same corduroy sport jacket he'd worn in college, so the one he had on now must have been an exact duplicate, looking as if he'd only that morning procured it from the cleaners. When we were in school he was an upperclassman and man about campus who interacted with everybody, somebody highly likely to succeed, president of the student body. I had been intrigued to hear that his father was an engineer at General Motors and an inventor, with some patents to his name. It was just wonderful to hear that there were actually black men who had done such things. So this was the last day, and he had a full house. Students came out and regarded me with interest, while I waited on Derek to finish the last after-class conversations.

He came out and shook my hand hardily, slapping me on the shoulder. "What did you tell them about me?" I asked.

"We were talking about what's a real education for black folks, as opposed to what only passes for one, how Ezra Pound the fascist had said that the only real education is obtained by men who work at obtaining it, the rest is mere sheep-herding. You happened to be right there! There's a man working on his PhD. See, he can't stay away from the place, even though he's on vacation."

As we stood there one last student came down the hall and approached Derek. "Professor Johnson," she said. "I hope you'll let me in experimental psychology in the fall. I need an over-tally." She was medium height, slim, and lovely, with large, soft, dark eyes, wearing a mini-skirt that stopped many inches above her knees. She looked at him in a way that seemed to say that she would accept him on any terms he was willing to offer, as professor, mentor, lover, friend, or father. He asked her name. Then he looked at her with a kindly smile and said that he was sure something could be worked out, provided she came back to see him the first day of class in the fall. She thanked him and left. He turned to me and winked.

"Had lunch yet? I'll be finished up here in a minute, and we can go grab a sandwich and beer. Better still we can go to my place. You can meet Tina. Can't wait to get away from this place. The damned school year is over!" We went back down the hall to the office, where Derek and the secretary chatted.

"Who is she; *what* is she?" I asked. "Is she a Black Muslim? She doesn't dress like one."

Derek laughed, "A real peach of a girl." We went down the stairs and outside to Derek's temporary office quarters, in trailers, necessitated by overcrowding, sweltering in the heat, since the air conditioning was on the blink. We walked to a faculty parking lot and got into Derek's car, a late model Mercedes, which he'd picked up "for less than you would think," having obtained it secondhand from a friend who ran an automotive repair and body shop. It had been "completely restored," he said. "These crazy southerners still don't know how to drive on expressways. But is there anything good you can say about these crackers?" We drove to my car. I had to follow Derek home. It wasn't far to go, and Derek drove like a madman, accelerating up to high speeds down thoroughfares and making sharp turns off these onto narrow streets. We arrived at a large development of condominiums, parts of which were still under construction, with the finished units being occupied, one by one, each day. Derek parked in front of a row of apartments descending down a hill, like a row of child's blocks set in sequence down a flight of stairs. Indeed, they looked like doll's houses, with their chic contrasting facades, as if a gigantic Santa Claus might appear one night and take them all back, sweeping them up into his bag. Derek called to Tina who answered from the rear.

"Nice place you have here," I offered.

"It serves for the time being," Derek replied. "Could be larger, as expensive per square foot as things on Peachtree Street. Outrageous, but certainly an improvement over the campus pad we used to have, and, you know, it's a condominium, something we can sell." Tina appeared and I was introduced to her. Derek asked her if she could make lunch for us, and she replied that she could. I watched her glide through the open space into the kitchen where, across a counter, she could be seen and could converse with us. She was tall and lovely, the mature apotheosis of the large-eyed pretty little brown-skinned girls I had grown up with. I thought that whatever the degree of comfort and safety a black man had been able to provide for his family, she had been a beneficiary of it. I thought how it clothed her like the insouciant ease middle-class white girls had when they went shopping in Lord & Taylor. She wore a long flowing chemise of African design that brushed across the bright red painted toes of her bare feet. I knew, as the occasion suited her, that she might either have straightened hair or sport a voluminous Afro hairdo like a giant halo. Today her hair was tied in a scarf at the back of her head. I thought of the electric hair of white girls, often Jews, as if they had been perpetually caught in the rain, a blond mass of wayward strands like charged streaks of lightning. When Tina moved past me, she left a distinct fragrance. I imagined she had been napping when we arrived. Derek went to get two beers.

Tina called to me: "Will you have ham or bologna or Swiss cheese or tuna fish or potato salad, and if so, in what combination? You can also have ice cream when you finish." I was not hungry, and asked only for a small ham sandwich, and I would have the ice cream afterwards. Derek questioned Tina about the roast beef. "He's not hungry, and he wants ham," she said.

"But you didn't offer him any roast beef to start with."

"But he doesn't want any!" She called sweetly to me: "Would you like roast beef?" I was obliged to reply in the negative. "Well, that settles it then."

"Well, *I* want roast beef," he announced loudly.

"Roast beef is for dinner tonight," she replied calmly.

"We had it last night," he replied.

"So why are you so keen on having it *now*?"

"Get me the roast beef! I happen to want it now. No one needs to explain his *tastes*." He wasn't angry. He just seemed to be mouthing-off in a usual way.

"Roast beef is for dinner tonight," she said again, calmly. "But because you're so insistent, I'll cut you some slices now, and you take what's left for your portion tonight." She wasn't angry either, just responding to him in what I took to be their typical banter.

"Do it however you want," he relented.

"Why don't you take Chris's beer out to him? Chris, your beer is coming up, as soon as Derek gets out of my way." Derek came out with the beers, set them down, and took a long and deep drink from his glass. It was a good thing, he suggested, that he did not drink beer the way he used to drink liquor, or that he did not drink liquor the way he now sometimes drank beer. He worked his rump off for a pittance, he said. He'd been thinking about applying for a new position.

"But you should have," Tina said from the rear. We heard the tap, tap, tap of her movements now, and I looked to see she was wearing wooden sandals, with a red strap across the instep the color of her toe nails.

"Maybe I will," he said. "Christ, I've got two books out now. Did you know that, Chris? I haven't been playing around. Damn good books too." I said that I had seen one advertised. "When I graduated from Yale, they wanted to do something for me," said Derek.

"You were a little afraid they *would* do something for you," said Tina, not hostilely. Derek ignored this.

"We need good black instructors teaching black students," he said.

"What do you do?" I asked, directing my comment to Tina.

"She's an artist," Derek replied for her, with pride. "See that painting." He pointed to a canvas on the wall. I had noticed it, and it wasn't clear to me whether it was an abstract design or a depiction of an object. "Looks like something feminine," Derek said, "affixed to a wall." I smiled at this, as I knew Derek had intended, but I then started talking to Tina about her paintings.

Afterwards she said to Derek, "You see, he likes and appreciates my work, while all you do is make lewd jokes about it."

There were other paintings in the rooms, and she conducted me on a tour. In a hallway, there was a charcoal drawing of Derek in, no less, his corduroy jacket. "It's easy to draw him," she said, "but hard to get the effect right, his aggressiveness, maybe belligerence, when he doesn't even seem to intend, or be aware, that he's like that."

We went back out and began to eat. Derek ate with great heartiness, a roast beef sandwich, a ham sandwich, and a mound of potato salad, washing it down with a second beer. Tina asked if everything was satisfactory. Between mouthfuls, Derek assured her that it was. I asked Tina where she worked, whether she had a studio.

She laughed deprecatingly. "I don't right now. Most of my stuff is still at my parents' house."

"Her father offered to set her up, to rent her a place to work. But she refused."

"I've been thinking about that, but there's Melissa. Then we might have another child."

"You two have a child?!" I asked in surprise.

"I was married before," she said.

"We saw her ex-husband on TV the other night. He's up and coming, an actor, you know, and now is getting bit parts, like on the police dramas, when they manufacture a part for a black guy. Not exactly a villain, but not a hero either, one of the good bad guys—I mean, you know what I mean—any black guy is automatically bad until proven otherwise—unless he's a comedian—so he ends up one of those guys faithful to the hero, who helps the action along but keeps out of the way."

"He wasn't bad," Tina said. "He had a good part."

"I didn't say he was bad. I said he was beginning to get a start, doing what's expected of him."

"Why should you be jealous of him?"

"Me? I'm not jealous of him," Derek said. "I envy him. One day he'll be famous and rich." He mentioned his name to me. "You see, Chris knows him."

"So Melissa is your daughter?" I said.

"Yes, five years old," said Tina. "She'll be home in a little while. She's playing next door."

"You got married in college?"

"Sort of. We were graduating. I was twenty-one."

Tina asked me what I was doing that summer, and I had to say not much.

"I eat, I sleep, I read, I try to write a few things. I'm living here with my sister."

From the kitchen Derek said, "By now you were supposed to have your PhD, a play,"—he paused—"a voluptuous wife with lots of children, an earth-mother type with strong nesting instincts, you know, to provide you some buoyancy and anchorage."

I looked at Tina, who looked at me, and Derek said, looking at us, "*My* life is complete. I lack nothing. *Hope* is still possible for unfinished guys like yourself. And some of the other out of their minds, malcontented crew from school. Whatever happened to Ed, the physicist, that crazy guy, for example?" Ed *was* extraordinary, I explained to Derek. I told him that, after he had graduated, Ed had left school at the end of our freshman year, never to be heard from again. Into the midst of these thoughts a child burst through the door, her pigtails flying.

"Mommy, I'm back!" she exclaimed.

"Then come give Mommy a kiss, and then you can give Derek one, and, if you want, you can do the same to that strange man whose name is Chris. After that, please go back and shut the door." The child did these things without hesitation.

"Derek, Derek," she cried. "We're getting ready to go to Six Flags. I want to go. I want to go!" She was jumping up and down in a sort of dance, beating her fists on his knees.

"All right!" he said. "Calm down. You'll have to ask Mommy."

The child looked over at Tina, who shrugged. "Six Flags is the amusement park," he said to me.

"Mommy says yes!" she cried.

"Who's going with you?" he asked.

"Karen and Bobby, —"

"What grown person?"

"You! You and Karen and Bobby's mother."

"No, I can't, sweetheart." The child began to cry.

"You can too!" she cried.

"No, I can't. Ask Mommy." She looked at Tina, who shrugged again.

Tina roused herself. "We're always the ones who go. I don't know why you always ask him first."

"I take her as often as you do," he protested.

"Derek, you believe that all you have to do is say a thing and it becomes true."

Tina rose from her chair. "Missy, come here. How have you gotten so dirty? Come with me now and change." Missy hedged and protested. "If you don't come, you can't go."

"She's all right," said Derek. "They'll want to leave in a minute. Why do you always primp and pamper with the child?" Tina gave Derek a sharp look. "Go in with Mommy now and change," he said to Missy, "like a good girl." Tina and Missy exited.

Derek invited me to come to the terrace. We went out and stood in the open air, and looked across a concrete patio toward a sloping grassy courtyard, in the midst of which was a large children's play area, with swings, seesaws, and sandboxes. At the opposite end of our view was another row of houses. I couldn't help thinking of it as a compound, a fortress. We stood silently watching, smoking cigarettes in the slight breeze. We had been standing close together, and when our arms touched, we moved apart, each seeking a different vantage point.

"You ever going to get married?" Derek asked me suddenly.

"I suppose so."

"Tina and I are doing all right. But sometimes I don't think it's working out too well. And I have to make more money."

"Sure," I said.

"Tina's father's a psychiatrist, one of the black shrinks in town. Has his place at the medical school. Has his practice. Does consulting. Sits on boards. The man is making the money." He emptied his beer can and threw it into a receptacle with a sudden, disproportionate forcefulness. He was pleased with the accuracy of his aim. "The black middle class here wants to bring its problems to one of its own. I mean, there *is* a black middle class. I should have gone to medical school, to get a piece of that action. It's not enough being mere academics. The only real advantage is a free summer vacation, and that you spend working. If you can't have some power, you ought to at least have some money. If I were you, I'd apply to med school. I might do it myself, be a *surgeon*. Go to law school. Or get an MBA. Work in finance. You still have a chance. There's places that'll take a good man like you." I knew what he meant, but I didn't want to do any of it.

Derek had paused, withdrawn his eyes from the direction of the playground, and looked intently at me, then back at the playground again. Children had been playing in it all the while, from one end of it to the other, but it was as if we had just now begun to notice them. "Tina might be expecting … though she doesn't really want to be. I want a kid of my own, as much as I like Melissa—don't mention any of this. She's a fine woman, you know? But a kind of resentment is building up in her—it's in all these women, you noticed that? And the young girls, the students … some of them will come right up and proposition you. I mean, it's touch and go to stay away from them. Maybe it's the pill. Look at that row of houses," he pointed across the way with his finger. "A couple of divorces in the making already. What happened to you out in the Midwest?"

"It's hard to say. I couldn't get it together, writing my plays. If I go back to graduate school ... well, I've got to do that. I'm going into literature. That's where my love is. I'm not interested in med school or law. Whatever it is, the only people who are going to represent black people to the world, with any generosity and understanding and accuracy, will be black people."

"Right!" he said. "Whites just insist on being first, right, and perfect. They think we all live in some ghetto on Lenox Avenue, or are going to end up there, though I believe I could kick some butt on Lenox." Derek had a certain combined look of urgency and anger when he spoke this way. "That's the pity of it," he continued. "It's our spiritual place. We ought to be able to call it home, in pride, without shame." We might have continued this discussion, but Tina and Melissa emerged, calling to say that they were leaving. They had changed clothes and now stood in their brown-skinned beauty, wearing complementary summer dresses.

"I expect we'll be there no more than two hours," said Tina. She said to me, "I hope we'll see you again."

"I hope so," I replied, in love with her smile.

To Missy she said, "Say goodbye to Chris."

Clasping her mother's dress, the child said, shy for the first time, "Chris looks just like my Daddy." To me she said, "I saw him on television!"

"Did you!"

"Yes," she said. "He was a *detective*."

"Yes, I heard about it. Bye, bye," I said. "Have a nice time!"

"OK!" said Missy. The two of them went out of the apartment, and we stood, looking after them.

"I've got to go also," I announced, "though it's been a pleasure." I was tired and wanted to take a nap. Derek insisted that I have another beer. I had to refuse, having already consumed three beers, the unfinished third can still in my hand. Derek protested, as if my leaving now would disrupt the plan for our afternoon, which had already been laid out according to some scheme of which only Derek was aware. He didn't know what we would have done, but we would have had a good time doing it. I knew that the summer would be half over before I saw Derek again, that Derek could not understand this isolating privacy or aloofness in me, though I saw myself as one of the reliable, accessible ones who could always be counted on. Derek walked with me out to my car, in the bright, warming up to hot southern afternoon. As we shook hands, promising to see each other soon, Tina and her party drove by in their car, waving profusely.

"I think I'll go in and take a nap," said Derek, looking after them. "I might as well have gone with them, even though I've got 120 final exams and sixty term papers to grade." I started up the car and drove off, following in their wake. I followed their little station wagon with a throbbing head until we reached the main artery, where we each went in separate directions. I thought how I must either cut down on my cigarette smoking or else discontinue entirely, so poisonous was this habit to the mind and body. In the very act of thinking these thoughts, I had already reached for my pack. Obviously people didn't know why they smoked. And he who had the will to stop didn't alter the balance any, or maybe not really, since smoking could also be a symptom of a divided nature, like the two hemispheres of the brain—surely that was a biological metaphor for human inner division—separate complementary parts trying to make a whole, the yin and yang, the left and the right, that was manifested all the time in all existent things. And another fifteen year old is absolutely going to light up his first Marlboro. For me it had been an L&M, which I procured to get some coupons.

Thus began the slow, incipient death, as I slowly worked myself up to a pack a day. Mercifully, that hadn't happened until I reached college and felt confident in the defiant nonchalance of the perpetual cigarette stuck in the corner of my mouth. Of course, by then, it was a pleasure to smoke, of the same order of pleasure as drinking alcohol, biting my nails, or masturbating, or saying yes when I ought to have said no. Moreover, smoking gave you something to do, so as not to appear unoccupied, someone without a purpose.

Driving along, my attention was drawn to a red light on the dashboard which, intuition told me now, had been flashing for some time. The red light read "Oil," and I began to notice a certain hesitancy, a certain enervation of the engine, signifying loss of power. Indeed, I was slowing down, my engine busted. I was certain that this was the case, having driven the car—used, to start with—back and forth from Florida to the Midwest. The speedometer had long since passed 100,000 miles and was now approaching another 100,000.

Creeping along, I thought of the time, a winter ago, after the destructive visitation of a blizzard, when I crept along at five miles an hour, returning from Christmas vacation to school, with the gas needle already on empty. It being two o'clock in the morning, all the little towns were sealed up for the night. I'd approach one, pass through it in a few minutes, and see the closed and frosted over service stations. And with defiance and nervy fortitude, I'd kept right on going, instead of pulling up to wait in one of the closed stations till morning, freezing in the zero degree temperatures, under civilized circumstances, rather than out again on the lonely road, with the five-foot-high snow drifts, to be passed every twenty minutes or so by some monstrous tractor trailer that bore down on me, a two-eyed mechanical monster in the rear view mirror, gaining on me, until it passed in a fury, almost sweeping me off the road. No, I had continued on, in this wilderness of desolation, because I had been ridiculous enough to do so. I had been going on in this way for perhaps the last forty miles. I would continue to do so until I found gas or else—the other thing, whatever it was, out on the lonely road, when I felt the cessation of the engine and rolled to a stop, where, after a while, the battery would spend itself, the lights and heater would be no more, and I would be alone in a frozen stillness.

Truly, I had expected the car to just ease to a stop, but it had continued to go forward as with a will. It would not stop, I had decided, until we reached an open service station, which is what happened. Another city ahead, I saw the *lighted* Shell sign, continued to creep up on it, at even less than five miles an hour, the steady pressure on the gas pedal urging it forward, as I rolled up, closer to the tanks, coming to a halt, my foot still depressing the pedal. But there was no longer a response from the engine. I had probably ceased receiving a response when I had turned off the road into the station. The rest had been a mere rolling forward, and I had not even realized it, the momentum of the car and my own urging forward had been so completely one motion. The strain of this ordeal over, I sat there in a kind of trance, moist-eyed, and swore that I would never trade in this car for another. I would drive it, repair it, service it, keep it until it utterly fell to pieces—and only, henceforth, buy Shell gasoline. Now, presently, as I lurched along, in halting fashion, engine knocking, toward home, I knew, with the same certainty as before, that I would reach my destination.

THREE

At length I arrived home without further mishap, the red light on the dashboard continuing to read "Oil." The engine became increasingly more sluggish and hesitant, but it continued to provide power. I thought of a heart attack victim in the solitude of his high rise apartment, the pressure of the pain in his chest such that he could no longer breathe, but perhaps was still able to crawl on hands and knees toward the life-sustaining ever-receding telephone. Finally, I reached the top of our hill and turned off onto a road that descended down into the plateau of our neighborhood—great for sledding and sliding, when the light powdery longed-for southern snows sometimes finally arrived.

I coasted down to the bottom, made a right turn, and eased up a slight gradient, past our house and around the circle and back again, in front of the house, next to the fire plug. Here, as in the Midwest, I was headed again in the right direction but was parked on the wrong side of the street. It was my habitual parking space, but no one, as yet, had summoned the police to correct me. I got out of the car and looked under the hood, with the earnest, deliberate scrutiny seen so often on faces along the sides of highways, the bemused, inquiring look you have when confronted by an inoperative heap of complex machinery. I listened to the residual metallic sounds, the contracting of steel and iron parts, the ebbing of fluid levels, as of discontinuous and subsiding groans. The odor of the machinery wafted up, a species of the same that lingered around lawn mowers, electric fans, and roller skates given vigorous use; and, beginning to be uncomfortable in the heat radiating from within, I was about to close the hood when I was joined by a pair of hands, clasping the molded edge of the body around the housing of the engine, and a bobbing inquisitive head, peering into the expanse like one abruptly stopped at a precipice, calmly looking over the edge at a falling scarf or glove. It was my nephew Charles, twelve years old.

"What you doing, Uncle Chris?" He asked in the definite way that required definite answers, as if convinced that everything could be subjected to a relentless examination that would yield conclusive results.

"Contemplating a mystery."

"You're *what*?—I know what you mean. What's the matter with it? Boy is it hot! The other day I saw some smoke coming out of the back too."

I was stung into remembrance. I had also seen the smoke. Upon starting up, it would increase in volume, then subside. I had been thinking of spark plugs or a carburetor adjustment. "I think it's going to need a ring and value job, for starters," I said to Charles, not knowing myself exactly what that meant.

"That's not any mystery. That's what happened to my Dad's car. He fixed it himself. You going to fix it?"

"Yeah."

"When? Can I help?"

"You can go with me when I take it to the shop, like your Dad did."

"You'll need $300." He offered this merely wishing to be of service, stating a definite fact.

"How do you know? Are you a mechanic?" I boxed his ears playfully.

"You'll see. Maybe even more."

"The car itself isn't worth much more than that." I watched Charles's eyes widen in wonder at this disclosure. It was a 1960 Impala two-door hardtop, which had struck such an appealing chord of acceptance in the imaginations of the many other people who thronged the highways and crowded their driveways with similar models.

Charles was disappointed. "It's not worth any more than that?"

"I don't know what it's worth. I can't afford another one, and I want to get this one fixed." I knew, however, that it would be a long time sitting where it was, a sufficient distance down from the fire plug, and away from the mailbox, so that the postman, driving *his* vehicle, could swerve in near the curb, make his deposit, and swing out again, in the continuous motion that he liked, without hindrance. But to let it sit there too long was to be in bad form, produce an eyesore, of which even my sister might begin to complain. I had closed the hood and was walking up the lawn toward the house. I observed the book satchel on Charles's back, which appeared to be an appropriated Boy Scout pack or a kind of knapsack deliberately sought after in an army/navy surplus store. It seemed an incongruous hump, crammed with more books and other stuff than ever had burdened me at this age. Charles, his brother Michael, and all their friends looked like strange little humpbacked people, their life packs on their backs.

Once inside the house, however, Charles deftly slipped out of a network of straps and dropped his pack with a resounding thud on the foyer floor, where I knew it would remain until one or the other of Charles's parents renewed a weary admonishment to remove it, reinforced by familiar and ineffectual threats of punishment that one remote day would be visited upon him for such slovenly behavior (his mother), such disrespectful behavior (his father). Charles and I headed instinctively toward the kitchen, as if that were a necessary point of convergence from which you gained entry to the rest of the house.

"Where's that brother of yours?" I asked, aware of a missing element of our afternoon get-together.

"He's hanging around out there somewhere, probably at Michelle's house, playing ping-pong. He's trying to get her to like him." He spoke of this with superior detachment.

"They're in fourth grade?"

"She *does* already like him, but he doesn't know it yet," he continued. "First, he's got to beat her at her own game."

"What's that?"

"Ping-pong." This seemed a straightforward reply, but I could not be sure.

"How do you know this?"

"Because I do."

"Does she want him to beat her, or do you just think so, because *you* want him to beat her?"

"I want him to beat her because he wants to, and then she'll like him all the more."

"But suppose that's not really the game she's playing."

"What?"

"Suppose she wants to win, whether he likes it or not."

"I don't know. That's for him to figure out."

"What do you think?"

"I think she wants to beat everybody she plays. But not too bad, just so long as they know she's the best."

"Is she?" Charles shrugged. "Would you play her?"

"They're too little for me," he said, dismissing the subject. He had turned toward the refrigerator in increasing impatience to yank it open. "*My* game is chess." He opened the door and let it swing out as far as it could. With one arm holding the door open, he stood in the streaming frosty air, contemplating what lay within. It was so jam-packed with fruit and vegetables and meat, cartons, bottles, pots, packages and packets wrapped in foil and cellophane, that to extract any one thing would involve a dislocation of everything in its vicinity. Charles looked every bit a cherub at a celestial banquet, gleefully rubbing his hands in anticipation. With rhetorical flourish he said: "What I want is a nice, big, cool glass of—water!" Instead, he brought forth a milk carton and poured a frothy glassful. Retiring from the refrigerator, he commenced to prepare a gigantic peanut butter and jelly sandwich, leaving the smeary remains of his efforts on the counter. I decided that I would have Charles's glass of water, since the beer I had drunk earlier in the afternoon had induced thirst and a bad taste in my mouth.

As we sat in the kitchen, Charles chewing absorbedly, me sipping gingerly from my glass, we were joined suddenly—he appeared like an apparition—by a tall, solidly built strong-looking man wearing only a pair of boxer shorts. His physique was like an inevitable and singular designation of his person-hood, his character. There was the suggestion of an unchanging distinctiveness, so that you could imagine having as familiar a knowledge of him at five as at seventy-five, someone cheerful, direct, and unselfconsciously lacking in guile. There was also the suggestion of moral strength that could be rigidly uncom-promising in defense of its cause. He said to Charles, "You woke me up when you came home. How come you have to make so much noise?" Charles looked at me in protest at this accusation, but said nothing, like a thief caught red-handed in an act he himself despises but would commit again for the pleasure of the offense. He had the identical look on his face that I remembered first seeing, ten years ago on my first visit to their new house, when as a child of four or so Charles had discovered the heady delight of pulling down his pants and running around the house with his engorged penis in his hand crying, "See Wee Wee!" In a single incandescent moment of disapproval, his father had abridged *that* interaction between young self and the world.

Now, in the kitchen, Mordecai continued in a mild but firm manner of address: "Is there something out in the hall you should go pick up and put in your room?" Seeing the counter he clinched his case: "I *know* this mess here is going to be cleaned up. I got to get dinner ready. Your mother's going to be late." He opened the refrigerator, as Charles had done and stood, a massive figure, examining the contents. Quickly he extracted a frosty, fat-bottomed pot, exclaiming with satisfaction, "We're going to finish off the pot roast." Charles had got up and begun cleaning off the counter, wiping it with vigor, in quick, short strokes, as if applying steel wool to a pot bottom, out of all proportion to the task at hand. He seemed neither angry nor relieved, and he left the counter immaculate, tossing his sponge into the sink with the cheerful expostulation, "There!"

As this was occurring, we heard the approach of footsteps accompanied by a clear boy's soprano, which cried out Charles's name once, then twice, then again. I looked at Charles, who I knew would not have replied had we not been present. When Charles answered, "What!" the voice declared, not with triumph but with brotherly solicitation, "You better come out here and pick up your backpack!" Then the footsteps retreated; we heard the sound of the steps go up the stairs and thud off into the distance. A moment later the footsteps approached again, bounding down the stairs and into the kitchen. A short, delicate-looking ten year old appeared, with the bright earnest face of a choirboy, though he sang in no choir.

"Michael, why don't you mind your own business?" said Charles.

"His business *is* to mind yours if you won't mind it," said his father.

"*You* are just too good to be true," Charles said to Michael, contemptuously.

"What's the matter?" Michael said innocently. "You heard what Mama said. She didn't want to have to stumble over your book bag when she came home, *ah-gin.*"

"Mama's little boy," said Charles, but Michael was unperturbed.

"When's dinner going to be ready?" Michael asked his father.

"I *know* you're not hungry. Didn't Michelle ask you to stay to dinner?" Charles said cheekily, with a quick sideward glance at me.

"In about thirty minutes," replied his father, busy at the stove.

"How's your table tennis game?" I asked.

"OK," he said quickly. He looked at Charles, then at me, then at his father. "I'm getting good." Michael and Charles went out into the hallway.

Presently, in the kitchen, I heard Michael's voice declare, in crystalline purity, "Here comes Mama!" I watched as my sister, Julia, entered the kitchen doorway. From a strap over her shoulder hung a large handbag or briefcase, and her head peered over a large grocery bag which she cradled in her arms. Michael and Charles approached on either side of her, as if shoring her up, though neither made a motion to relieve her of her burden. She didn't seem to want to relinquish it, either, but at last yielded to Charles's efforts as he took it from her and, in a combined effort, they deposited it on the kitchen table. In doing this Charles had to contend with a certain backpack, now suspended from a strap across his shoulder, which swung precariously and hampered his movement.

In putting the package down, she said, breathlessly, "Just a few things we need I had to get." She stood, petite, still young-looking enough, but matronly, a little woman in a neatly tailored blue suit and pink blouse, and wiped her brow with satisfaction, saying, "Well, here you all are—all my men, in the kitchen." It seemed to me that I could see in her demeanor the easing up of the residue of the office where she worked, mostly among southern white people. Immediately she began helping Mordecai prepare dinner. She put her hand on him, saying, "Daddy, you're a dear to be doing so much in here." It had startled me the first time I had heard it, making me think of the unnatural intimacy of those households in which the children referred to their parents by their first names; or maybe it was simply that I felt excluded, that Mordecai's relationship with her displaced my own. Also, tugging at me somewhere vaguely, was the idea of whether this "Daddy" could be in some way a substitute for her of our father.

Soon dinner was ready and we took our places in the dining room and ate in the late afternoon warmth, not yet intolerable, that had been building up in the house all day. The discussion at the table centered around this, whether cooling cross currents could be created through the appropriate opening of windows, day and night, or whether the windows should only be opened at night, allowing the house to cool off—there were cool breezes at night, no one disputed that—so that it could be shut up during the day, blinds drawn and curtains pulled to, to keep out the heat and preserve what remained of the cool. But would this work on high humidity days? Would not the house be a sweatbox? And to open the windows would mean that the air conditioner in the family room would have to be turned off. What if he wanted to watch television or play chess? inquired Charles. The point is to avoid running the air conditioner, replied his mother. Why did he assume in advance that it wouldn't be cool with the windows open? Mr. Spock on *Star Trek* would not be bothered by a little warmth, said his father. *He* would be all concentration. I bet you were bothered the last time I beat you, rejoined Charles. I'm not Spock, said his father. *You're* Spock. Spock isn't even human. He's a machine, said Michael. *Half*-human, said Charles, and better. Better than what? I asked. He's got the best of two worlds, replied Charles, now and in the future, what the future will be like. You mean, I said, we'll be automatons, like some of the creatures Spock and his friends have to deal with. Oh, *they're* just freaks, said Charles. Spock is something *else*, he continued. But you notice, I said, that Captain Kirk always beats Spock at chess. Why is that? Probably he lets him, said Charles. I think you know what that means, I said. He's got logic but not intuition. Everybody's got intuition, said Charles, but not everybody has logic.

The moment of silence following this exchange made us aware of the drone of the window fan stationed in one of the windows at the end of the dining room. I laughed to myself, seeing it as a semi-automated organism of indeterminate species which had been set in motion long ago and forgotten by benevolent beings who had found something useful for it to do. Mordecai suggested that in any case the summers seemed to be getting cooler, or rather that the hot periods were not as long or intense, just like the winters, which had, comparatively speaking, been getting milder. He had long since finished eating, and now he drained his second glass of lemonade with gusto, tilting it almost vertically, his eyes gazing abstractly upward, as if he were eyeing something above Michael and Julia's heads on the yellow dining room wall in the opposite corner of the room. I looked at him, imagining myself in Mordecai's place as he surveyed the dinner table. Looking at things through Mordecai's eyes, I saw that my son, Charles, filled almost to overflowing, had commenced to do with his glass what I had just finished doing; that my brother-in-law did not seem to have any appetite, as he desultorily picked among perfectly good pieces of meat and potatoes; that my wife and young son were still eating, in concert, a kind of duo, as if entranced by the motion of carrying fork from plate to mouth and back again. They looked like they might have been enchanted. As fairy creatures might look if suddenly spied through the window of their cottage in the forest. I saw that my wife now was looking at me, clear-eyed and receptive, and I quickly looked away, yet immediately returned my gaze, but she was no longer looking at me. She now said that even if they hadn't run the air conditioners that much last summer, the electricity bill was still high enough. Mordecai replied that that was because of the one in their bedroom. She grimaced in acknowledgment, as if in guilty recollection of nights of cool and peaceful slumber, a self-indulgence because not shared with their sons. Once the thing is installed, she said, you can't help but use it. It's a good thing we didn't have the central air unit put in, she said. That was your choice, Mordecai said, the air conditioning or the carpeting. We can still *get* the central air connected up. She quickly replied that she was nevertheless satisfied. Carefully he observed that the stairs were already frayed. That much she herself could see, she said in exasperation, angry that the blame for this blemish in her scheme of things could not be placed upon a specific guilty party against whom exact retribution could be made. She said with a sigh that if the children wouldn't keep running up and down the stairs so hard, it wouldn't have worn through so soon. And any covering put down for protection seems to come loose—(besides it's ugly)—making it dangerous.

Michael spoke with the urgency of a child startled by the revelation of events that had fallen outside of the time frame of his child's awareness, yet were intimately a part of the life he knew as his own. He addressed his mother, inquiring whether it had actually been a choice between the air conditioning and the carpeting in the house. When he received a definite answer he said, without envy, merely stating his observation, that Michelle's house had both air conditioning and carpeting. Here Charles felt it necessary to inform Michael that that was because Michelle's father was a dentist, and dentists were rich. *Some* are, said his father immediately. It seemed to me that Mordecai didn't want to make it a personal issue, because he didn't see himself as being in competition with Michelle's father. He saw that his wife, however, was not of a disinterested cast of mind. She declared that they too could have both things if they really wanted them. Michael said that it didn't matter to him whether they had both or not, and because his mother knew that he was perfectly sincere, she felt—this was my perception—the lack of them, for Michael's sake, even more; but Michael now only felt himself the cause of his mother's unhappiness. He bore this knowledge in a guilty recognition, as if he were unaccountably the offending one, looking at me as if in search of a corroborating acknowledgment, his eyes soft and solicitous in their desire for aid in fixing the situation, taking it back to its former, uncomplicated, state. He said, "But we have a bigger house, up on a hill." She said, "That's right! Listen to my baby."

I saw that she wanted to deal with the situation without too crudely seeming to have to defend their comparative status and accomplishment in the world when, in her eyes, they needed no defense; yet she could not bear that her son should feel diminished in any way. She and Michael sat on one side of the table facing Charles and me on the other, while Mordecai looked on from the head. She declared that she knew that they all liked their house just the way it was, that up on the hill it was the prettiest on the block, that they did not have to prove anything to anyone, like some people did, who were always showing off what they had, because they could not themselves really believe that they had it; that, indeed, to always want to impress somebody meant that you did not really believe in yourself. She said this in a calm, deliberate manner, the nervous agitation of her hands fidgeting with the silverware the only indication of her distress. Michael, bewildered, took all this in in thoughtful attentiveness, with the suggestion that he knew what he was supposed to think—what attitude his mother wished him to have—but he did not know why. He said, "You mean that's what Michelle's father is like?" To which his father quickly replied, preempting his mother, "Maybe he is, maybe he isn't. She wasn't talking about any *particular* person." Charles, seemingly having edged ever closer to his father, had a smug look of prior knowledge, as if he wished to proclaim, "I could have told you *that*," as he covertly assessed his father's face, on which was registered something strained and fleeting, perhaps disagreement, perhaps a finely tuned egalitarian resistance to his wife's high-handed expression, to which he nevertheless gave his assent, heavily, saying, "Your mother is trying to help you have the right attitude. What she means is you always got to be your own man, regardless of what other people have or think. You don't have to be better than they are. Just be what you are."

I had nothing to add to the discussion. I thought how like our mother my sister was, though she would resent the comparison. She made articulate and distinct what in our mother had been the dim, fragmented pride, the urgency of the battle for self-justification, or maybe self-representation. But, unlike our mother, my sister was not emotionally disturbed, undermined. So far as I could tell, she was contented with her life.

So I sat in the dining room, grateful for the haven provided, the freedom to pursue my thoughts and live as I liked without interference. I felt guilty, though, that I hadn't eaten my dinner, and began to do so. The others had finished eating and had begun to disperse. Mordecai asked me if I could help him on a job the following afternoon, cleaning up a supermarket. It was a job on which I had helped before; and it was a job which, if Mordecai intended to keep it, required the hiring of permanent full-time help, not the part-timers he relied on as the need arose. I was glad to see that even Mordecai was beginning to realize that he couldn't do everything himself. I agreed to help him; a spell of heavy physical exertion would constitute a tonic to my system. I looked at my brother-in-law's broad, strong arm spread on the table like a warm loaf of bread. He had extended to me the masculine recognition and acceptance which to Mordecai, in his conception of himself as a man, was inseparable from breathing. I knew that he thought I was different from him in some way, an "intellectual," but not like those "creepy characters," as he saw them, lacking real guts, who looked down on physical labor. He despised them; he would have called them "faggots" or "punks," without *necessarily* intending the homo-erotic stigma but certainly intending all the contemptuous connotative opprobrium that the words could muster. To him they were people of indeterminate gender, lost souls. That such men could also be black seemed doubly offensive to him.

I had always been physically active, capable at sports, though I entertained no particular interest in them, or in sports figures and teams, just as I had always excelled academically yet had no particular consuming ambition. This was due less to modesty, I now realized, than to indifference, or rather an attitude of indifference that masked a consuming fear, of self-assertion, of self-*display*—the horror of being visible in the eyes of the world. The inability to tolerate such visibility had been turned into the virtue of concealment, under the guise of civility and good taste, all of which were presided over by a protective vanity, which counseled restraint and tact that raised me above involvement in the mundane world's affairs. It occurs to me now, however, that that indifference was also a way to mask the pain of the tragedy of life—witness the many demoralizing things that had already happened to my family—that might lead you to wonder whether anything was worth doing. Perhaps that too was what he had meant, *the whole thing sucks*.

Mordecai had kept me company at the dinner table as I finished eating. He had gone and gotten his pipe and tobacco and returned and sat contentedly smoking, blowing, at precise and regular intervals, thin little clouds of smoke, that reminded me of the blue-white puff balls that issued from the tailpipes of the zany little cars in the Sunday comics I used to read as a child. With his pipe Mordecai looked like an irreverent Buddha, contemplating the succession of disasters and unending hopes to which the unenlightened are subject.

I volunteered information about my broken-down car. Mordecai sympathized and offered the family station wagon for my use, when not otherwise needed. I knew it would be offered, and I would, on nights when I went out, make use of it, and maybe even in the daytime too, since my sister on her job was granted the use of a car, which she sometimes brought home, on the doors of which were emblazoned the words Inter Agency Car Pool, State of Georgia. I was proud of her achievement, however modest it was; I thought how the lure of money and power represented everything that we had come (inexplicably) to despise, the clamoring for more dollars and cents. Such an attitude certainly couldn't have come from our father, who loved to make money and indulge in conspicuous consumption (so did our mother, for that matter). Now I was no longer sure that I knew what I had meant by entertaining such thoughts, faced as I was with the simplest matter of how to earn my bed and board.

FOUR

Mordecai and Richardson, Rich for short, one of Mordecai's workmen, and I arrived at the supermarket a little before closing time. "A heavy night," Mordecai said, "but we ought to knock it out by twelve and take out the two offices by four a.m."

"No problem," said Richardson, a half-smoked, fat stogie in his mouth, which he seemed to get more pleasure chomping on than smoking and, I noted, was much partial to discharging copious brown dollops into toilets and waste receptacles. I was carrying in a buffing machine as the last of the customers came out carrying grocery bags, a woman and three children, each occupied with a bag. I looked up and down across the aisle of checkout counters into the eyes of a brown-skinned young woman at the end with a round, candid face like an apple. She was tall as well as round, though not fat, seeming to give off good feeling, cheerfulness. "Hi," she said, and blushed, as I passed by. We had been content to just look at each other on prior occasions.

"Hi," I said, and kept on going until out of sight, but I made an about-face when I was out of sight and then returned. When I was next to her again she was busying herself attending to the day's receipts. "I guess you can't check anything else out now," I said.

"Sure I can," she looked at me smiling. My eyes scanned the display nearest her. I wanted to purchase a pack of cigarettes but decided instead on a pack of gum, though I never chewed gum.

"I think we live near each other," I said. "Maybe I could come over sometimes? I could ride my nephew's bike." One reason I said this was that I thought I was expected to say it.

"If you want to," she smiled. Her smile, though, made me glad I had said it.

"I could call you before I came."

"OK."

"But I need your number." She gave it to me. Her smile, with her beautiful, even white teeth was a lovely thing, as if she had bestowed a kiss. All night I thought of her, her face a palliative to my fatigue. She was not beautiful in the ordinary sense but was exceedingly comely and wholesome. I had had a full night, and it was sunrise when we finished the night's work. I decided to make good on my offer to go see her. In a few weeks' time I had visited her twice on weekends, riding Charles's bicycle to where she lived, an only child, with her parents. She had had the job at the grocery store since high school and now continued to use it to help pay her expenses at Spellman College, where she would be a senior in the fall. One of her parents was an elementary school teacher and the other was a postal worker. She was a biology major thinking of graduate school or medical school when she graduated. She liked having her own money and savings account, and for her there was the pleasure of interacting with people at the store that helped offset its tedium and aggravation. She understood my position at the moment and did not see it as floundering. I liked her open acceptance. She was both independent and extraordinarily congenial. She made physical contact with me, touching me as if I were her brother, smiling in her alluring yet innocent way. We had started taking walks along the winding, interconnecting streets of her neighborhood, usually ending up in a park with tennis courts, where we patronized the Good Humor man and sat under a favorite tree, or watched the players, or played ourselves when we had taken our gear, simply hitting the ball back and forth. Her reach was almost as long as mine, her serve powerful, and she taxed me, rousing in me a will to prevail, when this was possible. Her eyes were full of light and she played with abandon, with dexterity and speed, unmindful of the soft amplitude of her build and the surge of her breasts within the bursting curvature of her blouse. I was enthralled, looking at her, desiring as much to press her to me as to spend my days admiring her, as I might a loved sister. Indeed I had a sister, my other sister, and being with this woman somehow made me imagine what being with my other sister would have been like, had she been normal. The age difference between this woman and me no longer seemed to matter as it once might have in high school.

I didn't think of being in love with her so much as being blessed with the pleasure of her company. Wasn't that also love? I thought she loved me as her loving nature seemed to impel her to love everybody, but still I must have been special to her. We had held hands, but we were not lovers, yet the thought of her induced feelings of great affection and desire. I wanted to continue to love her in this way, and even make love to her, and yet not be her lover. The excuse of my life being unsettled sounded hollow. So was hers. People didn't let that stop them if they envisioned the greater possibility of being together in the face of all obstacles and uncertainties. Well, I had sent off queries and had received an invitation to come teach in a small black liberal arts college in Alabama. The ad had been displayed in *The New York Times*, two positions that had not yet been filled, at this late date, and now I had one of them. I would be away from her, and soon she would be away from me in medical school. Not only that, but my deferment as a graduate student had ended, and I might be subjected to being called to the war in Vietnam, if I could not get off as a teacher or, at the draft examination, put myself in a category that disqualified me.

One night in August, a week before I was to leave for Alabama, I took her in the family car to a disco and dinner club. When I appeared in the car to pick her up, she bounded out of her house down the sidewalk to the curb. Two figures stood in her doorway who waved first to her and then to me, and she and I waved back. I had watched her come, almost skipping, in a short blue pleated skirt, though not over the knees, and a tight reddish-burgundy blouse, her long legs flashing.

"You look smashing," I said, when she got in.

"Thank you," she said. "I thought you might like it."

"I like it." When we arrived at the club we entered a parking area in which we could be served in the car by young women wearing halter tops and hot pants. Prominently displayed was a glass box up on a platform, over which a sign in neon lights read Go Go Girls, and inside the box a virtually unclothed dancer gyrated to strong pulsing chords of rock music. She did not seem to be trying too hard, appearing almost to be bored, yet she continued with a sultry suggestiveness, urged on by shouts of "Go, girl!" from one of the many young men thronging the site, pulsing with energy themselves. There was energy, activity, everywhere like a force that we had to wade through.

"She looks tired," I said, but I thought how she also looked like she knew she was the captivator of many eyes.

"I know her. We went to high school together, a good girl but loved to party. Had a baby, I think." I waved aside one of the young women approaching for an order as we got out of the car and went inside, moving through a crowd. The restaurant accepted reservations, I had one, but that did not mean we would be immediately seated. We were, however, soon sitting, and we enjoyed the meal, closed off somewhat from the booming band in the disco area. When we had finished eating we went in and danced. She moved her body with the same ease and dexterity with which she played tennis, calling forth a similar response in me. I liked the way she followed my lead in a way that fulfilled our expectations and set up new possibilities that delightfully challenged our collaborative efforts. When she was across from me on the out swing awaiting the inward rebound of a return again, I held her when our bodies met and just twirled in a spiral, my lips brushing her lips, cheeks, and hair. In her eyes was an intensification of the shining look she always had. We came to a standstill and stood holding each other. The night went like that. After one last dance she whispered, "Thank you, but now I've got to go to the ladies' room." I watched her go and I went to have a beer. As I was drinking it I felt a tap on the shoulder and turned around to see Gladys, laughing.

"You were supposed to be taking me out," she said, amused, joined by a strong-built man whose chest showed through the unbuttoned top of his shirt, beads of perspiration on his face, who had come up behind her.

"What's that you say, Baby?" he said with a grin.

"This is my friend I see in the restaurant."

I acknowledged the two of them.

"I see you can dance," she said, "a little." Looking at her I saw her eyes look behind me and then I felt a hand on my shoulder. Evidently Sarah had returned from the ladies' room.

"I don't think you know each other. This is Sarah," I said to Gladys, offering "Gladys" to Sarah, and Gladys presented "John," who sized up Sarah, while Sarah rested her lovely smile on Gladys.

"And you …?" said John. He looked like he could have been from the Caribbean, a slightly discernable accent suggesting it.

"Chris," I said.

"It's been great tonight. The place is jumpin'," said John. "We saw you folks out on the floor."

"Yes," I said, "but I think it's time for us to go."

"Kind of early ain't it," said Gladys, laughing.

"I've got a job, and won't be in for breakfast much longer."

"Out of town?"

"Alabama."

"Don't forget to drop in sometimes, when you're in town."

"I will. You'll see." I gave Gladys a kiss on the cheek while John did the same to Sarah.

"I didn't know you knew anybody," Sarah said, as we exited. Outside, approaching the car we saw that the dancer who had been in the box when we arrived had been replaced by another. Then we saw the original one walking ahead of us followed by a number of petitioning young men; and when she passed a particular figure lounging, smoking, against a car who called out her name, to be ignored like the others, he grew incensed and called her again.

"What!" she replied, stopping somewhat negligently, sullenly, impatiently stamping her foot, like an imperious queen, in such a way that caused the flesh of her well-endowed body to shake.

"You can't speak to nobody?" he asked in a wounded tone. She exhaled an exasperated sound and kept on going, where she got into her car and drove off. But she had cast a certain look of recognition, and then disregard, in Sarah's direction as she passed.

"*Jo Ann* was her name," said Sarah, echoing the aggrieved tone of the young man when he had called out her name. When we pulled up in front of Sarah's house, I gave her a kiss on the cheek and out she went. As soon as the car door slammed two figures appeared in her lighted doorway, into which she went like an embrace. I called her house in the morning and was invited to come to lunch about one. When I arrived on the trusty bicycle, she let me in and said how nice it had been last night, following with, "My parents are gone for the day. They still like to go shopping together. They're checking on a new washing machine. They like you, you know." We ate tuna sandwiches and potato chips and drank iced tea. She wore a shift that hung straight down to her bare feet. When I sat on the

110

couch she sat next to me, tucking her feet under her and leaning against my thigh. For the first time it was not her smile that was prominent but an interested, watchful, waiting look. The pressure of her thigh against me caused me to put my hand on her thigh—I didn't want in any way to alter things by shifting position—and when I touched her she drew my arm around her and leaned back on the couch. I leaned in her direction, kissing her. This continued until she got up, took my hand, and led me into her bedroom. When she took off her shift she was naked. Her smile returned, and she got into bed. I undressed and lay beside her. "I've only done this once before," she said, "and it wasn't so good, so I thought we might as well be safe and comfortable, in my own bed. Did you bring a condom?" I shook my head. She got up, went out and returned with one. "One of my Dad's, though she must be hitting on menopause." She gave it to me respectfully, as if it were a precious gem. Taking it out and putting it on had begun to undo me. As if reading my mind she began caressing me, stroking me, kissing me, and I put my mouth on hers, tasting a sweetness suffused with gratitude, hers and mine, feeling a surge of strength which I wished to give to her only in tenderness, and she directed me into her like a dream of something we had done before with delight and were remembering again.

* * *

When I awoke she was sitting in a chair opposite the bed, smiling at me, dressed in her white tennis shorts and blouse.

"How long?"

"An hour." When I got out of bed her gaze followed my every movement, and for the first time I felt admired in my body even if still awkward, and her observing gaze also made me think she should certainly be a biology teacher or doctor. I went to kiss her. "You were wonderful," she said. She handed me my clothes which she had collected and neatly folded on a chair, as if she'd just taken them from the laundry. The spent condom, which I had placed on some Kleenex on the night table, had been removed.

"Tennis?" I asked.

"Can we have one more game before you leave?" she said. I'll ride my bike with you to your place to get your things."

"I'll write," I said. "I'll call you. I'll be back."

"I know." She followed me to the bathroom where I washed my face and combed my hair with a large blue comb she provided. She smoothed out my shirt and wrapped her arms around me as she looked over my shoulder at the two of us in the bathroom mirror. "We could be … together." She held me ever more tightly and kissed me at the throat. "I think I could be with you forever." She looked intently at me in the mirror. "Would you want it to happen?" We looked at each other. "See, it's hard," she said. "Don't make any promises. Just write to me, and come to see me when you're in town." She put her finger to her lips as if to silence the protestation I would make, that I felt I ought to make. "I'll be at Emery next year, or Meharry, or Northwestern. I like their program. I've got the grades, and I did well on the tests. I'm bound to get in somewhere. They're recruiting black students everywhere, one good thing the civil rights movement accomplished." I said nothing more, not thinking that there was anything more I should say, and looking at each other we were not unhappy. I felt that I would lose her as I had lost Della. I imagined she would pursue her studies, single or married, with the same practical good spirits and optimism. If I wanted to be hers I knew she would agree, but I knew she would want the responsibility of such declaration first to come from me. Look how far she had gone already. And she had also done what, in being good for her, had not hurt me. "Let's get going for our game," she said, and so we went out into the sunlight.

FIVE

The following weekend I set out with my brother-in-law for the college in Alabama. I didn't know how long I'd be there but at least through the end of my contract for the school year. It might be fun, and I certainly needed to make some money, of which I was reminded as we passed my car parked at the curb. I waved goodbye to the figures standing on the porch. I had a footlocker and two suitcases which to me seemed light and to Mordecai a lot. I was already going back to school but this time in a new guise as a teacher. I felt that I could quickly learn what to do in teaching a freshman English course or a dramatic literature course, which was expected of me, but I had no training in directing plays, also expected of me, only writing them. I'd also be responsible for the drama club and any extracurricular theatrical productions. I was not totally in the dark but certainly not the equivalent of a theatre arts major involved in the many aspects of the bringing to life of a production on stage.

Mordecai drove through the deep August afternoon, careful not to exceed the speed limit. Languid was the way to describe it, and humid, as well as beautiful, with the green leafiness of the trees giving way to sleepy hamlets and the beginnings of encroaching commercial strips and the omnipresent Men At Work road building and repair signs. The trip was little more than a hundred miles on Interstate 20 and then onto Route 21, no stark demarcation of a change from Georgia into Alabama. There were Confederate flags on the fronts of vehicles, just as there were the gun racks lining the back windows of pickup trucks. We could be menaced as well as treated with the deepest courtesy and smiling hospitality, as was the southern way. So I thanked Mordecai again for driving me. He was proud to have been of service, helping to establish me in my new job as a "professor."

The directions easily got us to the campus after we entered the small town and passed through the town square where, in a traffic circle, stood a statue on its pedestal, a soldier. It was a Sunday afternoon. Church would be letting out soon as the preachers were moving toward concluding hortatory cadences. Entering the main entrance of the college provided an unmistakable sense of having arrived, as the buildings seemed to fall on either side of a wide, tree-lined avenue of large, imposing, ancient oaks, shrouded, sometimes, in veils of moss, with branches arching, meeting over the road, as if you were going down a long airy arbor. We stopped at a building. I went in and got information about where to go and came out again. I had been greeted, given a key to my residence, and told whom to see in the morning. On my way back to the car I passed some tables set up by students and civil rights workers to assist the local black populace in voter registration. Talkative, earnest young men and women dealt with members of their parents' generation, workers and domestics and toilers of the earth who, dressed in Sunday best, had stopped here on their way home from church. You could tell who the professional civil rights workers were by their high-minded, committed appearance, and dress, whether white or black, which gave their work boots and denim jackets and pants a certain ethical and egalitarian cachet that was also a fashion statement. They wore protest buttons of every description. I made out: Free Huey!, or Free Angela; Voters Rights; SCLC; A Mind Is a Terrible Thing

114

to Waste. On the last, once you made out the first two words, you knew what the rest would be, rendered in decreasing-size smaller type. Also, leaning over a table, standing, talking to a gnarled-looking old black man and his wife, was a white man in white shirt and dark trousers, and wingtipped shoes, animated, intense, and polite.

Mordecai lugged the footlocker and I took the two suitcases to my residence, down a hallway into my apartment. We would have to go back and get my old KLH stereo and records, in crates. I had brought what I most enjoyed and thought essential, leaving the rest back at my sister's. Inside were two pleasant-enough rooms, recently refurbished, that received morning light, a bedroom-dining room, and through a passageway a kitchen and bath. I saw how I would place a desk or a long, low table in front of the windows where I could work commanding a view of flower beds and a gnarled old magnolia tree. I accompanied Mordecai back to the car where we got the stereo and records, brought them to the rooms, and returned to the car where I shook his hand saying goodbye but was surprised to also be embraced by him who told me to take care of myself. He said also that he bet he knew a certain someone who would be waiting to hear from me. I watched him drive off. I then looked around the campus. Would this be home? I asked where I could buy food and was directed up the street a few blocks, where there was a market. The town, with grocery stores, as I knew, was farther away. I would have to get my car fixed though it was pleasant walking. The beauty of the place was like a dream, and the surging swell and ebb of the singing of the cicadas seemed deeper than I had ever heard it. I might look down a street and see shacks with barefoot adults and children lounging about and sitting on steps, just as I might, on another street, pass dwellings where others sat on screened-in porches or behind jalousies, their shadowy figures suggesting a civility and comfort that set apart their neighborhoods, both of which were inhabited by black people.

When I returned with my purchases I met two of my fellow residents and faculty members. A man whose apartment was near the entrance came out of his door as I was passing. I thought that he looked like the man I had seen talking to the black couple at the table. He looked at me, "You're new," he said, extending his hand. "Howard Stein, sociology." Up close I saw a short, plump, high-waisted man with a large head, bushy eyebrows, and a friendly countenance.

"Chris," I said, "English."

In a nonstop way, he said, "Been to the market? Not much to do on a Sunday except read the *Times*, or play tennis, if you're into that—or work. There's a movie on Friday night. Some of us get together sometimes, and of course you can go to Birmingham if you've got a car."

"Did I just see you out at the voter registration table?"

"I'm doing research, social and economic effects, attitude changes, as a result of the civil rights movement. I get some direct contact, for our study. Questionnaires. Interviews."

"Been here long?"

"Three years."

"Like it?"

"Some good, hard-working students. I wanted to do work like this after I got my MA. A real change from life in Cambridge."

"Harvard?"

"Yes."

"Going to stay?"

"I didn't think I'd be here this long, but you can teach and write and be productive. I'm finishing work on my dissertation. I also collaborate with some people at the University of Alabama. I hear there's another new person in English. From New York. You met her?"

"No, I just got here a couple of hours ago."

"Well, see you around. I know you want to take that stuff in. Can I help?" I waved him on, and he went out the door. I went down the hall, and as I put my key in the lock, a tall, gangly, graying blonde, of about fifty, wearing bangs, came out and moved directly toward me.

"I thought I heard voices out here. Are you Chris? I'm Liz Buchanan, English department chair. So nice to see you! We were worried about that position. We were so glad when the dean got your letter. And then the president said he already knew you—you know our president was a dean at Fisk when you were a student there. So it all seemed to work out just fine. We got responses from some really radical people." She spoke in a refined though not unrecognizable southern accent, her blue eyes resting on me.

"I hope I can do the job. I didn't know who the president was."

"We're a small group, we *share*, help each other out, Mrs. Wright, Camilla Wright, the dean's wife, you, Jonathan Cole, who's been with us ten years, and Miriam Goddard, who's new like you."

"Five of us."

"We're small, not as large as Fisk. Since you're here, could you come over to my apartment tonight?" She pointed to her door. "We haven't finished reviewing freshman placement exams; you can pitch right in and help." I said I would be there. "Welcome aboard," she said. "See you at seven." There was both assurance and open accessibility in her. I went in and prepared a quick meal so that I could take a nap and be ready for the meeting. I woke up refreshed, washed my face and went down the hall, knocking at exactly seven. They were all already there, except for one other person, and introductions were exchanged. Liz presided, smoking a cigarette in a long blue holder. I immediately lit up, noticing the availability of many ashtrays, and sat on a couch with the other new person, Miriam, who had acknowledged me with a "Nice to meet you" and had continued her comment about the exams.

"It'll be great having some students like these," she said.

"You and Chris will get people in that range," said Liz, "while Jon, Camilla, and I will toil with the rest." She gave me a sheet that laid out the range of scores and indicated the sections offered.

"Everybody gets two sections of English comp," I said, "and two of lit."

"The Western Lit sequence and some electives. You get dramatic lit, *and* you get to do a play or two for us. Been thinking about anything?"

"*Who's Afraid of Virginia Woolf.* I was involved in a production of it in graduate school, and I think it's something the students could do and like, if you want something current."

"Great," said Miriam.

"Ought to shake *us* up too," said Camilla. She went to open one of the windows, a fair-skinned matronly-looking woman, and came back and plunged down in her chair, like a dumpling, fanning herself.

"We could use air conditioning," said Miriam.

"They renovated us last summer so we now have decent wiring and plumbing. This is one of the oldest buildings on campus, about 1880. In all these years I've never had an air conditioner, and now I can. Douglass Hall where you are, though, is new. Camilla, let me turn on the fan."

"It's mostly the smoke," said Camilla. There was a knock on the door. "That must be Jon, late as usual." Liz, nearest the door, let in a pale, slender man with veiled, expressive eyes.

"Forgive me for being late," he said somewhat floridly, with a winning smile. "We haven't finished yet with this business, Liz?" He kissed her, then Camilla, and after introductions were made again, kissed Miriam and shook my hand. "They're running their cars out there again tonight, the local yokels." He sat in a chair opposite Camilla and lit up. This induced me and Liz to do the same again. Sitting next to me, Miriam nudged me, asking me for one of mine.

"I don't want it to be a habit," she said. She had a rosy, peaches and cream complexion, thick, shoulder-length dark hair with a deep reddish tinge and green eyes that looked unwaveringly at me. I struck a match, leaned over and lit her cigarette. "What are the local yokels?" she asked, "as if I couldn't guess."

"Joy riding nightriders," said Jon, "updated in their souped-up Bel Airs, Fairlanes, and hot-rodding pickups."

"*Nightriders*?" exclaimed Miriam.

"Oh, he doesn't mean *those*," said Liz, "just local boys."

"We've called the police on them and they actually come, though they never catch anybody," said Camilla, rousing herself.

"Yes, they come," said Liz.

"They think they can cow people, but things aren't the same as they used to be. If some of these students catch them they'll get more than they bargained for," Camilla said.

"Is it safe?" asked Miriam.

"Absolutely," said Jon, "as safe as you'd be on Ocean Parkway in the hinterlands or the urban battleground at Broadway and Columbus Circle, with those hordes coming out of the subway. This is just the last gasp."

"You haven't had any real incidents then," I asked.

"No, no, no," said Liz. "Nothing to worry about. When the Southern Christian Leadership Conference and Dr. King were here we had some real nightriders, standing at a distance, with their arms crossed, looking menacing and pitiful, *peaceably* assembling, you know, but they didn't do anything, the police kept them apart, and the students were ready to jump on them."

"A few words *were* exchanged, my dear," said Jon.

I said, "Not very nonviolent, I see," and Jon gave me an approving look.

"'We WILL overcome!' they started shoutin'," said Camilla, who seemed to be remembering the event with excitement.

"They weren't singing it; they were saying it, and the scraggly-haired riffraff started backing up. Afterwards Dr. King was saying we have to love our brothers, overcome 'em with love, even them, awakening the divine in them. And somebody shouted—you know who it was," she said to Liz, "don't you; it was Clarence Fair—'But sometimes we need to kick some butt, Rev.' That liked to broke them up. Dr. King said, 'You gonna need a long foot, Brother, from here to kingdom come, ruled by rage and fear.' 'But I could be happy, Doctor, just gettin' tired doin' it.' Dr. King just grinned then. 'Think of the Man with the longest foot, Brother, who walked on water,' he said. 'Walk with Him.'" As she finished saying this we heard a roar of gunned engines down the street in front of our building and a rebel yell, and other noises that made us also think we'd heard gunfire.

"Gee!" said Miriam.

"Makes you want to get your own shotgun," I said.

"Are we talking about the KKK, people wearing hoods?" asked Miriam.

"These are just kids," said Liz. "They do it on the other side of town too, showing off. They're bored to death and haven't anything else to do."

I found myself speaking before I'd thought about what I was saying: "I don't want to alarm anybody, but those guys who string you up, bury you under the bridge, blow up and burn down your house don't have anything else better to do either, than blast you with a shotgun." There was a murmur of assent. A knock on the door caused both Camilla and Miriam to start, then laugh. Liz opened it and motioned to Jon who came and went out into the hall, where his voice could be heard in muffled conversation. Camilla looked at Liz.

"Jared," she said. Jon came back in flushed.

"Jared just wanted to know how long we'll be."

"Gets more and more impatient, doesn't he?" said Camilla.

"Forgive me all," said Jon.

"*He's* not scared, is he?" I asked, not knowing who *he* was.

"No, nothing of the sort."

"We need to wrap this up," said Liz. "School starts on Wednesday. I'm so glad to see you all." From her position at the head of the room she surveyed us all. "It's a good team, in spite of how Carolyn left so suddenly."

"Took a job at Howard, got out of the sticks," said Camilla.

"You know the book list. You should all go check in the bookstore to see what's there. Chris and Miriam, you'll have to make use of what we've been using, but if you really want something else you should go immediately to order. Anything else? Then good night, everybody."

"Did you live on Ocean Parkway, or on Broadway?" I heard Miriam ask Jon on the way out. He said that he had not but had done graduate work at Columbia in Manhattan. He went out into the hall where a younger man was waiting for him. They greeted each other and walked out saying good night to the rest of us. Camilla came out, and she, Miriam, and I went out of the building. I accompanied them to the curb where Camilla indicated that her house was in the opposite direction of Miriam's campus apartment, so I volunteered to walk with Miriam to her residence.

"I'm really not someone who frightens easily," she said.

"I don't think you've got anything to worry about."

"Have you ever been exposed to such things?"

"Nothing horrific, just the usual petty slights and insults."

"I can imagine that. I'm talking about bodily harm."

"No."

"Never? That's good. Imagine what we read about up north."

"Nothing's ever really happened to me." (I thought then of the bus ride to Atlanta.) "It isn't always so terrible." We paused. She looked at me. "I mean, how much anti-Semitic nastiness have you been directly exposed to?"

"More than you'd think."

"Like what, if you don't mind my asking."

121

"I'm thinking of the time I was a student. They had just started admitting a lot of Jewish girls." When I asked her about it, she told me the college's name, one of the Seven Sisters, to which she had been awarded a scholarship as one among the first wave of Jewish girls there.

"Down here, most blacks and whites alike probably don't even know if it's somebody Jewish, unless it's obvious," I said.

"But I'm sure they think they'd know one when they saw one. You did."

She looked at me; I looked at her: "Well, yes," I said. She laughed.

"I look like my mother, also like my father, who's English, French and, he says, Scandinavian Viking. How's that?"

"Sounds American." Our talking made us stop on the sidewalk periodically, and then start walking again. Looking at her I could see the suggestion of all of it in her appearance, now that I was looking for it. "It's the name that does it," I said.

"Yes, like *Tyrone* might do it for you."

"What's your Dad's name?"

"Gilbert."

"Sounds right."

"Everybody calls him Gil."

"Even better. What's he do?"

"Works in finance, in the legal department in a bank."

"Your Mom?"

"Was an historian. Wrote articles and a couple of books. Her name was Gerensky. The way she told it, they met on Columbia's campus, he in law school, she in graduate school. They kept crossing paths at 10:15 on Wednesday mornings. He saw that she looked Jewish, she saw he didn't. But that didn't stop them. They met for lunch in the West End, and everything went from there."

"Just what you'd expect at Columbia."

"My mother's parents were merchants, operating a deli, after they immigrated. She and her two sisters were born here. She was the oldest."

"Sounds authentic, like in the history books."

"Yes, and on the other side I could go DAR."

"Daughters of the American Republic?"

"Daughters of the American Revolution. Get that right."

"I hear you."

"It means something to some people."

"How about you?"

"Not really, but I could do that if I wanted to."

"Exclusionary ... reactionary ... tribal .... If one of my black ancestors had fought—and you can bet one of those Tyrones did—or for sure one of the bygone *white* fathers-to-be of one of the Tyrones or Tyeshas today—I don't think they'd let her in the DAR."

"Might depend on her color ... you know what I mean."

"Say on ..."

"Isn't color our national story? Then status, then money?"

"In this place it's money, then status .... But color is always the deepest thing ... here, and everywhere else, in Alabama, where we're talking, but we just as well could be in London or Beijing or Kampala, not just in the wilds of the Confederacy, which is always rising up again."

"That's why Never Again is there to deal with Ever Again."

"These people here were *defeated*, I like to think, got their ass kicked, for being so wicked."

"Tell that to the Nazis. 'Some will be on the bottom and some must be on the top' is a hard idea for many people to give up."

"Not the last gasp, as Jon said?" I saw that we didn't have far to go until the lights of Douglass Hall appeared. When we arrived I said to her, "I've really enjoyed talking to you." She nodded in agreement.

"Thanks for walking me home. I guess we'll be seeing each other often. Good night."

"Good night." I saw the light brown glints in her green eyes that seemed to be accentuated when she smiled, like electric sparks. I went back to my rooms. Entering I went past closets on either side of an arched entranceway and stood just so, observing. At my left was a recessed area where my bed rested against the wall in a kind of alcove. Facing me was another wall with tall windows. At my right was the passage into the kitchen and bath. I looked out the window and saw the magnolia tree looming like a vast network of leafy arms. I sat down and began a letter to Sarah, *I am looking at a creature ready to embrace me with many arms.* I told her of the beauty of the campus, the new people I'd met, and how I felt confident I could meet this challenge. I also spoke of my new experience with rebel yells, a combination wail, something piteous, and an aggressively defiant bravado, as if you were summoning courage. I thought of a wounded animal, say your favorite hunting dog, whom you loved, whom you had shot by accident. I was a southerner too, a black one, and knew about crazed desperation, displaced anger and shame, and a readiness to hope against hope for the result you wanted.

Finishing the letter I undressed and got into bed. It was a double bed with a firm unyielding mattress still covered in thick frayed plastic. I pulled the cover up to my chin and went to sleep. It didn't seem long before I was roused by morning sunlight streaming into the room. The night was over, I felt refreshed, yet it hardly seemed as if I'd been asleep. A fragment of something came back: The tree had been split by lightning and four children were observing it. I was one of them. *My tree, Miss Lottie lived there*, I had said. I remembered her, the spirit lady in the tree to whom I had talked at about four years old. The tree was at the front of the yard, opposite my father's cabinetry sign, used as a kind of driveway marker in the dark, with a reflector on it, and a hurricane had come. Everywhere the yards were littered with debris, leaves, broken branches, clusters of acorns attached to broken twigs from my tree, and one giant limb had fallen across the driveway and smashed the azalea hedge. This had been real. My father and others had come with saws and cut it into sections, to be burned in the stove upstairs. Yet it also seemed like a dream, I mean I had also dreamed it.

The sun was in my eyes, I had fully awakened, and it was lovely. I thought at once to play some music, my hymn to the morning, what I had played every day for the last two years, Brahms's great B Flat Piano Concerto. This concerto, a soul-stirring exploration—something restrained and at the same time passionate, rigorous, and disciplined but also audacious and even profligate—spoke to the fears and aspirations of my own imaginative life. I had never stopped pursuing my interest in music, which had deepened and broadened over the years. I had not become the musician I perhaps should have been, but the need for the uplift provided by music was a way I also gave expression to and fulfilled spiritual yearnings. I didn't play piano or cornet any longer, but I listened to long-playing records all the time, and went to concerts. I had many hundreds of records, and lugging them around was one of the chores of ownership. I had even dreamed once of Brahms, who had given me a coat to wear that was woven from the strands of his music. This was music that it seemed I needed to live. It promoted a state of feeling in which I was most emotionally alive, akin to being in love, being subjected to an experience that courted the possibility of being opened up, like being in love. I felt this way with Sarah, and something about being close to this other woman, Miriam, also suggested it, being opened up. I noticed that the dream I had just had recalled a time in my life of strong emotional connection, yet I had forgotten it. Something had awakened it. As a child I had talked to the lady in the tree and had been comforted by her.

I quickly set up the stereo and extracted the record, knowing exactly where it was. Maybe I had become something of a fanatic, collecting recordings of this particular composition.

As far as I was concerned, Cliburn with Reiner and the Chicago Symphony were the best, who had the right austere, passionate, transcendent sweep that took you—just like the Fourth Symphony did—right out of this awful place and gave you a feeling of triumph over it. However, I had written more than once to Columbia Records, appealing to Glenn Gould, asking—realizing my extremity—when would the world's greatest pianist give a definitive, if unconventional, rendering of the world's greatest piano concerto. Never a response, but I hoped every year for the privilege of adding that to my collection. I had many different recordings of it, disappointed that I hadn't liked the Horowitz-Toscanini version, which I had expected to be a benchmark. Richter got that rollicking introduction to the second movement absolutely right, with its jazzy lilting syncopated rhythms; Rubenstein and Arrau sounded like old world poets and gentlemen; Ashkenazy was forceful and precise, as usual; Gilels, lyrical and probing, and Arrau and Watts, I was glad to say, were the *only* ones yet I'd heard to get in the triplet grace notes or whatever the three notes were following the sustained trill at the end of the first movement's finale— and with a loving exquisiteness of difficulty overcome—which made all the difference in finalizing the mood of ascendancy, the feeling that the spirit will prevail, that is evoked and demonstrated in the music. Most of the time I only listened to the first movement before I had to stop and go out into the world, having been filled up with what I'd just heard.

I had arranged to eat in the faculty dining hall and proceeded there, where over the course of the year I sat with some of my colleagues and other faculty who ate there, so that a group of familiar faces met up and assembled; nevertheless many times I ate alone, or on the run. The one meal with a heavy turnout was dinner. Many of the others didn't eat much breakfast or did so in their apartments. Liz or Camilla would never be there. Almost never would Jonathan, but Miriam I saw frequently. This morning we ate together. We passed down the aisle where she selected fruit, cereal, juice, a boiled egg, and coffee. Following behind her I took juice, fruit, scrambled eggs, ham, toast, and coffee. We held our trays looking for a table, of which there were many unoccupied. "Over there?" she asked, motioning toward a window, and we went and sat down. As we did so there was a sound of chimes striking eight times from some belfry on the campus. "A sweet sound I've always loved," she smiled. We talked about our meeting last night and the need to go straight to the bookstore that morning. "Liz seems to be in control," she said.

"I like her cigarette holder," I said.

"I wonder how long she's been here."

"A well-bred Southerner, doing the good work. Probably ready to retire, with black nationalists applying for her jobs."

"Had they?"

"Sure, and some of the students too."

"You like her?" she asked.

"She's fine. Really committed. What'd you think of Camilla and Jonathan?"

"Must have been his lover outside, though kind of young. Camilla didn't seem to like it." Her brow furrowed.

"Camilla would not think that was correct," I said.

"You could probably get pretty lonely here."

"Yeah, but you don't have to come all the way down here to be lonely."

"That's what I mean. They've got their thing going in an obvious way." She paused. "What do you suppose Liz does for company?"

"Has her own lover," I said. She raised her eyebrows. "I mean boyfriend." She had finished eating but I hadn't, as I waited for a surge of nausea to pass. "What brought you down here?"

"I answered the ad in *The Times*."

"Me too."

"My first real job," she said. "I wanted to see the South, and I wasn't cut out to be a Freedom Rider or civil rights worker.

I could teach in some college in New York, or I could do it here, or I could go back to grad school."

"We won't be making much money"—I cited our salary—"but the cost of living is low."

"That's what you're making? That's $500 more than I'm getting!"

"Really?" The brown glints in her eyes were sparking.

"Why do they *do* that? I'm surprised they'd do that here."

"Maybe it's because I also do the plays."

"Both titles were the same, for instructors in English."

"Speak to Liz."

"I will! That's straight out sex discrimination." She was angry, visibly controlling herself. I thought that she wanted to hit something, maybe even me. "You'd better give us some good performances!"

"I will," I smiled. Having finished eating we got up to go. I saw how erect her carriage was, how purposeful she looked, and I could not help paying attention to how she dressed. She wore a robin's egg blue blouse and a navy skirt, with a wide brightly colored woven belt, accompanied by a matching woven handbag of similar design slung across her shoulder, looking as if she might have actually gone to Guatemala to get it, and on her feet were thin leather sandals secured by a loop across the big toe and a wide strap across the top of the arch, probably handmade out of some store in Greenwich Village, or so I imagined, on St. Marks Place, that I had seen once when I went there, full of flower children, hippie kids in their sandals, earth shoes or no shoes at all, flowers in their hair, copious beads, anklets, and rings, and clothing that either draped them completely or else showed off their bodies as they crowded the sidewalks, chanting, singing, loving, agitating, carrying signs in a dispersal of energy that was like Eros liberated. Here, even the police sometimes were smiling, or looking the other way, enduring or allowing the sticking of flowers in their uniforms by scantily clad pretty girls. It was really something, a living psychedelic experience, an electric circus, just like the name of one of the places that seemed to epitomize the phenomenon. I mean, it *was* liberating. One evening, in Washington Square Park, as I looked away momentarily from the fountain, I did a double take and looked again, toward a crump of shrubbery, where I glimpsed a naked female, then a male, not too hurriedly re-clothing themselves, from what must have been an impromptu tryst. The others who saw it just shrugged, or grinned, and continued doing what they were doing.

I saw how Miriam's rosy complexion was set off by the blue, and her figure was finely delineated, refined, and robust. I wanted to look at her without seeming to do so. Her hair did not hang down in the Madonna fashion which was so prevalent then, as it had when I had first seen her, in Liz's apartment, but now was held by a loosely tied blue ribbon. I saw how she gave attention to her appearance at the same time that I thought she would not have welcomed my, or any man's, interest in it.

We went out into the sunshine and walked across the street and up sidewalks to the bookstore, operated by the president's wife. Constantly harassed, she too could be irascible, taking book orders, placing them, dealing with late, lost, or incorrect orders, keeping the store stocked with the necessary items the students and faculty needed and demanded and the expendable goods like caps and jerseys emblazoned with the school's emblem that were less profit-making than textbooks but satisfying, like the sight of the school's name on the stickers affixed to the back windows of cars. She greeted us warmly and showed us that our books were all there, ready to go. I liked the cozy and cluttered store. I bought the daily paper and a calendar depicting influential black historical figures. Miriam purchased a large mug for her tea with the school's name on it. We also purchased our texts, just as the students might, floored by the prices.

"I'd forgotten how much these thick anthologies cost, and I've got to go home and do my syllabus."

"Me too." Outside again I said that I needed to get some furniture and didn't know how I was going to manage it. She told me that Buildings and Grounds would give me all the furniture I needed and transport it. She had furnished her rooms with nineteenth-century hardwoods and loved it. "We can go there now if you want." She seemed glad to be able to show me what she already knew about.

As we walked I was aware that we looked like a strange new couple, drawing eyes, who could only have been teachers, but were we also married? I wondered what she thought if she thought anything. When we arrived at the Buildings and Grounds office we were led down to a cavernous basement room comprising the full width and length of the building, piled with furniture of every description. I imagined that the farther I advanced, the farther back in time I'd go, until I reached some Spartan chair and table, a wicker lamp or tallow candle, of the slave era. I said this to our attendant, a little keen-eyed very dark-skinned man. He said that might be so. He said that way back up in there they saw once what looked like slave manacles and the bits they put in the mouth, and some mean-looking iron work, like branding irons, along with stuff that a blacksmith might have used, a "bellows," he said, "hammer and anvil, chains hanging from a post, rusty nails." Miriam exclaimed. Sure, the man said. "It's a living history down here, and maybe a ghost or two," he grinned.

"Have you seen one?" she asked.

"Naw, not really, just noises." He grinned. "Rats."

I told him I wanted a long, low desk of some sort, a chair with wheels like an office chair, and two easy chairs to sit in. The man took me to an area and said for me to keep looking over there. I found what I wanted, a cherry secretary, but light and winsome instead of massive and stolid. It was harder to find some chairs but I succeeded. I pointed them out. In pointing I was startled to see my reflection in an oval mirror in the dim light, and gasped. It looked like some strange and serious person pointing at me, and then I realized that it was myself. The attendant had seen it all, and grinned. "That's what I mean, some peculiar stuff." I stared into the man's keen, shrewd eyes and said that he must not come down there too often. "Whenever necessary," he said. "You new people seem to like this place." Turning to Miriam he asked how she liked the old piano she had got. She said that it was fine but needed tuning. He said to me that if I were the new theatre man he could also be called upon to do the sets. I thanked him. The man said that I would have my furniture this afternoon.

Miriam and I went into the building where our classrooms were and looked into them, on the top floor of a five story building without elevator.

"You'll be good and awake by the time you get to class," I said to her.

"And plenty of sunlight, to keep them awake at 8:15 in the morning." We examined also our nearby offices, waving to Liz who was already there.

When the school year began I had no time for anything but work. The reading of short stories, essays, and poems could be put to good use in the composition classes, but the numerous papers written each week kept me busy. I loved the dramatic lit class because it allowed me a sampling of plays from Sophocles to Tennessee Williams, and I was bound only by my own taste and the need to provide representative selections. I met with the drama club and saw that they were ready and probably able to do Albee's *Virginia Woolf*. I received a letter from Sarah that began *I hope the creature with many arms is only a metaphor*. She went on to speak of an internship she had at a local hospital and her applications to medical school. September was almost over when I received the first of what would be biweekly checks. I could go to Atlanta on a weekend and take my car to be repaired. Coming into the building one day I encountered Howard going out.

"You're the one playing the Brahms. Which one? Cliburn and Reiner?" The last seemed as much a question as a statement of what he had recognized.

"Yes."

"I just got Maurizio Pollini. You heard it?"

"Yes. I've got it."

"I get a lot of stuff from Goody's. Why don't you come in sometimes and we can talk."

"I'd like that."

"Good. See you around."

Going back out I saw Miriam walking with a pensive look.

"A rough day?"

"Tomorrow is Yom Kippur."

"That's a Jewish holiday?"

She stared at me. She said, "The Day of Atonement, the holiest. I didn't want to cut my classes tomorrow, but I told them I wouldn't be in."

"You told them why?"

"Of course. They'd never heard of it, well one person had. It wasn't even on the calendar."

"You can still observe it."

"I will, even though I'm not even a *strict* observer."

After my last class the next day I walked to the town square and took a Greyhound bus to Atlanta, then took a city bus to a stop near my sister's house, walking the remaining four or five blocks carrying a shopping bag with my few essentials in it. No one was at home so I took a nap. When they did arrive, first the boys, then Mordecai and then Julia, I greeted them and brought them up to date. The next day, a Saturday, Mordecai, Charles, and I towed my car very early to the Chevrolet dealership where we waited for it to open. Charles had insisted on riding in the car with me as Mordecai towed it in the family station wagon, a VW stick shift. We went early to avoid the congestion, reduced on weekends but still heavy on a Saturday, not certain either what the laws were governing the towing of vehicles. So we avoided all expressways. When the repair shop opened we were immediately taken in and courteously treated. I needed a new engine, and I could get a rebuilt one, installed, for about $400. Just about what you said, Charles emphasized. These models are popular, said the mechanic, a pale, lanky, blond, blue-eyed man who was not laconic but talkative, so we have plenty of them still in stock, he emphasized. People come in and do just what you're doin' and ride another hundred thousand miles if the transmission isn't shot or the car isn't already a heap of junk. Yours still looks good. What you wanna do is keep it serviced and get the oil changed regularly, he said. I made arrangements for a down payment now and payment of the other half upon completion, in two weeks. I was pleased. Watching it being pushed away I was aware that my eyes were moist, and not just because it *could* be fixed, but also because I had been able to be in a position to do what needed to be done to get it fixed.

I had dinner and stayed the night. I called Sarah who was not in, her parents said, working at her internship. I called Derek just to update him and found out that Tina had taken a job as an art instructor at one of the local colleges, that she was painting again, and that *he* had applied to medical school. Don't ask how we're going to manage it because we don't know, he said. So I told him my own news. The next morning, because Mordecai was off working, Julia took me to the bus station. She wished me well, and as I kissed her goodbye, I found myself pressing her to me and kissing her on the lips, so full was the welling up of feeling for her.

Back at school I was engaged the next two weeks casting for the play. It was pretty clear who the four characters would be, and George and Martha, Nick and Honey corresponded in unsurprising ways to aspects of the personalities of the students who wanted to play them. The boy who wanted to play George was Clarence Fair, a senior English major and man about campus, the one Camilla said had made the comment to Dr. King. The girl who wanted to play Martha was a music major, a prime mover in her sorority and the gentlest handler of children, whom she wanted to teach to sing in elementary school. She also had a friend, Gavin, visiting her, who had graduated from the theatre arts department of the state university and had experience working on productions in New York. Gavin volunteered his services and I decided to make use of him. In fact, he at once saw my inexperience and wanted to take over the production for himself. I saw that Gavin's expertise might result in a superb production, but I couldn't abide his egotistical self-regard, yet I kept thinking how I should put aside these concerns in favor of promoting the best interest of the school. I therefore told Gavin that he would be in charge of the production of the play but that he had to answer to my authority as the school official responsible for its mounting. Otherwise there could be no production. But Gavin agreed, appreciating the position I was in and deferring to it, since he thrived on the excitement of a successful production even more than the need to stoke a conflict with me. I felt relieved, yet I imagined I should have done the play myself. On the other hand, I'd made a decision that I was convinced would result in something extraordinary because Gavin galvanized the actors, causing them to realize the best of everything they had. They were grateful to him, and even to me, for having given them this opportunity. They saw the play taking shape with excitement, and it was going to be done in the gym, theatre in the round. They would absolutely be the center of attention, surrounded on all sides by the audience, both a frightening and empowering idea.

One evening I had been invited to a faculty get-together in Howard's rooms. When I arrived I found Miriam and Howard talking to one of the professors in biological sciences, Daniel Banks, and two people I hadn't met though I had heard of them, Scott Peterson and his wife, Melinda.

"Miriam was talking about sexist salary differentials," Howard said to me.

"Did you speak to Liz?" I asked.

"She said she was sorry but they wouldn't change it. She implied they do everything they can to keep male faculty, especially black males."

"They use blackmail," said Howard. "If you don't stay, we're going to tell all the Miriams."

"The same at Dartmouth," said Scott Peterson, "although these days there'll be lawsuits." At that moment his wife, a pretty blonde, was standing next to him with her hand on his shoulder. She looked pregnant, I concluded on second glance, and she took pleasure in keeping her hand on him, which seemed to contribute to his look of satisfaction. He was handsome, well-built, with brown hair, gray eyes, and a trim mustache.

"I can't file a lawsuit. I don't want to. How would that look? But I want my grievance to be understood."

"It is. It's unfair," said Daniel Banks, a tall, dark-skinned black, "but we still need black males."

"Chris would have come here regardless of the salary difference," she said. "Wouldn't you?" I gave a shrug. She continued, "I'm still surprised they'd do that here."

"Really?" said Howard. "Why?"

"There's enough discrimination already, isn't there? Why would they want to add to it?" She was perfectly sincere saying this.

"You mean victims shouldn't be perpetrators?" Howard asked.

"Well, no, they shouldn't be, even if they are, if that's what you mean," she replied.

"What we're talking about is the need for black teachers," Daniel said.

"Do you have a family?" Melinda asked me, and I shook my head.

"Family or not, I see the principle to this thing that Miriam is talking about," I said.

"What is it?" asked Howard.

"Equal pay for equal work," I said.

"Thank you, Chris," Miriam said.

"I think she means that you wouldn't want other nurses at the infirmary to make more than you because they're black?" I asked Melinda.

"No, but I would understand," she said.

"Do we understand a society that accepts more black men in jail than in college?" asked Daniel.

"Is that really true?" asked Melinda. "You and Chris certainly aren't in jail." She meant it as a compliment.

"What? No … Probably neither is your brother," replied Daniel.

"What do you mean? My brother isn't black."

"I know, I assume middle class and otherwise looked after," Daniel continued.

"Those in jail aren't middle class?" she inquired.

"Whatever their class, they've got additional pressures."

"People in trouble of every color have additional pressures."

"But I'm sure you or your brother wouldn't want to be *black* in addition, would you?" Daniel said with emphasis.

Howard interjected: "It's nice to hear our views on the wonders of a middle-class upbringing. I'm sure mine couldn't have been improved on. Anytime now I'm looking to graduate from Harvard—which I already did—marry well—a blue-blooded socialite—be the next US president and make a killing on Wall Street." Everybody laughed.

"Isn't that why this procedure here is in place in the first place? To try to offset disadvantage," said Daniel.

"Well," said Howard, apparently continuing in his spirit of mischief, "both Dan and I are men, and we're associate professors. Shall we compare salaries?"

Daniel, interested, said, "Say what yours is and I'll tell you mine." Howard cited it. "The same," he said.

"How do I know for sure?" said Howard, laughing.

"Of course it is," said Melinda.

"The president probably really appreciates the research you're doing," Daniel said.

"How about you, Scott?" I asked, seeing him keenly following this, looking from one face to the other.

"You might say my salary is paid by the National Science Foundation for this year, at the identical rate of what it would be at Dartmouth. I'm an associate professor too, but I can tell you that associate professor levels here would not compare with those at Dartmouth, judging by what Howard said, though that's a different issue we aren't even talking about."

"Let's talk about it," said Howard.

"That's one reason why I'm here. To set up this new machinery. To train faculty to run it. To give physics students here, and faculty, the benefit of it, and help bring everybody up to speed so they can compete equally. Otherwise, how could they expect to make the same?" Hearing this Melinda just beamed.

His saying that was so nice and pat and almost smug that I said, "I hope the black guys at Dartmouth who're using that same machinery with you are making the same as you."

"Why wouldn't they?" he said.

Melinda said, "We have many friends there too." Scott then directed our attention to our purpose for assembling tonight.

"What we wanted to talk about tonight was a program we're planning for next spring. A discussion on entropy, energy distribution, thermodynamics, the idea of whether the universe is running down, expanding, striving for a homogeneous state. And we want to make reference to a *literary* text, Robert Frost's poem 'West Running Brook.' I'll talk about ideas in physics, Dan in biology, and you, Chris, we hope—as our other black male—could talk about the text itself, the structure of the poem, etc."

"I like that. I'd be glad to."

"Good. If the black male had declined, we would next have asked the white female, considering there's no black female." Melinda laughed.

He was making an objective statement at the same time that he was also being provocative, maybe in a good-natured way. But my hackles were raised again, and I wanted to make an irksome reply to his comment. I said, mildly, "Might be too much heat for the white male, a black hole on either side."

"I'd be a quasar," he said immediately.

"Long since burnt out, just the intense afterglow of what once was, just getting to us," I said, with equal aptness.

Similarly responsive, he said: "But I'd still be *smoking*, as they say, still have my mojo. *You* know what I mean." Before I could reply to this, Miriam said:

"And I think I'll be the moonlight, ready to eclipse all of that, as it goes down at the horizon." It seemed she had felt the need to say something, and this is how it had come out. I saw how intense she had been during the exchange, sitting on the edge of her seat, her feet raised up on her toes.

"I'm going to be one of the ushers," Howard said, to laughter.

"I'm glad to see we have some levity. It could really be fun," said Scott. Melinda took a proprietary interest in Howard's potato chips, peanuts, and soda and reminded everyone that there was still lots left to eat. Miriam asked if the child were her first.

"Yes!" she said. "We've been *waiting* on it," and she put her arms around Scott.

"We've got to be getting on back," he said. "We'll all be in touch." When he stood up, this time he patted her, on the stomach. "We're turning in early these days." Her arms were around him again, and he kissed her. They said goodbye and left.

"What did you do on Yom Kippur?" Miriam asked Howard.

"I had class. We talked about religious and ethnic traditions. I asked what the value would be of having a day of atonement, of casting off your failings, and rededicating yourself. 'Like a New Year's resolution,' somebody said. 'Sort of,' I said, 'but it's like you made an agreement with God, pledging the best of yourself and your spirit.' 'The Holy Spirit?' 'Yes, if the spirit in you, your mind and heart, is a reflection of the divine spirit,' and so on. It was a fine discussion. I do it every year."

"I stayed home."

"Not to be crass," Dan said, "but I think they already had all the help in the infirmary they could use. We don't need more nurses. We need teachers."

"That was probably a condition of his coming," said Howard.

Miriam intervened, "She probably wasn't pregnant last year when they arranged this. She probably wanted to come, be with him."

"It certainly looked like it," Howard said. We laughed.

"Sure she did. He's the Man, just doing what it takes to do his job," said Dan, in a tone that left up to us the gauging of its level of sarcasm. He rose. "It's been a pleasure, but I've got to go too." After he had left, Howard asked me:

"You think his salary is the same as mine?"

"Yes, and if anything, you might make more."

"You think so?"

"You're the sociologist. Go figure. You're the Man, a white male."

"I'm a scholar, trying to do my job."

"A long way from home," Miriam said.

"Home is where you're with like-minded people," said Howard, and he indicated our little gathering. "I just got in," he said to me, "Wanda Landowska and Igor Kipnis, on the harpsichord, playing *The Well-Tempered Clavier, Book I*. Drop in sometimes and we can check those out."

"You guys are listening to that!" Miriam said, her eyes glistening.

"Is there a problem?" Howard replied, his bushy eyebrows arching comically, exactly like Groucho Marx's. Also, I noticed for the first time how his eyes sort of slid over her body.

"I didn't know. Do you play?"

"Violin, but I stopped by the time I got to college, having seen how really good the competition was."

"I know that feeling. I play piano."

"So does Chris."

"Not any longer," I said.

"I got this great old Wurlitzer from the Furniture Warehouse here"—she looked at Howard—"you know what I mean …"

"I've been down there."

"Sticky keys, slow in the action. I called the music department chairman and found out how I could have someone come and tune it—at my expense. A little repair work—and it sounds great now. You guys should come over to my house. I might play you something."

"You got the *Well-Tempered Clavier*?"

"Yes."

"Start practicing, we'll be over. Meanwhile, since I've got you here, let's see what Landowska does with it, then Kipnis."

"And Gould afterwards," I said.

"And Rosalyn Tureck," Miriam said. "You got her?"

"I've got everybody." We sat, leaned back, all of us lighting up cigarettes—Miriam again procured one from me—and started listening. Howard brought forth a bottle of red wine and asked also if anyone wanted beer.

"I'll have a glass of wine," said Miriam. He poured it for her while he and I began to sip our beer from the bottle. I watched as Howard sat, engaged in some not-so-surreptitious mini-conducting, or else he got up and walked around, gesticulating, sometimes humming; Miriam sat with her eyes closed, her wine glass in her left hand, her right tapping out notes with her fingers, as cigarette smoke from the ashtrays curled up around our heads; and I simply sat with pleasure, listening, delighted to be able to have people I could do this with.

A few days later I was coming from The Market when I saw Miriam approaching. Fall had arrived and Halloween would soon be there. Pumpkins had started appearing on doorsteps. Miriam had discarded her blouses and wore long-sleeved shirts in her skirts, low-heeled pumps in the place of her sandals. I accompanied her back to the store, which was within the outer perimeter of the town and in a neighborhood whose populace was different from that in the area near the school. Mutually tolerant relations existed, though white men parked their pickups and went into bars and restaurants in enclaves harboring them, as black people of all descriptions came and went on the street. The Market catered to the college crowd and relied on its patronage, but there were other establishments I knew that it would be problematic to enter. The incurably provocative sight of the two of us together, however, had yet to provoke an incident. She paid for her few things and we exited. She had actually been out mainly for the walk, she said. I extracted a cigarette and offered her one. She demurred. "Smoking in the street?" she said. "Camilla wouldn't think that was correct either."

I realized I'd soon need a fresh pack and decided to stop in a place that would be our last chance to get some, headed in the direction we were going. I knew I ought not to go in there—its name was Jimmy's—but the fact that I felt wary made me more resolved to enter it. I'd only be in it a moment, and she didn't seem to realize it might be off limits, but the very fact of her presence might have made me want to enter it. I went in, accosted by the strong smell of beer and tobacco smoke, expecting to find a vending machine against some wall. Not seeing it at first, I asked the clerk.

"Ovah thar, against the waul," he motioned with his thumb. He wasn't hostile or menacing, just indifferent. I saw it in-between pinball machines. It wasn't very tall, as I'd expected, and looked like another one of the pinball machines, so I hadn't recognized it. I put my thirty-five cents into it and pulled on the Marlboro lever, but nothing happened. I heard snickering laughter coming from a table behind me at the right. Miriam was right behind me, so close I could feel her against my back.

"Give that suckah a whack, boy, like you was diggin' with yo' hoe," a twangy, high-spirited voice sang out. I looked over and saw a sturdy, sandy-haired guy, in baseball cap, with a righteous, forward-facing bib, with keen, sardonic blue eyes, sparkling with intensity; but I didn't think he wanted to lynch me and cut out my genitals (though I could have been mistaken!—this white woman clutching my elbow) so much as he wanted to comment on my presumptuous inappropriateness. It caught me that what he'd just said was a real play on words that I thought hadn't even been consciously intended, though unconsciously it apparently was. I gave the machine a whack, disproportionately hard, though I knew to keep pulling on the handle, and my pack shot out. As this was happening someone had put money into the juke box, and out had come a truncated rendition of the *Amos and Andy* show:

"Lightnin', how you doin', boy?" inquired a not un-derisive interlocutor, and a dim-witted voice answered:

"Whaat?" Then a shrill, high-pitched female voice remonstrated:

"Kingfish, leave that boy alone. He cain't help it if he be dreamin' in his head."

"Sapphire, shet yo' mouf, woman! Wasn't NObody talkin' to YOU."

"Who dat?" another voice inquired.

"*MY* name Algonquin J. Cal-hOOOnn," declared a proud voice of insinuating lawyerly bombast.

"UHMMM NAYAHHH ..." replied the Kingfish, like the sound of a neighing horse. But Miriam and I were out the door before we could hear the rest, ushered out by raucous laughter in the room.

"Gee! That was something. *Amos and Andy* wasn't it?"

I felt myself giving way to laughter. "Wasn't that the silliest thing! It used to come on the radio when I was a kid."

"I remember it. We listened to it too." She motioned to me to give her a cigarette.

When I gave it to her, she said, "I guess we just earned this one!" She inhaled deeply and blew a cloud of smoke. It was drawing dusk of a lovely October afternoon. We imperceptibly relaxed as we got closer to the school and continued walking down the promenade of oak trees through the campus, past Douglass Hall and on out into countryside. In doing so we hadn't consciously intended to continue, but somehow the momentum of the walk had propelled us onward. I thought that we felt a need to prove that we weren't scared, could go where we pleased if we wanted. So when we approached Douglass Hall, she shook her head and said she'd never been farther out on the road and that it was like a lovely discovery. She motioned to where the moon was rising, a strong yellow arc glimpsed through the patches in the trees, like one of her own thoughts that was following her.

The sheared ends of corn stalks lay in stunted rows as we looked across a cornfield, and the woods emerged as we looked down the road, shrouded by oak, sycamore, and numerous tall pines held in suspension by the surge of cicadas, tree frogs, crickets, and all the other background sounds like a biological equivalent of the residual noise of the Big Bang, or the universal OM that is always sounding. I told her this, and she laughed. We walked for a while enjoying the evening. We continued doing this without consciously allowing an awareness of what it felt like to be doing it. At least, that's how it seemed to me. But I knew her a little better now, and I knew she had to be thinking of our being together like this, our elbows brushing, and being withdrawn, and touching again. What I think we began to be aware of was the mutual recognition of a distant muffled sound weighing in on the quiet of the evening. Gradually we knew we had begun to be aware of something. Soon we began to hear clearly from the direction in which we were going a muffled roar, which grew louder until we saw the headlights of a speeding car and the beginnings of yelling. I felt Miriam's hand at my elbow, and as the car approached I stood still as if to face it head-on. I felt that if this was it I would at least look them in the face as they blasted me, out walking with this woman, and I debated for a moment what kind of protective gesture I should make toward her with my arm. I didn't feel fear so much as the terror of the worst thing happening that could not be escaped and that I must be prepared to meet. As the car drew upon us I was aware of a sound like an agonized shriek from Miriam and the headlong dash of her form across the road to the other side, as she barely missed getting hit by the barreling car with its yelling youths inside. They went by in a flash and I was surprised to see that I was still standing, waiting. Across the road I could see her looking at me, still terrified, shaking, looking at me as if I were a dead man only pretending to stand upright. Recovering somewhat, she ran to me: "You're all right! They missed you!"

"What?"

"They *shot* you!"

"No, they didn't."

"What?"

"No."

"They didn't shoot?"

"No."

"No? I heard it! POW!"

"No."

"I could have sworn I heard a shot!" She put her hand on my chest, almost as if she were making sure I was still solid flesh, and then she embraced me. I held her until she withdrew. We walked in silence back to her rooms, where we stood in street light, waiting. She raised her eyes to mine and said, "Forgive me. You were so brave, so beautiful. I was frightened. I must have looked so foolish, ridiculous, running like that."

"I guess you wanted to live." Tears welled up and wet her face, but she didn't lower her gaze, continuing to look at me; and the only way I thought to still them was to gently kiss her, and then I pressed her to me. We stood like this for a while; then she turned away, whispered goodnight, and ran up the sidewalk, up the steps, and disappeared through the doorway.

The next day, a Friday, I looked to meet up with her, at breakfast or going up the stairs to our offices. I saw her in her office and she looked away as I passed. When I'd finished my class she had already finished hers and left. I simply wanted to speak to her, see her face. I also wanted to tell her that I was going to Atlanta that weekend to pick up my car, so I wouldn't be there, but it didn't matter now because she was avoiding me in any case. Passing their open doors, I waved to Jonathan Cole and Liz. When I got home I called her number, but there was no answer. Finished for the day I once again filled my shopping bag with a few essentials, made two sandwiches and walked out of my room and up to the town square where I could board a bus within an hour.

SIX

I returned on Sunday morning in my newly repaired car. When I opened up the hood, it looked clean and new. It felt tight but responded just like I imagined a new car would. I went through an automated car wash and cleaned it, and its white finish was still bright. It had been a pleasure driving through the crisp morning sunshine and the yellow-reddish turning and falling of leaves. It didn't appear as if there'd be much of a display, just the dull-yellowish turning and then the dropping of the leaves, and then the bare limbs reaching skyward; but there were always individual instances of brilliant display, and the poison ivy running up the trees and along fence posts turned also, sometimes a bright scarlet, often a burgundy color. A faculty parking lot was in an area that I could see from my window, abutting my magnolia tree, and I parked there, thinking how I could always be in a position to keep an eye on the car, even though there was no need. While in Atlanta I had called and spoken to Sarah, speaking with her in the most cordial way, as if we were old high school friends keeping in touch. Yet, sitting in my rooms, she did not seem far away. In fact she seemed near, someone always close to me, no matter what happened with this other woman. This other one was like some sort of experience waiting to be explored, a meeting of trajectories. Again I wanted to call her, and did, receiving no answer. Was she not answering? Just being near her now was wonderful. I wondered how long that would last. I put on some music, Gould's *Well-Tempered Clavier*, and lay on the bed looking at the ceiling light, the bottom half of a convex sphere suspended from chains which gave back a reflection of me staring at it.

Why had I stopped my piano lessons? I lay for a long time thinking about this, listening to a consummate artist who certainly hadn't stopped his. To him it must have been life itself, whereas to me life itself was threatening. I'd have had to *say* what I wanted and persist in doing it because I couldn't help myself, and not be concerned about what people thought or what I might look like loving and playing such music. Other things could have been involved too, like a lack of drive, or laziness, different from the stoicism induced by fear, or the something, for instance, which had kept me from completing my work at Iowa. There was the thought of the fear, or inability, of completely giving myself to anything. Then I also remembered the sound of Aunt Marnie's voice, one of my father's sisters, wife of Uncle Louis. With scorn she was saying, "They look just like chickens with their heads cut off, running and jumping around." She had been referring to male dancers in modern dance and ballet. Of my father's sisters she was the mysterious one to me, tall, thin, and somewhat spindly, though starting to fill out, now, with lots of hair piled up on top of her head, coiled in that cylindrical way remarkably similar in appearance to a bee's nest. She had progressive and even sophisticated tendencies but couldn't see how they were undermined by the limitations of upbringing and other retrograde thinking modes, making her a suitable mate for Uncle Louis, with his hip cynicism, without her seeming to recognize this.

"You still taking music lessons?" Uncle Louis asked me, seeming to take up her theme. I nodded in the affirmative. "Time for your Mama to be thinking about that. That man still likes to be putting his hands on boys."

Aunt Marnie had put her fingers to her lips, "Shhhhh ..." She had a strained, sympathetic look. I didn't know then how her ectopic pregnancy had made her desperate and fearful—and now childless.

"This is something he needs to know about," Uncle Louis continued, dismissive of her gesture. "You already know about it, don't you?" I looked at him, and he looked at me, with a kind of lurid complicity, but said nothing further.

* * *

A knock on the door roused me. It wasn't Howard's knock. I opened it and saw her, fresh-faced and smiling. My mind raced as I let her in.

"You haven't been home all weekend," she said. She entered with what looked like both self-assurance and a shy holding back. She did not look at me, when usually her gaze was focused and clear.

"I went to Atlanta, to get my car. I had it repaired."

"A white car?"

"Yes," I said. "You saw it?"

"Yes."

"Where were you?"

"Coming back. I went for a walk back out where we were." She sat down on the edge of my bed, her back against the corner edge where the wall from the closet joined at a right angle the wall running to the front of the room, about six feet, providing the recessed area for the bed. "It's just a road in the sunlight, melancholy cornfields. I thought how it wasn't my battle, and it wasn't me they wanted. I hated myself then, because of course they hated me too, and even if they didn't, they were still hateful people, and I should be putting my life on the line to stop them regardless ..."

"If they had been serious, they would have stopped for you too, taken you for a ride."

"I think I know that. I was still scared." We continued to sit, staring at each other.

"How did you know I wasn't here?"

"I called."

"I called you too, but you weren't in." We continued looking at each other. I felt I should go to her, as I looked into her brown-green eyes—the glints were alive—framed by her dark lashes—she didn't need any mascara—though I knew she would never in any case wear any—a strange effect, like jade in the afternoon down a forested path with sunlight filtering through. Looking into her eyes, I wanted to go there. I got up and sat next to her, kissing her without touching her with my hands. We remained like this for a while. Then she leaned backward until she lay on her back and, it seemed, sighed. It seemed, amazingly, to be done in exactly the same way Sarah had done it. I followed her, and in exactly the way I had followed the other one. When I began to undress her, she kicked off her shoes and worked on her skirt and shirt, then her underwear; and while I removed my pants, shirt, shoes, tee shirt, and boxer shorts, she had jumped up, gone into the bathroom with her knit bag, for a moment, and returned. We both were standing looking at each other again. I got onto the bed and made space for her. I saw the richness of her breasts and thighs, a richness I thought had been promised by her rosy, peaches and cream complexion, and I kissed her all over.

* * *

We awoke still holding each other, my lips in the crevice of her neck. "You're going to give me raspberries," she said.

"You've already got raspberries, like you're always blushing." Her eyes had a sleepy, dreamy look that thrilled me, and glancing down the length of her leg, I saw with delight the manner in which her toes seemed, I imagined, to wiggle at me.

"Look up there." She indicated the light fixture. I looked and saw our reflection.

"There we are," I said.

"Earlier when it caught my eye, I had to look away; it was so intense," she said.

"What about now?" I said, as I drew my tongue across her nipples and breasts, which led to a renewal of love making.

When this had subsided, she said, "Don't you ever get tired?"

"Should I?" She got up and put the Gould recording back on.

"No!" she said, with a sly, emphatic grin. She looked at the sensitive portrait of Gould on the cover of the album, looking as if he too were listening, and as the music began again, she said:

"I just love this."

I said, "We can spend the rest of our days doing this." The evening wore on into night. We had a dinner of tuna salad, fruit, chocolate, and white wine, made tart by the casual pacing of our many cigarettes. When it was time to go she gave me a quick kiss and was out the door. I stood looking out the window as she went past the magnolia tree below. Would she look back, look up at what had just been? I didn't think she would. I turned back to some tasks at hand, feeling both physically fatigued and mentally alive. There were papers remaining to be graded for class tomorrow. It was nine o'clock and I could probably easily finish them. I went to work, working steadily, and then gradually began to entertain the thought that had been pressing on me, a feeling of such suffused happiness that I exclaimed a sound out loud. She was gorgeous! And so interesting. I felt such pleasure that I laughed. And what was she doing here? Come to meet a new thing? So had I. She had run away, but had come back again. This somehow made her all the more endearing to me. I had no doubt how easily in her head she had heard the shot from the roaring car, even though there had been none. I also wondered whether her running to the other side of the road, at precisely that precarious moment, had so surprised the car's occupants that they were, instantaneously, distracted from carrying out the possible original intent of firing a weapon out of the window at me. They would have laughed and felt vindicated. I graded the papers with a fury, wise and impartial as King Solomon. When I had finished, at about 11:30, and the phone rang, I smiled again. It was she, and she said that that had been one of the most wonderful things that had ever happened to her, and she wanted to wish me good night. I said it had been the same for me, and thanked her.

I got into bed and lay where she had lain and embraced her again. I had fixed the stereo now not with Bach but with Mozart, who would accompany me to dream land, so I sank down into sleep. I awoke again with sunlight in my eyes. No building fronted mine so there was no need for window shades. Before I was fully awake, a fragment came back, then the entire scene: The four kids in the yard, but the split tree was no longer there, only my younger sister, myself, and two kids from the neighborhood, playing. I remembered it now as if soberly watching through my five-year-old eyes. *That's mine* she said, my three-year-old sister, and the other kid, already a little bullying psychopath, raised a brick and went with it toward her head. I watched, as if my watching could stop it, even after the impact had plunged her to the ground, as if I were going to run it in reverse and start all over again.

This was how it had happened? It was a dream, and yet I knew it was real. I was the only one with this knowledge? Because doubtless Ellen herself couldn't say. Who could I tell? Julia? My mother? I knew how it had come about, loss and shame and anguish. That's why I had stopped talking to Miss Lottie? The destruction of her tree coincided with this other destruction?

I didn't want to lie there and continue to think about this, any more, I imagined, than I had ever wanted to think about it;

so it went away but had come back again. But I had to get up, greet my day, and go to class. I had breakfast, the remains of the tuna and more fruit, juice, and hot coffee, and I sat, looking out my window, and cried.

It was another bright fall day, and by the time I reached the top floor of my classroom building I was as ready as I'd ever be to engage them, an English composition class of freshmen, as silly, irreverent, alive, solemn, serious, challenging as they could be. Sometimes I had great fun with them. Today I'd begin with a discussion of Robert Frost's "The Road not Taken," not letting them off too easily. I could be serious, and maybe that would explain the grief in my eyes. I walked into class and called the roll. If you've forgotten what goes on in an introductory English class of this kind, here's an example:

Me: You looked at Frost's poem? Everybody read it?
Class: —Yeah, of course we did.
         —That doesn't mean we understand it; though it seemed simple, it wasn't.
         —We always read it, no matter how boring (laughter).
Me: Let's do a reading of it again.

> "The Road Not Taken"
> Two roads diverged in a yellow wood,
> And sorry I could not travel both
> And be one traveler, long I stood
> And looked down one as far as I could
> To where it bent in the undergrowth;
>
> Then took the other, as just as fair,
> And having perhaps the better claim,
> Because it was grassy and wanted wear;
> Though as for that the passing there
> Had worn them really about the same,

And both that morning equally lay
In leaves no step had trodden black.
Oh, I kept the first for another day!
Yet knowing how way leads on to way,
I doubted if I should ever come back.

I shall be telling this with a sigh
Somewhere ages and ages hence:
Two roads diverged in a wood, and I—
I took the one less traveled by,
And that has made all the difference.

—Robert Frost (1874–1963)

Class: —It always makes more sense when you read it.

Me: Try reading it aloud yourself, Eddie. You see how the meaning comes out.

Class: —Where? In my dorm? There's nowhere I could do it.

—What's wrong with your own room, man? I do what I want in my own room.

—I bet you don't recite poetry in it.

—How you know what I do in my room?

—We know what you read in your room, John!

—And you're not setting an example, giving these Negroes some culture!

Me: What did you hear when I read it that you hadn't heard before?

Class: It hung together. I could see the author—the speaker—looking down the path, thinking.

Me: What else?

Class: It was like he was telling a story, having a conversation.

Me: He was! Who wants to give a brief summary? John?

Class: The guy is taking a walk in the woods and looks like he can't decide which way to go, the long road or the short road, and in the end it's not just the long or the short but whether people have been on it or not, whether it's new.

Me: How do you know, Samantha? Cite the passage.

Class: He said one had the "the better claim/Because it was grassy and wanted wear"—"Wanted wear" means no one had been on it, walked on it, doesn't it?

        —But "the passing there/Had really worn them about the same," so they aren't *that* different.

        —That "wanted" is nice. The path *wanted* you on it?

Me: Yet one was still less traveled than the other. Is that going to make a difference. Cynthia?

Class: Depends on where he's going (laughter).

        —Depends on what it means to him. Maybe he's lonely. Maybe he's trying to prove a point about something, that you can't get lost … I don't know.

Me: Maybe he's not just talking about walking in the woods or just choosing a road. Liz, I see your hand.

Class: He's making a comparison …

Class: Speaking metaphorically about something …

Class: Making life choices, choosing what you want to do.

Me: Is he? Willie?

Class: He must be, he's making such a big deal out of it. Like in the last paragraph …

Me: Stanza!

Class: Stanza, when he talks about what it meant to him after he'd done it, maybe at the end of his life.

Me: He certainly makes a nice comparison, doesn't he, between the roads in the woods and roads in life, yet he didn't *say* it outright. Right? Does this compare with ourselves? Some of you are going to be psychologists, some lawyers. Right? You're at the beginning. You could choose either way, each seems equally inviting, or almost so. What's the problem then? Tamika?

Class: You've got to choose!

Me: Is that what he's talking about? You can see him looking down each path as far as he can see, until it "bent in the undergrowth." Look how that breaks down. How many of you been hiking?

Class: This is heavy duty hiking, like on the Appalachian Trail. You don't want to get lost.

Me: You don't want to choose the wrong career either. Suppose you went on the Appalachian Trail—it passes near here—and the path divided, like your road of life will sooner or later bring you to a point where it divides, and you can go many ways. Some of us are going to go down that easier road where we know it's going to come out somewhere. Some of us are going to go where it looks like nobody else has been in a long time. Which way would you go? Like, for instance, being the first in your family to go to college or be a professor or doctor. Being the first. Does he refer to that in the poem?

Class: "And both that morning equally lay/In leaves no step had trodden black."

Me: What does that say literally?

Class: Stepping on the leaves? Nobody's been on them?

Me: No footsteps on *your* leaves? No one had been there before you? How far do you want to go with that? What's "trodden black?"

Class: Wet footprints.

Me: Wet, sodden footprints, blackening the way before you get there?

Class: That's pretty good!

Me: You've seen what it looks like when leaves stick to your shoes, or when you press them down, the kind of footprints you leave? How about how he started out in a "yellow wood"?

Class: Was he scared? Might end up in Timbuktu? [laughter, but some derisive dismissal of the comment].

Me: Sure, he could be. Uncertain he was going on the right path, which means doing the right thing. Since this is poetry, he could mean many things, all of them at the same time. What else could he mean? Look out the window at those woods.

Class: You mean, the leaves, autumn?

Me: It could be. Is autumn different from spring? Maybe he means he just happened to be doing it in autumn. Maybe there is a mood in autumn … melancholy longing? A time for new decisions?

Class: But what is it exactly!

Me: I don't know, maybe all of it. Can you tolerate a little uncertainty, Samantha? I know John can't [laughter]. All I'm saying is if he said "yellow wood," and it means autumn, he wants us to think about it. How's this shaping up thus far?

Class: Actually it's easier than the other one by him, "Stopping by Woods …"

Me: Really? You agree with that? I would have thought this was harder.

Class: The other is shorter but much stranger.

Me: Eddie?

Class: To me they're both kind of deep but artificial. I mean, you can feel it, but it's also like reading philosophy.
        —Yet they're so simple, and the words do have meaning, but you have to pay attention.
        —I kinda like them though.

Me: Maybe one big thing he was talking about in "Stopping my Woods …" is maybe being tempted to put aside your burdens. There are always many temptations, but you don't give in to them.

Class: But it was beautiful there, in the woods, like the horse couldn't appreciate. I felt like you could walk in there and be with God.

Me: Maybe he did too, Samantha, but it wasn't time yet. So—you're presented with the choice, being a lawyer or being a psychologist, and you've got to choose. You choose the "other" road, being a psychologist, though you keep the first, being a lawyer, "for another day." What does that mean? Juan?

Class: He wants to do both, and can't, so he wants to hold onto one, come back to it. Like keeping it on the back burner, like when you got one girl, and go for it, but don't tell the other one, just in case.

157

—That's what you guys always do, and end up losing both, and then try to put the blame on us!

Me: Once you've messed up with one, you just can't go back and take up with the other one, because she won't be there just waiting for you any longer?

Class: John can [laughter].

Me: *In the poem*, once you go down that road, is the other one still back there waiting for you? After 30 years of being a psychologist, with a family and a life, are you going to go back there and take up where you left off, being a lawyer?

Class: Yeah, we all think about that, so what's the point?
      —The point is to do right the first time or be left to your lonely self.

Me: The point is maybe both simple and deep. Does he appear happy with his decision?

Class: Looks like it.

Me: How do you know?

Class: He said, "I took the one less traveled by,/And that has made all the difference."

Me: Does that seem like a positive statement or a negative one? He took as John said the long road and has no regrets, it seems.

Class: No, he seems OK with it.

Me: So why is he sighing?

Class: It's over with, he's at the end, and everything worked out all right.

Me: What else?

Class: Relief. He didn't let himself down. Maybe he's also proud.

Me: What else? I am always wondering about that title.

Class: "The Road Not Taken" …
      —"NOT" taken.

Me: The Road NOT taken. Doesn't everybody have one, or some? You wonder what it would have been like to have been the lawyer, but you'll never know. Not that you're unhappy being a psychologist. What if you'd gone with the other girl? Not that you're unhappy with the one you've got. But you'll never know. So I wonder if that's another reason why he's sighing. Eddie?

Class: 'Cause he had to do it, choose. It's philosophical, just like I said.

Me: So he couldn't travel both roads and be one person on both at the same time. So the poem *might* be about the necessity of choice.

Class: To choose one thing, you got to give up another?

Me: I don't know. John?

Class: Not unless you really can have two girls at once!

* * *

They hadn't been gripped by the poem but at least had given it their attention, and a few had been moved by it. Talking about it had taken me completely away from what I had been thinking about in bed that morning. I had papers to return and talk about. Then I had thirty minutes to talk to students in my office before I'd have to talk about Frost again to the other section, though the next section wouldn't need as much guidance as this one did. Then in the afternoon I was talking about Camus's *Caligula* in my dramatic lit class. I saw Miriam pass by and I waved. She looked in at me and smiled but did not wave. I didn't have any further contact with her that day. When I'd finished the next class she had a line of students to see, and then Liz waylaid me, inquiring about the project Scott Peterson was organizing for the spring. I looked for Miriam at lunch but she wasn't there, so I quickly ate, went home, had a nap, and returned for my afternoon classes. After that I met with Gavin and the drama group to see how the play was coming. I got home at eight o'clock, put on some Debussy and Ravel, and made dinner. I called her number. She answered, and I could hear Mozart's *Prague Symphony* in the background. I told her how lovely she had looked in the morning and that I had missed talking to her. Yes, she said, but she had been so busy.

Hearing my voice was wonderful, though. She supposed I'd be grading papers like she was doing that night. I spoke of the campus movie that Friday night. A date? she asked. Yes. You and me? she said. Yes. What's playing? I didn't know, but that wasn't the point. Pick me up and we'll walk there. Goodnight, I've got to go. She kissed me into the phone. I kissed back and hung up. I ate my dinner and commenced to work as I imagined she was doing. In this way the week passed. Friday finally came, almost as a surprise, just as I'd stopped longing for it to arrive.

It was now dark at six o'clock when I went to pick her up. Every time I saw her I thought she was more beautiful than before, and I felt something strong and proprietary in escorting her. The room the movie was shown in was a large auditorium with a makeshift screen, and it was already full of students and some faculty, in a festive mood from the week's release from duty. The only thing missing was popcorn and soda.

We found an aisle with empty seats and sat down. No sooner had we done so than Jonathan appeared, accompanied by the mysterious young man we had seen him greet out in the hall the night of our first departmental meeting. "Have you saved these for us?" he sang, indicating the two empty seats next to the two of us. "Thank you, my dears. You *two* are looking good! By the way, this is Jared. These are Chris and Miriam." Greetings were exchanged. "You're going to love this movie, if you can bear it. It's just so deliciously trashy." It was a movie called *Back Street*, a melodrama of love lost, won, and compromised, with plentiful use made of romantic background music from Rachmaninoff, Tchaikovsky, and Brahms.

"This is too good to be true," she said. We enjoyed the movie and laughed a lot, Jonathan and Jared plainly enjoying themselves. Miriam had not let me hold her hand while we were walking to the movie but did consent to a clasping in the darkened room. She had seemed to like walking with me, asserting a picture of our being seen together, brushing against my body as we walked, but still without any conventional display of affection that would have announced our romantic connection. Yet, automatically, our being together seemed to announce something. I thought that she seemed to like our being the object of such mystery without ever having to clarify it. I thought we were even more provocative looking than Jared and Jonathan, the exact nature of whose relationship was also unclear.

Walking home she told me that she wanted to buy a car, probably a used one, and that she wanted me to accompany her when she went to get it, like for instance tomorrow morning. I agreed. Then I told her that she must play something for me tonight. She consented, and when we got to Douglass Hall we went into her rooms together. Her apartment looked like my mother's idea of a parlor. She certainly had kept the Buildings and Grounds people busy. "I had everything taken out and different stuff brought in," she said.

"All you need now is a harpsichord."

"Wouldn't I be thrilled with that!" She sat down at the piano and began the C Major Prelude of Book I of *The Well-Tempered Clavier*. She played with exceeding animation, with an artful air of spontaneity. Her execution wasn't always the best, but there was something loving in it that won me over. Her fingers flew, her head moved up and down, but her back remained ramrod straight, which somehow gave me the image of looking from behind at a juggler. She played the fugue but said it really wasn't ready yet, what she wanted it to be.

"Are you ready for me?" I asked. I had begun kissing her at the nape of the neck, having arrived there by placing my mouth at her ear and sliding inward underneath her hair until my face was almost concealed, and under there I could just breathe in her essence. She sat there, letting me proceed. I felt such a surge of confidence that I picked her up and carried her to her four-poster bed, though without canopy, and, flinging back the fluffy comforter, deposited her there. Then we just got in and pulled up the cover again, still at this point with our clothes on. I asked her, at one point, when her head was resting on my chest, "What about birth control." I had imagined she had done something each time she went into the bathroom after getting unclothed.

"I have a diaphragm."

"From the beginning?"

"Yes. You didn't ask then."

"No, I would've had all of you, whatever came."

"I got fitted at the Margaret Sanger Institute, my senior year in high school. You think I was supposed to take whatever came?" It did not seem that she was angry at or disappointed in me, so much, rather, that it had never occurred to her that her hopes for safety could have rested on the expectation of my having taken proper precautions. In this connection she hadn't expected anything of me, and this made me feel disappointed with myself, and not for the first time.

She told me that I'd better be getting ready to go, that I shouldn't be in there after ten o'clock. It was, after all, a women's residence. I got dressed and we parted, promising to go off tomorrow morning to get her car. I'd pick her up in my car about nine.

When I picked her up in the morning, thus began the many excursions that we would take riding together, either in my car or hers. A large Chevrolet-Pontiac-Oldsmobile dealership, just outside of town, seemed to be a main supplier for the entire county. "I want something nice, small and reliable, and it doesn't have to be new."

"Why not new?"

"It's not the money," she said. "You don't need a new car when a used one might be just as good."

We arrived and got out, surveying a large lot. She looked at a few of the small new cars, liking none of them, saying they all looked the same, regardless of who had made them, and she thought them overpriced. But her eye had already been drawn to a certain item among the used cars. I saw her looking in that direction, and knew exactly which one it was, a blue VW convertible, looking relatively unscratched, a VW bug.

"Looks good," I said, "but there's no way you can tell if it's any good."

"Don't they have warranties?"

"Probably, but it's not new."

"I don't care whether it's new. I like it." We walked round and round it. I got inside it, inviting her in. It had 30,000 miles. It was neither dirty nor scarred. It had a radio, and the top looked in good shape. We got out, and I looked and saw her kicking the tires, frowning.

"What's that for?"

"I don't know." She laughed. "Isn't that what you're supposed to do? That's what they'd do in a Woody Allen movie, and then the wheel would fall off."

"And the salesman would be Groucho, getting ready to charge you for destroying his property." We laughed. She looked around for him, and sure enough one was approaching, dark-haired with a mustache wearing a plaid sports coat. He spoke directly to Miriam.

"Yes, Ma'am, can I help you. See something you like?"

"This one."

"A nice car. The owner traded it in for a Pontiac GTO just last Monday, a professor at University of Alabama. Just likes convertibles, since he got him another one."

"Sounds like he gave up quaintness for speed," I said. The salesman blinked. "We saw it had 30,000 miles," I continued. "What year is it?" The salesman acted as if he hadn't heard me. He continued looking at Miriam, who was looking at him, waiting for an answer.

"We checked it out. It's in good condition," he said to her.

"We saw it had 30,000 miles on it," she said. "What year is it?" She echoed exactly the sound of my voice. There was something new and urgent in it too. She was both angered and pained, as if she were recognizing something for the first time, her eyes alive with their emerald charge, but also moist.

"A '65, not even three years old yet."

"About what you'd expect at moderate driving, isn't it, 10,000 miles a year?" I said.

"About that," he said, struggling with his desire not to attend to what I was saying.

"You offer a warrantee?" This time he looked at me and smiled sickly.

"Sure, we offer six months on it, or 500 miles, but I think you're getting a good deal on this. Professors are careful people. Look at it."

"We know," I said. "We're also professors." His eyes slid over us, lingered, and his face resolved itself into the sickly smile again.

"How much?" asked Miriam.

"$900. It's a convertible, and not bad for a VW. 'Flower power,' isn't that right, but I don't think fifty crazy students have tried to fit into this one." She looked at me; I shrugged. The salesman looked at both of us and then said to me, "Come on in, and I'll write it up for you."

"It's a stick shift," she said suddenly. "I can't drive it."

"I'll drive it, and you drive my car." Not having thought of this, she smiled a luminous smile that made the brown glints in her eyes shimmer. I went in with her and sat next to her as the salesman arranged the deal. He acquired much information from her, observing her identification and New York driver's license. When he saw that she taught at the local black college, he said it was a good one for the colored students.

"You folks married?" he asked. When she blushed I said that we were colleagues, friends. The salesman arranged financing of $200 a month, 7 percent interest with a down payment of $200, and had become quite cordial by the time he had finished. He said that the workmen had already taken it to get it ready and that they would pull it around to the front shortly. She looked at me, I looked at her, and we looked at him, as he seemed to look at both of us simultaneously.

"You won't be disappointed in this one," he said. His smile wasn't so sickly. It might have been that something in him, that he had been struggling with, had won out in spite of himself. He shook hands with both of us and bid us goodbye. We went and stood out front, and soon, sure enough, she saw her blue beauty pull up. We got in and drove to my car. Having driven Mordecai's VW station wagon, I knew how to drive her car. What a lucky coincidence. I revved up the peculiar sounding VW engine, that always sounded like something straining. It certainly was not a Detroit V8, but it had taken off in a flash, and the clutch action meshed with my working of the gas pedal just right. I almost liked it, but I could see that she was in love with it.

"You have to teach me right now!" she cried. "Today!" Her eyes flashed at me. We began lessons at one of the far ends of the car lot. I showed her how to start and, with her foot on the clutch, to go from first gear to second and third, as we sat there, and then to actually ease up on the clutch and begin. She was an apt student and quickly got the knack of it, driving up and down our strip, going with increasing speed from first gear to third, and she did not get tired of doing this.

"All you need to do now is tie a big rose, a passion flower, onto the radio antenna. You can call it The Blue Beauty."

"I'm ready to go in my blue beauty, and I want the top down."

"Not yet. You think you're ready?"

"Yes." She was impatient with delight, almost stamping her feet with delight like a child.

"On the highway? You heard the man. Professors are careful."

"Can't be any worse than the LIE or the Brooklyn/Queens Expressway, and I've been on them."

"That's not what I mean." I shook my head. Seeing that she was upset, I relented, thinking that she probably could do it without mishap. "Drive down to the end, shifting all the gears, and come back, and if you do it *all* right we'll see." I got out. She got off to a precipitous, ragged start, but recovered and did well. She went down about fifty yards, slowed, turned, came to a standstill and came back again, beaming. "Let's go then. You follow me," I said. I entered roads and exited them in such a way as to allow her plenty of time to get up speed, get out behind me, or slow down again. When we reached campus she drove down the main thoroughfare with a flourish. Soon we were taking trips, and with the top down, to Birmingham and Atlanta, to concerts, to the ballet and plays. I worried that we would be stopped by the police, just because, but we never were. She refused to put the top up. Having succumbed to fear once, she said, she would not do so again, and this was one way she could make good on it. I liked that verve, and didn't want to dampen it, though I knew how easily we could get stopped, insulted, or worse. We would stay overnight on weekends in Atlanta pretending to be married, and drink champagne and eat oysters and chocolates in our room, in a hotel shaped like a round tower in Atlanta where we could go dancing on the top floor with a view of the city's skyline. I had spoken of her to my sister and brother-in-law, and she was coming with me for dinner on Thanksgiving.

Out of my mailbox in the student union one afternoon I extracted a letter of greetings from my draft board, informing me that since I was no longer a student, my student exemption had expired and that I must report for examination of my fitness to serve my country at a convenient site listed near the college. That same afternoon I called the board in Florida and explained that I was a teacher, and that surely working in such a capacity was at least as worthy as being a soldier. I would get no exemption for being a teacher, and I must report, I was told.

I knew that if I went there did not seem any reason why I wouldn't be sent to Vietnam. I wasn't a passionate objector to the war, as so many of the people I knew were. I simply thought that what I was doing was of as great a value as anything I could do as a soldier. I might be induced to kill people, I imagined, if I were fighting an evil, Hitler, for instance, or the Ku Klux Klan, or some other repressive organization of hatred or intolerance, ready to curtail my freedoms—or even my life—in defense of some ideology; but I didn't really see the imperative of my being needed to fight in Southeast Asia. I could get killed there, as some of the people I knew in college already had, since men of color were serving and dying out of proportion to their numbers in the population. Here was one instance in which they were overrepresented in a national institution, in the machinery of bodies offered to fight and die, just as they were in prisons, but not as scholars in classrooms. I felt it my rightful privilege that if the white boys could get off by going to school, so could I. The warriors, people who would fight for our country right or wrong, could go fight—people who thrived on meeting this obligation—of whom I imagined there were many, and there was no doubt that we needed them, but I was not one of them.

However, the more I thought about this, the more agitated I became. I mean, *how* black people loved this country that mistreated them so! What was more lowly—*and* inspiring— than a black soldier, a black man in uniform, ready to fight—as they did in the Civil War *and* the Revolutionary War—for the country and its ideals that they believed in so desperately as their own salvation, when the country still didn't believe in them? The white soldiers *might* share with the black soldiers a mutual commitment, but might not share a common humanity. Yet the black was expected to equally shoulder the burdens of living and dying carrying this additional weight, and they continued to do this, somehow, fighting and dying for this wonderful thing, and still be thought of as less patriotic. *They* were the true patriots, because they still believed the ideals worth fighting for, hoping that they wouldn't be lynched or spat upon (like the black veterans of the two world wars) when they came back home. *Would* they be accepted and congratulated too? How about GI Bill benefits so they could go to college, get a job, get a mortgage to buy a house? But from this they were summarily excluded. I tried not to be the cynic that thinking of this kind turned you into. This place, America, *was* my home, I had no other, and I had been here as long as the earliest Americans; yet a fundamental resistance to me had kept me from being at home and feeling accepted in my own place. It was a hard thing to deal with. I knew many of those who went and fought, but I would stay home and teach. That too was the American way, wasn't it? Each doing his part to glorify this great country. Weren't both equal versions of patriotism?

I had been instructed to arrive early at a site where I and others I saw assembled would be picked up and transported by bus to an army base. On the ride were many Southern white boys and black boys, about equal in number and equal in status, I thought, by virtue of their life prospects and the military's egalitarian leveling. Some of them looked like they had known poverty and were ready to meet this next installment in the plan life had begun to lay out for them, and others looked like they had not the least objection to going to fight. They grinned at each other, or just eyed each other in that sizing-up way people have when thrown together in a common endeavor, and one black voice called out, "Come on and git ready to fight the man's war, 'cause you know where you goin'." "Ain't nuthin' wrong wit fightin' for yo' country," another voice replied immediately, a white one. But another white one countered, "I ain't lookin' to be in no body bag for no Vietcong." "Hush up, guys," said the sergeant, and they hushed. He was tall, blond, and strong of build, with close-cropped hair like the look of state troopers. "You're now part of the US Armed Forces," he said, slightly pausing, "the greatest fighting force the world has ever seen."

The ride seemed like a couple of hours, though I hadn't timed it. We arrived at a facility, were ushered into a room, briefed about what we might expect to happen to us that morning, and made ready for the first part of it, a physical examination, after which we would be given a mental examination, and then we would have lunch. It was about as thorough as a cursory physical examination could be. I was asked many questions, my lungs and cardiovascular system assessed, all my orifices checked. Particularly interesting was the pulling back of the foreskin of the penis to see what lay underneath—it seemed still to be intact on almost all of the men present—and it looked like some needed a cleaning in that area. Thus far I imagined my condition to be acceptable.

The aptitude examination was next. I was in great shape that morning and, though agitated, I was also energized and in a mood to do well, which most of the time I did, though sometimes not so well, depending on how discombobulated I was from the bad effects of something I had eaten, something containing milk, for instance, or some other thing to which I was allergic, putting me in a neurasthenic funk; although it didn't seem to make much difference today, unless my performance could qualify me for some kind of special work or position. I could see how many of the men in the room were having a hard time with the examination, verbal and math portions, sitting grimacing, fidgeting, staring into space. There was more sighing on the verbal section than the math, it seemed. It seemed a shame. I thought that any intelligent person who was determined and properly prepared could do well, and yet so many of us had never been properly prepared, and through no fault of our own. And this mass exercise in mental competence we were engaging in was one of our main means of determining the best and the brightest—and right there was a problem. Surely that was not the proper order of ascendency, unless there had been irony intended, a dig at the limitations of the all-knowing. There were the brightest, and then there were *the best*, those who were unquestionably bright but with an additional quality that could not be easily defined or quantified but was instantly recognizable, the capacity for imagination, not just the ability to amass data and do well on tests; no, the something that set its possessor apart from the others, the merely bright: the unforgettably inspiring ninth grade teacher, for instance; the Einstein or Churchill or Nelson Mandela—or the Martin Luther King; the few good men of strength, character, and smarts that the Marines were looking for—*the best*.

When we had finished teasing our brains on these tasks, we had to fill out psychological questionnaires assessing our character, mental state, and degree of deviance from normalcy. I could do many things with this: answer it correctly, that is, say what I thought they wanted to hear; lie and misrepresent myself, especially if I thought doing so would get me off; or quibble about a question that induced an ambiguous answer when it was phrased in such a way as to require a concrete yes or no—as, for instance, the question of whether I'd ever had physical or sexual attraction to another man. No, I had not, so far as I knew. Had I ever had sexual contact with one? No. Had I ever wanted to have such contact? No. Yet I knew there had been men with whom I'd enjoyed close physical contact. I had embraced and even kissed Ed, for instance (or, rather, he had kissed me), and it was hard to say what exactly it was that Brock and I had been doing. Did that make me, as Mordecai would say, and maybe even the authorities here, a homo? I thought: It might even be a good thing if men were at ease enough with themselves to give expression to their desire to hold and emotionally support each other, without being subjected to a judgment of sexual abnormality, or even, strictly speaking, homosexuality. Having held and kissed Ed did not mean that I wanted to "have sex" with him; neither did it mean that when I thought of having sex I only thought of it with another man. That certainly wasn't true. Men were physically beautiful too, as Ed had said, and another man could see this as well as a woman, but did that

170

mean I wanted to sexually relate to the man the way a hetero-sexual woman might? Or sexually relate to him the way a gay man might because it was appropriate for him to want to do so? I saw that if I answered yes to this question I would prob-ably be exempted from service. Answering yes would not be saying strictly the truth in the sense I imagined the authorities meant, but it might be true in the larger human sense of the way I felt all humans could be attracted to each other. Answering yes would be all at once a half truth, a whole truth, and a self-serving truth, an option I felt I should take. It would keep me alive to see Miriam again, or Sarah again, and my family, my mother, my students, and my friends. One more reason why I could see that Derek was ready to be a medical student, among the many other reasons he had.

We had a hearty lunch and in the afternoon were told the results of our morning's performance. Just as I had expected, I was called for a consultation with a psychiatrist. An earnest and also severe-looking young white man took me to a cubicle. He seemed to me to be a Southern gentleman, in his glasses, tweed jacket, tie, and slacks, speaking in a soft Southern drawl. He was blond and blue-eyed, handsome like a leading man, but clean-cut and self-possessed, like a corporate lawyer. I knew there was also iron in his reserve, and he wanted to know if I had understood what I had said.

"You remember this question?" he asked, not unkindly, and pointed it out, his gold wedding band glinting.

"What's wrong with it?" We looked at each other for a moment. The psychiatrist turned from that sheet to another he held in his hand and then back at me, his attitude subtly changed. It was also then that he seemed to take notice of *me*, for the first time, and to observe that I had worn my own blue blazer, tie, and grey pants, what I would have worn to class each day. We were similarly dressed. His eyes were engaged in a casual scrutiny, down to the similar pair of tasseled, bur-gundy loafers we both were wearing.

171

"Do you mean what you say?"

"To the extent that I understand the question and can only answer it in this way."

"Are you gay?"

"I'm a cheerful person, most of the time." The psychiatrist stared at me, and sort of allowed a slight suggestion of levity, the corners of his mouth drawn back with a glimpse of teeth.

"What does that mean?" he asked.

"The form already says it all."

"What does it say?"

"I'm someone who's trying to like himself as he is." When I said this, though, I had had the thought of my sister and the brick coming. Then I thought of what Ed had said to Janice, that he might not like her any more than he liked himself. The psychiatrist considered my statement, then wrote something down and gave the papers to me. I imagined that he and I had seen eye to eye.

"Go see the sergeant at the desk out front." I thanked him—he replied, "You're welcome"—and I went out to the front desk, where a large, jovial, black sergeant took my papers.

Reading them, the sergeant exclaimed, "Whew! We won't be needing *you* under any circumstances, no circumstances at all, man, or should I say, *fey*," and he held up his arm with his hand hanging limp at the wrist. He'd said it loudly too so that others could hear. I went out with the eyes of others upon me. I would have to wait until the bus was ready to take us back. It was about 6 p.m. when I arrived back at the starting site, about a twelve-hour day, since I had arrived that morning at the pickup point about 6 a.m. When I got home I wanted to call someone and speak about what had happened. I could call Julia and tell her I was 4-F and could not be drafted. I could call Sarah, or Derek. I could call Miriam. It occurred to me then that I should call my mother, and tell *her*, who probably had a greater investment in my safety than any of the others, though wanting to speak to her had only occurred as an afterthought.

I reflected on the idea that what I had said was now on record, and wouldn't it come back to haunt me in some form, when I least expected it to? Could I run for public office or hold some position of prominence in which questions of good character would be issues to be investigated? People would take this to be more serious than the desecration of a church that Ed and I had engaged in. Everything would always be found out, eventually. Nevertheless, I had said what I had had to say.

Yet it had been easy to refuse, to say no, much harder to have gone forward to fight, even die, for my country, like a man, as Mordecai would have said, to be engaged, rather than separated, apart from. In spite of being looked down on by his country and denied basic civil rights, Mordecai would still have gone off to fight for it, just as he had fought against it as a civil rights worker when it had deviated from or corrupted its ideals. When the boys had come roaring in their car, it was easy for me to stand my ground—*she* had thought it such bravery. But all I'd had to do was to stand. If they had blasted me at least I would have looked them in the eye as they did so. If they had stopped, would I have fought them? I would have fought for *her*. I would have fought them because they represented something I despised. But would I have fought them for myself because they had disrespected me, personally flung derision and offense at me? I would never have summoned the violence out of myself with the same readiness as they did, scowling, already pounding their fists into their palms, as I saw them, flinging away their smoked-down cigarettes like bread spat upon a starving pauper. Even then I would still at first have wanted to see what we had to say to each other. It would have taken a blow to the face to awaken me. Of course, there was also and always the other thing, the internalized psycho-neuro-muscular surprise factor—that I am sure had been instilled in me by both my parents' example—in which your hand shot out, before you realized what you were doing, and went SMACK into the face of the other! And then—if I hadn't already lost the advantage—I could see myself a similar maniac, little round holes in their foreheads, just slightly oozing blood, if I'd had a gun, and I *did* know how to use one, faces ground to a mush I would not have gotten tired squashing my shoe in—as Camilla said Clarence Fair had told Dr. King—succumbing at last and playing my part in the final violent arena in which such things played out to the end.

Involved in this was the moral ambiguity of the efficacy of choice. Why fight at all? They revealed themselves to be the stupid blockhead louts whose only conception of successful implementation of thought—and the ultimate measure of power and authority—was the violent imposing of it upon me, another, and by joining them I had agreed to this scheme of things. In the end I would lie on the ground bleeding and inert, or they would. But whoever emerged could not think beyond the thrusting of a hammer or a fist into the brain of the other as the only means to silence and remove the thorn of opposition. The measure of the power of thought was its power to maim and coerce—to be most motivated, as Dr. King had said to the student, by anger and fear, disdain and contempt. And so the world continued to go around with no deeper an understanding of the sources of these feelings and our moral obligation—if we wished to live with ourselves and with others—to try to resolve them—accepting our capacity to hate without succumbing to it. I wanted to kill the sons-of-bitches too, yet to do so made me forfeit whatever it was that you might call the soul, that made me myself—it could be forfeited simply because I could hurt whomever I wanted to, who was in my way, and do it simply because I could. To *assert* yourself meant to go up into the face of the other—the default position of psychological liability—and we all had learned to devise elaborate interpersonal and rationalizing means to negotiate it.

SEVEN

On a sunny, chilly, Thursday morning, Miriam and I were on our way in her car to Atlanta for Thanksgiving dinner. I was driving, and it was too chilly for the top to be down. Though I thought we should run up the windows and try it anyway, she said no, that it was too cold. I sensed in her the reserve, almost a fear, about coming, and it touched me. Everybody there will love you, I said, and I loved her blue dress, with a burgundy tie at the waist and a similar tie binding her hair low down so that it framed her face like a Madonna's. When she wasn't just plain beautiful, she also had a way of looking exactly like a young wife to be in the making, or a compliant on the surface defiant schoolgirl. Her hands rested in her lap neatly folded around a blue purse. We rode in silence until she suddenly spoke, thanking me for inviting her to dinner, to meet my family. She spoke of how she could have eaten in the dining room at school, and even with me, or with the others, but it wouldn't have been the same as Thanksgiving dinner at home, although, since her mother's death, it might only be her father, herself, and her mother's two sisters, and the family of one of the sisters, since the other had never married and was a sort of bookkeeper at a real estate firm. She'd asked Howard how he managed at school, and he'd said he was OK, contented, but she didn't believe him. What's he doing on a day like this?, she asked.

I said, "Reading, listening to a Beethoven symphony, maybe eating at Liz's house, or something like that, having got himself invited. There's also a faculty get-together, and dinner, you know."

"You notice how he looks at us when he sees us?" she asked.

"I've noticed."

"I think it's completely unconscious."

"Of course it's unconscious. Otherwise he wouldn't be doing it."

"It makes me sad." Now, that she would talk to me, about this, made me see what an extraordinary person she was; but she continued as if she had said nothing unusual. "You were right about Liz, what you said a while back, that she's got a friend. According to Jonathan, who seems to know everything, it's Leon Wallace, the music department chairman. He gives a recital in Town Hall sometimes, and guess who goes with him. They've supposedly been pretending not to be interested in each other for twenty years."

"Maybe they stop pretending in New York."

"Jonathan was in New York at the time and said he saw them holding hands coming out of Carnegie Hall."

"Why not?"

"Do you think it would still have been hard for them?" I kissed my fingertips and reached over and pressed them against the back of her hand.

"Never say anything is too hard," I said. We rode in further silence. "It's certainly not too hard for Jonathan. According to *Howard*, who also knows everything, Jon's friend, Jared, is a local planter's son, and he doesn't like what's going on. Jared has a history of embarrassing him, getting himself into trouble. So he just comes to get him, and forgive him, until the next round of problems. He's a Southern liberal, and a trustee of the college."

"How in the world did they meet?"

"At the bookstore up at the square, The Iron Rail," I said. "If his dad shows up, there'll be some repercussions at school."

"Poor Jon. He needs to have someone, even if it's Jared," she said.

"Even? Aren't they made for each other?" As we heard this statement, it also seemed to raise the question of whether and to what extent it might refer to us. We were entering Atlanta's city limits. I told her that it would only be another ten minutes or so to our house. When I turned onto our street I didn't say anything, but she could see that it went into a dead end around a circle and back down again. "Guess which one."

"That one," she said without hesitation, and pointed exactly to it on its little hill.

"How did you know?" I asked, surprised.

"Something in your voice told me." She paused. "Like when you feel somebody looking at you, and you look up into their eyes." We gathered our belongings. We had brought gifts, and we would stay the night. I showed her the two bottles of wine I had brought, red and white.

"They don't really drink, but I brought them anyway, sort of to make things festive. What have you got?"

"Something simple, but you'll like it. Something everybody likes, whether they indulge or not." We went up the stairs to the door.

"Shall I open it or ring the bell?" I decided to open it and enter as usual, but before I could do so the door opened itself and Michael was standing looking at us.

"Hi, Mike. This is Miriam."

"Hi," he said sweetly, almost inaudibly, then, a little louder to the others, "They're here!" Julia came, then Mordecai, then Charles. I introduced them all.

"So nice to meet you," said Julia, who also stood looking, and then she embraced Miriam, and let herself be embraced by me. Mordecai told us to come on in; he shook both our hands and took our things.

"We're going to put you upstairs in Chris's room, for the night, and Chris can sleep down here in there," he motioned to a utility room where a sewing machine could be seen.

"Such a lovely house," said Miriam, and as Julia said her thank you, Charles blurted out:

"I like your car. It's really cool."

"Thank you. Your uncle helped me pick it out."

"I didn't know Uncle Chris liked VWs."

"You've got one. I like yours," I said.

"And it was a good thing, too, because it's not an automatic and he knew how to drive it. He taught me."

"Please come on in and sit down. Dinner won't be ready yet for another hour. The wine is for dinner?" she said to me. "And this lovely box?" she asked Miriam.

"Just a little treat, maybe after dinner."

"Oooh, it's so heavy."

"I wanted there to be enough."

"And so mysterious," I said. Miriam and I sat together on the couch, Mordecai sat in a big easy chair across from us, Charles and Michael either stood or took turns sitting in another chair situated down from Mordecai, and Julia looked at us from where she was in the kitchen across an open airway. Miriam and I were asked about our trip there this morning, how the weather was in Alabama and whether it was as mild a fall as they'd been having in Atlanta. Charles thought that the weather was great because we could go with the top down.

"But not today," said Miriam.

"You don't have any problem?" Mordecai asked, emphasizing this in such a way that we knew what he meant.

"We've been fine," I said.

"We've been thinking about you," said Julia, "just walking around, I mean the *two* of you, and now you're riding around in a convertible."

"We were almost run down one time we were out walking," said Miriam. She seemed to intend this as an amusing, or at least, interesting, statement.

"Oooh," said Julia. "What happened?"

"Chris stared them down."

"Oh, dear! They still *kill* people. Be careful! They're still recovering from freedom rides and integration. Daddy—Mordecai—was a freedom rider."

"I'd be thinking about what you're doing, though," Mordecai said. "You stared them down? We got our heads bashed in."

"Miriam is exaggerating. They just rode by and we stared at them."

"Did you have a gun? I'd have me a gun," said Charles.

"No you wouldn't!" said Julia. "You aren't going to be out there fooling with those maniacs, sick animals."

"Ma, suppose they fool with me? What then?"

"You see them coming, you go the other way."

"That also, but never run like a coward. You scare them the most when you show you're not scared," Mordecai said.

"Like Uncle Chris did," said Michael. The sudden high, clear sound of his voice made us all turn and look at him.

"I saw a man turn away, had started to be ashamed, when we were desegregating a lunch counter once, and he had spit on us and tried to set a girl's hair on fire with a cigarette lighter," Mordecai offered.

"Gee!" said Miriam.

"That's when we had to do something."

"What?" asked Charles.

"I knocked the lighter out of his hand. We eye-balled each other. Then the cops decided to do something, when those guys with the ax handles were getting ready to come in."

179

"And that was in Florida. You folks are riding around in *Alabama*," said Julia. "Didn't I just read some state just now abolished its anti-miscegenation laws? Alabama, Mississippi, one of them."

"Virginia." said Mordecai. "Those people named the Lovings, can you beat that?"

"Just being *seen* together qualifies." She stopped. "Oh, dear, forgive me, Miriam, we didn't mean to be talking about all these awful things."

"It's real. I'm a part of it. I know about it."

"What's mis-edge-genation?" asked Michael.

"Enough, Mike. You heard Mama."

"You don't know."

"I do too—it's *race mixing*." He said it with emphasis so that its full impact could not be missed, and the sound seemed to linger there.

"As if that were something new," said Julia, recovering. Miriam and I looked in each other's direction as all eyes looked at us. A rosy crimson seeped into her cheeks.

"That's us," I said, "on the edge, Mike."

"The *cutting* edge," said Charles. This brought laughter.

"Dinner is coming. Chris, why don't you call Mama? She'll be waiting on us, if you can get through. Miriam? You can call your family."

"I spoke with my father last night," she said. I got up, went to the telephone and dialed.

"It's ringing," I said. "Hi, Ma," I said loudly, "it's me, we're at Julia's house, Happy Thanksgiving. How's everything": Thus began a son's dutiful engagement with his mother. I had been speaking loudly so the others could hear, and I knew that Julia would appreciate that. I turned the phone over to Julia. When Mordecai got the phone he spoke genially and with laughter to a mother-in-law he liked and who responded to him in kind. Then Charles and Michael gave their greetings to Grandma and the ritual was concluded, fulfilled.

Julia called us to dinner and everybody stood at the table, waiting to be assigned places. Mordecai sat at the head and indicated, with a confirming look at Julia, Michael at his right hand; Julia next to Michael; at the other end, me; at my right hand, Miriam; next to Miriam, Charles.

"This is beautiful," said Miriam.

"Chris said you didn't require anything special."

"Oh, this is special!" I loved how her eyes shone. She smiled at Charles as he began to rub his hands in anticipation, calling out the turkey, dressing, and pumpkin pie.

Julia began a recital: "This is what your Grandma would have made. There's fresh squash, and broccoli, mashed potatoes," she looked at Michael; "Macaroni," she looked at me, "all this stuff with milk in it, but maybe today you won't mind the headache, not to mention the pumpkin pie." She looked at Mordecai. "Daddy's going to say a blessing."

"Here is a passage from the Old Testament. We've heard it before. This might be a good time to hear it again. Ecclesiastes, Chapter 3, verses 1–13:

To every thing there is a season, and a time to every purpose under the heaven:

A time to be born, and a time to die; a time to plant, and a time to pluck up that which is planted;
A time to kill, and a time to heal; a time to break down, and a time to build up;
A time to weep, and a time to laugh; a time to mourn, and a time to dance …

He continued reading, until he had finished all the verses. Then he said:

"This is a time for us to give thanks for our own good fortune—seeing that we are in good health and can sit together like this. I want each one of us to say a little something on this day of Thanksgiving. Mike, our youngest, can go first."

Michael: "I am glad to see our guest, Miss God-DARD ..."

"GODDARD. Just Miriam."

"I am glad to see our guest, Miss Miriam, I mean, Miriam, and hope everything is going all right with her." He spoke as if that were the one particular thing he had wanted to say.

Julia: "I am grateful that at times we can have open hearts and minds, and I wish it for the entire world."

Me: "I am thinking of my mother and my sister, and I guess all those in the world who are missing someone. I would like them not to feel alone."

Miriam: "Most Highest ... One ... descend upon those gathered here, in this room, and bless them ... always ... with your presence."

Charles: "I would like the war in Vietnam to end, and all war, and the atomic bomb, and racism."

Mordecai: "This is the spirit of Thanksgiving we wish for everybody. And since Chris has brought wine, we should have a toast. Red or white?" he asked me.

"You choose," I said.

"Red, for flavor, and"—he smiled—"some color. But I don't think we have a corkscrew."

"We do!" sang Charles, "and I know where it is." He got up, went running upstairs, and came back down with it. He presented his father with a screw sticking out of a handle severely bent at an angle.

"In your room?" He showed it to us. "Think this'll work?"

"If you can screw it in you can pull it out," I said. "Just make sure it goes all the way in. You can go right through the covering—no, better take it off." Mordecai screwed it in and pulled out the cork.

"I thought it was supposed to go pop!" said Michael.

"No, man, that's for champagne, right, Uncle Chris?" Charles held his glass in readiness, looking at his father, who smiled at him.

"You too. You and Mike." He poured everybody's glass. "Now, Charles, you can do the honors."

"What?"

"Make a toast."

"To happiness," he said immediately, beaming. His father touched his glass, we all touched each other's glasses, and drank, "To happiness."

"I thought you were going to say, 'Good bread, good meat, Lord, let's eat!'" I said to Charles, to laughter. Mordecai began carving the turkey.

"That's a fat-breasted one. Plenty of dark and light meat. Miriam?"

"I'll take dark, a leg, without the thigh, unless Mike and Charles both want one." They shook their heads, snickering, nodding toward each other in a confirming manner.

"What's the matter?" They didn't answer but kept giggling. "What is it?" Mordecai was now looking at them.

"So Uncle Chris will have to have *light* meat," said Michael.

"And maybe you're not going to get *any* meat," said Julia. Mordecai carved many slices onto a platter and let it pass around.

"What meat are *you* having?" I inquired of Michael.

"I'm having light."

"You know you always have a drumstick," Charles said.

"Not today. I want breast meat, just like you."

"Miriam and I will eat the legs," said Mordecai.

"I always loved drumsticks, from the time I was a little girl. When we had chicken, I also made my mother take out the wishbone."

"We can do it with this one," said Michael. "It ought to be a big one."

"Oh, no, don't bother."

"Sure, go for it. I was getting down to it," said Mordecai.

"I don't think we ever took out the wishbone," Charles said.

"Anybody want more wine?" This bottle is finished," I said. I reached for and opened the second bottle. "Anybody want any?" Mordecai, Michael, and Miriam declined, but Julia and Charles extended their glasses. She let her glass be refilled, but told Charles he had already had enough. I poured myself a glass. Mordecai wrenched loose the wishbone and presented it for all to see. Miriam protested that she didn't really want it. Michael asked that maybe he could have it. Charles told him he'd have to pull with somebody, and he and Michael looked at Miriam.

"But only one person can get his wish, and I'd want you to have yours just like I'd want to have mine," she said.

"You can both wish that all of you get your wish, whether you lose or win," said Charles.

"Is that kosher?" said Julia. "Will the wish fairy go along with that?"

"That means that you have to wish that your wish and the other wish both come true," said Charles.

"You see how kids do it these days," Julia said to Miriam. Mordecai handed a large, interesting, whitish-brown bone to Miriam. It looked like the balancing bar used to support two measuring scales, with a little flattened tip as if for holding at its center.

"It's gigantic," she said. "We'll have to make big wishes, Mike." She extended it across the table where he took hold of one end while she held the other.

"You're supposed to close your eyes and wish," said Charles. They did, and then they pulled, each gingerly at first, with no result, until more force was applied, and still no result, until a decisive "crack" was heard, and then we clapped. Michael emerged with the larger end.

"But you both still get your wish," I said.

"What's that I heard you tell Mama about the draft?" Julia asked.

"I went and got off. I'm not a student any longer, so they told me to report."

"How'd you get off, Uncle Chris?"

"On the psychological part. I told them I was a strange character."

"You are," said Julia. "But you have to be morally unfit or mentally deranged, don't you? Having flat feet won't work any longer, will it?"

"I guess. I saw a nice psychiatrist who understood me."

"Wow! That's far out, Uncle Chris," said Charles.

"You going to have any problem later on?" asked Mordecai. I saw that Mordecai understood what had happened and disagreed, but I was glad that he didn't say anymore about it.

"I'll be all right."

"Let's clear away some of this so we can have the pie," said Julia. When this was done the pie was served. Julia brought from the kitchen a package of ice cream. "We might as well go all out. You remember how Mama only wanted vanilla? This is vanilla almond mint. See how that goes with the pumpkin."

"Tastes like Mama's, maybe not as sweet."

"She used a lot of milk. It's no wonder you were so sick. I've got water on for tea or coffee."

"I think this tops your mom," said Mordecai.

When we had finished the pie and washed it and the ice cream down with glasses of water, Mordecai asked for requests for tea or coffee. Miriam and I asked for coffee, Julia and Mordecai tea. When Michael and Charles also requested coffee, their father abandoned the automatic objection they seemed to think was coming and assented, saying that there was a time for everything, so with their first drink could come their first coffee.

"And I hope it *is* the first," said Julia.

"Ma, you think we haven't had the chance before?" asked Charles. "I'm having mine black, like Mr. Williams does when he and the teachers go into their little room and start bad-mouthing the students."

"I'm having cream and sugar," said Michael. We sipped and eased our full stomachs.

"Oh, there's something we forgot—Miriam's present," said Julia.

"We're full now. It might go better afterwards," Miriam offered.

"Then let's play Uno," said Michael. This was greeted with enthusiastic assent. After everyone had pitched in to clear the table and wash the dishes, we sat down in the living room to play. Miriam's present was opened revealing assorted chocolates.

"Three pounds of everything, especially chocolate-covered pecans with and without caramel, and chocolate bark with pecans, almonds, and hazelnuts."

"That's for me!" said Charles. We played many rounds of the game, for more than an hour, stuffing ourselves with chocolates, amid acknowledgments of the gaining of many pounds tomorrow, and exclamations of how great the games had been. It was nine o'clock before we stopped. When Michael went into the adjacent room and sat down at a piano, and struck a chord, and then closed it up again, Miriam joined him. She asked him if he played. He said he was learning.

"I guess you get off practicing today," said Julia, joining them. When Miriam sat down and played a few random chords and arpeggios, Michael exclaimed how good she was.

"Not really. I never liked to practice either," Miriam said.

Michael continued: "Will you play something?"

"Maybe she'll give us a little concert," I said, joining them, seeing how happy she was and pleased to be able to give something back of the kindness she had received. "OK, everybody, Miriam's going to play for us," I said. They all came into the room—Charles was told to turn off the TV he had already begun watching—and sat down as her audience.

"I'll play two things," she said. "One is from *The Well-Tempered Clavier* by J. S. Bach, and the other is a surprise, for Chris, who asked me to learn it, or rather relearn it. It might not be the best, but here it is." She began the familiar C Major prelude with much more restraint and calmness, but also more intensity, than I'd heard the first time she played it. She was more subdued, maybe more poignant or singing, and more improved in execution. She played with determination rather than conviction. She finished to great applause. When the applause had subsided, she turned around, thanked us, and turned back to the piano again, where she remained seated with her back to us and began the next piece, after a pause, as we were waiting in anticipation. I heard the wistful opening of Schubert's "Impromptu in G Flat." This time she hardly moved except for a slight swaying of the head. This engaged her more than the Bach did, and her playing was lovely, moving. I felt the depth of a sadness and love. I was filled with that loveliness, such a mood of longing, that I felt my eyes moisten, and I might have exhaled a sigh or exclaimed in broken, subdued humming, and this caused them to turn and look at me. When she finished this the applause was of a different kind from what had been given the first time. "That was Schubert," she said, "whom I love, his 'Impromptu in G Flat,' Opus 90. I'm glad I was able to play it tonight, for you."

"I want to play like that," said Michael.

"Then you must practice," she said, "and also have love for it. That is only one tenth as good as it ought to be, might have been, if I had practiced when I was your age." Julia looked at me and said to Michael that I too used to play, to which Michael said that he didn't know that Uncle Chris played. And he also didn't practice either, she added. There were many thank yous and then a shocked recognition, on Mordecai's part, that it was time to go to bed. We all said good night and dispersed, with the thumping sound of footsteps up the stairs as Charles and Michael ran back to their room. Miriam was told of the fresh towels and linen provided in her room and to just knock on the door down across from hers if she needed anything, and Julia shouted up to the boys to let Miriam go first into the bathroom.

I retired to my little room excited and happy. Everything had worked out well, the best brought out of everybody. I couldn't be still. I went out into the darkened house and turned the light on in the kitchen. Hearing scratching at the kitchen door I knew it was my cat and opened it. Was Cat surprised to see me? He acted like he hadn't missed me and resumed his usual rubbing of table legs before he rubbed up against me and jumped into my lap, his motor running. Of course he had missed me, and I would keep him in my room tonight. Stroking the cat was calming, but I still could not quell the agitation I felt, a familiar one, as if I didn't know whether I might shout out my happiness or burst into tears. In the back of the refrigerator were two cans of beer, on a bottom shelf, that I had secreted there, though I thought no one else would have been interested in them, but I'd felt guilty putting them there just the same, taking up space with my indulgences. I reached in and moved my hand around and only found one. Bending over, looking in, I saw only one. Was it Charles initiating himself after all? I popped the pull tab and began drinking, sitting alone in the kitchen. Later, around twelve, I heard footsteps gingerly making their way down the stairs. Mordecai and Julia appeared.

"We thought we'd find you here," she said.

"She's a beautiful person," Mordecai said.

"There's something exquisite about her, I have to say, and talented, and sweet, and *sincere*, nice eyes the way she looks at you," said Julia. They kept their voices down.

"Spiritually beautiful," Mordecai repeated.

"She's a *white* girl all right, if you had to bring a white girl home, even if she is Jewish …"

"She's mixed …" Her eyebrows raised. "Multi-ethnic, her father's English and French—Yankee, I guess."

"... and not a blonde, blue-eyed. But nicer looking than some of those girls at my office, with their orange or pie dough complexions and blotches, with all that awful makeup on, looking like they're embalmed. We already have people who look like her on Daddy's side of the family, whose Mamas the white men kept getting hold of."

I said, "I wasn't thinking about her looks the way you are, though I love the way she looks."

"I'll bet you weren't thinking about her looks! She ain't black, that's for sure." It seemed that she just couldn't help saying this.

"She's a lovely girl," said Mordecai.

"I can see that, and I like her too, if you want to know," Julia continued.

"And she likes Chris," Mordecai said.

"Does Sarah know?" asked Julia.

"No."

"You going to tell her?"

"Yes."

"That'll be interesting. I'm sorry." She came and touched me. "Goodnight," she said. "It was one of the nicest Thanksgivings we've had. Tell her that." They went back out and up the stairs. I finished my beer and went out and had another chocolate and fed one to the cat, who wasn't interested. I went into my room and lay down. She had touched me with the Schubert. I saw deeper into her. She had delicacy and depth, as when she saw what she must have looked like when she'd run to the other side of the road; I had thought more of her fear than any lapse of character. She had been suffused with Schubert's poignancy—and sweetness—and had held it and shaped it, giving it clarity. It was as sweet as heartbreak, and without emotional excess, nothing overwrought. She was like a poem herself as she played it, and she hadn't been put off by all those flats. I missed her terribly, and the next thought I had began to seize upon me like an obsession. I knew I was not thinking right and I didn't care, as I moved to go out in my pajamas.

I shut the door behind me, shutting the cat up inside, but hearing him immediately scratching, I opened it again and let him out. At least, I thought, it's after one o'clock, as I moved, feeling and liking the effects of the wine and beer, a flighty wooziness. I crept up the stairs, with the cat behind me, his tail upright like a broom handle, to her room, expecting a crying out of creakiness, but there was none. And I watched myself as I mounted the un-creaking stairs, feeling, in spite of the booze, a supercharged erection (would it last!), stiff against the pajama's fabric, and throbbing, a stud in a *Playboy* narrative, coming to deliver his charge to his girl. When I opened the door she rose up in bed, awake, just as I had expected. "What are you doing here?" she whispered. "You shouldn't be here." I put my finger to my lips and slid into bed next to her. "Stop," she said. "You shouldn't be doing this," but I continued. "Stop," she said. "It'll be *noisy*!" I had begun to embrace her. "Don't!" she said. There was a new note of both fear and urgency in her voice, and the sound of the beginning of something hysterical, and her body became rigid. It must have been this that made me come to myself as I lay still beside her.

"I'm sorry," I whispered, eventually, after the thought had taken shape. "Goodnight," and when I kissed her cheek I tasted a salty rivulet. It was at that moment that the cat—who, in his way, had evidently entered the room with me and been assessing the situation from the floor—decided to leap onto the bed, landed with a delicate plop, then reconsidered his decision, and jumped back down again. I crept back down the stairs and lay on my hard little bed and stared at the ceiling. After a while I got up and went to the downstairs bathroom, relieved myself, returned and lay again on the little bed for the rest of the night, staring at the ceiling, as if staring were a substitute for thought.

The next morning, a bright, cool, sunshiny day, everybody was up early since it was still a Friday and school and work beckoned. Julia prepared a hearty breakfast at seven so that all would be out of the house by eight. Mordecai had already eaten and left to do work at a site that had remained closed following the holiday. Miriam and I ate with Charles and Michael, as Julia had already finished, was getting dressed, and would soon be out the door to work. Sitting at the table, Miriam and I did not look at each other.

I said to Charles, "I know what you want. You want a ride in the car, with the top down."

"Yeah!"

"Ask Miriam."

"Can we?"

"Sure," she said.

"We'll take you to the bus stop." When Julia appeared she embraced Miriam, told her what a wonderful time they'd had, and hoped to see her again. Telling Charles and Michael not to be late for school, she exited, as I told her that we would give them a ride to the bus stop. Soon we all went out, locked the door, and got into the car, Miriam and I in the front and Charles and Michael in the back, their backpacks resting in their laps like Sisyphean rocks. They watched as I undid the latches for the top and folded it back.

"That is so cool," said Charles. As we drove past a house Michael waved to a girl with long pigtails coming out encumbered by a similar backpack. "Look at that; there's Michelle. Now your day has just been made." Charles and Michael got out at the bus stop and voiced their delight at having met Miriam, and waved goodbye as the car pulled away. The two of us drove in silence and were soon on the interstate highway. The bright sunlight darkened my tinted lenses, and Miriam had put on her sunglasses. She looked like a celebrity to me.

"Please say it," I said.

"You dishonored me *and* your sister's house," she said immediately.

"I stopped. I don't know what got into me."

"Booze and lust."

"Lust? How's that any different from any other time? We've never been able to control ourselves."

"I controlled myself."

"How can I not desire you? You're as lovely as the sunshiny day."

"Desire is not rape."

"I *stopped*."

"Why?"

"Goodness! You know why."

"Why?"

"I realized what I was doing."

"You shouldn't have been doing it."

"You were so wonderful, so lovely, I missed you so that I could hardly think."

"It's true, you weren't thinking." She seemed to have relented somewhat.

We continued to drive in silence. I felt I had to say further, "No one will ever love you as I do."

"How do you know?"

"I know. Isn't it so?" She didn't say anything. We continued driving in silence until I slowed down, pulled off into a service lane and stopped. I couldn't help it. I turned to look at her, and gently reached over and removed her sunglasses. "Say you forgive me. I can't continue if you don't."

"I've already forgiven you." She sort of smiled. I put her glasses back on and held her hand as we drove.

"What did you wish for at dinner?"

"Happiness."

"Whose?" I pressed her hand, but she just continued to smile, not saying anything more. When we got to the campus

I drove to her residence where we parked the car. We got out and went into her rooms. Inside we dropped our bags and held each other, and kissed, in an embrace, just standing there, as if we had been long separated, parted, and been joined again.

EIGHT

The Friday following Thanksgiving there were no classes at school so all day we had the luxury of being together, doing our work together, reading composition papers, reading texts in our courses, listening to music, talking to each other, taking meals. All of Friday I remained in her rooms, after having gone back to my apartment to get needed essentials. All day Saturday she stayed in my rooms, and on Sunday we remained in our separate quarters, talking on the telephone, sorting out the nuances of the previous day's togetherness. On Saturday when she accompanied me to my apartment we encountered Howard coming out who greeted us with his usual effusiveness, chatted a minute, and in departing regarded us with an intense, engaging look. "I think he has a crush on you," I said, inside.

She didn't say anything. I told her of a conversation I'd had with the president, whose secretary had sent a note asking me to come in. "He told me about a fellowship fund for black graduate students that would be ideal for me. A great opportunity to get an advanced degree, which he said I obviously ought to be thinking about doing, and if I did he hoped I'd want to come back and teach here."

"You should. I like teaching here."

"I think I'm going to do it. Apply next fall."

"And continue another term here?"

"Maybe leave here at the end of this year, and stay in Atlanta, and study. I majored in philosophy, not English, like you did." I told her further of my plans: "I want some time to read all the novels and poetry I missed out on, like I was doing last summer. You know where I want to go? Columbia."

"I'd come with you?"

"We'd go together."

"I'd apply to NYU."

"Not Columbia?" She shook her head. "Assuming, of course, we got in."

"You'd have a whole year off. I'd come to see you on weekends."

"We could rent something cheap of our own." She didn't say anything. "Right?" She smiled, but still said nothing. I was thinking about this conversation on Sunday. Wasn't this what I wanted, to be with her? She seemed to want to be with me. Why did I love her so? If it was love it was also something else to which I couldn't say no. She was extraordinarily interesting to me, yet, objectively, I thought she wasn't, as a person, any more interesting than Sarah, or Della, and not any prettier, in her own way, than they were in theirs. Yet she was more mysterious, captivating. Was that because she was white? Her multiethnic peculiarity? But who was *she*? Why did she appeal to me so? Because I wasn't supposed to have her? Because she always tried to tell the truth and yet be kind, kindhearted, not self-serving, except, for instance, when she played something she didn't like or understand, and then called attention to herself instead of to the music? Because she was high-waisted and long-legged with just the right flush of the calf and sweep of the ankle down to sweet little toes and feet? I felt a thrill each time I looked at her, but this was the way it was supposed to be between lovers, wasn't it, and I saw how she smiled at me, sometimes, unguardedly, in a giddy helplessness. Just now I thought of the time of a different kind of unguardedness, when she'd offered thanksgiving at dinner. It had been a prayer, and her eyes were closed.

"Do you believe? Are you a believer?" I asked her.

"In God?"

"Yes."

"I haven't any choice. God exists, the idea of God, the unseen, unavoidable thing. I don't know what the reality is."

"For most people the idea *is* the reality."

"Then I guess I'm one of them. I'll go on believing. Belief is all there is. And in case you're wondering, I can see how Jesus is a wonderful idea. Everybody ought to be loved, or believe in the idea of love, be capable of loving others. I already believe that. I was brought up Jewish and Episcopalian, or something like that, though we didn't practice much of either."

"What we do together is a kind of religion. A humanism." She didn't say anything. I thought that if I married her our children would still be Jewish or something Episcopalian, or black kids brought up to be white who might or might not be religious; but they wouldn't be *blacks* unless I made them so—that is, in their own minds. How society viewed them would be something else. She might want them to have bar mitzvahs, whereas all I'd want was for them to know that racism and sexism and ethnic and religious intolerance were real and that they should never go along with anyone who practiced these things, looking down on others on the basis of such things. They would disappear into some vague conception of Jewishness, or some other religious category, or whiteness, maybe, as I had perhaps already done in my own imaginative life, having succumbed to the usual corrupting or co-opting influences of white hegemony, or maybe just wanting the life of a person trying not to always think in terms of race. Of course, they might also be social radicals ready to upend everything! (Could there be such a thing as plain humanbeingness?) Of course, they might *insist* on thinking in such terms just because I didn't. They'd have plenty of help from society. They might even be fanatical believers. But I couldn't be one of them myself. I couldn't be part of any religious system—and that had nothing to do with whether you were a *spiritual* person, a good person, or not—a moral, ethical person—and maybe, again, that was one of the problems, not belonging, or not belonging to one of the established, conventional groups, or finding one's place according to some ideological alignment. It had often been a choice of being black but belonging to something else that legitimized you, like being a Negro who was a Catholic or Unitarian or Black Muslim, or else being black and not being thought of as belonging to anything at all except something threatening or destructive. That was the dilemma presently being addressed by black pride and black power, being black as a good thing in itself, being oneself, without some perception of limitation, a sufficiency unto itself, like being Jewish, Irish, and Italian, or Kenyan and Ghanaian, with these categories referring to something respectfully, mutually, similar, even Afro-American.

I had just mentioned an –ism, humanism, but I believed all men were a part of that by virtue of their shared humanity, whether they knew it or not—a version of Dr. King's Beloved Community. What's that common bond based on? Ask a three year old, Who are you? And he answers, I'm Me. Ask him three or so years later and he starts talking about being black or white, Italian or Kenyan—or Christian, Muslim, or Jew. But the Me is the identity that came first, the core or irreducible one, and it's the Me that we all have in common, that makes us one, the Me as a mere human being. Accepting others involves a receptivity to seeing how the other experiences that Me, something different from our own, yet the same Me-ness. Can we separate that Me, the individual, apart from his race or religion? For some people this is about as impossible, or undesirable, as standing apart and watching yourself breathing. Yet it is this Me that makes us Us and One. And how desperately we are in need of that! Imagining the other.

On Saturday morning I had awakened to the sight of her sitting cross-legged on the floor, on a pillow, her eyes closed, meditating. The expression on her face was serene, and her lovely body, wrapped in her nightgown, seemed as chaste as the sunlight filtering into the room. When she emerged from her trance she began to do postures, bending and stretching. I would have been content merely to watch her, but she, feeling uncomfortable being looked at, invited me to join her. Thus began our joint routine of yoga.

The buds on the magnolia tree, which had now lost its leaves, looked like a mosaic of tears, encapsulated tear drops, but in the spring they would burst into the loveliest of blossoms. I wondered what their color would be. There was no happiness apart from these tears, as when I listened to Bach with my heart full, or looked into their eyes, Miriam's or Sarah's, or greeted the morning sunlight in my bed like this, hating myself for my weakness, but still grateful for whatever else it was I knew myself to be. In a few more weeks it would be Christmas and I would go home. Say goodbye to Miriam and go first to Atlanta where I'd find out the news about Derek and Tina, and call up Sarah, with whom now I seldom had contact. Thus far it had been a good semester, and the play would be produced in a week, promising to be a great success. Next spring we would do Hansberry's *A Raisin in the Sun*, and I would direct it, having gained much confidence from my experience with this play, interacting with Gavin. I liked my students, but did I really see myself making a career of teaching? I had recast one of my short plays as a short story and had submitted it to a literary journal, waiting for a response. The story hadn't come back rejected, so I kept my fingers crossed. I reached for the day's first cigarette, lit up, received the jolt of toxins, and, after a few drags of metallic after taste, crushed it out. It would certainly taste better after breakfast. I put on the Brahms, the version by Maurizio Pollini, about which I had talked with Howard, showered, shaved, and ate, ready for a day of paper grading.

The play ran for a week, set up in the middle of the gym, on a raised platform that revealed the action occurring in a living room, with chairs for the audience surrounding it. The lights went out, the actors walked in, almost as they must have done 2500 years ago in a Greek amphitheatre; the lights went on again where the audience discovered them, and the play began. I welcomed the audience and introduced the play and Gavin, the department's guest director. Then I sat down and the play began, the audience mesmerized from beginning to end. Thunderous applause greeted the four principals, who graciously accepted their bouquets of flowers, eyes glistening. Something about this made me think of Albee's pronouncement across the acknowledgments page of the text, in which he said that no production of this play could be allowed before a racially segregated audience.

School closed for the holidays on December 22nd. Examinations were over, we had graded them and had turned in the grades. Miriam and I decided to drive in tandem to Atlanta where we would separate and she would continue on to New York. She had insisted on driving, not having to be back until the middle of January. We departed with her in the lead as I followed, a trip we'd taken many times before, and in two hours we were there. She pulled off into an exit for gas and to say goodbye. There was a choice of Gulf, Texaco, or Shell. She pulled into the Texaco, and when I came up alongside her I asked if we could go across the street to the Shell.

"I know you only go to Shell, but this was the easiest."

"Could we still go across the street?"

"If you want, but isn't it all the same?"

"It's a long story, I'll tell you some day." It took some doing getting to the other side of the four-lane highway at that congested intersection, but we did, this time with me in the lead. We stopped at the pumps and filled up. I went in to pay for my gas, and she accompanied me to pay for hers, to the calculating interest of the clerk who produced a key attached

200

to a worn wooden handle when she asked where the ladies' room was.

"In the back," he said, his eyes shifting from me to Miriam and back again as if he were trying to recognize us from some buried memory. I waited for her to come back with the key, and when she did I took her hand and went out.

"A filthy place, and you know what else? There was another little door I passed that was painted over but you could still see it said Colored."

"Unisex," I said. I kissed her, held her, and looking over her head I saw the clerk and another with their noses pressed to the glass.

"So that's why you stop at Shell?"

"At least they *had* a john." I kissed her and said goodbye. I arrived home, greeted who was present and went up to take a nap. I lay down where she had lain in my bed and wished her a safe trip. Later that night, after dinner, I called Derek and Tina, who weren't in, but when I called Sarah she answered.

"It's great to hear from you. You stopped writing."

"I've just been so busy."

"I know why."

"Why?"

"I saw you and a white young lady riding down Hunter Street."

"One of the teachers at school."

"It's OK. We had a good time together."

"Yes."

"I hope she knows what she's getting."

"She's a good person."

"You like her?"

"Yes."

"Stupid White Bitch!—sorry, just kidding."

"Don't hate me."

"Chris, Chris, Chris, Chris, Chris ..." In the following silence she waited for me to speak.

"I didn't plan it."

"But it went."

"Just like our tennis." When I said this I heard her gasp and start to cry.

"Why, why, do you do it?" I had no answer as we sat listening to our silence. "Goodnight, Chris," she finally said.

"Goodnight, Sarah."

I had spoken on the phone in the kitchen and Julia had come down and heard me. I sat in the kitchen as I had done before with the cat rubbing up against me. She came in, looked at me, went to the refrigerator, opened it, looked in, closed it, and went back out again. I was grateful to her for not saying anything. I felt a combination of sorrow, anger, and shame, recognizing the many sources of these feelings as inevitable factors I'd have to live with.

The next morning I said goodbye and was on my way to Florida, down Interstate 75 to route 319 to Tallahassee. This was still south Georgia and northern Florida, so the bright, clear, chilly morning only revealed the pines and bare oaks, hickories, locusts, and pecan trees that would not give way to a real plethora of swaying palms for another 500 miles, hours farther down from where I lived. It was always a fine sight to approach the Capitol from this route, looming in the distance, as if the road, when you finally arrived, would roll right up the steps of the Capitol building into the portico, which was bathed in light at night. But I was no tourist, having been born here, feeling a certain pride in spite of myself, understanding while I condemned the ones who expressed it with their crossed Confederate flags. It was an easy drive down Adams Street through the downtown area straight out to the outskirts of the black university, where I would turn right onto Palmer Street and go up a long hill to Boulevard, the main thoroughfare through the university, where, facing me, on the right, would be the chemistry and physics building (where I used to talk to Dr. Ellis) and, at my left, Lee Hall, an auditorium and administrative building, and I would turn left and go past familiar landmarks: the fountain, the centerpiece of a promenade with a perpetual leak at its left in the grass; the student commons and then the student union and administrative buildings; imposing brick buildings that were dormitories and faculty residences, past the science building, and others, through a block of private homes and bourgeois Negro prosperity to Osceola Street, where I turned right and went within the block to my house. Nothing had changed much, up and down the street, except for the university's creeping approach with more cars and parking lots in what had once been single family yards. I pulled into the driveway and saw that my mother's car was parked farther down in the garage underneath our rental house, which had been built on the same spot where my father's shop used to be. I saw it was a different car, a used Buick. The empty campus showed that the students had already left for the holidays, so I hoped not to find any in my house. I got out and saw that the house needed a coat of paint, and walked up the steps onto the porch and entered after I'd knocked on the door. My mother was ironing clothes in the kitchen, looking from there through the house into the living room where the TV was on—a soap opera that had been running at least ten years—and my sister sat by the heater keeping warm.

When my mother saw me she exclaimed, "Oh, he's here!" She put down her iron and ran to me, allowing herself to be held and kissed. She and Julia looked more alike than ever, and she held onto me, her head on my chest, and then turned me loose. I went and kissed Ellen, who was beaming but didn't get up from her chair. I said to them, looking at Ellen, that I had Christmas presents for them still out in the car. I spoke to my mother about my job, how I wouldn't be going to Vietnam, and I caught up on news about my childhood friends, some of whom had gone, one of whom had died, and the ones who'd gone to dental, law, or graduate schools. Some had just gotten married, and she emphasized this.

"No, Ma, I'm not getting married yet."

"You have somebody? A girl?"

"Yes." I thought maybe it was true.

"I remember when you used to be reading that *Lonely Crowd* book."

"So, Ellie, how are you?"

"I'm fine. I got up early today 'cause Mama said you coming." She was still beaming.

"You and me can go get the Christmas tree tomorrow."

"OK!" She was two years younger than I, and though she had a woman's body, she still retained the innocent look of a child, much like, I thought, Michael still did, a trusting purity in both their eyes.

"Mike and Charles and Julia and Mordecai in Atlanta send their love," I said to her. "You still watching *The Secret Storm*, Ma? Or was it *The Edge of Night*?"

"No, child, I can't do without my stories." I couldn't appreciate how she could actually hear it from where she was in the kitchen, and how closely she followed it I didn't know, but it was like her constant companion. It used to come on at four in the afternoon, just as I was arriving home from school. Seemingly all the TV sets in the neighborhood would be on, as I heard the theme song that had been appropriated from what I didn't know then was the Brahms Double Concerto. Then, at five o'clock, I and the other kids in the neighborhood got to listen to the radio broadcast *The Lone Ranger*.

"Ma, I see you have a new car."

"I told you I had trouble with the other one. It wasn't worth the bother."

"I see it's a Buick." She smiled. "That's what you used the money for I sent you?"

"Something worthwhile." I went out to get the presents and came back in with them, taking them to the little room off the living room under the stairs where we always set up the tree. Before my father had put on the second story this had been a full-fledged bedroom, and I had been born in it, on a Monday morning. I noticed the piano, to her a new piece of furniture like a room air conditioner, new carpeting, china cabinet or a Buick in the garage, that every household ought to have.

"A nice piano, Ma." She stood behind me, smiling.

"A Baldwin. Pecan finish."

"A little too late for me, though." It was a spinet, fitting snugly into the space provided for it. I went to sit down at it, but before I did I thought to open up the top of the seat, and inside, as I'd suspected, were all my old music books. I took out the edition of *The Well-Tempered Clavier, Book One*, and tried the opening bars, a cascade of fractured notes and awful sounds. I sat still for a moment. It had been fifteen years at least. Even so it was beautiful, Bach's great epic hymn, the ambassador of all that can be said in music. No one should play this but with rapt and rapturous attention, as if welcoming the sun. I thought it was the sound of life, something fundamental, the complex simplicity that something fundamental always had, an intuiting of the movement of DNA itself, for instance, as it moved along the double helix, if the movement of such a thing were audible.

"You can practice some." Her hand sort of reached out, brushed my back, and fell away. Both of us, Ellen, too, had taken music lessons, right down the street in the home of a man who played organ at church and at the university two blocks away. Ellen had been right-handed, and after her trauma had had to learn to become left-handed, still to a degree paralyzed on her right side, and she walked with a limp. My mother had nevertheless sent her to music lessons, and to school, until provision was made for special education classes. It was strange how she had learned to read notes but not, with any certainty, words.

"Does Ellie want to play it?"

"She's not interested anymore. She doesn't do much anymore, after you left, and the kids around here grew up. Just stays in her room."

205

"You giving her her medicine?"

"Child, what you mean?"

"You know what I mean."

"I always give her her medicine."

"If you did she wouldn't have *any* seizures." She turned her back on me and walked back to her ironing.

"Nothing wrong with that child," she said from the rear. I took my belongings up the stairs and went back to my old room. I knew I wouldn't be in there; I'd be in my father's room, but I looked in there anyway to see what the student boarders had done to it. They were all women, in this room, in two rooms downstairs, and six rooms out in the back. It looked like a woman slept there, with a fluffy comforter evenly spread on the bed and the articles on the dresser neatly arranged. I shut the door and went into my father's room, my room now. *If she gets too antsy I go down there and quiet her down*, I had heard my father say, when I was about six, speaking to one of his workmen. And indeed he often went down the hall to my mother's room; but always, when he came home late, he went to sleep first in his own room. Outside, facing this room, was an alcove space with one wall lined with books. I looked until I found Riesman's *The Lonely Crowd* exactly where I had left it, one of the books I'd read that had disturbed her so, though it wasn't at all what she thought it was. Who was lonelier than she? Perhaps that had been her fear for me. The first time I'd come home from college for the summer, I'd seen a painting of a nude, a woman, hanging on the wall opposite the books. It wasn't there now. When I'd asked about it she'd said she'd found it among some things when she'd been cleaning up.

"Where'd it come from?"

"I had it."

"Where'd you get it?"

"It was mine."

"Someone gave it to you?" A look in her eyes made me realize, "You painted it?" She smiled, a sort of shrug. "I never

206

knew you could paint." Even after admitting it, she acted as if she hadn't done anything, and if I were to ask her for it now she'd act as if she didn't know where it was. I had wanted it. It was hers, she was able to paint, but it was lost to me, like so much of her was.

"Did you paint others?" I had asked.

She shrugged. "I did some in art class."

"In college?" She nodded. "Ma, that was thirty years ago."

The wall was bare again. I unpacked and lay on the bed and was awakened an hour later by the sound of her voice calling up the stairs, telling me dinner was ready. It made me feel a teenager again. I washed my face and went down. The three of us sat while my mother said grace, a litany unchanged from my childhood years: "We thank Thee, Heavenly Father, for the food we're about to receive," and then we all responded, "Amen." As we were eating, my sister's face began to twitch and distort itself, as if she were rapidly gnashing on food. She was having a small seizure, lasting about twenty seconds, the conclusion of which left her with an idiotic grin.

"Oh, look at the child!" I went and held her, trying to ensure that she wouldn't bite her tongue.

"Are you OK?" I asked when it was over. She smiled and I could see that she was conscious of herself again. I turned on my mother. "Damn it! Did you give it to her today?"

"The child is all right." She was both belligerent and guilty. I went into the kitchen, looked in the cabinet where she kept the Dilantin, got some and brought it back to Ellen. We continued to eat in silence. At least she kept the prescription filled, or *maybe* she did, but was neglectful about administering it. I saw that Julia and I would eventually have to come and take Ellen away from her, something we should already have long since done.

"Ma, it's so easy to do." She continued to eat, with her right hand in the air with its elbow on the table, while she ate with her left, but she wrote with her right. I thought, for the first time that moment, that she had probably been left-handed and had been made to write with her right. "Ma, were you left-handed?"

"I'm even-handed."

"Did you do things first with your left?"

"Yes." I had gotten a straight answer. "They made me write with my right, though." There was the slightest hint of grievance in her voice.

"You paint with your left?"

"Yes."

"Where's that painting that was on the wall upstairs?"

"I don't know."

"Ma, I want it, to take with me."

"It's around somewhere. Maybe I can find it." I thought it best to leave the matter there and see if she produced it. After dinner I went to the piano and practiced. It was not out of tune, with a nice sound, and the agony of the hard work of practice came back to me, along with a pain in the back from sitting upright in that posture with my arms extended over the keyboard. It was pleasure and pain. I had just begun to get the notes right, not to mention the fingering, when I became aware I'd already spent three hours at it. I stopped, exhausted but happy.

When I went out I heard my mother working in the kitchen, and Ellen had gone up the stairs to her room. I went outside on the front porch and smoked a cigarette. I would leave after New Year's. I looked up through the pecan tree and could see the stars in the winter sky, the bright low Christmas Star and the other, not so bright one, that always accompanied it, shining above it. Venus or Mars? I was startled to hear the phone ring, having been expecting it. My mother called me, "For you," she said. It was Miriam, who wanted me to know she had arrived all right and she missed me. I told her how I had been practicing. We talked for a while and said goodbye. When I hung up, my mother asked, "Is that the one?" I said that it was. "She has a nice voice." I bid her goodnight and went up the stairs. I went into Ellen's room and saw her sitting on the bed, changing into her pajamas. I thought how I hadn't knocked. When had I ever? I had knocked when Julia shared this room with her, though, twenty years ago, because Julia had made me. She looked at me but continued what she was doing. Her breasts were exposed, and now she had taken off her underwear. She was fully developed, more so than Julia or her mother, and more beautiful as well. I believed also that she had been the most intelligent. She put on her pajamas, kneeled down in front of the bed, her hands clasped, and said, "Now I lay me down to sleep,/ I pray the Lord my soul to keep./ If I should die before I wake,/ I pray the Lord my soul to take." She said this flawlessly, and then got into bed under the covers. I kissed her goodnight.

"I'm glad you came," she said.

"So am I."

"Tomorrow we get the tree?"

"Yes." She beamed. "I want you to do something for me. Can you do it?"

"Yes."

"You don't know what it is yet."

"I don't know."

"I want you to remember to take your medicine YOURSELF when you wake up in the morning. Can you do that?"

"Yes."

"What is it I want you to do?"

"Take my medicine."

"When you wake up, YOURSELF, every morning."

"OK."

"Don't forget."

"I won't."

"You know why you should do it?"

"So I won't have a fit."

"That's right!"

"OK."

"Goodnight." I leaned down to kiss her again, but she kissed me. I went into my room and smoked a cigarette. Lying on my bed I began to hear the truncated, muffled sounds of a conversation coming from below. Who was she talking to? Was she on the phone? Then I knew. It didn't cease but continued, increasing in urgency and vehemence, as if she were accusing some others—I knew them as her tormentors—of having done her an injustice. When I was small I had gone under the covers and stopped my ears. This time I was moved to go back down the stairs. I did so, down through the house, into the kitchen where she had been engaged in Christmas dinner preparations, onto the back porch where she spoke in the darkness through the screen door to the denizens of her fantasy world. She had not heard me and continued, asseverating and gesticulating into empty space, entangled in a web of hurt and offense involving what had happened to her daughter and the actions of looming, tormenting figures to whom she had given names and specified roles to play, acting out their sinister involvement in the precariousness of her life and marriage and her very appearance and existence as a black female. "Ma!" I had intended my voice to be soft, but it was a shout. "Stop that!" She turned around, startled, almost as if she had expected to see one of the inhabitants of the spirit world at last take physical form. She had been wild-eyed for a second, at once both frightened and triumphant. "Ma!" I said, slightly frightened myself, the goose bumps rising up my neck. "It's ME. STOP THAT." It was the first time I had been able to speak like this. She stopped. She looked toward the screen door, and back at me, and grumbled something, and turned and went past me back into the kitchen.

I stood there thinking. I remembered a time when I was home for summer vacation, early, and the student boarders hadn't yet left. Some of them might have been interested in me but I could not, being ashamed, be interested in them.

My aloofness might have meant rejection to them, or my own limitation, being the son of the woman whom they'd seen behaving in such a strange way, she and her daughter. Once, an incongruous family gathering, three women, my sister, and my mother were sitting watching a TV program as I entered the house and went up the stairs. It seemed cordial enough, though I saw my sister's response to her condition, her desire to be a participant on an equal footing and the impossibility of being so. She could at least affirm her identity as another female among others, and this she apparently had done. She sat among them with her hand slipped between the buttons of her dress cradling one of her breasts. Or maybe she was simply maintaining contact with herself in some elemental way that made her feel safe and gave her some sense of adequacy. Everyone sat as if they had noticed nothing.

Once, on an earlier occasion, I had come home from grade school and not found my mother there but an aunt instead, who told me she had been taken for treatment. When she returned, weeks later, she was a different person, but it hadn't lasted. Even then I knew she had refused to take her own medication, and before long she was declaiming through the screen door again. When we visited her parents in the country, my father had tried to solicit their help to *make her stop it* but to no avail—they didn't seem to understand what he meant (or did they?!), though they saw his anger and grief—so he worked harder and drank more deeply. I hadn't realized then, as I do now, the extent to which he must have loved her.

I went back through the kitchen where she was getting the pie ready. It was ridiculously incongruous, with her chubby cheeks and apron on, and the thought of what she and I had just been doing. She ignored me and I continued going. Upstairs again I smoked another cigarette and lay on the bed. No wonder I had always been so frightened. Nature was alive to me and the unseen world was real. As a child it literally was, when in the dark the curtains billowed from the window, and

I expected to see some creature's feet revealed. That night I dreamed of the Friday morning when the phone rang downstairs, and I knew what it was, not needing the confirmation of her grief-laden crying out. I went down and she said *he had an accident and killed himself*. I stood there, unable to go to her and hold her, and she stood, unable to go to me and be held, or was it the other way round.

The next morning at breakfast I watched Ellen go to the cabinet in the kitchen to get her medication. Her mother saw her and told her to "Put that back. Your pill is already on the table." She put it back and dutifully went to take her seat. I looked to see the capsule was at her place, and I knew that it would be there for the rest of time I was there. Around eleven we got ready to go get the tree. I took my mother's car to see how it drove. It was a much better machine than mine, and Ellen and I enjoyed the ride out in the crisp bright December air, no more than fifty degrees. I thought of how I had used to go with my father, far out on the Old Meridian Road to deep-forested woods, and as an impromptu visit, even farther back into the woods on a rutted road that led to the homestead of my mother's parents, the farm on which she and her seven siblings had been born and raised. It had been great fun going there for Sunday afternoon visits, over the log pile where a stream crossed the road, and have figs, fresh boiled corn, in the summer, and sweet potatoes in the winter, baked in the fireplace. I was a grandchild and made much of, caressed and kissed by folk with rough hands but with cheeks a sort of soft, glowing brown, who spoke a vivid, evocative language: "Bring that young'un in here so we can see where he done growed" and "That thar's a big'un, so juicy in yo' mouf it gone explode," referring to a fig or a peach or a plum I had just been given. But the old homestead, a hundred acres, a mile or two off the main road, nestled in the midst of a rich white man's many thousands of acres, was swapped by agreement for land of equal size closer to the road and divided among the eight siblings. It was said that the white man shared with them an ancestral progenitor who was also Grandma Gracie's mother's lover and owner. He married her off to a prized house servant of one of his neighbors. One day I (or Julia) might be expected to move back there, develop my mother's parcel, and live there. This morning I drove right past the turn off and went farther out where no one had made forays into the pines and only the occasional passing of a solitary car disturbed the silence. My mother, Grandma Gracie's youngest, told us the story that in the 1920s, Grandpa Parramore (Gracie's husband) had stayed and rebuilt after night riders had come and burned the house down, white men who resented their large acreage and their capacity to grow their crops, sell them, and survive. I said to Ellen, "Here's a good place to stop and go in," where the posted signs were few and far between and only a strand or two of barbed wire was strung along as fencing.

"Daddy and I used to come here. You remember Daddy?"

"He always got big ones."

"I used to help him cut them."

"He rode me on his back and I see way up."

"You got on his shoulders."

"And we played horsey."

"I did too."

"And he never came back." She said this as an important observation, something she had noticed. I held up the barbed wire and we entered. Not forty yards from the road I saw three excellent possibilities. I had brought the saw instead of the ax. I showed them to her and told her to choose, and she selected the biggest, bushiest one. As we approached it we surprised two adolescent deer, quietly concealed, with little nodules on their heads, who sprang away with their white tails flashing. "A Bambi!" she cried, pointing. We watched them disappear, and then we went to the tree. She was beaming. I sawed it down, and we dragged it back, catapulting it over the fence,

213

and stuffed it into the Buick's trunk. We were on our way again, having had the scene to ourselves, and no one had passed by.

When we got back home we had lunch, and then I went out to make a stand for the tree, using the saw and a hammer and nails from the drawer of the table on the back porch, that my mother kept amply stocked, and pieces of lumber from a pile in the back. I brought it in to a kind a fanfare, and stood it up in the little room, satisfied to see that at its top there was still room for the star. From the closet under the stairs I got out the boxes of trimmings, and Ellen and I began. First the lights went on, then the ornaments and everything else that soon made the tree seem to be dripping with delight. Last I put the star on and turned on the lights, all of which worked. Ellen clapped her hands, and my mother came and spread white sheets on the floor, covering the tree's stand. The house was filled with the fresh smell of the pine. That night we would wrap the presents.

I went outside to smoke a cigarette and string up the out-side lights, in the privet hedges and azalea bush and in the front windows and on the porch. I turned them on and they looked great. Then I decided to take a walk. I passed the place where Miss Lottie's tree had been, and nothing was left, not even remains of the stump of the giant oak it once had been. I went up toward the campus, thinking of the holiday peri-ods and the late summer days when the place was liberated of students, and my friends and I had freely skated on the sidewalks and ridden our bikes, Ellen too, which was not surprising to us since she had always done what we did. I went up on Boulevard and went past some dorms, the stu-dent union, toward Lee Hall, one of the main auditoriums. It was open and I went in. The auditorium was dark and so were the wings containing the practice rooms on either side. I had learned my Burgmuller and Michael Aaron piano course practice books in those rooms on heroic and beat up Wurlitzer and Steinway uprights. A junior high school student, I was not even supposed to be there, but no one knew the difference, and when they did I was allowed because I had grown up there. I went back out and sat on a bench under a tall palm tree that bore middling-sweet yellow dates I had had the occasion to climb up and taste. I sat there and was happy. I saw my sister's face as she passed for graduation through that very door with her mortar board and robes. I had grown up there, and it had been a safe, unthreatening, encouraging place. The high school was right down the hill, but I wouldn't go down there today.

People were still about, on the sidewalks, passing in cars, sighted as figures moving past lighted windows. I wondered if I would run into, or be seen by, someone I knew. Was it Christmas Eve? I went back down the sidewalk, the route I would have traced coming from school, past the student union. It had frightened me to walk in there, across the expanse of students and tables and chairs to the counter to order a triple-decker ice cream cone that the student servers laid on so generously. I would be *seen* striding to make my offer, and seen withdrawing to eat it, as if broadcasting a dare. To me it had been one. My mother had called so much attention to herself that oftentimes I had wanted to be invisible, not daring to step forward in the simplest way to present myself and my desires and wishes; and she had probably not wanted the attention either, which was only a by-product of the compulsion that gripped her to speak the aggrieved and torturing anguish of her heart.

I walked past the science building that I had seen being erected when I was in the seventh grade, and I had gone into the structure after hours and collected the workers' discarded Coke bottles and sold them. As I was nearing my turn off I saw approaching a couple out strolling. The masculine figure seemed someone I knew, this being confirmed when he recognized and greeted me.

"Chris!" He stuck out his hand and shook mine. "Home for the holidays? How you doin', man! Gloria, this is Chris. Did

215

you know Gloria?" I admitted that I had not. "You haven't been home in years. I heard you were at Iowa."

"I'm teaching now." I told him where.

"I'm in the comptroller's office at school. Doin' OK for myself."

"You're doin' great, honey. You didn't know me," she said to me, "but I knew you."

"She went to Lincoln," he said.

"We thought you'd be in medical school. Gerald went, to Meharry."

"I heard."

"Making big bucks already," she said.

"Naw, he hasn't finished his residency yet," he said.

"And then he'll have all kinds of loans to pay off. But he'll recoup. Isn't he a surgeon?" Gloria asked.

"Nice home, a Caddy, send his kid to Columbia," he confirmed.

"That doesn't mean we can't do that," Gloria said.

"The next step of the contract is coming up in January, and I get a raise," he replied.

"What do you do?" I asked Gloria.

"Oh, I'm just a secretary. We goin' to have a family sooner or later, so I might have to stop anyway."

"No, baby, you got to work."

"Do I?"

"Damn right. Ain't that right, Chris."

"The *two* of you're going to have to work that one out."

"Well, I'm working it out for her. Takes *two* to get ahead, don't it, unless you're a goddamned surgeon."

"Oh, honey, stop it. It's such a nice night to take a walk on Christmas Eve."

"You married, Chris?" she asked.

"No."

"I bet you got a girl."

"I'm seeing someone."

"Anyone we know?"

"I doubt it."

"A white girl?" she asked, with insinuating familiarity.

I said it was a girl at my college.

"A student?"

"A teacher," I said

"How's Julia and Ellen?" he asked.

"OK."

"I heard she was in Atlanta. You an uncle."

"She has two boys now."

"Now there was a smart kid. Graduate from FAMU at twenty, didn't she?"

"Yeah."

"She stay home with her kids?" asked Gloria.

"She works."

"Then I bet her husband help her."

"He does."

"See? And I know what's going to happen. Right now I can't get you to get up from no football game to do nothing. And it run all afternoon and all night too. That TV is always runnin'."

"You sayin' I'm the only one watchin'?"

"I'm sayin' when I come home from work I got to get your dinner and mine too."

"You sayin' you don't want to get my dinner?"

"No! I'm sayin' I could use some help sometimes. That's why we out walkin' right now, to take a break."

"OK. I gonna get you breakfast tomorrow morning. 'Cause you been working so hard on Christmas dinner. That gone be my biggest present to you."

"I want you to stretch it out all year long!"

"How long have you been married?" I asked. She was full-bodied, so I couldn't tell whether or not I saw the beginnings of a prenatal bulge in her abdomen, but it looked like it, swelling against the light coat she had on.

"Six weeks!"

"And it's great!" He patted her on the backside. "This my Honey, Chris. She good for another twenty years." She hit him playfully.

"Then you better start treating me right, like you used to be so sweet."

"Baby, I do. I treat you just like you deserve."

"I wish you the best," I said, departing.

He said with feeling, "Say hello to your mother and Ellen." I watched them walk away, showing to whomever was observing their delight in the idea of a Christmas Eve stroll. She was plump and soft like a pillow, the epitome of mammary respite. I strove not to succumb to bitterness, but the guy was still a self-satisfied blockhead, alive and in his way prospering, insisting on the privilege of having things his way, as he did, years ago, when he crashed the brick into her head, with all the might his little hands could muster. It was so hideously incongruous, monstrous, absurd, their contrasting fates, my sister's and his, galling my conversation with him, who had wreaked so much havoc without his even knowing, and I could never tell him. He wouldn't know what I was talking about, and in any case he himself had been a child, no more responsible than a two year old in the throes of a tantrum. We should have been supervised. He should have been disciplined, way before the event occurred. I ached in the thinking of this, as if it could reverse the sequence of events and relieve me in some measure of the guilt of having been unable to stop him. He knew nothing and would forever be blissfully intact. And then it occurred to me, *was he? He had always been so solicitous of their well-being!* This idea left me breathless for a moment. I couldn't pursue it any further.

When I returned home we had dinner and afterwards began the Christmas present wrapping. Most of mine had been wrapped at the store, but a few remained that required my attention. Ellen went up to her room with wrapping paper and scissors and the presents her mother had given her, and later that night mother would do the same in her room. So I wrapped some thigs on the living room floor, watching television, *It's a Wonderful Life*, with Jimmy Stewart and Donna Reed, punctuated by a thousand commercials. My mother had told me of the bags of pecans she and Ellen had collected from the two trees in the yard Daddy had planted at the beginning and end of the property line. I put my presents under the tree and went for the pecans. She had wanted me to crack them as I had done so often when I was young. Working swiftly, a pound or two, and then brown them in the oven with a little margarine. When she saw me come back with some pecans she provided the cracker and a bowl. I spread down some newspaper and began to work, embarrassed that the movie made me cry, and I kept needing tissue to blow my nose. But the more the tears flowed the harder I cracked, and before long I had filled the bowl. My mother pretended not to have noticed anything. The oven was free, and I went to it, applied the margarine, a little salt, and placed them in. Then I went back to read the local paper.

When Ellen came down with her presents the nuts were ready.

"Mama, you have to say which one," she said. Her mother looked at them, felt them, determining which would go to whom, and taped little name tags on them. We ate the pecans and drank orange crush, Ellen's favorite, our mother sitting with us, and then she got up and turned on the Christmas tree lights. I went in, brushed pine needles off the piano, sat down and began to play again.

That night, before turning in, I stopped in Ellen's room.

"I see you remembered your medicine."

"I did."

"Any time Mama DOESN'T give it to you, YOU take it yourself."

"I will."

"Don't forget."

"OK."

Lying on my bed, smoking, I remembered that I had forgotten about her all day. I went down and got the phone, pulled the chord around to an easy chair in the living room, and called her. She answered. I told her all of what I had done that day. She thought that having a Christmas tree was fun. I kissed her goodnight and wished her a Merry Christmas anyway. Back upstairs I longed for Brahms, or Mozart, or the B Minor Mass. The only music on the radio was popular songs, big band music, Christmas fare. A certain FM station far away in Jacksonville couldn't be relied on to come in. I began to hear the beginnings of some grumbling downstairs, but it didn't last and died away. Otherwise, I would have had to go back down and tell her to stop it. That first time she had done so. What did it mean she had complied with my demand? I went to sleep and dreamed of a beautiful, smart, interesting woman I was dating, but I could never see what she looked like. Afterwards, I thought that it was Ellen, what she would have been. Maybe—I shuddered—it was my mother. Miriam? She too, in a way, was impermissible.

My mother did not get up early the next day, so I went downstairs and made breakfast, hot cereal, bacon, fried eggs, toast, juice, and coffee. Ellen and I ate. I was glad to see that her appetite had not been diminished. She was ready to open the presents. I saw how my mother's additions had been piled under the tree while I had been sleeping. It had always been so, nothing under the tree when I went to bed, but piled high with things in the morning when I had run down the stairs. This had been her routine for forty years, and she would probably continue it with Ellen when I was no longer there. Ellen and I went to the tree as she and I and Julia would have done while our parents continued to sleep, and I knew this was still what my mother expected. Although I didn't want to disturb her, still I wanted her there, so finally I called her, and she said she'd be down soon.

Ellen and I took turns. I saw also the packages I would have to take to Atlanta. My mother had bought Ellen clothing and personal articles, a sweater, blouse, shoes, new hairbrush and comb, underwear, a new Negro doll. I supposed it was to put on her bed. I knew how my mother had turned towards the menswear in that same department store and gotten me V-neck tee shirts, boxer shorts, socks, shirts, and even a pair of pants. I heard her coming down the stairs. The pants and shirts were the right size. I asked her how she had known and she told me she had called Julia who had checked my clothing. She hoped I liked them. In her mind buying clothing for me now was no different from what she had done when I was ten, except that my sizes were larger.

We made her open some of hers. One package wrapped, "Mama, Merry Christmas," was a gift to herself that she had given to Ellen to wrap as her present to her mother. It was a box, with a lot of Ellen's tape on it, containing a new coffee pot. I should have thought of that myself. She was now drinking a cup of coffee, one of her few indulgences. I made her alternate with Ellen who had opened and claimed for herself a simple phonograph I had bought her and some recordings of fairy tales. I knew she had loved listening to "Cinderella" on her old player which no longer worked, and the record had been played down to scratch. There were also picture books with large print, *Winnie the Pooh* and the like, stories of Harriet Tubman and Sojourner Truth, and travelogues to faraway places for children, such as to India, Peru, and Ghana, to be read to her by me or her mother. When she took out the three-pot Le Creuset cookware, which had really set me back a pretty penny, she was pleased, liking as well some stainless flatware, and new cups, saucers, and plates. She exclaimed when she unwrapped an original painting I had gotten at an arts and crafts fair in

Atlanta, of a black man and woman working in a field together. "That reminded me of grandma and granddad," I said.

"See what I got for you," she said. "I found it." She handed me the nude that had been hanging upstairs. It had been rolled up and I would have to frame it. It was ragged at the edges but still distinct, as I remembered it, something solemn and unabashed, that I associated with her, a woman kneeling, as if in supplication, but I wouldn't have said in prayer. Ellen immediately set up her phonograph. I showed her the little packet of needles, that she should place on her dresser, and I showed her how to change them when the sound got bad. We listened first to "Cinderella," not as dramatic or fervent as the one she used to have, but it made no difference to her, and she clapped her hands when it was finished. She said that she wanted to be Cinderella and get married. She took her things up to her room, the phonograph, records, books, and clothing, and spent the rest of the day in there until dinner.

When dinnertime finally arrived I helped my mother set the table. She had changed out of her apron and smock into a dress, and earrings, and had done her hair. She was a pretty, brown-skinned woman, but I knew that she thought, as a black female, that she could never be good enough or pretty enough no matter what she did. When I tried for a third time to reach Julia's family I succeeded, and we all talked. Then the food came out, a pot roast, gravy, green beans, broccoli, mashed potatoes, and afterwards sweet potato pie, chocolate cake, and vanilla ice cream. She made me sit opposite her, in my father's chair, instead of next to Ellen, and I would be expected to say the grace, bless the table. I asked that the spirit of the divine be in men's hearts on this day, and all the time, and that our house too be blessed and not forgotten. She was pleased with what I said. I didn't know how much I could eat, but I was determined to show that I had not lost a liking for her food.

"Put up that painting you got me in the living room," she said.

"I wish you would paint more things." She made no response, but asked how Julia, Mordecai, and her grandchildren were getting along. Then we ate heartily. I was always surprised to see how much she could eat, being little more than five feet tall, though she was starting to get ample. I was more than six feet and also starting to fill out. By the time we got to the chocolate cake I seemed to be hungry again. I had passed on the pie. It was her cake she was most pleased with, and I had a big slice with ice cream.

"Ma, why do you only eat vanilla?"

"We eat strawberry, butter pecan. You eat chocolate."

"But you only want to buy vanilla."

"It goes with everything." I thought that there was a meta-racial-sociological commentary you could make on her prefer-ence for vanilla, but of course I couldn't go into it with her. I sat stuffed. She and Ellen were still eating. Ellen might sit there for another hour and eat, little portions of everything all over again, enjoying herself, taking her time. Meanwhile I cleared away some of the dishes and washed them. Then I went out on the front porch and smoked a cigarette. The Christmas lights in the neighborhood were glowing. Some were simple candles in windows; others were elaborate affairs, strung along the eaves, framing the porches, wrapped around window frames and supporting posts. It was beautiful. I sat down in the swing and smoked. Her houseplants had not been taken inside because there was no danger of frost. I thought of how Mordecai had caused the swing to collapse once with a thud, and when she ran out it was about the plants she had exclaimed first, though he was tangled up in chains on the floor. They had laughed. Would there ever be contentment for me? Everywhere I looked was only grief and loss. It might be a long time before I would be back here again, and being away was as painful as staying.

When I went back in I told her that I'd be leaving after New Year's, and she accepted this announcement. I went in to practice again, and after a few hours went up to read to Ellen.

We listened to "The Boy Who Cried Wolf" and "The Three Little Pigs" on the phonograph, and I read about an Indian boy learning to guide an elephant. I showed her the pictures of the beautiful, brown-skinned Indians with their large, expressive eyes. Then I got a book for myself and went to bed. I spent the rest of the week following this routine.

However, passing by Ellen's door one night I heard a rattling sound coming from within, as of something being dragged across the floor. This time I remembered to knock. When she said, "Come in," I opened the door. She had resumed the action she had been engaged in, of playing with a toy. It was a battered but still intact wooden dog—a cocker spaniel with floppy ears—attached to a handle, and when you pushed it by the handle, its wheels, attached to the dog's legs, the right hind leg of which was missing, put the dog in motion, animated it, and its head bobbed up and down in a bright-eyed, toothy grin.

"What you got there, Ellie?"

"It's *mine*," she said, "my doggie," and she pushed it like she was engaged in serious business. Seeing this I remembered it, a toy we'd had. I watched her take another spin or two before she stopped and put it back into her closet. Hearing what she'd said, now its significance, I had to turn away then, and I went back out, my eyes brimming. Was this the *mine* in the dream that she was still enacting, the thing he had tried to take away?

When New Year's Eve came I went up the street to a party of childhood friends but returned shortly after midnight. I stayed long enough to clink glasses with them and wish a happy New Year to each one. When I returned home the explosive celebratory sounds still filled the air. I decided to add my portion with my grandfather's shotgun, an old-fashioned double-barreled twelve gauge, with cocked-back hammers. "That's your granddad's; watch where you fire it." She looked pointedly at me, a smile in her eyes. "That's the one, you know, that he sat up with on some nights after that first time the Klan came to burn down the house. I saw him." I fired both barrels, its roar soon answered by others.

The next day, passing her as I walked through the kitchen, I saw her reaching under the sink where I knew she kept a cache of fermented drink, a homemade product from our two plum trees in the back yard, one planted when Julia was born, the other when I was. Now they were old and gnarled, and I no longer remembered which was which. She brought out a sealed Mason jar and examined it, pronouncing it OK, and put it and two glasses on the table where she poured herself a drink. She also went into the kitchen and came out again with something she knew I would like, apple-pecan tarts!

"It came out all right," she said. Seeing that she expected me to taste it I poured myself a glass.

"Happy New Year, Ma," I said, and touched her glass, and we drank, and enjoyed the tarts. The wine was absolutely delicious, not too sweet, but wild and strong. She sat in her armchair as she would to watch television.

"From which tree did this come?"

"It's a mix." We savored the pleasure of drinking together. "Don't forget to take those presents to Charles and Michael. You're leaving tomorrow?"

"After breakfast."

"Lord, have mercy. It's been a long way since your father died."

"You managing OK?"

"Everything going up. I put two students in a room now. They so crowded up on campus they take what I give them."

"You have enough money?"

"Enough."

"Ma, I want to tell you something."

"What?"

"You listening?"

"What you mean? I can't help but hear you."

"It wasn't any conspiracy of invisible people that hurt Ellen. It was Anthony, when we were out in *that* driveway playing."

"What you mean?"

"He hit her in the head with a brick."

"Listen to the child! Anthony!"

"All these years I had forgotten it. But it came back to me this year. I was a child myself."

"Anthony?"

"I'm sorry, Ma."

"You're sorry? The child's sorry!" She looked at me with that look that was both vague and attentive. Listening to me she was perfectly lucid, and realized what I was saying. "Anthony." She poured herself another drink and just continued to stare. "Why? Why'd he hit my baby?"

"I don't know. They were arguing. I don't remember."

"For God's sake." She let me hold her hand for a moment, but she soon pulled it away. "Lord, have mercy." For a long time we just continued to sit. She got up, after a while, locked the house door, and indicated her desire to turn out the lights.

"That day ... that Saturday morning, Ma, when he took her to the hospital, when she had her first seizure, it was a Saturday, wasn't it?"—she looked keenly at me—"Did you go with him?"

"He left without me," she said immediately, the beginning of tears flowing down her plump cheeks, though she made no sound. She was looking at me seemingly not so much out of surprise that I would know about this but with astonishment at what I was referring to, that she, the child's mother, had been left. "He was out of his mind," she said. This time I was able to go to her and hold her. She allowed me to do so, her head on my chest; then she withdrew. When I went up the stairs, she followed, went into her room, and shut the door. I lay on my bed expecting to hear an intense recital of accusations, but all was silent. I thought again what the boarders must have thought when she went to the screen door and talked. No wonder she had a crazy daughter, she was crazy herself! And yet, in spite of these things, in so many other ways, I felt I had lived a normal, even privileged, life—a picture of reality's strange intermingling. She had originally taught third grade and then in a vocational program for adults, but had been absent from that vocation since my adolescence. I thought nevertheless of her courage, in her madness. What did she want? For me to be near her in her old age? To be near? What did she dream of? I had never thought of that, since half of what we normally experience only in dreams she dramatized right out in the light of day. The house was quiet as I lay on my bed, but every so often the explosive sounds of celebration could still be heard. I thought of Sarah before I fell asleep, as a beautiful doctor, a brain surgeon whose laying on of hands could heal.

He had asked Ellen to do that, one Sunday morning, my father, to approach the radio and place her hands upon it as Oral Roberts, the evangelist, prayed for all the infirm, damaged in mind or body, crying out, "HEAL!" She went willingly with the touching hope that something might happen, that she desired something to happen. My father watched, ready for anything, ready to banish the fear that nothing really would happen. She looked to him for confirmation of the certainty of the thing she hoped would happen. Afterwards, who could tell? One simply had to wait to tell. I certainly was hoping, but the strangest part was that when he said, "HEAL!" her hands on the radio cabinet acted as if she'd received a jolt.

The next morning I rose late to prepare breakfast. When it was ready I called to both of them and they came. My mother ate and drank her coffee, having regained composure. I washed up after breakfast and began packing. She gave me a blanket and quilt to take that had been mine as a child. I looked in the box under the bed in my old room. I saw my high school and college yearbooks; my *Phi Beta Kappa Key* (Delta of Tennessee), good I had been told for punching holes into ends of cigars; my Eagle Scout merit badge sash; my badge for marksmanship that I had earned at the ROTC program for high schoolers, the only one able to put five bullets more-or-less through one hole, a little honeycomb; a page from the local newspaper of me standing next to one of my rockets; a tattered library card, one of the first issued to colored students at the county library; the God and Country Award, in Scouting, for which I'd had to do clean-up work around the church and then on one Sunday morning recite from memory the sixth chapter of St. Matthew and then give a commentary on it. And I had believed in the spirit of every word of it then—who *would* be looking after the sparrow, the least of us, if not Him?—even as everywhere I looked I already saw that the world was mostly unrelieved suffering, that only a few were ready to assume responsibility for the well-being of their fellows. I didn't know how to do it myself. Reality was terrible and there seemed little remedy for it. There were other things in there—I saw my elementary school report cards and other things detailing the time from first grade to graduate school that she had saved. When I kissed Ellen goodbye her eyes were sunny and bright, perhaps taking delight in my attending to her; but when I kissed my mother her cheeks were wet, and her arms hung limp at her side as she said goodbye. I held her then and kissed her.

When I left I followed a different route out of town that I noticed, without my having consciously thought about it, was taking me to the other side of town into a sort of black business district called French Town. On the way there I passed by a house on whose porch a woman was sitting, incongruously, in the bright winter sunshine, swinging in her porch swing, and then I remembered who it might be—a woman named Eloise, who was what was called then a high-yeller, and she also was a very handsome female, who lived in a good neighborhood down the hill from ours, who was kept by a white man (reputed to also have a family living on the other side of town), in a nice house, with her daughter, Margaret, who was both envied and condemned, with her fair-skinned beauty and flawless complexion and thick chestnut hair, said to be friendly with the boys, who couldn't believe the ease with which their fantasies could proceed. I remembered then her brother, Everett, who used to watch the clock in a countdown in the last section of the day in eighth grade as the long hand slowly moved toward twelve and the short one toward three, marking three o'clock and the end of the school day. He always had a candy bar or some other good thing in his pocket. He had made the extraordinary statement one day that his ambition when he grew up was to be a criminal, at which he succeeded, moving from petty arrests to front page notoriety in *The Tallahassee Democrat*, one summer when I returned home from college. It had been armed robbery. He had got away but been captured: *Local Boy in Armed Heist*.

As I drove it occurred to me that the drive was like the ones I'd taken as an adolescent after I'd gotten my license, to a friend's house over there, or to nowhere in particular, or with a friend from my side of town as we came over here to see what kind of trouble we could get into, as for example the time we pulled up into the drive-in liquor store and were reported on by someone who had called my mother. Now, driving along, I passed right by the building with the large plate glass window that had housed my father's office. The building seemed unchanged. New writing was on the glass and I hadn't been able to decipher it in time, but it seemed to me more insurance was being conducted within. The image still in my mind was of the large red ribbon and flower on the door, placed there, probably, by his secretary after his death. I'd seen how the woman had been too close to him—I'd seen her sitting in his lap once—on those Saturday afternoons they'd left me there to receive anybody come proffering a payment, and to emphasize our readiness to take postdated checks.

I don't think that my mother ever knew of his actual infidelity, only of its possibility, which for her was sufficiently real to have been vividly imagined. When she received the call from the woman, the secretary—and I think she did it cheekily, too—she would give the phone to me with her enigmatic smile, telling me that my father needed me to come over that afternoon to mind the office. She never seemed angry, but she gave the phone to me with a look that suggested that though he wanted me to come, the choice was still mine to make. This was one of those times, however, in our family's psychic drama, that I went with him, abandoned her, and went over to the other side. Just like her, I had learned to know the truth and accept it, without complaint, except that the displeasure, or disappointment or outrage in her had found certain other ways to make itself known. Maybe for me the equivalent was the disabling recognition of the inherent expectation, or necessity, of the compromise of life. I liked the woman because she was so pretty and interesting and good to me, yet disliked her for disrespecting my mother; was angry at mother for being so crushed by it; was angry at him for allowing it; yet because I loved and feared them I could never speak the truth of what I felt.

Then, when I was in the office, I'd liked the work, sitting there looking out the window at the constant stream of people, or reading a book, or speaking to someone who had come in. I'd liked testing my skills of persuasion against any hesitant compliance of an actual or potential customer who had come in. In this I wanted to be good at what my father did, who would be out soliciting, tracking people down, pressing on them their need for policies.

I remembered the time my father's boss had come, along with his wife, a regal southern lady, to see the new district office and his new man, Hinson, whose son was also present, and his secretary. My father's boss was large, florid, and gregarious, with the shrewdest blue eyes I'd ever seen, making me think of something deep and calculating, but perfectly friendly, as I imagined the look of a champion poker player would be as he took your car, house, and last paycheck, smiling all the while with the same agreeable, bland expression, completely noncommittal, nothing personal. He got along with blacks with the same ease he got along with whites. His ease in interacting was in contrast to his wife's stiff reserve, a woman who, though she'd seen the colored all her life, and had hired them as domestics and laborers, had never thought of having personal relations with them. She saw two brown-skinned Negroes and a third, a straight-haired, gray-eyed, fair-skinned, picturesque one, the secretary, whom she stared at, it seemed not with hatred but with *wonder*, while her husband joked, as if whatever he did he expected to have a good time.

When they were trying to locate a phone number of a contact, my father asked me to look it up in the phone book, a certain Isaiah Jackson, my father said. I looked it up and reported it wasn't there, to their consternation. My father said of course it was, since the secretary had just called him the other day. He spelled out the name, not accusing me of anything, but to make clear, in his own mind, what the object was of our search. Still it was not there, and the boss's wife took me in hand as if to demonstrate the obvious flaw in the manner of my mis-alphabetized search. When she took the book out of my hand I loudly said, "It's NOT there, no Isaiah Jackson." Startled, she almost dropped it, and the boss, not offended, laughed, saying, "Tell 'em, boy"; and my father, shocked, exclaimed, "Jacobs! Not Jackson. Isn't that right, Gwen?" he said to the secretary. The boss's wife looked it up, reporting, "No Jackson, but there's an Isaiah Jacobs." My father looked at me with a kind of pride as well as shame, a look similar to the one he'd had when, on another occasion, he had, for the first and only time, struck me, when I had been told to stop turning over an electric cigarette lighter that rested on the desk but, when up-ended, would glow red. When he went out of the office, briefly, and came back, I was still doing it, fascinated, and received a slap to the side of the head. He had immediately apologized, not knowing what had gotten into him, he said; but I also seemed to detect in him a certain pleasure in seeing my willfulness, my ability to resist.

When I reached the cemetery I knew why I'd come this way. It was a chilly morning. The sky was neither clear nor overcast but opaque, leaden, as if the air had congealed and had weight. I drove in, got out, and went to the spot. My mother had gone to some expense to place a marble headstone and slab. On it was a bouquet of fresh flowers, and also next to it, sticking out of the mouth of a single whiskey bottle, was what looked like a withered chrysanthemum. There was a brown residue in the bottle. Perhaps he was being given a little taste, a reminder of one of the earthly pleasures he had loved so well, since it was to be assumed that none would be obtainable in the afterworld, no matter to which place he went. Since he had been loved by many people, anyone could have brought them here, with their sincere expression or joking irony even unto the grave. What I had to offer was my prayer, Rest in Peace, Dad. Next to the slab was the sunken space of an earlier grave, a younger sister's— born after Ellen—who'd died too young for me to recall. Then, twenty paces off, were also the graves of my grandparents, my mother's father and mother, and I went to visit them. Would I want to be brought back here and placed next to them, where my mother and Ellen would doubtless be, and Julia? I'd have a wife one day. Would she go with me? Would Miriam?

From Florida I drove back to Georgia, and from there I would return to Alabama. When I arrived their tree was still up and I deposited the gifts under it. Charles and Michael knew what to expect from Grandma, and Julia told them that that was one less socks and briefs and tee shirts she'd have to buy, though they liked the "cool" baseball caps Grandma had gotten them. That night I thought I should call Sarah but could not do it. I wanted to go visit Derek and Tina but continued to lie on my bed. The next day I bid them all farewell and returned to campus.

NINE

Entering my rooms I felt both relief and homecoming. On the way home I had stopped at a shop in the square to get a gift for Miriam. When I'd come in I'd heard music coming from Howard's rooms and I decided now to go visit him. He received the same sunlight as I did and was watering plants in his windows. He was playing a Mozart symphony. I asked where he had gone for the holiday, and he replied, "Los Angeles. I have some friends there, a nice change from here."

"You're not from LA?"

"No, Chicago."

"Did you go home?"

"It's not home any longer."

"Your parents aren't there?"

"They're both dead."

"Any siblings?"

"I'm the only one." He finished his watering and put the empty can down on his desk with its long thin round-barreled spout sticking out and looking at us like the eye of an alert machine. "My parents were emigres. They were linguists, working for the state—that's how they met and married—in Berlin. They saw what might happen early on, and left, first to England, then to Palestine, then to the States, eventually to the University of Chicago, where they both got posts. They died in an automobile accident when I was at Harvard, struck by a drunk, head on, coming the wrong way down an exit ramp."

"No family?"

"Everybody else stayed in Germany. I keep in touch with people I knew at school—I guess I run up a phone bill—and of course here I have a place. I relate, and of course talk to Miriam and you." His manic way of talking had slowed down. "She's back too. I talked to her yesterday."

I said, "I went to my sister's house in Atlanta, and her family, and then to Florida to visit my mom and my other sister. It's curious. I missed this place and couldn't wait to get back."

"Maybe to see Miriam."

"Sure, but I mean this place, the job."

"I know what you mean. You and she seem to like each other."

"Is that what people think?"

"She likes you," he said. I nodded. "A fine girl, Chris."

"You talk to her often?"

"We talk, about music, things, just like you and I do."

"I think sometimes she misses New York."

"How'd it come about between the two of you, if you don't mind my asking?"

I sort of squinched my shoulders. How could I even begin to try to talk about *that*?

"Were you thinking of it?" he persisted.

"Thinking of it?"

"Attraction, between the races."

"I don't know."

"How's it working out?"

"Like any relationship, I suppose."

"But is it like any relationship?"

"Why not?" Let me hear, first, I thought, what his idea was of why it wasn't like other relationships.

"There's a difference, racial, ethnic, religious," he said.

"Then there's the pleasure in overcoming it." That *was* true, and something that moved me immensely, and yet it was also completely irrelevant—or was it? I was silent as we each waited for the other to speak.

"I wish you well."

I said, "You spoke of overcoming religious difference in your discussion of Yom Kippur in class."

"I spoke of *appreciating* religious difference, to bring about an understanding and acceptance of difference, to live and let live."

"I agree with that. But I guess I'd like to abolish that difference too."

"Black and white, Jew and gentile will always be, and a thousand other differences."

"I guess I'd like to mate them, you know, merge them, graft them into one homogeneous thing." Probably I did not really know I felt this way until I found myself saying it. Even as I said it I knew he was right, that if we got rid of racial difference, for instance, and everybody looked alike, a new, different hierarchy of difference would be established, would emerge, for instance, people with bushy eyebrows vs. people with sparse ones.

"You've got your work cut out for you. Life is being ourselves, living our differences. How does she feel about this?"

"She doesn't say."

"She knows what it's like to be different, if you know what I mean."

"You know she's multi-ethnic, right—her father is Yankee, English and French."

"I imagined it." His saying it made me wonder, though, what he had thought.

"How's that for difference—the American way. You and I are different too, yet the same in basic ways; what people in their distinctions forget."

"I understand you. You two are so interesting to look at. She's a lovely girl. You're a good-looking black man. But not just that. Probably I'm also talking about the impact you make. I *know* you. But it's still arresting, startling, to see you."

"Doesn't it ever wear off?" I asked. Howard smiled, and I returned the smile. I continued, "We try not to notice. By ourselves, we almost never do, unless it's a way to make ourselves happy about something."

"Would you have children?"

"Sure we would." Even she thought that, and wanted to bring it about. I imagined she thought, as I did, that they would be beautiful, the world a better place, I thought, and said.

"That's one way to look at it. I came down here, I wanted to do something in that spirit, commitment in a worthy way, you know, to people, mutual respect."

"Everybody respects *you*, appreciates you, what you do."

"There's love too, a need to give—I feel I should say that—in this world." He went to change the record. "Let's do some Papa Haydn," and he put on a symphony. Our thoughts turned to music, and I remained until I left later in the day.

* * *

In a few days the new semester would begin and I was anxious to get it underway. I was excited. The coming time held some sort of transformation. It would mark the end of my stay there. Miriam and I would leave together, for the summer. Spring would come and awaken the beauty of the campus. As I was thinking of this, the phone rang. It was Miriam asking me to come over, that Jonathan was there in trouble. When I arrived the two were sitting having a glass of wine. She spoke to Jonathan in soothing tones, and he looked both wounded and belligerent, ready for a fight. "Jared's father came and got him, and told the dean to tell Jon to stay away from him," she said to me.

"He also told *me*, came right into my house," said Jon. He was sitting on the edge of his chair.

"Where's Jared?" I asked.

"Under house arrest, you might say. His father can't *make* him. He's of age and can do as he likes," he said.

"What are you going to do?" I asked.

"They can't impose this on me. The dean—a pitiful ass—'This can't be *tolerated* any longer,' that they had already 'looked the other way too long' and so on, as if the sanctimonious creep had been doing me a favor."

Miriam added, to me: "He said that the president spoke to him and was nice to him, but emphasized that he didn't want Jon to have to force them to take action, because they appreciated him as a valued member of the faculty."

"Jared's father's a big donor isn't he, a member of the board of trustees?" This I had heard from Liz.

"A Big Cheese," Jonathan suggested.

"Jon said he's going to send Jared away."

"*I'm* going to call the American Civil Liberties Union and the AAUP."

The words came out of my mouth, "Isn't there a statute still on the books in this state? Sodomy?" The word, as uttered, didn't sound nice.

"It's time we tested it, my dear, just like interracial marriage and miscegenation. What else are the courts good for?"

"It would be nasty, Jon, and you would still probably have to leave, and all this would follow you," said Miriam. Jon sat quietly looking into his glass.

"I love him," he said, trying to stop the beginnings of tears. Miriam went to him and touched his arm. He rose. "Thank you for being here," he said, and then strode to the door and left.

"Did you have to use that ugly word?" she said immediately. "He probably couldn't take that."

"What, somebody is always going to have to be the nigger?"

"Don't be so disgusting!"

237

"He put it right out there with interracial marriage."

"And good for him!"

"No use pretending what you're up against."

"You think he doesn't know that? It's as false for him as for you."

"But the goddamn world doesn't think that. Don't you think that when you see those old photos of those yellow Stars of David?"

"But it isn't the truth. I am still here, he still loves Jared, and those guys that howl in their cars don't make you bow your head."

She was right, but something in me kept wanting to say otherwise. I said, "They've kept him this long because he's still a white male."

"White? Or male?"

"Both."

"Spend the night with me," she said. "I missed you over the holiday. When you called my Dad had an idea, but I haven't said anything yet. He just thinks you could be someone I'm interested in, one of the faculty."

"I am." I went home, got a change of clothing and other things and returned. I commented on the prospect of my staying overnight in her rooms by now having been noticed—tolerated, we might say, as Jonathan's liaison with Jared was. I gave her a gift, brightly wrapped. It's heavy, she said, and opened it to find a brass light for her piano. I wished her Merry Christmas, and Happy Chanukah, something practical for a mistress, I said, as in mistress mine, and I saw she was pleased. But I have nothing to give you, she said. It is only your first Christmas, or my first Chanukah, I replied.

She said, in response, "But you know it's hardly my first Christmas. I always had a Christmas tree, as well as a Menorah." I didn't say anything to this. When morning light showed in the room we were still holding each other, sitting upright in bed, resting against the headboard where we had fallen asleep.

We began the semester with a departmental meeting. I was congratulated on the production of the play, and more expressions of pleasure followed when they heard that *A Raisin in the Sun* was scheduled for the spring. Liz announced the preparations being made for a visitation of our accrediting body as part of our evaluation due that year, and the dean had asked her to appoint somebody to be in charge of rewriting the portion in the school's bulletin that described the historical development of the college and its mission. She asked me if I would do so in collaboration with the librarian. She's got all the information, and your job is to rewrite and finesse it, she said. Liz introduced the idea of a collection of exemplary student writing from across the college, a kind of natural outgrowth of writing across the curriculum, and she designated Miriam as coordinator. They would publicize and send solicitations to the faculty in all departments and have a little ceremony on the occasion of its yearly publication, maybe in the president's office, with a luncheon and the students reading selections from their papers. All thought it was a great idea and wondered how it could have been for so long not thought of. After a prolonged discussion of the degree to which we thought student writing was or was not measuring up to expectations, to "standard," as Jonathan said, the meeting was brought to an end. Expressions of sympathy were directed toward Jonathan who, seemingly chastened, thanked his well-wishers. We discovered that Jared was in San Francisco, "vacationing," as Jonathan described it in a clear-eyed and sober manner. He remained, talking to Liz and Miriam. I was told, on the way out, by Camilla, that it was a good thing Jared was away and that their relationship was a bad influence on the students, unacceptable and offensive. I nodded, bid her goodbye, and entered my rooms.

Spring was approaching. One morning I looked out the window and saw the first of the magnolia's buds opening, a strong blood-red. The old tree was still sensual, fecund, no matter how gnarled its limbs and the need to cut out dead wood. Casting was complete for the play, which would take place in the theatre in a set Buildings and Grounds had helped make. Not only that, but a production of the play was occurring in Birmingham, and the English department was taking students in two of the school's vans, plus my car and Miriam's, to see it. Then, in April, Miriam, Howard, and I would return to Birmingham to see the pianist Gina Bachauer playing the Brahms Second Piano Concerto with the Birmingham Symphony Orchestra. The year would be finished with the program Daniel Banks, Scott Peterson, and I were planning on entropy. The tulips were up in the grass spaces of the rectangle bracketing the parking lot, and on the hillside fronting the lot, and in multilayered circles around the magnolia tree, along with daffodils and jonquils. This much my eye could see from my window, and the rest of the campus also teemed with such multicolored splendor.

One day in February I extracted this out of my mailbox in the Student Union, enclosed within an envelope and printed on a red card in the shape of a heart:

Chris W. Hinson
You are so fine.
Won't you be my Valentine.
Please agree that you will be
The Valentine of MLG.

I replied with:

Miriam L. Goddard
You've captured me.
I eat, sleep, and think of thee—
Smile on my horizon—
And Valentine of Chris W. Hinson.

I had got a white sheet of paper, cut out a heart, colored it red, with my red composition pen, ran an arrow through it, printed the poem in black ink on it, then took it and mailed it.

* * *

The caravan of school vans and cars stayed in convoy on its trip to Birmingham and back again. We passed along the highway the signs advertising Berma Shave that I remembered from my childhood, already icons of Americana, and also other signs, in the large bold print of billboards on private property looming out of the pines, IMPEACH EARL WARREN or KEEP AMERICA WHITE. The play was given by a newly established company that received funding under the National Endowment of the Humanities, a new governmental initiative that sought to encourage and sustain the arts. This being a Negro group the school wanted to support it in the best way by providing patronage, and the production was moving and professional, with hardly a dry eye among those in attendance. It was a powerful moment when Walter Lee Younger affirmed the black family's self-respect in that slow beginning of the rocking of his mother's chair. As much as they wanted money, and had never had it, and would sell their souls to get it, it wasn't everything! The students who were looking forward to enacting that moment themselves were given an indelible imprint of its power, what it meant. The black family was black but no different from any other in its loving togetherness and the good life it wanted for itself. It had become possible in the national consciousness to imagine that no such thing existed for them, and they too had come to be inheritors of this doubt.

When I saw the advertisement for the Birmingham Symphony Orchestra concert I sent off for tickets immediately, having asked Howard and Miriam, and secured three balcony tickets. I used my new credit card, a MasterCard, that had arrived unsolicited in the mail. The actual card had been sent, and all I had to do was sign it, fill out a PIN number and agreement, and return the envelope with my acceptance. In doing so I discovered that all the other faculty at school had also received one, sent out through the mail by one of the local banks up in the square, The Farmers National Bank.

Our journey to Birmingham was quick and uneventful on a pleasant night in April. I was driving, with Miriam up front and Howard in the back. As we neared the theatre looking for parking we looked up on a hill overlooking the city and saw a giant statue of a strong-looking muscular figure.

"What's *that*?" exclaimed Miriam.

"Vulcan," said Howard. "This is a center of Southern commerce—manufacturing, steelworks, lumber milling. Coal mining. It's certainly dirty enough—the slow catching up with the fast."

"The North?" she asked.

"That too. That's good, Howard," I said, taking him up. "Haephestus, his Greek forebear, and lame."

"I got you," she said, "and caught the swift one, Ares, in bed with his wife, Aphrodite the golden."

"Shook down the fine-spun webbing with their lovemaking, and the male gods came and laughed at them, held fast in their embrace," Howard said with pleasure.

"But the female ones turned away in modesty," she said.

"Hermes said he didn't care," I said, "he'd be held in an embrace with Aphrodite the golden no matter who was looking at him."

"Sly devil that he was," said Howard—"I see we've all read a certain translation—Lattimore's?" We laughed in agreement.

I thought that the theatre was a large, ornate, lofty building, sumptuous in the way of suggesting antebellum splendor. We went up some stairs to our seats in the center balcony, which we all preferred over even orchestra seats, provided they weren't too far back and afforded a sense of scale and proportion.

On the program were Ravel's *Le tombeau de Couperin*, the Brahms Concerto, and Sibelius's Second Symphony. We were simply in love with the occasion, giddy with delight. It was a wonderful, varied program. Hearing the Ravel would be just as interesting as listening to the Sibelius, with the great delight of the Brahms in the middle. The concertmaster came on, the orchestra tuned, and the lights dimmed. The conductor appeared, wearing tails, looking, for all the world, as if he could also have worn a top hat. The hush descended, and thus it began, the enthralling sound that only Ravel could make, so peculiar, produced through the combination of the woodwinds (reeds), strings, and horns in a strange tonality, both eerie and soothingly appealing, in line with the imaginative conceit I had, like maybe the sound of a commemoration in heaven, when instruments such as these, now player-less, decided it was time for them to make their own music by playing themselves. It was completely wonderful, and the audience clapped heartily. Then the change of scene began with the wheeling onto center stage of the Steinway grand. Then the moment arrived and the soloist appeared, followed by the conductor. She was of substantial-enough build and reassuring looking. She had better be, I thought, for this journey we were about to take! The horns sounded those first three notes, for me a statement of what the world was like, the subject of inquiry, ushering in the piano's collaborative investigation with the orchestra. The journey had begun. We sat bemused, shaken, transformed, until the end, and gave Mme. Bachauer a standing ovation. Brahms had been true to form again, passionate, tragic, overwhelming, and triumphant. It was what I understood music critics to mean when they said that Brahms made a moral statement in his music that was inextricable from its esthetic import. It was big enough, deep enough, and powerful enough to reconcile you to the anger and pain of being alive.

At intermission we got up quickly and made our way to the rest rooms, the men's on the one side and the women's on the other. Howard and I went into the as yet relatively uncrowded room. We both went past the urinals to the stalls, of which only one of the four there was occupied, affording both of us the opportunity to disappear within. Reemerging we both acquiesced to the expectation of the washing of our hands, running lots of water and engaging in prolonged drying. I thought that we had done so, especially, because of the expectation each had that the other would.

Back in our seats it was a while before we were joined by Miriam, moving to her seat between the two of us. When she sat down she said that there had been a long line already stretching out the door, with the women inside also freshening up their makeup. Also, she told us to look back up to the far left and we'd see Liz and Leon, the music department chairman. We looked and saw them.

"Should we wave," I asked. They were looking at us.

"It might be embarrassing," said Miriam.

"But acknowledgment, in here, might not be bad," Howard said, game and ready for mischief.

"Let's stand up," I said. This was uncharacteristic of me, but I was moved to do it. We stood up, all three, at first pretending to stretch, then pretending that we had just noticed some friends, and waved. Liz and Leon waved back, and the people sitting above and below turned their heads and followed the acknowledgments with their eyes. Then they looked back at us, but of course we had already been the recipients of direct, or covert, glances in our direction all night. What possibly could have been our relationship to each other? Was she his sister, or his wife, having brought along with them an improbable friend? Was she *my* wife and he her brother? Were we the very image of the social radicals, integrationists, from God knows where increasingly cropping up in their midst, with their new legislation and court battles on behalf of the blacks? Their eyes almost seemed to directly ask these questions.

"Also, you're the only two brown skins in here," Howard said. We looked as if to confirm this and saw nothing to contradict it.

Miriam said, "Jon says she's a member of the Buchanan clan, prominent around here, in publishing and real estate and, a hundred years ago, plantations and slaves. She's supposed to have a lot of money and is a big contributor to the school."

"Can you beat that?" said Howard, "and likes sitting in the balcony." The lights dimmed and the Sibelius began. I thought as always about the intriguing strangeness of the music. Tragedy and pathos. It was moving, and at the end people sat, almost suspended, before the clapping began. It might have gone over even better than the Brahms.

On the way out we met up with Liz and Leon making their way down the winding flights of stairs. Outside, Liz said that it looked like Mme. Bachauer hardly kept her hands on the keyboard. Her speed was amazing.

"*That's* dexterity," said Miriam.

"Yes," said Leon. "A great performance." The three of us bid the two good night. It was about midnight when we arrived back at campus. I dropped Howard off and drove to Miriam's apartment. We parked and went inside and sat down, first, to unwind.

"He's a tall, distinguished looking, gray-haired, brown-skinned gentleman, what you'd look like in thirty years."

"She's also tall, with blond gray hair, a blue-eyed *lady*. Is that you?"

"I don't paint my nails and wear blue mascara and eye shadow."

"You don't have to. It goes with her blue cigarette holder."

"No woman does."

"Why can't she adorn herself for her own pleasure?"

"Adorn? How come she's not good enough as she is?"

"Then we don't need to have colorful clothes, or comb our hair, or anything like that?"

245

"Not if it's meant to say you're not any good without it, or it's only to please a man. People aren't works of art! They're already real. They don't need to be made over into something else, manufactured."

"But we're still artisans. We can use our bodies, *our selves*, as raw material," I continued.

"I like you as you are. You don't need to do anything to recommend yourself."

"You like it when I come on as an innocent subversive, a part I'm playing right now, and I like it when you deck yourself out in a *tighter* blouse and skirt—don't say you don't do it—and a wide belt and bag from Guatemala, which raise up your breasts and bring out your color, just more of you, and I think you like it too."

"I don't think we understand each other," she said, but she gave me an amused look.

"And besides, what's wrong with pleasing a man if you want to do that?"

"Let us not get into that tonight."

"Can I hope there's something we *can* get into tonight?" She smiled that smile with the emerald light in it, went to the piano, sat down, played those first three notes, struck an arpeggio and chord from the Brahms concerto, and got up again.

"She played with ease and grace," she said, "and understanding, and power, not just using it as a vehicle to show herself off. Here's the score if you've never seen it. I ordered it." She got up and went to the bathroom. I went and looked at it, to me an arresting document, a vision of the movement of spirit (or energy) in the universe, and even more so with the Fourth Symphony. I thought that of all creative artists composers were the most blessed, no matter how seemingly miserable their lives might otherwise be. They had *melody* (among other things), a direct expression of the thoughts of God. Looking up from it, my eye went to the top of the piano, right next to the lamp I'd given her, where something else seemed to catch my attention at once by simply being there. It was a letter in clear, distinct handwriting, laying open, easily read:

April 26, 1967

Dearest Mimi,

Come away from that environment. I feared for you when you went down there. You speak of your interest in this young man that is upsetting to me and would also be to dear departed Sophie. Come away, dearest daughter, and leave that behind. How can he be for you? How can he, my Miriam? Think what you are doing. Do you imagine it'll be the same as what your Mom and I did? It won't...

I couldn't read anymore. I imagined she had intended it for me to see, and I had felt ashamed reading it, and then angry. She had written about me to her father, and I guess it had been a momentous thing. She came out of the bathroom.

"I read it," I said, "like you intended."

"I was going to show it to you."

"But you left it for me to see first."

"I suppose I did."

"Why?"

"'Cause I'm afraid. You see what I'm up against."

"What?"

"He objects."

"What if he does?"

"He's my father."

"What if he is?"

"Stop this! You know what I mean. I don't want to hurt my father."

"You've already hurt him."

"You're not helping me!" She was both angry and upset.

"You want me to go away, like he does?"

247

"Did I say that? I don't know what to do. What to tell him."

"Are we separating? Are we?"

"No! Why are you so extreme?!"

"Then tell him that. Maybe he'll see that you're not a fool, that you have your reasons, and you're not going to change them, and that he might come around."

She said, her voice raised in volume and intensity, "You're absurd! You think it's that simple, just something you're supposed to reach a rational agreement about?"

"Sorry," I said. "But you *did* write to him, I suppose, saying something *reasonable* about us, your involvement with me."

"It was the right thing. There's nothing *wrong* with you. I want him to accept you. I want him to *like* you. I don't want him to think what he thinks."

"But *everything's* wrong with me … You know that."

"Yes, you're so wonderful!" She sort of laughed and cried.

"I see how he loves you." She began to cry in earnest. "And I see how you love him." I was still sitting on the piano stool. She came and sat next to me, where we remained a while.

She said, "I'm angry at him. He's not really like he sounds. Not conservative or liberal, just trying in his way to look after me." We continued to sit, holding hands. Then I kissed her goodnight and left.

When I entered my apartment, I called Miriam and told her that it was right that she had told her father, and I was glad. I only wished that there was something I could do to help her. Saying goodnight again I went to get something to eat. Opening the refrigerator my eyes fixed on a half-drunk champagne bottle, and I thought of the chocolates we had gotten to accompany it. I poured a glass and ate a thick, dark piece with almonds. It had been a great outing, and the strangeness of Sibelius was still sounding in my head. The composer, though a family man, was supposed to have liked women, strong drink, and cigars, conventional indulgences for a mind so weird in its musical imagining. He took you to some very strange places, some sort

248

of prophetic visionary, as if giving you a view of what a soul-transforming experience would be like.

I got into bed and prayed for happiness, a successful life—you should be able to love and work, said Freud. Here was another visionary, the depth of whose prophetic insight into human behavior still wasn't fully appreciated, like recognizing the unavoidable (or inevitable) necessity of learning to live with ambivalence; or realizing how the decisions we make are unconsciously overdetermined by a multitude of factors that have impacted us from the past, most of which we are unaware of at the time of our decision-making. We have a personality, a character, for instance, but can't remember how it was formed. We simply act out of the deepest, most emotionally resonate, forgotten pressure points. We seem to see people in terms of what we want them to be, not what they are. Love and hate seemed inextricably meshed. How could Miriam and I escape destructive effects of this entanglement? I turned off the light and thought how the two darkened windows were like the eye slits of the room looking at me, and how the space in-between where the desk was looked like the nose and mouth. As a child I could easily have thought this, waiting for the shade to go up or down, indicating a wink. These thoughts led to the spectral image of the magnolia's limbs and fading blossoms outside the window—and soon I was sleeping.

I was dreaming in the nineteenth century, watching a white man and woman in a carriage who were observing some slaves, toiling at some task, some stooping and ready to drop in a swoon, some muscular and strong, some defiant and straight-backed. The woman turned and looked directly at me, though I myself wasn't even a part of the scene. The woman and the man then went in to dinner, passing through a room with a desk in it like my own. Then it was night. She was sitting on the desk in a clingy nightgown, but it was right now on my desk in my room, with her legs crossed with one slipper on, dangling from her toe, smiling at me. I saw the points of her nipples pressing at me through the flimsy gauze and the ferment of her pubic area's dark morass. Then she pointed her finger at me and wagged it. Her smile was enticing and pleasurable, but hard and cold as well, as if she were inviting me to a lynching. That woke me up. I reached up and flipped on the light switch and looked at the desk, still shaken. Of course there was nothing there, only the desk itself, against the wall.

I thought that if I stared too hard at the desk she would reappear. I still felt an eerie tingling down my neck and back, as if I'd been made privy to some sort of secret. I got up to calm myself and opened the refrigerator and took out a peach. I sat down, cut it into halves, then halved the two pieces, and ate them as I fitfully paced up and down the room. Soon I lay back down but left the overhead light on, as I used to do as a child. I slept with the light on for the rest of the week and told no one, and neither did the dream recur.

All the while I had been in the thick of rehearsals for the play, and then came the night of its first performance. Of all that I had done in my life this was my proudest accomplishment. I had not backed away, had trusted myself, and they had trusted me. When the lights went dim in the theatre I could see that the kids were charged to realize their characters as they might the lives of their parents, their siblings, or themselves. They were measured and dramatic, rather than merely emotionally earnest. Each time they played was a more perfect realization. Who else could interpret the truth of their failings, so often condemned, as versions of the love and cravings everyone else knows, from which also emerge a triumph, a passion to live right, with self-respect, which corrects the errors resulting from deprivation or excess? With each change of scene, I was there to make brief contact with the actors. They sat with a suppressed sense of their triumph at intermission, and at the end, to thunderous applause, they bowed deeply, called back repeatedly, and they insisted on bringing me out to join them. This was the first night of a task they were called upon to execute three more times that week until Saturday night, when they'd have their theatre party and be released. Gavin came backstage to congratulate me, and so did all the members of the English department. When I looked at Miriam her eyes shone, and she told me that that night alone was worth my extra salary. She waited for me until the last person had left, and the theatre was darkened, and she took my hand and we walked home together.

Once it became known that I wasn't returning the next year, I began to feel a sense of sadness and regret. Dean Wright, my provost, was not only saddened but annoyed. Here was another frustrating instance of the loss of a promising black (male) teacher. I told him that perhaps I'd be back after I had earned my advanced degree, hopefully by means of a fellowship program that had been introduced to me by the president. My students all told me they'd miss me and that they wished I'd come back. I myself would also miss the campus, its beauty, and the extraordinary way it had opened me up to the possibilities of life. It had constituted my first adult, self-sustaining job, and I had responded to the prospect of love.

I was coming out of my door one day when Liz came out of hers. She spoke of my leaving and inquired where I was going to do graduate work. I mentioned Columbia as my first choice but saw I'd have to explain that it wasn't the fall of that year but the fall of the next year that I intended to be enrolled, that the coming fall I simply wanted to be engaged in a routine of study. She asked if I knew what Miriam's plans were and I told her she planned on attending NYU but would, as I was sure she knew, be back at school this fall. She had liked being here, I said. How about you? she had asked, her blue eyes fixed on me, and I had to say it had been a privilege to be there, to have worked with all of them. I mentioned how I had acquired some furniture from Buildings and Grounds and wondered whether it should stay in my rooms or if I should request to have it returned. She replied that I should not bother, that it should stay. Her own family, she said, had contributed furnishings to the school, particularly some of the furniture of her grandfather's sister, an eccentric, beautiful woman who never married, a character, who had an eye for the good things she collected, but also a weakness for the junky antiques of her day, the handmade tables and chairs that the slaves and tenant farmers made. She said she had in her apartment right now a cherry bureau that was said to be hers, a nice thing, light and elegant. Underneath is a brand into the wood, C. Buchanan, for Cecelia. With Miriam still here maybe you'll be coming back sometime to see us, she said, and I said that I would.

At our symposium on entropy, Scott went first, opening up the dimensions of our discussion. Daniel followed and I came last. I had requested that a copy of the poem, "West Running Brook," be distributed to each person in the audience, and I read it first, then talked about how it related to our subject in an explanation of how its lines built up the structure that was a demonstration of the theme. Then, when I had finished, a recording of the poem being read by Frost himself, with his gravelly voice, was played. We all thought the audience was appreciative. Poetry could be difficult, even philosophical, as my student had said, and still be interesting—or at least, for that moment, its interest could be demonstrated, and people would consent to hear about it and maybe even wonder about it. I had certainly taken pains to *read* it such that what had always already been there could be heard, and Frost's own amused (or ironic) and conversational gravity had finished off the effect.

When final examinations came, I administered and graded them with generosity. I could still hold the line at the A's, but all the teachers had begun to recognize the gradual erosion of the difference between C's and B's, D's and F's. Succumbing to this meant the gradual metamorphosing of B's into A-'s. And the A itself—the paper I could read in class to show what an exemplary performance actually was—was increasingly more desperately evoked, as if in defense of the quality of its difference and an undemocratic elitism. It would be nice already to be freed of the need to make such distinctions and to cease being the bearer of disappointment to students. Still I thought my hopefully objective (and sometimes benevolent) discriminations were better than the biased ones that filled the world, of which my students would soon get their fill, since it was of the nature of the species, as Howard had said, to make distinctions, a process I both participated in and disliked.

I turned in my grades, said goodbye to my friends, and started packing. Miriam and I would drive together to Atlanta and then to New York City for the summer. Finishing up in my rooms there was something I had put off doing, half out of fear, half out of preserving a state of uncertainty that remained as long as the truth were unknown. I told Miriam what we should do after I had cleaned out the drawers of my desk—tilt it over on its side so that I could see underneath it. Unless I saw what I was looking for, I was not going to tell her why we were doing it. We tilted it over, I looked underneath and found nothing. I was disappointed. "What is it?" she asked. Then I thought to pull out the middle drawer and look underneath the desk where it had rested, and sure enough I saw etched there *C Buchanan*.

"Look there," I said. She looked and saw it.

"Buchanan?"

"The same. A great-great aunt or something." Then I told her of my dream and my talk with Liz.

"Extraordinary. Good grief!"

"Yes, and I am glad I'm getting out of here."

"Doing what we're doing, you drew her near?"

"Her niece is doing it too. She came back and sat on that desk, and winked at me."

"Should we tell her?"

"What would we say?" I got some of my things and went out to the car. Coming back in I knocked on Howard's door.

When he came I said goodbye. Howard shook my hand, and then we looked at each other, and then we embraced. "You should learn to play it yourself," he said, "for your own pleasure. Brahms would like that. He was an iconoclast." I nodded and went back to my rooms. I took the footlocker out and came back. Then Miriam and I carried out the phonograph and records. Her car was in the parking lot next to mine, and she was already packed. I looked at my building and said goodbye to it, to my magnolia tree that still held some blossoms. Farther down from my windows I saw a figure standing framed in an adjacent window's darkness and knew that it was Howard. I cast a glance of goodbye to him again, and we got into our cars and left.

TEN

W e took off with speed and exuberance, with Miriam in the lead. She was completely at ease now driving her Blue Beauty and had a tendency to speed, her preferred speed being seventy miles per hour, when the speed limit was fifty-five. First we would arrive in Atlanta and stay overnight, then depart the next morning in her car, leaving mine behind for safe keeping until I returned. We arrived in the afternoon, unpacked, had a rest and then dinner, at which Miriam was no longer a mere guest but was made to feel that she belonged. That night Miriam mounted the stairs while I went to my little room off the hall. In the morning we said goodbye to the others as they successively went out the door to school and to work. When we were alone, we smiled at each other and together went back up the stairs.

The trip north on Interstate 85 then 95 seemed both monotonous and unending. The route was heavily traveled, burdened with tractor-trailer trucks, and debris of all kinds littered the roadway. We saw furniture and even abandoned appliances at the side of the road. We stayed overnight once in a motel in Virginia and were courteously given our accommodations. It was a Howard Johnson's, big enough to house a convention, therefore used to ethnic diversity, Miriam said, so that our faces would only be two more among the anonymous. We arrived in Manhattan in the dark as we went across the lit up George Washington Bridge and saw the lights shimmering along the Hudson, always a stirring sight, the skyline like an appetite for the liveliness of life. She conducted us downtown to a hotel called the Broadway Central where she said we could stay a couple of weeks in a place that was cheap but comfortable enough. She'd had some friends staying there once. When we arrived I could see that it was a residential hotel still respectable but had seen better days. Everybody now seemed to be in it. The elevators were clean but slow moving, and when we arrived on our floor we went down the hall past the sound of a saxophone playing. In the lobby had been whites as well as people of color looking like office workers and others of similar description except that they were foreigners speaking their native language. "They're Russian, from the Ukraine," she said. When we opened the door we saw a sitting room, with alcove-kitchen, a bath, and a bedroom. To me it was quite cozy. What I had to get used to was the view out of back windows onto concrete enclosures and an array of iron fire escapes, with a lone tree or even a plot of earth below in the little boxed spaces behind the apartment buildings with things growing in it like something good that had been forgotten but might be remembered again.

To conserve our money we ate inexpensively at home, with plenty of fruit and vegetables and a roast beef that would last half the week. We went to movies and to the many concerts in the offering that were free, checking the listings in *The Village Voice* and *The New Yorker*. We celebrated, in the Oyster Bar and Grill, in Grand Central Station, the news forwarded by my sister that the short story I had salvaged from my play had been accepted for publication in a journal. When we returned that night we walked past the saxophone playing, then a violin, and, putting the key into our lock, we heard farther down the hall a male and female voice loudly arguing, with the woman shouting, "Deen geet out, deen!" in a high-pitched Eastern European

sounding voice. Then an outburst of tears. Then sudden stillness. We stood unabashedly listening, and then went in.

The next morning at about nine, as we were eating breakfast, the buzzer rang. When I looked questioningly at her, and
she remained seated, I went, answered, and announced to her,
"Selma Gerensky and Ruth Marcus."

"Oh, I told Aunt Selma I was here, but I didn't think they'd
do this." I sat back down to wait. When we heard the knock
on the door she got up to answer it. She let in two ladies in
their sixties, one, about Miriam's height, round-faced and
energetic, the other, taller, with watchful eyes, an observer. She
introduced them, "Selma and Ruth, this is Chris." I got up and
shook their hands.

"We were glad to hear from you, so I thought I'd peek in on
the way to work," said the energetic Selma, her eyes on me.

"Ruth came with you?" Miriam inquired, trying to muster
irony.

"She's going shopping."

"There's sales at Gimbels and S. Klein's. We thought you
might like to come," said Ruth, staring at Miriam and then
at me.

"I haven't finished breakfast."

"We can wait."

"I don't need anything."

"You never know," said Ruth, "and we can talk, have
lunch."

"We'd love to hear about your year at school and what happened down there," said Selma.

"I thought you were going to work."

"I am. Get dressed. I'm sure Chris will be glad to get you
out of his hair."

"Please," I said. "Don't mind me. Go right ahead." I looked
at Miriam. "Go right ahead." She finished her grapefruit
and then went into the other room where I knew she would
probably change from the jeans and blouse she was wearing

into something else. Seeing that the two were still standing I asked them to sit down.

"Is this your first time here?" Selma asked.

"I've been here before."

"Must be a change from Alabama," said Ruth.

"It is. This place never sleeps. You can go shopping from 8 a.m. to midnight if you want." They laughed.

"Are you going to stay or go back home?" asked Ruth.

"I don't know. Florida is my home, but I haven't lived there in ten years."

"How's it been for the two of you?" asked Selma.

"Fine."

"No problems?"

"None."

"How lucky!" said Ruth. I thought how they sounded just like Mordecai and Julia, with more irony and acerbic twist. Miriam emerged wearing a blue blouse, a blue and white striped skirt, a certain knit belt and handbag with her hair tied by a colorful scarf of similar design, and new leather sandals with a single woven strap across the toes that I loved.

"Fancy, schmancy. How nice you look," said Selma.

"You'll be all right?" Miriam asked me.

"Sure. Bring back something interesting." She leaned to kiss me. I watched Selma's smile as one who seeks politely to understand what she's seeing, and Ruth's watchful observation, as of a curious something.

She returned that afternoon with two shopping bags, looking pleased.

"Look what I got with my Farmers National Bank MasterCard." She presented me with two striped shirts, "Van Heusen, 17 inch neck, right?" and then she thrust before me two khaki shorts, "Thirty-four inch waist, for our trip to Martha's Vineyard, in August, though you can wear them now if you want, and two pairs of crew socks. These came from Gimbels. I also got this," and she produced from the remaining bags a bottle of Chardonnay and a box of baklava. "That ought to be nice."

"My mother still buys me clothes, and now you're doing it, though she never bought a bottle of wine. She makes her own, from a cherry tree that was planted when I was born, and keeps it in Mason jars under the sink at home. So what did they say?"

"They were something." She rendered the interactions: What did I think I was doing, that I was doing this? What does it look like, I said. Your father won't like it one bit. I know that, I said. You had to go all the way to Alabama to get one? said Selma, who's always been the sexiest one in the family. I didn't answer that. So what's it like? she said. I'm fine, I said. Gil will be coming to see you, Selma says. And maybe Sophie too, Ruth had to add. *That* was uncalled for, Ruthie, says Selma. You never know, said Ruth, nonplussed. I had to laugh in spite of myself, Miriam said.

"My father will come," she said, "next."

"I can take it if you can."

"They'll report back and he'll show tomorrow, or the next day."

"Won't he call first?"

"He'll come just like they did."

"But he won't be amusing," I said lightly.

"He'll be looking for evidence of what he thinks."

"Like the Six Day War. Or maybe somebody wearing a striped green and yellow shirt and orange pants?"

"Maybe you should go pray that God helps him understand us."

"Maybe to Allah. Maybe I'll beseech the Universal Spirit."

She laughed. "You and he have a similar sense of humor. It's so sad you can't understand each other."

"I might understand him," I said.

"Oh, he might understand you too. He just might not want to."

"Tell him I'm a lapsed Episcopalian Humanist."

She laughed again. "You mean, *Humorist*, he'd say."

"See," I said. "We could get along."

We were into our second week in June and had been trying to find an inexpensive sublet, a nicer place. Our first attempt was a piano teacher's apartment in the Chelsea area. The lady turned out to be prim, spinsterish, and enamored of cats. She would sublet to a responsible young person or couple who would also care for her cats. Since I knew about cats I would make the feline appeal while Miriam made a more indeterminate one. She would sit right down and play a Bach prelude in her best form. Maybe I would too. I had started playing again. We would, of course, pretend to be married. When we arrived the room was filled with five or six young women, sort of standing in line, eyeing each other, finding something ironic in common to talk about like New Yorkers do. Seeing us they seemed to take it in stride as one more example of the expected eccentricity of the city. We had a pleasant talk with the piano teacher, especially after we both exclaimed over her baby grand Steinway and each asked to play something on it. She knew we were showing off for her benefit and appreciated our efforts. When her cats began to climb over me, she didn't know whether to be annoyed or pleased. I thought of the girl in Iowa. She liked that we were English teachers who loved music, but we had to fairly admit that we expected to be gone for a week in August, and the music teacher wanted constant presence for her cats.

On our second attempt we were successful, subletting an apartment in the West 160s and Riverside Drive. The place belonged to two painters and sculptors, husband and wife, who were making their annual expedition to an arts and crafts colony in Connecticut. They offered, after a brief cleanup, a nicely furnished place with two large windows looking on an appreciable skyline, with the Hudson flowing below and the Palisades across the shore. I thought how we had passed right by the place on our arrival two weeks ago. We were packing, making preparations to move one morning, when the buzzer rang. I was alone, since it was Miriam's turn to be out moving the car for alternate side of the street parking. So, of course, it should happen this way, and I would be the one to greet him.

The switchboard operator had rung up, "Gil Goddard," and I had told him to send him up. At a knock on the door I opened it and saw a tall, firmly built, blue-eyed man with a full head of grey hair but the beginning of a receding hair line, a compressed look about the mouth but a courteous manner. At least he didn't seem hostile. We stared at each other. He looked correct in his robin's egg blue button-down shirt and grey trousers. It hadn't occurred to me until then that I had expected him to be wearing a suit, or a jacket and tie, with even a felt hat—the way men used to always wear hats, and now they don't, substituting now for headgear baseball caps.

"I've come to see her."

"I'm sorry, she isn't in." My voice was as cordial as I could make it. We were staring at each other. Then I became aware that I should invite him in to wait for her. "She'll be back in a moment. She's out moving the car. Please come in."

"You are the one? … Chris … whom she's with?"

"I'm Chris." He came in, found a chair and sat down. It seemed she looked just like him. He immediately got to the point; neither threatening nor insulting, he simply said what was on his mind.

"Do you think this is going to work out for the two of you? Why do you think you should be giving her your attention?"

"She gives me her attention." We continued to look at each other, making some kind of calculation of the extent of the other's resolve. "You think I can't appreciate her? You think there's nothing in me for her to appreciate?"

"I think you should reconsider."

"This thing has happened."

"That doesn't mean it's good."

261

"You don't think I'm a worthy person, a decent person?"

"I don't know what you are. You seem … decent."

"You think she would choose otherwise?"

"That isn't the only thing."

"What is?"

"Appropriate."

"What's that?"

"When people share essential things without thinking about it."

He was apt, which caused me to get right into it, replying in kind. "You mean, color, or things in themselves?"

"Might be both."

"Isn't that for them to decide?"

"Yes, when it's too late."

"Then those who are 'appropriate' would never break up and always be happy."

"Aren't they usually the most happy?" I thought for a minute how he seemed to be thinking about how it sounded that we were talking like this. Even as I felt the need to continue to respond to his argumentative force, I also felt a sense of unnecessary transgression we both were engaging in. He said: "There are always basic human failings, whether or not people are otherwise right for each other."

"Basically, I think you're seeing difference where there is none."

"I want her to be happy."

"I do too!" I couldn't help adding, "Like she wanted her mother to be with you."

"She was." He was nonplussed in this response.

"That's my point!" We were silent. Instead of saying more, he looked around at the apartment, as though noticing it for the first time.

"Look where you are … are you comfortable in this place?" It could be interesting, I thought, if I told him how we got here. As I was considering this the door opened and Miriam entered.

"Dad!"

"Selma told me."

"I was out moving the car." She looked at the two of us.

"He and I have been talking." He stood up. "Please come out with me."

"Selma did that too. Say it here." Her eyes were bright and pleading. She had made an entreaty but had also stated a condition from which it did not appear she could retreat. He looked at her, taking her measure. It seemed that she could not bear to see what his answer would be, so she sought otherwise to move him. She came and took my hand. "Chris is a good man," she said, in a kind of sob. "Nothing's wrong with him that you think."

Outside, at the door, incredibly, someone said loudly, startling us, "Nuthin' wrong wit him, you tell 'em, girl," and then laughter. The intruding voice was that of a black girl, in a party of others, partially seen through the cracked door, as we saw that Miriam had left the door ajar, but I thought that maybe I had done it when I had let her father in. Hearing this she sank down on the couch. He went to touch her gently, and she became calm. He stood looking at her. Then he turned, looked at me, and proceeded to the door, where he paused again and turned, saying to her:

"I would be glad to see you at home tonight." He left. I went and knelt down beside her and held her. Then we sat up, and we looked at each other.

"You *are* a decent person," she said.

"You heard what we were saying?"

"Some of it. I wanted you to continue."

"You and he and everybody will just have to accept me as I am."

"I do."

"He is just as I imagined him …"

"What?"

"That he didn't want to be personally insulting, but he said what he had to say."

"He saw that maybe you had merit." She paused. "He might even have seen how interesting you are, in spite"—here she threw up her hands—"in spite of being an ... *inappropriate* person."

"You know that my 'merit' doesn't depend on what he thinks." I felt the edge in me that I wanted to convey to her.

"I know," she said. "You know I know that." We looked at each other.

"You are all he has? What happened to your mother?"

"She had a brain tumor. It kept recurring. She died when I was sixteen."

"So did my father, in an auto accident, when I was sixteen."

"Well."

"Mimi. I was waiting for him to call you that. Is he an opera fan?"

"He would never have named me that, named me after her. It's just a nickname."

"How can you stand all this?" I asked.

"How can you?"

"With much practice. You're going home tonight?"

"Yes."

She returned to our place at midnight, after having seen her father. She was subdued but said it had been "all right." I did not inquire further. Looking at her, I thought that her talk with him had not been good, and she was refraining from further mention of it. I went to her, though, and said, "Thank you for loving me." She said nothing, but she touched me in acknowledgment. Then, later, she said, "Thank you too." But then she roused herself, looked at me, and said, "'He's still a black man,'" he said. She put her face to mine and kissed me. As she continued, her vein of earnestness descended into something else, agony and despair. "I think my Dad will change his mind about you. I've done this thing to him ... I hate it ... the last thing he would have thought! Something good has to come ..."

The next day we moved into our new space. We continued to go to the movies and did simple things like taking walks, occasionally going out or seeing friends. Painting and sculpture abounded in our rooms, and we amused ourselves trying to determine which work was done by the husband and which by the wife. We were sipping wine and looking at the Hudson in the company of Miriam's friends Al and Karen one afternoon. Al was a lawyer who wore his suits with a ponytail and handmade cowboy boots. Everything about him was outsized and unexpected.

"I'm sure Woodstock was great," he was saying, "but it's a one-shot deal, a kind of fantasy that after it's over is almost like it never had been, like a dream."

"Did you go?" I asked.

"Sure I did, some great music, but it was a scene, and with the mud and latrines, naked, drunken craziness."

"He became another person," said Karen, "or maybe more himself." Al laughed.

"You went too?" asked Miriam.

"I wanted to be there." I listened to her with interest. Miriam had spoken about going, but we hadn't found ourselves doing anything to get us there either. "The hippies were beautiful," Al said as he continued, "but completely ineffectual, spoiled brats, and someone had had to work hard to provide them the luxury of lighting up and dropping out, playing at being Bonnie and Clyde, with their hip identification with the downtrodden, the fun of being an outlaw. But in the end, we know they are still going to be the lawyers and dentists their parents want them to be."

"Just like you," said Karen.

"No, No, I'm not nearly hip enough," he replied. "Anybody over twenty-five is already too old." He was likeable but off-putting. He seemed to like me but acted as if he knew what I was going to say before I said it, and he put words into Miriam's and Karen's mouths and finished their sentences, yet it seemed hard to take offense. Karen just sat with a bemused smile. Al said that the neighborhood was changing and that the Hispanics and blacks farther down were moving up, and the Jews who used to be here, like his parents, were now up in Riverdale, and that that, after all, was progress, change. Karen ventured that the quality of life hadn't changed. Al agreed, "So far," he said. We looked out the window and saw a tug escorting a freighter that seemed to be glistening in the white of the water in the afternoon light. There's a sight that will always be beautiful, Karen said, no matter who's in here looking at it. Then we talked about how the apartment must have been perfect for painters and that the owners would probably never give it up.

Three days later Miriam said that Al had told her not to marry me, if that had been her intention. He's Jewish and Italian himself, she said. But it's Karen who's the mystery, she said. She was hot stuff at Barnard, in anthropology, but is content answering the phone in an office and goes along with whatever he says. She seemed personally aggrieved as she said this.

"Why do you think Al said that?" I asked.

"That's what I asked him."

"'You're such an idealist,' he said, 'but I don't think you're going to be equal to the reality. Even my parents weren't.'"

"'Why?' I said, 'if I can ask that.'"

"'My father took up with this girl, after thirty years,'" he said.

"'A younger girl?'" Miriam said to him.

"'Yes.'"

"'What did that have to do with their mixed marriage,'" I asked.

"'It was never easy,'" he said.

"'What's the girl?'" Miriam asked.

"'A blonde young person, thirty-eight years old, five years old when I was born. He's having another family, has a two year old.'"

266

"'I'm sorry,'" Miriam said.

"'He likes you, Chris does, and I might be off the mark, and out of order, but, you know, the novelty wears off.'"

"'That's what happened to your Dad?'"

"'He's just a foolish old man.'"

"'Maybe he'll get it right this time around.'"

"'Maybe you should go up to Riverdale and tell that to *her*.'"

"'Your Mom?'"

"'Hey! Go tell it to the other one, too.'"

"You weren't offended by that novelty statement?" I said, after she'd made her recital of her talk with Al.

"You're certainly the most novel thing that's happened to me yet!" She laughed.

"Well," I said, "the novelty hasn't worn off for me either. Tomorrow I am ready to go along with whatever you say when we hit the road." August had already come and I was excited. "I'm wearing my striped shirt, shorts, and sneakers," I said, "and we'll keep the top down all the way."

ELEVEN

This was what happiness was, speeding along in our little convertible, the sparse grass in the white sand stretching to the ocean, on the left, and she on my right, her ruddy face, sun-bronzed limbs, eyes obscured by dark aviator lenses. Her hair did not so much stream in the wind as it was wafted and buffeted, the way sea grass shifted with the current. This was the way you were supposed to remember yourself, leaning into, speeding around a winding curve that seemed familiar, a replay of something that it seemed had already happened, something we had done before.

The afternoon light was bright and hard, but softened, occasionally, by blankets of passing clouds.

"Time to start thinking about a place for the night," she said. "We can stop any time, at the next town."

"And get gas." I liked the idea of staying in a guest room just as she did. It would be informal, yet private. We would be greeted by the lady of the house. Miriam was going to pick out the loveliest, or most interesting, house among those advertising and simply say, that one, that's where we should go.

We were slowing down as we approached a town, a habitation that seemed suddenly to appear as if it had been dreamed, houses with shutters, fences, and weather vanes. I felt that the people ought to still go whaling and wear Revolutionary War gear, even as things had begun to be one long commercial strip, following some maddeningly similar blueprint of chain store eateries and merchandizers. We stopped at a gas station—I had been watching for a Shell sign—that might once have been a carriage house, that now seemed to double as a whitewashed dwelling upstairs. Miriam put on her sandals and got out. I ordered gas, and a blond, muscular guy with hair worn in a ponytail came into view. Stopping often brought back reality in the form of immediate or covert staring, though the attendant seemed to be smiling through his shaggy blond mustache, self-possessed.

He checked the oil and reported it "looked like it was down one."

"OK," I said.

"OK, what?" asked the attendant, poised, seemingly amused.

"Put one in then," I replied, "the best." I watched him walk around the front of the car with a broad-shouldered, narrow-waisted gait, a tattoo on his arm, and what also appeared to be a slight limp. Miriam returned with a Coke. I watched her approach in her shorts and halter top, diffident and self-conscious, as if she thought she were exposed, or on display. Natural reserve was involved in this; so also was the imagined effect, that summer, of having gained some weight. Yet I'm sure she knew how alluring she looked in her top and shorts, which I thought was why she wore them. Now she *might* have been wearing them for me!. And with her Dr. Scholl sandals on she was simply captivating, to women and men, apparently, of whom some of the latter would turn around and look at her as she passed, so amply, perfectly made she was. It didn't matter what she had on. Did Mother Nature really need to go that far? And when I was with her you could see how the race war was being played out in people's faces, for and against.

She extracted a paper cup from the glove compartment, into which she poured some Coke, watched it fizz up to the rim, and then gave me the remainder of the can. I didn't want it but took it anyway. I downed it at once and gave her back the can, which she perched precariously on the dashboard. In giving me the can it was as if she had given me a kiss. I reached over and gave her one.

When it was time to pay, Miriam had already procured her Shell credit card and was handing it to the attendant. I took it back and reached for my wallet, offering cash instead. She had wanted to conserve the cash we had but had also asserted a certain prerogative of proprietorship, proud of the ownership of her car. I didn't even possess a Shell card and wondered at her alacrity in obtaining one, but I thought that she also wanted every convenient new thing, even as she also appreciated the old. I felt that since I was driving the car I should pay. But this merely meant that I wished to be in charge, in the same way I knew that she did. It was after all her car. I roared away out of the station, tires spinning gravel, with the peculiar whining sound of the VW's engine in my ears.

"You'll get a speeding ticket if you don't slow down," she said, sipping her Coke, "and you'll really have to pay cash." She brought her hand down in that gesture she shared with her father. Since her visit to her father that night, I felt she was both closer to me and also more distant at the same time, or less ready to refrain from saying what she thought, in her responses to me; yet I also thought she was more ready to display affection.

"They take checks," I said, ready to let the matter rest. I liked the look of the town, and we had begun to see the little signs, "Guests," sticking up, near the walkways, on lawns. "What do you think?"

"Let's drive around some more." We cruised up and down tree-lined streets, shading the darkened, quiet, cool-looking houses, with their look of small town pride and independence, yet all of them seemed to cater to the tourist business. I saw a brick house, advertising, that I liked, with its own parking lot.

271

She liked it too; she liked the flowers lining the sidewalk, a profuse row of multicolored chrysanthemums. We pulled into the parking lot.

I would go in to see whether there was room available. I would also go to see what the reception to my person might be, which we thought had less shock potential than the two of us together but was still the determining factor in whether, and in what way, we would be received.

"Have you got your ring?" She voiced with pragmatic necessity the idea that I should put my birthstone ring on my left ring finger and rotate it such that only a thin gold band appeared. She would do the same. I rang the doorbell. Almost immediately a gray-haired woman appeared with bright, alert gray eyes, like those of a predatory bird, but lacking the fierceness, with a strong, aquiline nose. I said that my wife and I were looking for a room. In a pleasant way she assured me that she had one, and I got the impression that she was glad to be able to give it to me.

"Come right in," she said, "and I'll show it to you, or maybe you'd like to go back out and get your wife and your things. Go right ahead, and just come back in through this door." I went out and returned with Miriam, bearing two suitcases. We opened the door and went into a wood-paneled reception area. Three doors opened to it as well as a stairway leading above. There was furniture and a commanding mahogany desk, sturdy and serviceable, with nineteenth-century Victorian weightiness. We stood idly looking at each other, almost like newlyweds. Miriam pointed to the door at left.

"That's ours," she said with a shrewd look, as if she were clairvoyant. She had barely finished speaking when the door opened and the gray-haired woman emerged from the room. Taking the two of us in, her eyes intensified in brightness.

"Well," she said, her hands on her hips, "I think you'll be comfortable here."

"Thank you," I said. "We're the Hinsons, Chris and Miriam." For a second I'd almost said "Goddard."

"I'm Mrs. Pine," she said. "I have a book here. I'd like you to sign it." She placed it before me. As I signed it Miriam announced that she wanted to sign it too.

"By all means, dear," said Mrs. Pine. So I held the book as she wrote "Miriam Goddard-Hinson" in her bold, clear characters.

Mrs. Pine explained what services she provided and what was expected of her guests. "Where're you folks headed? Vacationing?"

"To Martha's Vineyard," said Miriam.

"Oh, you'll love that, some fine beaches, but crowded about now."

"Yes, I've been before. You can always find a secluded spot," Miriam continued.

"The ferry ride is nice. I see you've been riding in a convertible."

"It's hot going, though," I said.

"You get tanned without trying," said Miriam.

"Mr. Hinson too, I'll bet." She said this with laughter.

"He's already got one," said Miriam.

"Sure," I said, "and I don't have to try."

"Of course, dear," she said, "and, besides, it's unhealthy, though it's a nice look if you like it."

"Parched," I offered to Mrs. Pine. I liked the way we had gotten on so readily.

But Miriam said, "I think it makes you look and feel great."

"With your complexion?" said Mrs. Pine. "Sensitive, yes?"

"I do fine with protection."

"So one of you does and one of you doesn't. I know what you mean, dear. I did it a lot when I was young. And it was Mr. Pine who got cancer, and he didn't even smoke." Everything she said was phrased in such a direct, disarming way that she simultaneously put us at ease and made us alert. Her gaze remained on Miriam. "Well, Mrs. Hinson," she said, moving toward the door on the left, "this is your room. I think you'll find everything you need. If not, just come out and ring this bell," to which she pointed on the desk. We thanked her and went in. Inside was more wood paneling, a large double bed with posters, matching furniture, and a small built-in bathroom.

I slumped down in a capacious armchair, realizing how tired I was. She came and stood next to me and began, and then ceased, to run her fingers through my hair. She had told me once of the curly locks of a certain Steven, my predecessor, a childhood sweetheart whom she was supposed to have married, with whom everything for the first time had been experienced, to whom she had remained committed, more-or-less, throughout college, though each had gone to different schools. When she had told me of this, my pleasure in her doing it ceased. The difference in hair texture, and thus sensation, was appealing to her, but my reaction to this difference made her self-conscious. Instead, she massaged the nape of my neck, running her hand underneath my shirt, up and down my back, in a caressing way. I liked it—a lovely, arousing, intimacy—but also a controlling one, I imagined, as when a man might run his hand down a woman's backside and let it linger there, handling a piece of fruit. "You didn't mind the talk about sun tanning?" I said that I hadn't; in fact, I hadn't. She was now sitting on the chair's arm and precipitously slid down off the arm into my lap. The pupils of her amber-green eyes were widening to ever darkening space, and I could see nothing, staring into them, except the strange mesmerizing appeal of their depthless sucking in. The tip of her nose and her cheeks were red from the sun, making her look like she was blushing. We looked at each other in this way until each ignited, in the other, the beginnings of a widening grin. Holding her in this way, I wanted to feel the movement of her mind the way I felt the certainty of her body as it relaxed against mine.

However, as we continued to sit I began to feel the pressure of her weight and shifted position, as if to get up. She restrained me by intertwining her fingers with mine, clasping me. We became aware of the mutually deceptive rings.

"Mr. Hinson."

"Mrs. Hinson."

"You almost said 'Goddard' to her."

"I knew you wouldn't miss that."

"I'd keep my maiden name, except when it's family. It will be *legally necessary* for me to rename myself. And Goddard-Hinson sounds absurd."

"How about Hinson-Goddard?"

"Just as ridiculous." She laughed.

"But the last would be first," I said, "at last."

"Where would you be?"

"I'd be one of the first not to be last."

"Isn't that legally not allowed? Besides, you wouldn't like it if you didn't possess your wife like other men possessed theirs."

"You're the possessive one."

"You don't know how to admit what you want. You think it's a virtue not to make demands—see, I know you."

"But that's *you*, isn't it, what you're like, provided there's a point beyond which you can't go, where the line is drawn. A guy has to have a high tolerance threshold. That's called being understanding—see, I understand *you*."

"What you mean is all we want is to be held," she said.

"We?"

"Women," she affirmed.

"I don't know about women. Don't you want to be held?"

"No more than you do."

"Sure I want to be held. Did I say different?"

"You're sweet, but you're no angel. The men I've known tended toward self-absorbed and overbearing, though they knew how to feel guilty about it, but that didn't stop them from being it."

"I know what it's like not to want to hurt anybody," I said.

"Every woman is taught not to want to hurt anybody."

"Then we have a basis for mutual understanding," I said, lightly. Her sandals were off again and I looked at her feet, watching the toes wiggle occasionally, wondering at the inexplicable delight I took at watching them. Feet were exquisitely expressive, I thought, like a body part not intended to be revealed; and it was not true that beautiful women all had ugly feet, inharmonious and crude, like lovely elms forced to reveal a gnarled battery of tenacious roots. The feet could not speak without the toes, sweet little appendages, and the nuance of their articulation was everything. I would almost as much prefer the sight of her feet as her face. I could not get enough of looking at them, feeling that I would forever be in their thrall, and that it would be enough to come home each day knowing that she was there, always carrying this part of herself with her.

We decided to shower and have dinner. We rang for Mrs. Pine and asked about local restaurants, all of which seemed inevitably seafood or lobster houses. She recommended one, inexpensive and good, called The Wharf, not far to walk to, in which you sat over the ocean and could walk along a boardwalk and enjoy the view, a local as well as tourist attraction during the summer months. The owners during the rest of the year were retired college professors, said Mrs. Pine, a man and his wife.

We left the house and soon joined a throng of people walking the streets, little different from a scene on Coney Island on a summer's night—ice cream parlors, pizza joints, restaurants, and boutiques, and people strolling, almost as if to affirm that being present made one more beautiful and real. Passing our second shop advertising antiques, we succumbed to temptation and went in. We walked up and down in the deliberate browsing manner that gives the indication of the desire to examine every object, and circumambulated the shop, walking past the proprietor as he sat benignly in a cane rocker, occasionally peering above a newspaper he was reading, and back out the door again, a task accomplished.

Miriam wanted an ice cream. I suggested it might be nicer to have one after dinner; we could eat it on the way home, as dessert. She agreed. Then she wanted me to accompany her inside the next shop. In the window were manikins dressed in the urban-peasant-cowboy denim sports wear currently in vogue I'd seen in the pages of magazines. She wanted a new pair of jeans, and maybe a size larger. I watched as she found her size and began to make a selection. The place was filled with young people, and rock music blared. She said that the prices were high and that she had to try on the two pairs she'd chosen. She had to wait for space in the fitting room, and when she got in she returned twice, first with one pair on and then the other, insisting that I help her choose. One pair fit snugly and the other was somewhat larger. I recommended the former while she favored the latter, saying that when both shrank the larger would be just right. I suggested that maybe she feared she was going to grow to fit the larger pair. She surprised me by getting both.

Our walk toward the restaurant drew nearer the coast and soon put the ocean in view. Gulls that had been heard overhead were now more profusely in evidence, diving and swirling, and occupying lonely perches atop posts, like totems. The heat of the day had given way to the soft textured caress of cooling breezes off the water, mild exhalations of the sea. We entered the restaurant. It was a home-run affair of practical and unadorned simplicity, and limited menu. You entered, approached the counter, gave your name and order, sat down and waited until the order was called out. We ordered our lobsters and waited, glad to see that we could be provided with a carafe of white wine. Soon we were eating, chowder, oysters, and three lobsters, one and a half each.

The place was crowded and noisy. We sat along a wall with a view of the water and of the gulls perched on the

277

pilings. Contented and happy, we ate. Miriam had changed into a blouse and skirt, and viewing her I thought of cherry blossoms, the flowering clusters of pink and red and white, almost something succulent, so much rosy life bloomed in her face, her presence. She was beautiful; I wondered whether she knew this, since I wanted her to know it. I imagined that we looked a perfectly conventional couple! What did I mean by that? Not weird or provocatively unconventional? Perhaps it was an awareness of this that made us calm; no effort need be expended to create an impression of normalcy, which would have been the surest indication of unease and a calling of attention to ourselves. I was grateful that I felt no strain when we were together and that we were able to be mutually engaged and self-accepting. Being with me did not make her feel strange or feel that she must do things, or project a certain air, to justify herself.

We had been busy with the food, not really talking about anything. But as if she had been silently following my thought, she said, as we divided the third lobster, "When I went down there to teach I never expected any of this to happen." She replenished her wine glass and reached to do the same with mine.

"Our sitting here like this?"

"I've never been anywhere with someone like you. I mean, I've seen men like you. I grew up in New York, in Brooklyn, but I've never really known any black men. There were a few nice boys in my school. I've never known *anybody* like you; though, actually, in some ways, you're not much different from some of the guys I've known."

"What kind is that?"

"Urban, intellectual, iconoclastic, humorous, strange. Nice, regular, intelligent boys going to Harvard or Columbia. Trying to measure up to being something special."

I said, "High expectations make you perform at a high level," conscious of my desire to make a particular point. "Middle class, intellectual black boys—there are such things—went to

278

places like Morehouse, Dr. King's school, or Tuskegee Institute, Booker T. Washington's school, or Fisk, W. E. B. DuBois' school, as well as to Yale—or to Spellman, if you were a girl."

"DuBois took his PhD from Harvard," she said.

"How'd you know that?"

"Why shouldn't I know that? Isn't that general knowledge? It says so on the back cover of my copy of *The Souls of Black Folk*, which I had to read in high school. Everybody knows that's a classic." She smiled at me sweetly. "That's where the idea of the problem of the color line, for the twentieth century, really gets brought out. He made the obvious original and articulate." I think she expected me to take this up, but I just continued to give her back her sweet smile.

We had finished eating and were preparing to leave. On our way out we passed by a table presided over by someone familiar. Unmistakably it was our smiling service station attendant, at a table with a woman and four children and many lobsters. The woman was Asian, the children biracial, fair-skinned to cocoa. The woman attended the children, and the service station attendant looked up as he held the youngest, an infant, and saluted Miriam and me with his eyes, and the older child at his elbow followed his father's gaze in looking at us. The woman, with a long braid down her back, never looked up from her task with the two others, who were hungry, insistent, and beautiful.

Miriam and I, outside, proceeded in quiet happiness. "That, I'll bet you, is his Vietnamese war bride," I said. We found the ice cream parlor and ordered three expensive scoops on our cones, and licked them all the way home. That night we lay quietly in an embrace.

"I'll bet her room is right above ours," she said.

"And I bet she knows we're not married," I said.

"Yes, we're frauds," she said. "That guy at the restaurant, and his wife, they're the genuine article, with four kids to boot."

"He married her and brought her home," I said.

"Knew what he wanted, didn't care what it looked like," she said.

"And have four kids, and still be illicit, according to your conventional standards," I said.

"You're always so concerned about appearance," she said, somehow irritated.

"Howard told me once just how powerful our appearance is."

"What?"

"Something illicit, married or not. Actually he spoke about the 'impact' we make."

"Only if you're concerned about appearances," she said.

"Aren't you? Isn't the world? According to conventional standards?"

"I'm at least as unconventional as you."

"I didn't mean you personally. I meant conventional standards in general, as when Hamlet refers to 'your philosophy' to Horatio. You know what I meant."

"Don't quote your spurious Shakespeare to me." For some reason she was annoyed, and she rolled away from me and lay on her side. "Signifying nothing."

"Not so loud," I said, derisively. "You wouldn't want Mrs. Pine to hear you."

She raised herself back up and said, "The rest is silence, between you and me," and lay back down again. Somehow I had provoked her, in this silly way, and I didn't really know why. I was sorry, and I didn't like lying like this. Of course, I did know why. It *was* true that I was concerned about appearances, just as I knew she was. God, I wanted us to look normal, and the two of us together would always appear to be something else. But, as she said, why should *we* be concerned about that? I thrust myself next to her where she lay on her side and lay likewise, barely touching her. She neither moved away nor acknowledged me or stirred. Feeling the warmth of her body, I thought of the paradox of intimacy and impersonality, affection and anger, or dislike, and of how neither cancelled the other but was lodged in a complex mosaic. The awful intimacy of intercourse could be engaged in by total strangers, emerging neither humbled nor wise, as strange to their partners, and to themselves, as before. I put my arm around her, held her, and planted my lips at the nape of her neck, and persisted, until she relaxed and turned toward me. Then we lay on our backs, holding hands, and slipped into sleep.

We rose fresh and renewed in the morning. We dressed and went out to breakfast, though we could have had the juice, pastry, and coffee Mrs. Pine offered. When we returned we encountered Mrs. Pine sitting at the mahogany desk. She inquired about our dinner, the night before, and breakfast that morning. Miriam, glad to see her, thanked her for her hospitality.

"Come back to see me the next time you're in these parts, even when you have little ones," she added. "I have room. You can call ahead of time." She handed us a card. "I'll remember you." She looked at us with warmth with a strong light in her gray eyes. "I suspect you'll want to get going to be early for the ferry." We went in and got our bags, returned, said goodbye to Mrs. Pine and went out to the car.

When we arrived at the ferry there were already many cars waiting; cars were filling the parking lot. We parked and took our bathing suits and towels in a small bag. The sun was already bright, and we strode, in our sunshades, holding hands. Soon we boarded the ferry in a throng of people. On deck, underway, we watched the coast recede and the ocean unfold and envelop us, an ark of humanity, mainly couples, and contingents of families with children. It was so simple and so lovely, sailing into the morning on the sea, in a slight breeze, soft spray, and the smell of nostalgia, bracing, a memory of origins. We kept our posts, like kids, at the railing and stared at the water and drank in the air.

It was not long before we reached land again and were docking, ready to disembark. We filed down the gangway amid people waving and being greeted. The atmosphere to me seemed both festive and quaint, as of a Sunday morning outing or gathering of a clan. Without being surprised, I recognized and pointed out a figure to Miriam—having almost expected to see such a person—standing incongruously next to a large station wagon, seemingly trying to look inconspicuous but not wholly opposed to being recognized—a prominent American novelist, a sort of quizzical expression on his face as he rearranged the contents in the back of the vehicle.

We were hungry again and walked around surveying the eating establishments. We went into a fast food joint, had hamburgers, fries, and soft drinks, in about twenty minutes, and were out again. Desiring to rent a car, we declined the appeal of mopeds and bicycles, though the latter were tempting. Directed to a car rental, we selected a VW similar to the one we'd left behind, though not a convertible, and considerably the worse for wear. Miriam paid for it and insisted on driving it since, having been here and done this before, she wanted to show me around.

The first thing we did was stop at a general store to browse, from which we emerged with newspapers and sunbathing lotion. We drove to a beach and remained there the rest of the afternoon. A breeze persisted and brought in strong waves, into the midst of which we ran and collapsed in the cascade and then made our way back to shore. She would grab me by the hand and run, leading me after her. Then I would pick her up, cradling her in my arms, as she kicked and squealed, and run with her and plunge into the oncoming wave, from which we emerged dazed and gasping. Though she wore a two-piece bathing suit, she was no longer concerned about what she might have looked like, and neither was I, though it occurred to me, in another connection, that I was the only person of color in sight, all the other people like me, I supposed, to be found in a historically black area I had heard about called Oak Bluffs.

After our play in the water, we lay on the sand. But this soon seemed too hot, and undesired, perhaps intensified by the proximity of a mass of other reclining figures or even the feeling of anticlimax following our time in the water. We were still vaguely excited and could not sit still. We returned to the car and decided to drive farther around the island. We soon came to remote stretches of road that seemed to be the province of seagulls. Many, apparently, had refused to move from the road and had been crushed under wheels. We arrived at a high point on the road that afforded an unbroken expanse of dunes leading down to a secluded, unoccupied beach. We stopped the car and walked down to the water, which was shallow, crystalline, and still. "I always wanted to do this," she said. I saw that it had been her intention to arrive at just such a place. She took off her clothes and walked nude into the water. She called back over her shoulder, "Aren't you coming?" I didn't reply. She proceeded farther and sat down in the water. I looked back up the road and could see our car, waiting, its two headlamps like eyes observing us as she proceeded. She cast no backward glance. Gulls, eyeing her approach, did not scare. I had watched her back and rumpled thighs, the flesh of which rippled as she walked. Granules of sand adhered to her skin, giving the appearance of a fine satin garment, acquired when she must have sat down to take off her sandals. I thought how the merest stitch of clothing made one clothed, compared to its absence altogether. She sat still in the water, like an idol, almost as if she were at prayer. Also, it gave the impression of an indescribable aloneness, nothing in it of the serenity, for instance, of a meditative yoga pose. To me there was also in it something of a sadness, a need. The water, serene in ebb and flow, lapped at her buttocks, and held her and seemed to let her go.

I didn't want to join her. I didn't want to do what she was doing. It answered no need in me, as it obviously did in her, and I thought that one reason she was able to do it was that she was with me, empowered by whatever it was I represented. She didn't mind being seen because she could not be known and would remain anonymous in her nakedness. I, however, didn't want it thought that there was something about myself that I wished to reveal—some statement I wished to make— that could only be made through the public exposure of my body. The impulse to do so seemed trivial to me, unless it were a case in which you were naturally called upon to be naked, whereas she seemed most concerned about providing for herself the experience of having done so, in the absence of which there could be no substitute. She seemed to want to prove to herself the right to be able to do so. I didn't feel that you ought to have personally felt any constraint regarding doing so in the first place. But why not just get naked for the hell of it because she wanted me to? Then why wear any clothes at all in public if that turned you on? But it didn't turn me on. Yet I was the one who went naked in our apartment and walked past windows, and even looked out of them, with the shades up and curtains parted, something she would never do. The thoughts kept pressing in on me. Where else would it have been appropriate to be naked, if not at a beach? But for her was this so because she was with me, the dark-skinned nature boy, the naked one? If this empowered her, why couldn't it empower me? But why should that be empowering because of me? And wasn't there for me something empowering about her being white? A difference of the drawing room or the jungle. What did I imagine I was doing, eating this vanilla Swiss almond? It certainly wasn't chocolate fudge! And liking it wasn't the same as accepting it.

I sat down in the sand with an image of the scene, a tableau, the sight of which hurt and oppressed me. As I watched her, she rose from her reverie and emerged strong and dripping from the sea. She approached me with a smile but also a queer luminosity, a certain triumph of resolve that seemed to focus on me. It seemed to me she wished to convey a sense of herself as carrying a power greater than my own, a will both to honor and subdue the opposing male in me, a side of her I had not seen before. She came to me, kneeled, and reclined, with me, on the sand in a motion that seemed to compel. I didn't like the chill of her body, its wet, gritty feel. The strength of her resolve seemed to clarify the need for my resistance, and so I held her, by force, in an embattled embrace, until her own struggling was stilled. I held her this way until my grip was relaxed, but neither of us disengaged from the other, holding on to something still.

"Is this what we want?" I said, with effort.

Her eyes were closed, as if she were wondering, or sighing.

There had been something in it of everything: man against woman, boy against girl, black against white, Jew against Gentile, male against female, your discrete separate inexorable uncompromising self in opposition to mine. *There* was something truly overly-determined. We got up and went back to the car, as if nothing had happened, not being able to say what had happened, or what it meant. By the time we reached the ferry we had gained composure.

"That was interesting!" she said. "I don't know what came over me. I wanted to wipe you out."

"I know," I said.

"I didn't think you'd resist."

"Did I have a choice?"

"There's a grievance in women," she said.

"To be on top," I said.

"That's a man's way of saying it."

"Of things," I said. She just continued to look at me, saying nothing.

Then she said, "Not to be hindered."

"Yes," I said. "Respected, wanted for yourself only. Maybe that's a black's way of saying it."

"That's what women used to say to men."

"Used to?"

"But you're not a woman."

"You're not a man."

"I *am* a white female. Doesn't that factor in? Why must it always be something bad?"

"History doesn't stop just because we want it to."

"Then we have to continue to write it." I didn't have anything to say to that. Soon we were in the car again and on our way back to Manhattan.

TWELVE

We did not stay long at the lovely apartment on Riverside Drive since it was time to head back South. We would be gone before the owners returned. Miriam called to thank them when we reached Atlanta. The two were pleased that she and I had enjoyed staying in their house and had left it in a clean condition. They also spoke of the arrival of the proofs of my short story which, trying to be helpful, they had opened and then had read. They would forward them to the address Miriam gave. I now stood on the porch and waved goodbye to Miriam as she pulled away heading back to school. I could see other people watching her leave too, from their front porches or yards, and, across the street, looking out from the entrance of her garage was the other white woman in the neighborhood.

I turned away and went to my reading project, which was providing me great satisfaction. Currently I was reading through the two thick volumes of *The Norton Anthology of English Literature*, keeping deep company with all the poets. I would reread, or finish reading, all the anthologies I'd accumulated over the years, thick paperbacks weighed down with their riches of print as if they were bouillon, and then I would turn to individual works. For instance, I had pulled out Oliver Goldsmith's *She Stoops to Conquer* and had read it with pleasure. Next I was going to read Robert Burton's *Anatomy of Melancholy* and proceed down through time as far as I could, to Ellison's *Invisible Man*, for instance, a different kind of melancholy. I loved what I was doing, and I had complete freedom and time in which to do it. I had to apply to graduate school and for financial aid, appealing to some of my old professors for letters of recommendation. If they were still at their old posts I could locate them.

Meanwhile I had been looking for an inexpensive apartment where Miriam and I could stay on weekends, in a nice neighborhood, for students or a young couple. When I saw the For Rent sign and turned off Hunter Street into a residential area, I came upon a three-story brick complex of apartments and thought that this was it. I went up to the second floor, went down an outside walkway on the front of the building, and looked through the window into a vacant space, a one-room studio. I called the number and made arrangements to secure it. Miriam and I had saved our money, so we could afford it. She arrived a week after I had rented it and thought that it would do just fine. We bought furniture from secondhand stores. One large rocker we got that we both liked to sit in, sometimes together. When my short story came out and we located a bookstore where I could obtain additional copies, we bought five, almost the entire allotment; and the store displayed memorabilia, such as Confederate flags, some in the form of blankets and pillow cases. To the white clerk's amusement I bought a pillow case and told Miriam she would see what good use I had for it. When we got home I took the cushion from the rocker's bottom and slipped it into the pillow case as a seat for our bottoms.

The man from the gas company had not liked it when he came to turn our service on. Both Miriam and I had been at home, and he had been surprised to see us though not antagonistic, but the sight of the chair had riled him. I had asked what size gas heater I needed to heat the place, and he had replied contemptuously that I'd need a bigger one than the ones he usually saw in these places. I said we'd get as big a one as needed, that we'd only be using it on weekends, and that we personally were used at home to raising the thermostat lever for heat. He had simply looked at us then, and I felt that the response he had wanted to make to this rebuke was to spit. Instead he thrust a form for me to sign and left. "The chair got him," she said, and we both went and sat in it.

Miriam came on weekends, arriving around dusk on Fridays, and leaving after we'd had lunch on Sunday afternoons. It was a routine that carried us right into November before we realized the passing of time. She was especially happy to come, to see me, because she had not been sleeping well and had been waking up at five every morning. Sometimes I thought I got a hint of something desperate in her. After we had had champagne and oysters one evening, and she had drunk more than she normally might, she sat in the rocker, rocking back and forth, increasingly forcefully, and said that sometimes she didn't know why she was doing what she was doing. She wanted me to talk to her to cheer her up. She wanted me to tell her that everything would be all right, that her father wasn't right in saying that it wouldn't work. She wanted to be held. I held her, and dried her tears, and made her blow her nose. Afterwards she felt better. I had never seen her really tipsy, and instead of the lighthearted and silly condition she could get into after having had a few drinks, this time I saw the fear and anger that surfaced, something morose, and maybe some resentment. She had gotten up out of the rocker, and when I came and sat in it, she returned and sat in my lap.

"He said you may be nice ... and intelligent ... and interesting, but still the ... other thing." She ran her hand down my arm to my hand and entwined her fingers with mine. "Are you working some magic?" ... She turned around to look at me, face to face. "That's what he thinks ... you're working a spell on me ... sweet and seductive ... could be sincere, but perverse ... You're just you, you say? … You're the most interesting person I know … I've never been happier, and more scared … and I don't care." She brushed my lips with a kiss. "I wake up at five sometimes and can't wait to jump into the car to get here … Throwing away my treasure … you know that's really what Howard thinks … though he'd never *say* it … You're the only one who's ever really *seen* it, shown it to me … I love you for that. Whatever I am, is yours. They don't understand …" She laughed. "I don't understand either, but I think you really *love* me. *He* knows that too, that's the problem." She squeezed my arms, wrapping them around her. "Listen … Regardless … Don't ever let me go."

* * *

We went to concerts occasionally and to the theatrical productions of the local colleges. For Thanksgiving Miriam stayed at school to be with a group of faculty who had instituted their own gathering, and I appreciated how she had had a sympathetic feeling of sharing the occasion with Howard. One weekend I returned with her in her car to the campus, arriving after midnight and remaining in her apartment all week, returning with her to Atlanta at week's end. I played her stereo and her piano, joking about how anyone who saw her leave yet heard sounds coming from her place might think it's a phantom piano. She replied, not joking, that maybe it is a phantom piano. She thinks sometimes that she hears it at night, playing itself, though there isn't any actual sound coming from it. Yet she thinks she hears Mozart's *Eine Kleine Nachtmusik*. She keeps thinking she hears the well-known first three notes of the second movement. Then we know whose piano it is, I said, laughingly, C. Buchanan's. Gee-whiz! she said, don't scare me with that. We could turn it over and see, I said. Fortunately it's too heavy to turn over! she came back at me. And I don't want to know! Seeing that she was agitated I said no more. She motioned for me to give her a cigarette. I did so and we both lit up.

For Christmas I went home to be with my mother and sister and found things there about the same as they had been the preceding year. I'd had another drink with her to usher in the New Year, from her stash of homemade wine she kept in the Mason jars under the kitchen sink.

Spring came sooner to Atlanta than I had thought. Tulips and daffodils, irises and crocuses were pushing their way up in early February. Some of the shrubs, like the forsythia, were already budding or making leaves of yellowish green. Thus far there had been no snow that winter, though it had been cold on occasion. I thought of the night Miriam and I had been snug in our apartment with our large-enough gas heater. We turned off the lights and viewed it as a fireplace from our king size mattress resting on the floor, on a night when we might have ordered pizza, drunk beer, and smoked cigarettes. We exchanged Valentine's Day cards with poems on them again, and drank champagne and ate chocolates on our birthdays in March and April. We had been successful in getting into graduate school and were brimming with plans for our return to New York.

One Thursday afternoon I was at my sister's reading Dickens's *Bleak House* and thinking about Miriam's arrival on Friday when Michael burst into the house shouting, "Dr. King's been shot!" He was crying, almost hysterical, and I had to hold him. We turned on the TV and saw the special broadcast in progress relating the awful news. A sniper had shot him in the throat (aiming for his head?) as he stood on the balcony of his motel. As we were watching the TV I saw a figure flash past the window, and in burst Charles who, seeing the program, demanded, "Is he dead?" We nodded, and he slumped down and stared, the bulge of the backpack he was still wearing pressing into the couch. Apparently King had been pronounced dead in the emergency room in a hospital in Memphis.

"I hope they catch him! I hope they catch his ass, whoever did it!" shouted Charles at the TV. Soon Julia and Mordecai arrived, solemn-faced, hopeless. They stood, holding each other.

291

"This is so horrible," she said. Michael got up from the couch and interposed himself between them, crying again. Charles and I remained on the couch, staring at the TV. As the night wore on there were news analyses, testimonials, and pleas for calm from prominent people. Already, apparently, rioting had begun. Most extraordinary was the recording of a speech King had given the night before, when he spoke as if he had a premonition of his coming death, when he said to the people in the church that he had been to the mountain top and had seen the promised land, but that he might not get there with them. Death threats had been constant companions, but this somehow seemed different, when he said that longevity had its place, but he wasn't concerned about that any longer. He just wanted to do God's will. That inimitable voice, those surging, lilting, rhythmic cadences just caused us all to break down in tears. In my mind was an aching echo of Charles's sentiments—if I *could* catch the person who did it, *what* would I do? A slow castration death with a very sharp knife of the perpetrator and all his cohorts, anybody of the remotest similarity of thought, with their murderous, lunatic hatreds, as Ed had called them. And at once I thought how King would have condemned such thinking. It made me weep again, piteously: every good thing always assaulted and imperiled, every good thing that uplifted our hearts undermined, assailed.

Then I remembered my first encounter with King. He had come to speak in my church when I was a teenager, in 1955, a year after, come to think of it, the Supreme Court decision against segregation in public schools had occurred. That morning he spoke not with the prophetic cadences that we were used to hearing but now with the intellectual forcefulness, the rigor and logic that characterized his performances on programs like *Meet the Press*, but with the same gravitas of the pulpit. He was still the Doctor, different from what Malcolm X had been, but ready to prophesy, always the powerful advocate and spokesperson for what the ills were and what the remedies should be.

Hearing him in church that morning I recalled how I had wanted to be a doctor just like him.

We came up afterwards in the line of people waiting to speak to King, and my friend—thirteen years old, the eldest son of our minister who had asked King to come speak—asked him if he could see his shirt-sleeve cuffs.

"Why's that, young man?" King asked, amused.

"To see what you have written on them." We all laughed. "You never use a text." King looked at me and then he looked at him, and he grinned. He knew what my friend was talking about. His brown eyes were soft and enveloping, with a twinkle in them. Then I thought of how we had heard that the smart boy preacher, who went to college at fifteen, was also, on the dance floor, the jitterbug king, a great dancer.

"It's not what you've got on here"—he pointed to his cuffs—"but what you have up here"—he pointed with his index finger to his forehead—"that counts."

I looked out the window and saw that there were people in the streets, standing alone, like watchful sentinels, or in groups, talking, waiting, where they might remain all night. Miriam called to say she would be there Friday night. She would have to return to school as usual on Sunday, before the funeral, but she would be able to see the body, as we learned it would be on view at Spellman College, before the funeral at Ebenezer Baptist Church and a second ceremony at Morehouse College. On the weekend we all went to a chapel on Spellman College to view the remains. Michael was first, followed by Charles, Mordecai, Julia, Miriam, and myself. It was a bright spring day, and we stood in a long line but one that continued to make progress moving forward. People from all over the world in the thousands were present, patiently waiting to pay their last respects. As we got nearer we could see the bier. Mourners passed before it, paused, stared, uttered a prayer or made the sign of the cross, and moved on. Sometimes, though, they uttered cries of anguish, or fainted, or shouted angrily, or beat their breasts, or remained standing, staring, until they had to be led away. When our turn came we all paused, looked, and moved on. Remains were the right word, for what was left was a kind of copy of the man himself whose self had departed. He did not even appear to be sleeping, because even that has its way of seeming natural. It was more like a consummate reproduction, a substitute, of someone who was supposed to be asleep. Nevertheless, it was all that we had left.

The six of us walked back to the car we'd all come in, and went to a restaurant, Paschal's, where we were early enough to get a table without delay for dinner. Mordecai suggested that we should have a dinner for the common man. I imagined he was suggesting that we could just eat, eat our grief away. We could eat as a *tribute* to King, he meant. That meant a superb rendition of common man's fare: fried chicken, mashed potatoes, green beans, biscuits, beer and soda, and a slice each of chocolate cake with ("butter pecan ice cream," Julia interposed, "not vanilla") your ice cream of choice. He said that no one was to be concerned about gaining weight tomorrow. We will eat for the Doctor, he said with a damp eye, just like at a heavenly banquet where he now is … They need to *catch* the ones who did this, he said. … And before long, after the food arrived, and we had begun to eat, our spirits revived.

After dinner when we arrived back home, we said goodbye to Miriam who got into her car to go back to school. "They have been so good to me, all your family," she said to me as she was leaving. On the day of the funeral I was one of the thousands lining the streets as the mule-drawn casket containing King's body went past. Many of the people close to King or involved in the civil rights movement walked behind it. Among the mourners I could easily recognize prominent figures, and there among them was one of my former roommates, himself an established figure now in the movement. It was a long day and when the casket finally arrived on the campus at Morehouse College, I was there to hear, over loudspeakers, the eulogy delivered by the emeritus president, Dr. Benjamin Mays, one of King's teachers. After this I went home to the apartment Miriam and I had. I had bought a candle resting in a little glass container that I wanted to light. I lit it and stared, thinking of the flame as the light of eternal benevolence, faltering but steady, always there, but always needing some encouragement.

Two weeks later one night I was upstairs in my bedroom reading Keats's poetry when Charles called to me from below, "Uncle Chris, come down here!" An urgency in his voice made me put down my book and come running. When I got there I saw that Charles was watching the news and the commentator was talking apparently about another atrocity. "A black guy shot up the Klan rally, and might be somebody you know!" Charles reiterated.

"Who?"

"Somebody named Kavanaugh."

"Edward?"

"Yeah."

"Ed!" Ed? "What happened?"

"The Klan had a cross burning at Stone Mountain. This guy took his gun and offed those suckers."

"Who did?" asked Michael. He and Julia had come in and were standing watching.

"Somebody I knew at school shot up the Klan rally." The commentator was saying that mayhem and confusion had ensued, and there had been many dead and wounded.

"Everybody was shooting at everybody else. They didn't know who was who. My man had him an automatic weapon and plenty of ammo," repeated Charles. I could hear that the gunman was among the dead. It was a feature on the ten o'clock news, and then the commentator passed on to other items of pain and disruption. I told them briefly about Ed, my friend, who had left school. I had just heard the commentator say he'd become a worker for the US Postal Service. I went to call

Derek, who was not in, but I spoke to Tina. She remembered our discussion about Ed when I had visited them last summer. Later that night I watched the eleven o'clock news without being much further enlightened. When Derek called about twelve o'clock we knew that the gunman was indeed our Ed. The following morning when I awoke I went out and picked up the copy of *The Atlanta Journal-Constitution* lying on the doorstep. On the front page I read:

Negro Gunman Opens Fire at Ku Klux Klan Rally
By
C. J. Piltch and Michael A. Stickney
(And Additional AP Sources)

(Atlanta. April 18). Yelling an obscenity, a Negro gunman opened fire at a Ku Klux Klan rally and cross burning near Stone Mountain, Georgia, yesterday, with eighteen confirmed dead and ten wounded. The gunman, identified as Edward Wilkins Kavanaugh, III, 26, of Atlanta, seems to have acted alone, though in the confusion of the assault, and return of gunfire by klansmen, it was not clear if there were accomplices. Some victims may have been struck by gunfire from fellow klansmen, unsure of who the assailants were and the direction of the attack. Men, women and children were killed and wounded.

The police, hard pressed to restore order and disarm klansmen, were confronted with many individuals firing at various points indiscriminately, as bullets ricocheted off stones of the area as people ran scrambling for cover. The gunman, concealed and firing an automatic weapon, waited until the moment when the ten-foot-high cross leaped into flames before opening fire. Some thought that the gunfire was the jubilant expression of celebration among those in the crowd of more than two hundred upon seeing the flames leap up into the night sky. It soon became clear, as the gunman began yelling, that people were being fired upon and injured, among them the Grand Dragon and other robed officials, all of whom were killed.

After a while the wailings of many sirens were heard, as police reinforcements arrived. When the gunfire finally ceased, at the instigation of the police, who themselves had been forced to take cover, the bodies of the victims were examined until that of the gunman was found. Lying bleeding from head and chest wounds, Kavanaugh was still alive when discovered behind two boulder-size rocks in a litter of spent shells. Kavanaugh reportedly gasped, as he lay dying, "This is for King," apparently referring to the recent assassination of Dr. Martin Luther King, Jr., "and all the other black people murdered. How many of you **** did I get? I hope plenty!" With those words the gunman reportedly ceased talking and died.

Kavanaugh is reported to have worked as a U.S. Postal Clerk for the last three years. He was described as hard-working and friendly, but someone who kept to himself. He had been a student at one of the historic Negro institutions but had dropped out. Gunman was the product of a respected and prominent middle-class Negro family of Philadelphia, son of A. M. E. Bishop Rev. Dr. Edward W. Kavanaugh, Jr., and Irene Marshall Kavanaugh. Gunman had given no indication of anger or violent intentions before this incident.

Kavanaugh's fair skin had enabled him to approach the scene without arousing suspicion. A duffel bag, like that used by campers, was found near the body, in which apparently had been concealed the assault rifle and ammunition. Much anger was expressed afterwards regarding the incident by those present, with talk of revenge and race war. After concerted effort the police were able to secure Kavanaugh's body and prevent it from being the object of attack by angry spectators, many of whom were hysterical in their reaction.

I read this with a mixture of shock and pride. In his extreme way Ed had given up his life in opposition to what he loathed and in defense of what he believed, may his soul rest in peace. I wanted to hug him, bless him, and didn't feel in the least sorry for those he had killed, murdered. He had gone all the way, and he had been efficient in doing it! Too bad he hadn't killed all of them. At least he had taken out the murderous, loony officiating goons with the hoods over their heads. I noticed that, even as I was laughing, tears were flowing down my cheeks. He had done what he'd said we ought to do, to defend ourselves and retaliate, to get revenge. When the phone rang I knew it was Derek, so I went to get it.

I could hear the intense excitement in his voice: "That was Ed all right! Took out those sons-of-bitches. We need to go to the funeral."

"Yeah. I'll call them in Philadelphia and try to find out when it is."

"Let me know. We should go."

"Yeah."

"Here's where you'd want to hope even King wouldn't be disapproving," Derek said.

"Just look the other way this time?"

"Yeah, and let those bastards go straight to hell."

"Ed said hell was a lost cause."

"Looks like he took the matter into his own hands." We laughed, but we were crying. Later that morning I called Bishop Kavanaugh's residence in Philadelphia, which was listed in the phone book. A female voice answered and said that the

Kavanaughs were not available at this time but would be glad to return my call if I'd be so kind as to leave my name and number. I did. Two days later I received a call from Ed's mother, Irene Kavanaugh, who apologized for the delay in returning my call, saying she was sure that I could understand considering the disruption in their lives. She said how fortuitous it was that I had called, since Ed had left a letter for a Chris Hinson, and she had assumed that the Chris Hinson who had called must be he. Perhaps I would like to come get it? Also, Ed had left a will and he had mentioned me in it. They had been thinking of calling the school to get my address, but now this was unnecessary. I said I'd be glad to come, and another friend and I wanted to attend the funeral. That would occur tomorrow, she said, a private ceremony, and they would be glad to have us. Ed had requested to be cremated, she said. I thanked her. I called Derek. If we left that night we could arrive in Philadelphia early in the morning, so we agreed to do it, buying round trip train tickets.

When we arrived that morning we took a taxi to the Kavanaughs' residence, a brick structure next to the church. "This is called the City of Brotherly Love," said Derek. "You know why?" I shook my head. "Neither do I, but I bet it's something we ought to know." The taxi driver, an aging white man with a red face and gruff voice, leaned back and said, "It's because of the Quakers, brotherly love, which we could use some." We agreed. When we stepped out of the taxi and went up to ring the bell, we were let in through an antechamber where we waited in a sunlit room. Other people were also in there. Soon, a regal-looking, fair-skinned black woman came in and took both our hands, introducing herself as Ed's mother. The service would be next door, she said, at ten. Let me show you where you can leave your things and freshen up, she said. Indicating the others present, she introduced Derek and me as Ed's school friends and presented us to Ed's cousins, childhood friends, and grandparents, apparently two

299

sets of them, both sets aged but intact, who nodded, and you could tell which were which by their skin color. We were led to separate rooms, where we both showered, shaved, and put on fresh clothing. When we came back down it was 9:30, and we were led in an entourage through a door into the chapel. It was three-fourths filled with people, and we took our seats near the front. Soon the parents, grandparents, and others were led in to seats in the front. The lady who had greeted Derek and me, Mrs. Kavanaugh, had been walking next to a tall, large-bodied, dark-skinned man who had been holding her arm, obviously Ed's father, to whom Ed bore resemblance.

The organ had been playing and the choir was in place. On the platform were a robed minister and two other individuals, including a very pretty young woman. The program in my hand read Memorial Service for Edward W. Kavanaugh, III, April 21, 1968, 10:00 a.m., Bethel A.M.E. Church. Interment in Private Ceremony at Greenwood Cemetery. There would be a processional (which had just occurred), a hymn sung by the choir, a responsive reading of a psalm with the reader and audience participating, a reading from scripture, reflections (with audience participation), acknowledgment of telegrams, condolences, and flowers, an organ solo, a eulogy, and the recessional. Things progressed just as I had remembered them at my father's funeral, except that I had been up front in a cloud of grief. Now my head was perfectly clear, even if the tears just kept silently flowing down my cheeks. When the responsive reading came it was read by the lovely young woman whose sweet voice compelled me to respond in kind, rousing me from my reverie. I thought that it also sounded like the voice I'd first heard on the telephone. There were quite a few acknowledgments of condolences, I imagined, because of the Kavanaugh family's prominence. Then one of the other two people on the platform got up and began speaking of Ed as a child, student, and young man he had known from the time he was born until he went off to college. I learned that Ed had been dutiful, hard-working, and smart, a paper boy to earn his own money, an Eagle Scout, class valedictorian, a boy soprano in that very choir in the back, before his voice started changing and they put him in the tenors. He never gave anybody any trouble, and he filled everyone with the pride of someone destined to succeed. He said that this was the Ed he had known. Then some family members spoke, with concluding comments by his father; and when they finished the general audience was invited to come up and speak of the Ed they knew. I could feel Derek stirring and knew that he was going to get up immediately. He went up and said, with a kind of fierceness, that Ed was one of the smartest persons he had known. Perhaps many of us, he said, would not condone his action, and maybe it shouldn't be condoned. He was not there to judge, but for him Ed had taken his stand against evil, and he was sure that that is what Ed would have thought people needed to do if they wanted to be good men or even if they wanted to do the right things approved of by God. He withdrew his intense gaze from the audience, turned and went back to his seat. They might have agreed with such problematic statements, but the saying of them might also have left them feeling uneasy.

In the silence that ensued I knew that I must speak now or never. I went up and smiled at the audience, hoping that I would not begin to cry again. Ed may have been one of the smartest, I said, but to me he was also the gentlest, which was why he was so hurt by injustice in the world. Sometimes it's the gentlest who are the fiercest because they feel so deeply the world's cruelty and don't know what they can do to stop it. I said that I would just like to say this, since it was not the way people usually thought about someone who did what Ed had done. I smiled again, and somebody said, "Amen!" and I made my way back to my seat. A few other people came up, until all had been satisfied in giving expression to what they'd had to say. When finally the recessional came, Derek and I found ourselves part of a procession following the chief mourners out the front door. On the steps outside and on the sidewalk, people came to a standstill and engaged in an exchange of hugs and condolences. People shook my and Derek's hands and thanked us. Also, when we had emerged from the church, raised photographers' cameras had captured us.

Later, inside, waiting again in the large sunny room, we were summoned to another room down the hall. We went in to meet Dr. Kavanaugh, his wife, the grandparents, and other family members. They all were sitting in leather easy chairs around a table, at which Kavanaugh sat, his wife next to him. Bottles of white wine and glasses had been provided, and Mrs. Kavanaugh nursed her glass in her hands.

"Chris Hinson and Dr. Derek Johnson," he said. "We appreciate your being with us today."

"You knew him, you knew our boy," she said.

"We were close, until he left," I said.

"First, he left you this." Kavanaugh handed me a letter. "Which you may read now if you wish." I opened it and read:

April 16, 1968

Chris,

Thanks for being there. You did what you had to do and so did I. No hard feelings.

Ed

P.S. If you wondered how I did it, I took my weapon into the woods, into the Georgia pines, and practiced shooting at dead trees. I found out how to get it through the mail. I worked, as you've probably heard, in the post office.

Peace.

"It's short," I said. "He's thanking me for something we did together once."

"Second," said Kavanaugh, "he left you $3,000 of his own money, saying you'd know what to do with it—you'll hear further about this from our lawyer."

"I think he'd like me to give it to the school, for scholarships."

"I hope he was happy there," he said.

"I think so."

"You know he turned down Harvard and went *there*, to Nashville," she said.

"I know."

"Always had a mind of his own," Kavanaugh said. "He left and went to work in a post office."

"I'll never understand that," she said.

"Maybe you can help us understand it," he said.

"I don't know," I said. "He was a complex person."

"And then to go murder those people, foul as they are," Kavanaugh said.

She said, in a quivering voice, "He couldn't hope to get away from there."

"No!" said Derek.

"No!" she cried. She burst into tears.

Kavanaugh waited until her crying subsided. "He has been cremated. We agreed to his wish to be buried elsewhere, not in the cemetery. If you'd like to come to the ceremony, you can."

"We would like that," I said.

"Then we'll be leaving soon. It's about an hour's drive from here, a place in the country."

We drove out of the city and into farm country, a rural area of back roads and lovely countryside, and when we pulled off a road and climbed a little hill, I could see the scene, the sun rising, as Ed had described it; and there at the left was an apple tree, and in the back a barn. The undertaker's men were already there, standing with their hands clasped behind their backs, as if providing black-coated fortification for whatever the action was that was about to take place. The same minister who had officiated earlier was standing next to them.

The minister stepped forward into our midst and said a few words. He turned then and received an urn from the undertaker and stood holding it. Kavanaugh then approached and the

303

minister gave the urn to him. Holding up the urn, he said that perhaps we would like to hear Ed's last wishes: "Reduce me to powder, to my elements, and scatter me back into the universe where I came from. Do it on this site, where I was happy."

Kavanaugh then reached in, took a handful and forcefully scattered it. Mrs. Kavanaugh came, looked at her husband, and then into the urn, staring. She extended a finger into the bowl, withdrew it and put it to her lips. Then she reached in both hands, one after the other, and vigorously, perhaps, it seemed, exuberantly, flung away the powdery substance. It looked a hazy something with bits that both wafted and fell. Then the rest of us took turns doing the same with what was left in the urn, some people agreeing to do so almost fearfully, some declining to do so. Afterwards, we did not know what to do with our hands, as if nothing further could be touched with them. In his closing words, the minister was aware of this, and raising his palms, led us with a clasping of hands.

We were silent almost all the way back home that night. We arrived in Atlanta in the morning, awakening from slumber.

"I'm so glad we went," Derek said.

"Yes."

"They seem like they have no clue of the deep shit Ed was in," Derek suggested.

"Do parents ever?"

"Yeah, I think they do. Did you understand what was bothering him?"

I was surprised that Derek could ask that. I said, "How have we survived so long being so despised? Subordinate, secondary, always?" Derek didn't say anything, and I knew he knew what I meant. When I arrived home there was no one there, but on the kitchen table was spread out a page of the newspaper. It was a photo of people coming out of a church, and the caption underneath read, "Mourners at memorial service for Klan gunman." I looked and saw myself and Derek just as we had appeared coming out of the church.

THIRTEEN

In the middle of May I received a card in the mail sent by a gallery announcing the showing of some work by Tina Shepherd Johnson and other painters. I certainly would be going and would take Miriam with me, on the Saturday afternoon of its opening. The two of us were almost deliriously happy about the coming to an end of the school year and our readiness to leave for New York. When we arrived the place was half-filled with people, standing, conversing, viewing the work of the three painters, drinking the wine and eating the fruit, cheese, and crackers that had been provided. Immediately I spotted Derek and was welcomed by him, who was wearing a lighter-brown version of his corduroy sports coat, so that the material looked almost like suede, and he sported a typical bow tie of red, green, and gray. He came to me and took possession of us, introducing us to Tina's parents, to Melissa, who was as excited as a fairy, moving about, to his other friends, to the two other painters. He was completely happy, and I could see why. Tina too was happy, was productive, and was also pregnant—his child was coming; and he had just finished his first year at medical school. For a while he played the guide for Miriam and me, in his amicable way, as we reviewed some of the paintings. We were led to Tina's work first, most striking of which was a painting of two women, black and white, looking at each other. I stared at the painting, as if reminded of something I couldn't place. Miriam and I looked at each other, struck by it. We discussed it briefly then moved on to the next. When I saw my opportunity to talk to Tina, I excused myself, pleased that Derek was so entertaining with Miriam. When I went to Tina I saw the extent to which she was pregnant.

"I see you've been busy."

"I can do what he wants and what I want too."

"Nice paintings."

"I think one brought about the other."

"When is it due?"

"In July, and it better be a boy. I haven't been sick at all; the little morning sickness I had passed quickly. I feel better than I've ever felt in my life, and I love my job. It'll be interesting to see what happens after the child comes, though my mom will love to baby sit." I had to admit, as soon as I saw her, that she looked the picture of health, almost exuberant, as if the hormones coursing through her body had plugged her into the life source. Her skin was supple, glowing, as if she were giving off light.

"I like your work," and as I said this something came to life in my head about one of the paintings. I smiled at her, and I could see that she was smiling back at me. "The painting of the two women. Am I wrong in seeing a resemblance to someone?"

"Maybe someone riding in a blue car with someone else we know, down Auburn Avenue?—more than once."

"And the other one?"

"Someone who works in a grocery store?"

"But how?"

"She was a student of Derek's. Imagine how surprised she was to hear he too was applying to medical school. He went to Fisk. *She* knew someone who went to Fisk. He had her over for dinner. I talked to her. I could tell."

"That painting is mine. I want it."

She told me its price. "Talk to that lady," and she pointed to a woman sitting at a table.

"A bargain, Tina." We looked back in its direction and saw Sarah looking at it. "Sarah's here!" I said.

"Back from Northwestern. When she comes over I'm sure you'll have lots to *say*."

"You've already said it." We looked back at the painting and saw Sarah coming. She greeted Tina who excused herself.

"I see you brought SWB with you." She smiled.

"Her name is Miriam."

"I thought so. And you're Itzhak …"

"No, Alistair."

"Of course. And I'm *Clarissa*"—we stared at each other—"your sweetheart." She kept her smile. "Since you're so busy, I brought myself. Actually, I have someone to take me. He's into being a surgeon. Neurologist. So many of our folks die of strokes, he says. Eating that greasy fried chicken and fries. Smart and reliable he is. But no one will have your heavy and lightness."

"A paperweight."

"Flighty and grave."

"A letter opener."

"Piercer of parts, I mean hearts." She smiled. "She got any humor in her?"

"Yes."

"She understands you?"

"I think so."

"What you're really like? How scared are you? How brave?"

"Here she comes. You can ask her." Miriam arrived and I introduced the two of them.

"What did you think of that painting?" asked Sarah.

Miriam seemed completely happy and unself-conscious: "The two women? I liked it. They seemed to be looking at each other or into each other, but you can't be sure."

"Maybe looking so hard that they're looking past each other," I said.

307

"Or maybe two versions of looking that are the same, they just don't know it," said Sarah. "They can never know it because they can't see it."

"You mean a third party makes it complete?" said Miriam.

Sarah said, "Yes, that's why I think they seem to be looking past each other as well as into empty space, and that's why *we're* here to say what they might be thinking."

"Instead of their looking at each other and indicating what they think?" I said.

"That too, but not just that," Sarah said. "Many things are being reflected, what they think, what we think."

"That's why it's called *Correspondences*," said Miriam.

"So what are they thinking," I asked.

"History is always present," said Sarah.

"Couldn't it be I Speak My History and You Speak of Yours?" said Miriam.

"I *am* my history and you are *yours*, I think," said Sarah. "I don't know if they're really communicating anything to each other, so much as just being there."

"That's what I mean, My Presence Speaks Regardless," said Miriam. I saw how she had something of the same look she'd had after our discussion at the beach last summer.

"But are they aware of that, or are only we?" said Sarah.

"You going to ask the painter?" I said.

"It's almost better not to know," said Sarah.

"Yes," said Miriam. "The meaning is our talking about it, and I've enjoyed talking to you."

"Actually so have I. Maybe we're like the painting, except we're talking. Excuse me, it was nice meeting you. I see Tina is sort of free and I want to go over." She left.

"That was interesting," she said.

"Did you notice anything about the painting?"

"What?"

"Anything familiar looking?" We went to look at it again.

"I don't see anything."

"Does the black woman look like Sarah?"

"Well, actually, sort of!"

"What about the white woman?" She stared.

"Who?"

"You."

"Me! How can that be?"

"The painter is clairvoyant."

"What?"

"She knows of the two of you, and me."

"Sarah and you?"

"And you and me. She saw us riding in the car."

"Gee-whiz! We were sort of talking about ourselves. Does she know?"

"I doubt it."

"Good grief!"

"Yeah."

"You should buy it, before somebody else does."

"I am. As soon as I figure out how. I could charge it, but that would be over my limit."

"We could go half and half."

"It could probably take that."

"Let's do it."

"If they'll do it."

We were able to purchase it. It would be packaged and ready for me to pick up in two weeks. One week later we were in our apartment packing up getting ready to leave. We had just returned from a gynecologist's office recommended by Julia whom Miriam had wanted to see, saying there was something she wanted to check on, but afterwards had nothing further to say when she returned. Leaving Atlanta this time was difficult. First, Miriam had to precede me in order to check on a part-time job and to try to get an apartment. Second, the painting wasn't ready yet, and in any case I had pledged myself for two weeks to work with Mordecai on a new job. I would take a summer language course at Columbia, but that did not begin until the last week in June. It was another bright spring day with sunlight streaming in. I could see how bare and plain our place had been, and yet how happy we'd been in it. Had we been living a real life there or substitute playacting? She was actually humming as she took her few garments out of the closet. If this is what passed as living a conjugal life we had done just fine at it. Why couldn't we just continue doing in New York what we'd been doing here? We'd both be students, at least I thought that Miriam still intended to follow through on her NYU enrollment. We'd seen in *Time* magazine and on TV the pictures of the protesting students, the occupation of buildings at Columbia, and the arrival of the police, it seemed, in the thousands, in riot gear, who advanced on the students with their clubs raised, breaking heads. There were lots of shocked white kids, now feeling justified in calling the cops pigs, or was it bulls.

The last night of our stay in the apartment we were watching our fifteen inch TV, something we seldom did except for the news and programs on PBS. On the toss of a coin it was decided that she would take the TV set with her. President Johnson had earlier decided not to seek reelection, and Robert Kennedy seemed now to have a clear trajectory toward the White House. When the news program we were watching was preempted by even more pressing news coverage, we were primed to be confronted with some new disaster, and we were not disappointed, hearing now of a second Kennedy being shot as he crossed a ballroom floor mingling with supporters. We sat and watched in numbness, the assault again upon what we took to be the good, the flickering of the flame of the latest standard-bearer of some notion of civilized, humane discourse, and social justice, a man who maybe still had his soul, or might not resist an appeal made to having one, who would help stop the exploiting of the weak and the helpless if he could. Kennedy lingered, but we did not expect him to live.

The next day Miriam had to leave. We were at my sister's house when Miriam said goodbye to the family. She told them that she also felt one of the family, and seeing her drive off I felt as if I were saying goodbye to my wife. When Miriam arrived in New York she lived first with a friend, then in a rooming house. I met her at my last roommate's apartment, where I lived briefly, after driving up from Atlanta. While I took a morning German class at Columbia, Miriam took an occupational breather, not having any classes yet, but intrigued by and working on occasion with the news media, at the moment with an alternative agency, the Liberation News Service, as a reporter, and I accompanied her once to a gathering featuring the Black Panther Party at the Columbia Sundial.

When September came we still had not found a new place to live together, but yet we'd have to move; so we made plans to live separately, temporarily, if we couldn't find a suitable space together. In addition, Miriam wanted to live downtown in the Village while I wanted to continue living uptown near Columbia. I was surprised we had not posed more resistance to separating. Though she was not receptive to the idea of our living apart, she acquiesced, as if this was a means of working out the larger plan of our eventual cohabitation. Was this a reluctance to give up a last vestige of independence, or the fear of protesting at separating being taken as a sign of neediness? Was there still remaining something in me—maybe in her too—that wanted to reserve the right one last time to do other things?

Soon the apartment listings in *The New York Times* and the Columbia Registry of Off-Campus Accommodations became constant sources of reference to me. Miriam located an apartment before I did, finding a suitable building in the East Village and being first in line at the realtor's office one Monday morning, but I did not join her in her place, and my search for a space near Columbia was much more difficult.

Arriving early at a lovely brownstone advertised in *The Times* on West 102nd Street off Broadway, I was delighted to see no one else around and made my rush for the super. He was unavailable, though a rather too respectable-looking man sweeping the sidewalk said that I should wait, since the super would soon arrive. I waited until five p.m., watching our little group gather in number. Finally there were about twenty of us. Suddenly we saw a well-dressed couple approach accompanied by none other than the man I'd seen sweeping the sidewalk that morning. He turned out to be their agent and looked at me and right through me as he approached. We were left to wait some more in the hall.

Presently a voice—the agent's—inquired loudly, and a little defensively, who had been first. I volunteered immediately. He asked again, against a lengthening silence. I answered again the same. It was clear that he didn't want to accept this evidence, so the wife of the couple—tall and imposing—suggested that, for a start, the first two people should go up. A young girl and I went up to see a beautiful studio on the third floor, abundantly furnished, with French windows facing the street and the sun. "I'll take it!" I cried. This claim, however, was ignored. We were commanded to give relevant information about ourselves and our income, as were all the others, and then asked to leave. We would be notified. At the top of the sheet was the couple's own identifying information, Richards Realty (Broderick and Lynette).

After waiting until all of the others had left, I approached the owners, having become more fully aware of the enormity of my innocence. I suggested that I had been first, that I was a graduate student with a fellowship, that I had a job as well (in the library), and that my relatives weren't poverty-stricken. I told them how perfect it was for me and how close to school so that I could walk to class. The woman, who did most of the talking, kept her face at an angle, as if she wished to look elsewhere; I could see that the man seemed on my side, but he no longer looked in my direction. I then began the moral appeal: They were, after all, obligated to a sense of fair play by their own admission; it was so easy for them to do this simple thing which was so important to me; I lived a straight and clean-cut life and was going to take my PhD degree. It had all come out without my having thought about what I would say.

This led to a slight effect on the woman. She softened her piercing look enough to say, civilly, that the agent or super or whatever he was would call. But I knew he wouldn't, and knowing this I found I had to speak the whole truth, and this time I was thinking what to say, and maybe I was a little bit extreme. That she did not respect me, I said, was no matter, because what I was didn't depend on her valuation; I cared equally little for her, too, and she would not be in a privileged position forever; one day when I would be working for some agency like the Human Rights Commission, I'd see to it that they continuously came down hard on people like them. After this, for a frigid moment, we were all three of us aghast. Then, turning simultaneously on our heels, we walked away. That they and I were both walking in the same direction seemed the final indignity. Fortunately my car was only two or three car lengths away, where Miriam sat, having come to join me, innocently watching as we approached. And yet, less than a week later, I *did* get a call from the agent, who seemed surprised to get an answer. Indeed, he had seemed surprised, when I had given him my number, that I should have a phone at all, but surely that was too incredible. Now, here he was on the phone, obviously agonizing over the decision he was trying to make. He inquired again, very intensely, into my financial arrangements. I could only repeat what he already knew. Perhaps if I'd told him any new thing, that I would be making $10 an hour at the library, that my father was an insurance executive in Florida (he had been!), he would have accepted my word for it and given me the apartment. I refused to do this, and the super hung up, it seemed to me, reluctantly, and I heard from them no more. Just

313

to satisfy my curiosity, I called the Human Rights Commission and was told that landlords have the right to require that the rent not exceed one-fourth of the tenant's income (it didn't); but could I prove a malicious intent of deliberate discrimination? I supposed that I couldn't.

Miriam moved into her East Village apartment and I stayed with my roommate. Visiting Miriam one night, the misfortune befell me of having my car stolen, with many of my books and irreplaceable personal belongings still in the trunk. When I'd left it on the street I'd had a premonition about this, so that when I reached the corner I'd been prompted to look back at it, to see if it was still there, with its out-of-state license plate. When I returned the next morning and saw that it wasn't there, it was almost as if I wasn't surprised. I went around the block to a similar spot on the street above and below this one. I came back and stood standing at the vehicle occupying the space where mine had been. I wanted to cry. I saw the pain in Miriam's eye in her hope that I wouldn't blame her for the incident. That hurt me almost as much as the car's loss; I had told her about what the car—and Shell—meant to me. We went to the Ninth Precinct House around the corner. The officer there told us that 90 per cent of the cars stolen in New York were recovered. I didn't believe this, never thinking that mine would be recovered. I viewed that as a profoundly untrustworthy statement, feeling it is the 90 per cent which one sees on the streets, many of them with their license plates intact, where they sit abandoned, a little bed of trash surrounding them. The patrol cars cruise right by them, the slouched figures inside averting their eyes, just as everyone else does. I had been badly shaken by this event. Strangely, it was merged in my mind with the view of a Hispanic man inside a wire mesh cage inside the precinct house, whose eyes just looked at us and followed us the whole time we were there. Was this what was referred to as the pen? The man inside a human animal?

Our misfortune continued. A few days later I had to come down to the Village to comfort Miriam after someone had heaved a brick, with unerring accuracy, directly through her window, from the roof of a building across the street. We examined the object, without touching it, dumbfounded by what we saw, a red ribbon tied around it, the bow still crisp. Miriam had glimpsed the person and described him to the attending officers as a tall man with shaggy red hair and beard. Might there not be fingerprints on the brick? The officers were not impressed, though they did get a laugh out of the ribbon. "The guy's throwing you a valentine," one said. We wondered if the red-haired man was taking it out on the two of us, and was reading books from my car's trunk in the mornings, riding in my Chevy in the afternoons, and sitting at night in his darkened apartment across the street looking into Miriam's lighted one—whose windows I'm sure I had paraded past with nothing on more than once. It was frightening to her. She trembled to think of the man's eye on her, somewhere, thinking his thoughts. She put up shades and kept them down all day and night. Then, changing her mind, she raised the shades back up again in the daytime, since she hated succumbing to such fear. It was depressing, but the desire of raising them up again was stronger than the elusive sense of safety secured by lowering the shades and enduring such curtailment of her life. It all was having a very bad effect on her, compounded by our separation. Sometimes at night when I had come to visit we lay on her mattress on the floor, but on occasion she did not want to be touched.

She had been reading Doris Lessing's *The Golden Notebook*—and engaging in other feminist consciousness-raising activities in women's groups—and had been soliciting my agreement, or imposing her desire upon me, to lie together, refraining from intercourse, and only touch, or not even that, but simply to be two engaged figures, lying together, experiencing what that felt like. This was sometimes interesting, but often it seemed a way for her to make me accept that she had a right not even to be touched, if she didn't want to be. Of course, this was so. Sometimes she really *didn't* want to be touched. However, all this sometimes also felt doctrinaire, an exercise, such that I was sure that it wasn't true that she didn't want me to touch her, but, rather, that she wanted to have, at my expense, the experience of seeing what it was like to not be touched—the two bodies lying, nevertheless, side by side—because she thought she ought to have such an experience. I wondered also if it was a counter-response to what she might have thought was my exercising of the fabled right of male assertion when I had come into her room that night at Julia's house.

Lying next to her naked body, looking furtively at it, its suppleness, ineffable, like a *formula* for the indescribable, I thought that there were three things you could do: admire or observe it; seek intimate contact with it; possess it; and that these three things constituted desire. I felt constrained to try to comply with her request, since to object would betray all the self-serving tendencies of male sexual egotism that we were pretending to deny and rise above, even as we engaged in what I felt was a new kind of coercive ritual. Nevertheless I held my peace, got up around midnight, dutifully kissed her, and went back uptown. I was angry about this, but questioned the legitimacy of my feelings. None of this was good, like a slowly accruing alienation that we did not want to look at, a substitute for things more fundamental that we couldn't face, like explaining why we allowed ourselves to live apart.

I acquired an apartment in the middle of October, desperate and disposed to accept almost any halfway suitable thing. I got a one and a half on West 107th Street, a room ten by thirty feet, from which one went through an archway into a small back room, closeting a range, sink, and refrigerator, and farther in the rear I opened a door to what first seemed like a real closet and found a bath. One large window looked onto the street, but there was no sunlight. I was not unhappy there since

I had always thought of the place as temporary. The landlord allowed I might move out when I desired, he himself seemingly a little ashamed of the rent he was charging. I did not feel claustrophobic, and felt it even less when Miriam was present. In this room I would at least write my master's thesis and get anchored in my quest for the PhD.

One day I got a call from Miriam saying that Howard was in town giving a paper at a conference, and he had showed up at her apartment asking to stay with her. "Just so you know that he asked me, and I sent him to you," she said. I thought of the something she had wanted to tell me that time she'd visited the gynecologist in Atlanta and had then refrained from speaking. Something involving herself and Howard? She must have had some feeling for his being alone in their outpost of progress. I didn't know what to think about this beyond the recognition that I understood it. Howard didn't contact me for lodging at my place. For Thanksgiving I had dinner at Miriam's apartment. She had cooked a small turkey and we had a big meal, happy being together but not exuberant. She remembered the wishbone and wanted to try it. I told her, "Remember, each wishes that both get their wish." When we pulled she lost again, but with a look of defeat or sadness, unlike her look with Michael. I knew what she had wished for, and I had wished it too, but I didn't tell her this. She had a new cat, whom she'd named Catsky—I laughed, and told her of my cat named Cat—but her cat had a penchant for depositing in the bathtub instead of the litter box. She appreciated my suggestion that she keep water in the tub. I sat with her as we did some yoga poses, and her mood greatly improved. I spoke of my job in the library at Columbia and she of life at NYU. When I went home that night I took packets of turkey, cranberry sauce, and dressing that she had wrapped for me.

As the school year progressed, I had time to think about some of the things that occurred in the life of the city, in my neighborhood, that were new to me. Coming home one day from a dreary class, I saw people standing outside the building perfectly still in silent anticipation, looking up the street. I stopped to look round and could see nothing. Later, one of the women across the hall explained that it was "mother's day." It was a time near a holiday and people were especially anxious. There were instances of stolen welfare checks in this building, and I began to be watchful myself lest someone should lift my monthly fellowship stipend.

Walking to school one cold morning I had a momentary feeling of emptiness, as of an endless routine to be endured. But I knew perfectly well why I was enduring it. I cast my eye at Alma Mater, on my way to Philosophy Hall, and noticed how the bronze folds of her garment settled so demurely in her lap. She sat contented, yet forever expectant.

When I walked the campus I was in a sea of whiteness, what looked like Jews, then WASPS, or members of white ethnic groups (some appeared to be hardscrabble working class) and Asians and Indians. Aside from one other black person, whom I seldom saw, I was the only black in my area of specialization, contemporary British and American literature, with a minor concentration in seventeenth-century English literature, though there were blacks in other areas of specialization, and I'd seen one, a black girl, Phyllis, who'd come in a year ahead of me. Among the thousands walking across the campus the eyes of the blacks would, somehow, furtively, meet, assess each other, or greet, and go on our way. I had an Anglo-Saxon class with Phyllis that she had been putting off taking. The students were to give some evidence of understanding Anglo-Saxon by being able to read certain works written in it, but half of the class was never in attendance since attendance was not mandatory. Some of the works were wonderful in translation. I particularly liked Ezra Pound's "muscular" rendering of "The Dream of the Rood," in which the Cross speaks of the experience of having had Christ's body on it. I had simply planned to memorize all of the poems so that whichever ones appeared on the examination I'd know, instead of actually reading them in Anglo-Saxon, which only a handful seemed willing and able to do. It was hard to say why I just as well could have learned Anglo-Saxon, and didn't.

Phyllis said that the whole thing was ridiculous, but since it couldn't be avoided she wanted someone to study with. When she invited me to be her study mate I accepted. When I went to her apartment, she let me into a small cozy space at 113th Street and Broadway. She was barefoot, wearing shorts and a bra-less top. She said it was refreshing to see some black guys who knew how to study, instead of keeping themselves locked up in their rooms like the white boys did, and then do nothing but go out and drink beer into a stupor afterwards. She had spread out all the material on the bed and looked at me, then got back into it. I decided to go look at the material, so I took off my shoes and got into bed with her.

One day I returned home to find my place broken into, the door, opened to a crack, greeting me as I approached it, a sinking feeling in my stomach—stereo, a small radio, typewriter, and some clothes stolen. At least the records, which were more valuable to me than the things taken, were untouched. I felt the break-in was due to my own negligence. I had been away overnight at Miriam's and had left a rear window open—a window with a locked gate before it. The thieves had reached through the open window—after they'd come down through a narrow air shaft—and bent ends of the gate forward to make a space large enough to crawl through. It just seemed that this would have required great strength and determination. But the hole was still so small that only an exceedingly slender adult—or a child—could have come through. I had a jar of unopened hard rock candy that my mother had sent in one of her Christmas packages. There were half-sucked pieces of candy strewn about and the jar was half empty.

I felt the need to move again, and I didn't want to move down to the Village to be taken in by Miriam. So I became once more one of the peripatetic figures in and out of the Columbia off-campus housing office. They did not announce when new listings were put up. I simply had to come in each day and see. Consulting a listing only a few hours old could often be bad news, so many students stood outside the office and waited. I was more lucky than usual, and in a few tries made my claim on a new place, through a broker who handled the deal. It was a breezy place off Riverside Drive in the 140s.

I was shown the place by the landlord's chief workman, a Puerto Rican all-purpose handyman covered at the time in paint. His name was Angelo; he was fond of song and revealed himself to be a great lover. Angelo advised me to take the place, since it was one of the nicest in the building and could be really great once it was fixed up. Other people had seen it, and the rent was low.

The broker assured me that the place would be mine and arranged a meeting with the landlord, whose office was in the same block. The landlord arrived exclaiming how easily he'd found a parking space. This was good luck for one of us from the start, he said. He examined the papers. The broker had raised my income, and I had agreed to have a subtenant, which allowed the landlord an additional increase, along with the new equipment and "improvements" which were being made. The landlord took out his pipe, slowly and deliberately lit it, cast a pleasant look at me, and said that I must paint the place or share the cost of having it done. This seemed outrageous so I refused. The landlord did not immediately answer, having become interested in the information about the subtenant, disliking the fact that the subtenant worked for the welfare department (I had given my roommate's name, who did). He was further upset when he discovered that though I was a student, I might be in the place a while, might even finish up an advanced degree, get a job and live there. He wanted students because they'd come and go, giving him a fast turnover. Welfare workers were subversive, would perhaps fill his buildings with clients, or incite any who might already be in them to some kind of action.

The landlord then broke off with me and began speaking to the broker with complete equanimity, in Yiddish, as if I weren't even present. Since I knew German, and they were talking in such a relaxed fashion, I was able to understand some of what transpired. The landlord was concerned about my being there too long. Suppose he married; they would not be getting the right return on their money. And about that welfare worker— that would be trouble. This was puzzling since I had thought that we all understood there would be no real subtenant. The broker, to my surprise, was arguing in my favor. He liked me, said I was a nice guy. I supposed he'd rather get his money from someone he liked than from someone he didn't. They finished chatting and the landlord got up and walked out, without a word. When I asked the broker what had been said, he replied that the landlord wanted to think it over some more and see what could be done about the painting.

I rode home on the subway and sat in my cubicle again, fuming, so I called the landlord. To my surprise, he was perfectly agreeable. He suggested that once I understood that I, like all other tenants, existed at his sufferance, everything would be all right. He told me that the place was mine but I'd still have to paint it. Paint would be supplied. "And brushes?" I asked. "Everything you need," he replied. I moved in with the help of Miriam and her car. I was approached later by Angelo, offering an appraisal of Miriam: "I like that you had with you yesterday," he said. "Real nice." His judgments were always definitive. One day while painting in the hall, he was greeted by a female tenant. "Angelo! You're working too hard," she said. "I work hardest with you in bed," he retorted.

My relations with the landlord underwent a change. The final development came one day when Miriam was over helping me paint. The door was open, and when the landlord knocked and entered, I greeted him in German, and I then

321

introduced *meine Freundin* to him. He just smiled, a glint in his eye. Then he asked her, "So you go to Columbia too?" Since that encounter, the landlord has treated me with only the greatest courtesy.

I had finally finished the painting of the place and the varnishing of floors, cleaning up the mess the workmen had left behind. My tub and sink were filled with old plaster which had been scraped off the ceilings and walls. The drain was stopped, and when the plumber came he applied his acid, used the plunger, and then just shook his head. "That is really bad. I'll have to go get the snake," which I knew to mean the flexible metal device that was forced directly down the drain. I could see that there were some things you would just have to accept. I walked down to Riverside Drive to stand at the railing or sit and watch the Hudson. The people were interesting to look at, especially the children, who were already full of the aggressive preoccupations that give character to New York City life.

I got up and went back to my building. As I approached I saw pages of a pornographic magazine, *Screw*, that had been taken out of the garbage cans and scattered around, offering a glimpse of what first looked like body parts or truncated torsos that wrenched the eye in their direction, until the scene resolved into a recognition of women's bodies in various postures of display, contorted, reclining, splayed. I imagined this to be the work of Angelo or his workmen, or else some garbage can scavenger. And I knew the magazines had (*probably*) come from the three girls from Columbia on the top floor. I knew which apartment they were in because I had seen it and rejected it for the one I was in. Theirs was much larger and, though full of sunlight, too big for me, and up five elevator-less flights. They came and went, just as I did, and I'd often pass them. The eyes of one of them would always catch mine as we passed. I knew her name was Jenny because I'd heard the others call her so. I'd seen on occasion the magazines, and other counterculture publications, along with their schoolbooks, under their arms. The girls chatted with the other residents, blacks and Hispanics, and sometimes brought home bearded young men who looked like they'd be going camping, with their plaid hunting shirts and thick-soled yellow working boots. Jenny was blue-eyed and blonde but kind of rough looking, as if the acne or the skin problem, perhaps eczema, she had was a metaphor for some kind of unhappiness that had blemished her life, casting a pall over her prettiness. "You're the one playing the opera," she said once when we were at the mailboxes.

"Probably," I said.

"I never liked it, but some of that sounded sweet, like a Joni Mitchell or Nancy Wilson song."

"You can come down and listen sometimes if you want," I said, having a strong idea of exactly what I was getting myself into.

"Thanks. Maybe I will."

A week or two later, one Saturday afternoon as I was again checking the mail, I saw her coming down the stairs. She asked if I had time to show her my operas. I said that I did and would show her *Tosca*. When she got inside the door she just walked right into my arms—not that I wasn't expecting this—and we started kissing. Then we just plunged down on the bed, eased out of our clothes or, rather, stripped them off with startling alacrity, and started intensely to engage. When we had finished, we lay there sort of catching our breath. It had been as sweet as it was brief. Then she said, "That was nice, but we haven't played the opera." I got up and put it on. She listened, her head lying against my chest, for about fifteen minutes. Then she said, "That's nice, but I have to go," and got up, clothed herself, and left. I was no longer aware of her skin problem as I watched the lovely, slender form put on her panties, then bra, then jeans, then blouse, after which she had slipped her brightly painted red toes into her sandals. Her long blonde tresses had cascaded over her head as she leaned over to pick up her clothes, to be tossed back into place when

323

she raised herself up again with that snapping motion of the head—the same one performed by my blonde seatmate on the bus years ago, but she did it with more thoroughgoing effect, the whole thing, the picking up of clothing and the pausing, as if you were not sure she wasn't stepping out of them again—all done in some sort of gesture you would have thought had been originated by Aphrodite. She brought so much feminine appeal with her that I understood what Rilke meant by saying that beauty is a thing that slowly distains to destroy us. Each time I saw her after that we'd smile and go on walking past, and this seemed perfectly representative of what we'd done together and what it meant. And Rilke, whose *Duino Elegies* I carried around in my pocket, had also asked who is there we can make use of—maybe not even ourselves. He seemed to have been referring to the need we have for another human to love and be loved by. Did he mean that no beautiful thing—physical or spiritual—can last, that it will wilt (like Barbara's orchid), and that it's better not to get attached to it and inevitably be disappointed? He said that we should fling the emptiness out of our arms … and, quivering, endure. That *was* strange, and I didn't exactly subscribe to it.

* * *

Weeks later, at the end of the term, Miriam and I had finished having lunch together at which occasion we each congratulated the other on having passed the MA degree examinations. We had beer and hamburgers in the campus hangout The West End, then went out holding hands. We went down to Riverside Drive and decided to walk all the way up to my house, more than thirty blocks. It was a fine, sunny day and we had nothing else to do. We were giddy again, our bodies touching as we walked, provoking smiles and stares. I would continue in school and so would she, but we avoided discussing how this would be done, knowing this would soon be the only thing that could be discussed.

We went past the building we had lived in two summers ago and located, we thought, the windows of our apartment. Miriam wondered if I had been writing any more stories, and I answered, not yet. We were enjoying our walk. The sunlight still shimmered on the Hudson, and the New Jersey shoreline beckoned like a strange resort, reminding us of those lazy summer afternoons when the two of us used to watch from our windows above, with our favorite things, chocolates, smoked oysters, and a glass of wine, and Horowitz playing Scarlatti and Chopin on the record player or on our favorite classical music station, WQXR. I had still begun the day with the Brahms B Flat Concerto, and knowing she understood why increased our delight.

When we got to my neighborhood we were hungry again. I took her to a newly established bakery across the street from my building. I was particularly interested in it, since it was run by a black man and two white women. One was plain, but the other, the wife of the man, was quite pretty—Irish, I decided, and I wanted to call her Kathy. I had assumed they were sisters, the plain one going with her sister, the sister, the more adventurous, going where her heart took her. The plain sister's hair was securely bound in netting, whereas the other's swished about in a ponytail. We went into the shop; it seemed snug, and maybe the mixed neighborhood of blacks, and those from the Caribbean, and the Hispanics and Jews—those who, according to Miriam's friend, Al, hadn't yet moved up to Riverdale or Westchester County—would sustain it. As soon as we were inside I remembered the couple's son, a kid spoiled rotten. That should have been his name. In that very moment he was reaching into a display case to extract a donut, in full view of the customers, in order to eat it with satisfaction as he looked back at us and as his mother pretended not to have noticed.

325

Two black girls had been waiting, looking at the display case, trying to make up their minds. When she came to take our order, the girls piped up in a chorus, "We were here before them!" She went over to them with a look of consternation of having misjudged their readiness to order, which they evidently took as an expression of something else.

"I'm sorry! I didn't know you were ready."

"But we were." She took their order, carefully wrapped it, and smiled in giving it to them as they paid. When the husband appeared from the rear with his tall baker's hat on, as they were going out the door, they said, "Black and white together ain't no good, NOO way!" taking in the universe of all of us, and slammed the door. Miriam and I made our order and smiled back at the others, who seemed stricken, even at spoiled rotten, who had placidly continued to eat his donut as if he had heard nothing.

"I think I understand her, but she doesn't know what she's doing with the kid," she said, outside.

"He's going to need more than donuts," I said. She took my hand again, and I was glad.

After that day I hadn't spoken to her in a week, but when the phone rang one night about nine o'clock I knew it was she. She said it as quickly as possible, getting all of it out, precisely stated, as if she were reading it: that there were people interested in her whom she liked; that we shouldn't have two apartments like this; that either we live together and get married and stop this pretending, or we should call it quits and I should bring her the keys to her place. It sounded as if she actually had been reading it, and she didn't want to talk any further. I could think about it and then call her back. I could hear *La Boheme* playing on her stereo in the background. I didn't call her back. I took the keys—the key to our, to *her*, VW, the Blue Beauty, was still on the ring—and went out the door. I didn't like her ultimatum, yet I knew she was right, and maybe the reason why I had wanted separate places, why we had let ourselves get separate apartments, almost by default, was the resentment I'd felt at having had to fight for her and prove myself worthy (though not at her insistence!), and the desire to be in New York and have experience with other women. *There*, had been the real booze and the lust. Hadn't that also been true, somewhere, for her? I walked with a kind of forceful reluctance, as if I were going to a goodbye party and didn't know how to say my piece to the departing one without breaking down.

When I got to the subway station for the long trip downtown and looked up the tunnel for the train, I felt coming out of me an outburst and a flowing of tears, and I couldn't stop them. The train came and I sat with wet cheeks, not even trying to conceal them, and people furtively watched me. I arrived at East 10th Street, walking past the spot where my car had been stolen and on into her vestibule where I rang the buzzer, and her voice, as if echoing out of an underwater chamber, let me in. As I went up the stairs I thought how my tears had dried and I was calm again.

She let me in and sat back down at the kitchen table where she was having tea, in the large mug she'd bought in the bookstore in Alabama. I declined her offer to join her. *La Boheme* was making progress. I had feared that by the time I arrived Mimi would be on her deathbed, but it had only gotten to the point of her complaining about her lover Rudolfo to their friend Marcello, how hard it was for them to get along, even though they still loved each other, as if Marcello's love life was any more secure or orderly. Of course, she may have put it there when I had rung the bell, since their reconciliation follows!

"I didn't think you'd call back. I knew you'd come. Though somebody else could have been here."

"Would you have planned it like that?" I looked up and saw something new, a work of art like a plaque that was on the wall, depicting the word LOVE in a fractured design spelled out in block letters of different sizes as a child might do learning to spell at school. The artist was well known, enjoying high exposure with this design that was popular at the moment and could be seen everywhere, almost as if it were a plea for love's continuance, or an advertisement for it. Near it, and as if it were making a comment on the other, was Tina's painting that we had bought of the two women in the presence of each other. I walked across the wooden floor to the window where I looked across to the top of the building where someone had wound up and thrown the brick (with red ribbon still around it!) straight across the street through the window into her room. I thought how the sound of my walking across the floor was similar to the creaking sound I'd heard of another man's bare feet when I'd talked to her recently on the phone. That time she'd said she was busy, and I couldn't come over that night even as I heard the agitation in her voice, though I hadn't wanted to come, and the footsteps of the other had made themselves known, this time against the background sound of Mozart's Prague Symphony. The cat came and wrapped herself around my legs.

Seeing Tina's painting made me say to her, because I didn't think I had told her, "Tina had a boy." We absorbed this information in silence. It hadn't been possible for us not to think what any children of ours would be like. So in this moment we continued to say nothing.

Eventually she asked, "How are you?" having finished her tea. She got up and stood in the middle of the floor, then went to the piano she'd had brought in but did not sit there. They'd had to raise it up from the street and swing it in through a window. We both looked at the brass piano lamp I had given her.

"I'm fine," I said.

"Don't you have any tears?" Her eyes were still wet and had the look in them she'd had when we'd pulled on the wishbone.

I thought her statement might bring some. I felt the keys in my pocket, and fingered them, making a clinking sound we both heard.

"You should give me those then." She walked toward me in her bare feet, wearing jeans and a blue blouse, but stopped and then just looked at me, with a sad calmness. The cat went to her and she picked it up. "Catsky," she said.

"Mimi," I said. Looking into her eyes, I looked down that forested path again that led to a meadow, and I wanted to go there. Looking at her, I thought she had seen what I had thought, had seen me going there, and I was glad. She understood me, and made me understand myself. She was the one who'd have our children, and we could start making some headway in that connection right now. Holding the cat, stroking it, she lay down as if she could no longer stand. Her eyes had again that dreamy, sleepy look, and my eyes followed a certain movement of her toes that banished all resistance and regret in me, as if I were awakening from a trance. I recognized that smile as my own, and I went to claim it.

* * *

I married her—and she me. I put it this way because the mutual pledging, and acceptance, that marriage implies—almost a sacred thing—are not always actual in the way one intends to affirm them, in spite of the bright and misty-eyed affirmation of bride and groom before family and friends. The two of us had much to overcome—family resistance, public disfavor, the personal banishing of doubt and fear to support the illusion of certainty.

They were all there in attendance at our wedding, a sky-blue spring morning in the Brooklyn Botanical Garden, in front of a flowing stream, in bright but not yet burning sunlight. It was a spot she used to visit as a child. We stood under a flower-draped canopy, the ceremony officiated by a rabbi and an Ethical Culture minister. We pledged our commitment to each other and exchanged rings; two friends spoke in tribute of each of us; and the ministers, seemingly happy to be able to collaborate in this ecumenical gathering, spoke of the sanctity of marriage, especially as this occasion brought together as one family disparate members of the human family. Her eyes were shining as she looked at her family, her father, and aunts, Selma and Ruth, and Ruth's husband and children; and my family, my mother, my sister and her husband and sons, and my other sister, beaming; our many friends—we had brought together a lot of people, maybe 150—whose collective will toward affirmation seemed our final consummation. Our school colleague, Howard, was among them, and Liz and Leon, and Derek, Tina, Missy, and their new baby boy. There were others, who had traveled long distances to get there, from addresses that had not changed over the years, and many that had, friends and teachers from college, even my old professor from Iowa who used to recite Homer in Greek. He had come with his English wife, an actress, as I later learned. Then we all left in an entourage, as I led her across the grass, through the heady fragrance and showy extravagance of blossoming roses and peonies, making our way to the banquet that would last the rest of the day. As we passed, I noticed Brock, with an expression only to be described as a happy smirk; and near him was Sarah, with an intensely interested look, standing next to what I assumed was her surgeon boyfriend.

We married in 1970, and three years later we finished our doctoral studies and were lucky enough to get jobs in New York City. I am now a professor of English there, and so is she. In 1975 our son arrived, after a long wait—and not for our not having tried (though the second, now, is on the way)—a creature so beautiful we didn't know whether he was a boy, a girl, or an angel. He didn't look like either one of us so much as you could see that he was our product. "He's so light," she said, referring to his fair skin, almost as fair as hers but with a luminous, honey-hued tinge, the unspoken signature of the long-standing comingling of the races; but, of course, any time *any* two individuals mate, doesn't the original ancestral Homo sapiens stock get shifted around some more? He didn't look white and he didn't look black either. Maybe he was just what it looked like to be human.

The first family member to hold him (in the delivery room, after he had nestled with his mother), even before my mother did—who saw his face—something wondrous—and placed the child in his arms—was her father, with a big grin, making the most amazing clucking sounds with his puckered lips; and the child's eyes attended to him, he who had been opposed. Then he recognized me and came and placed the child in my arms. I looked at my son as I might look at a miracle, staring at him, and then gave him to my mother, who placed him back into his mother's arms. Her father was standing next to me then, and, with a heaving chest, embraced me for so many seconds. I could see how the motion he had originally intended, when he had approached me, was to shake my hand.

I have been thinking about this—not how our married life has developed and progressed, but about the ways in which our past life played a part in bringing us together. I decided to marry this woman long before I did it or even knew her. How could this be? Meeting her dramatized the question of choice as maybe the defining factor of my life, or of life, as indicated by the Frost poem. Apparently, then, what I had said to Sarah, and to Howard, that I hadn't planned to have anything happen with Miriam, wasn't true at all. And I wonder if the same might be said of her, in a trajectory that placed her at a little black liberal arts college at the same time I was there. We were both moved to cross barriers, to see a different image of ourselves, the result of being led by the deepest promptings of one's being, and not understanding why they're there, only that not to follow them is not to be oneself.

I notice that a main occurrence of this story is the depiction of the way what is put out of the mind comes back again

331

when prompted by the right circumstances, usually a situation of emotional agitation or transport, like falling in love, being loved, wanting to love, or losing love. As Janice said in the club, it is something about which we have to tell lies. We're either striving to be loved, or seen, or appreciated, or else we're defending against such needs, trying to look self-sufficient. I was able to live because my wife entered my life with such intensity as to compel me to feel; and, loving me, she came to see what the real measure was of her own capacity to love.

I want to try to be opened up, to get beyond myself, as my friend Ed in the extreme was trying to do. One way, for instance, is not to be ashamed or contemptuous of a conception of obligation, looking beyond the securing of your own good comfort to a feeling for the many in the world in need. I think the prime impediment to being able, or willing, to do this is the inability to accept and mourn your own failings.

Meanwhile, Miriam and I sometimes still greet the day with the Brahms concerto, which we discovered has been scored for two pianos. Now we play it. Each time we do so is a learning experience, old difficulties overcome with new competence, but what a glorious learning experience it is! We play it (and, sometimes, other works, in get-togethers with our friends) on a baby grand and an upright in our home, one of those splendid old Upper West Side apartments, ornate and spacious, with high ceilings and thick walls, she the soloist, I the accompanist (or vice versa)—with a certain little person with luminous eyes and a storm-cloud of curls, watching us, holding his own little violin, saying, as if he knew exactly what he was talking about, "That wasn't bad, Dad. You and Mom are getting good!"—and we are sometimes (looking across at each other) lifted to a height ...